A Lucky Bump

Jenna Motels

Contents

Prologue | Rock With You 1

Chapter 1 | Start of Something New 5

Chapter 2 | Party in the USA 14

Chapter 3 | Summer Shade 23

Chapter 4 | Friends 32

Chapter 5 | She Looks So Perfect 42

Chapter 6 | Crush 52

Chapter 7 | A Million Dreams 63

Chapter 8 | Same Girl 76

Chapter 9 | M. I. A. 88

Chapter 10 | Treat You Better 102

Chapter 11 | My Dilemma 119

Chapter 12 | Rewrite the Stars 136

Chapter 13 | 10,000 Hours 155

Chapter 14 | You Belong with Me 174

Chapter 15 | Last First Kiss   193

Chapter 16 | Better With You   214

Chapter 17 | He Could Be the One   236

Chapter 18 | Nobody But You   259

Chapter 19 | Walk with Me   283

Chapter 20 | Marry You   306

Epilogue | Perfect   332

Prologue | Rock With You

{ Started June 22, 2018}{Completed August 26, 2018}

Zac let out a laugh, enjoying whatever his best friend Nate was saying. He wasn't really listening, but he knew it was funny. Everyone else at the table was laughing. He took a look around, his eyes landing on an elderly couple on the opposite side of the diner.

That couple looked in love as the guy spooned icecream into his wife's mouth. She let out a laugh as some chocolate syrup stained her cheek. The man grabbed a napkin, wiping away the gooeyness.

Zac suddenly felt like he was missing something. He had the looks, the smarts, and the athletic abilities. He even had the money. He didn't think he needed anything else, but upon seeing this couple in love, he felt like he was missing that. Yeah, he had endless hook ups and one night stands. He was known to just be one and done. So, why was he suddenly feeling like he needed that?

He had his whole life ahead of him, being accepted into all the elite schools, not only for his grades but for football as well. He didn't need some high school romance to satisfy his needs. He knew that as soon as that diploma was handed out, the relationship would be over. Plus, his parents weren't the best at being examples of happy couples in love.

They were together for the money, but each one had their own secret-ish relationship, hiding it from the public. They just couldn't tell his grandparents they wanted a divorce. They'd take their wealth away. That he was sure he couldn't live without.

"Hey Zac. Why are you staring at that couple?" His best friend Nate asked. Zac took one last glance at them and turned to see the entire table's attention on him.

"I was curious as to why an old lady was giggling. After watching that scene, I think i'm going to be sick." He lied smoothly. Nate raised an eyebrow. He could tell when he was lying. He was the only one. Being best friends since kindergarten had his perks. He just hoped his best friend would buy it for the time being. He didn't want to discuss his weird thoughts in front of the guys. He was sure they'd think he was going soft.

"Any way, party at your house this weekend?" Nate asked. Zac smirked. He was known to throw the best parties. He had the money and the mansion for it.

"Right after we beat the Liberty Lions' ass." He smirked. The whole table started to bang on the table, cheering. He let out a laugh. This was all he was ever going to need. He doesn't need a stupid girl or love. He just needed this.

-

She stared at her idiot brothers. They were wrestling each other in their backyard. If you could even call it that. It was a small patch of grass, surrounded by dirt. A fence surrounding them. There wasn't even a tree. It was just dried up dirt.

"Hails, what's for dinner?" Her youngest brother Seth asked. He was fifteen, with blond hair and bright blue eyes. He was the smarter of the bunch, always striving for excellence in his school work.

"Pizza. I have some extra money from my shift at Carl's." She told them. Carl's was the diner in town. She had gotten a job there as soon as she turned sixteen. The owner, Carl, gave her work immediately. She thought it was out of pity, but she ignored it. She really needed the money.

"Hailey, let me pay." Her oldest brother Josh said. He was tall, buff, and tanner than the rest. He worked in construction, being four years out of high school. He was their guardian and has been since he was sixteen. His hazel eyes stared into her own. She sighed.

"Josh, I want to pay." She said firmly. The next eldest brother Ben took the distraction of Josh, to tackle him. "Ben!"

"That fucking hurt." Josh said getting out of Ben's grasp. He rubbed the back of his head, annoyance radiating off him.

"Dude, just let her pay. She's the only other person that contributes to this family." Ben said. Josh stared at him as Luke let's out a cough.

"I second him." Luke found himself saying. Josh glared at Luke next. Luke had dark blue eyes and dirty blond hair, practically brown, while Ben had bright blue eyes and light blond hair. Both were amazing in sports. Ben having gotten an athletic scholarship to the nearest community college for baseball. Luke played football for the high school, being a junior and a year younger than her.

"Joshie!" They heard a soft voice. The five of them turned around, seeing their youngest sister Trinity. She was only ten and full of energy. They all switch off with putting her to bed. She never wants to sleep and always wants to play.

"Yes Trin?" Josh asked. They all stared at her intently.

"Hailey said she's buying pizza. Is that true?" She asked. Josh sighed, before nodding.

"Dial the number Hails. And get breadsticks too." Josh said giving in. She smirked. Josh can never say no to Trinity. That girl has his heart. Sometimes she envied the power she had.

"Hey Hails, can we go grocery shopping later this week? We're out of Gatorade." Ben said. She nodded. They drink those way too quick, but she knew they need to. They do have sports practice every day.

"Great. It's settled. Now let's go inside and wash up." Josh said. The boys all nodded, going into their small three bedroom home. She sighed in content.

Even though her brothers were a pain in her butt, she wouldn't trade them for the world. They had been on their own for eight years now and nothing was ever going to change. She just wished that they'd be able to afford sending her to college.

She wanted nothing more than to become a nurse and have the ability to help others, but she didn't know if she'd ever be able to. All she could hope for was a happy ending, even if that meant giving up her dream for reality.

~~~~~~~
~~~~~~~

Chapter 1 | Start of Something New

- -

Rolling out of bed, Hailey felt different. She had no clue what it was, but today did not feel like an ordinary Friday. Something new was going to happen. She could feel it in her bones. She just hoped it was good.

She made the small trek to her bathroom, careful not to wake her little sister up. She had school while Trinity would not be attending until hours later. Perks of her being in elementary school. Her oldest brother Josh would wake her up. She was jealous that she got to sleep in. She wished nothing more than for a few more hours of sleep. Maybe even a days worth.

She shut the bathroom door, flipping on the light. She was instantly startled by her own reflection. Her locks of brown hair tangled into a mess, almost like a bird's nest. She sighed. No matter how much she tried, her hair always tangled in her sleep. She turned the knob to the shower, letting the cold water heat up. She slipped out of her baggy t-shirt and running shorts before stepping into the hot water. She felt her muscles soon start to relax.

She was tense about the upcoming college applications. She had a couple of weeks before she'd have to turn them in. She didn't know where to apply.

She didn't know if they'd even be able to afford it. Ben went to school, but because he got a full ride for baseball. They didn't need to pay much, or anything at all.

Her, on the other hand, she didn't do much except work and babysit. Sometimes she wished she had the same athletic abilities as her brothers. Maybe she could learn soccer before the end of the year She shook her head and began to wash her body. She made sure to pay close attention to the knots that formed while in bed.

Once done, she slipped out of the shower. Wrapping herself in a warm fluffy towel, she stepped out of the bathroom. She was careful to not run into her annoying siblings before stepping back into her bedroom. She looked over at Trin, seeing her sound asleep. She was instantly jealous.

She walked over to their shared closet and chose a pair of dark wash skinny jeans with a few rips in the knees and an old maroon baseball t-shirt that belonged to Ben. Handy downs from him were her favorite. She enjoyed watching baseball more than she'd ever admit. Sometimes she wish she played softball, but knew she'd suck.

She slipped on her old, not white anymore, Vans and walked over to her desk. There was a mirror placed on top to double as her vanity. She snatched her brush and began to tame her locks. She then let it dry into its natural waves.

"Hailey! Breakfast." She heard one of her siblings shout. She looked at Trinity and saw her slightly stir. She held her breath before seeing her snuggle back into their shared bed. She let out the breath before walking out of their room. She didn't want to deal with Trinity's crankiness of being woken up too early. That child definitely has an attitude.

Hailey then walked into the kitchen. All her brothers were waiting for her. Four plates sat out as Josh's back was next to the stove. She could smell his world famous French Toast. They were phenomenal, especially because he uses nutmeg with the cinnamon.

"Hailey, can you watch Trinity tonight?" Luke asked. She sat down at the counter and turned to look at him. She quickly shook her head. "Why not?"

"It's your turn." She stated. They all took turns hanging out with her sister. She can be a little over the top.

"But Zac Logan is having another party." Luke whined. She quickly shook her head. She didn't really know who he was. All she knew was that he was supposed to be some bad boy who parties and sleeps with strange girls. She did not want any part of that.

"I don't even know him or who he is. Besides, no drinking until your twenty-one." Hailey stated again. Luke began to pout, earning a glance from Josh. She ignored Luke, not wanting to waste her Friday night indoors.

"It's not like you have anything better to do. You don't wanna go to one of the most legendary parties. At least live a little." Luke said glaring at her. She shrugged. She wished she could be a normal teen but her life wasn't normal. She had a family to help take care of.

"Besides, you guys need me to go grocery shopping. You know I can't take her. She'll run off or she'll beg me to buy her something." She told him. Luke pouted, before getting up. "Where you going?"

"I have to talk to Coach before school. I'll see you there." He told her. She nodded, digging into the delicious food. As she let out a moan, her older brother Ben walked in.

"I'll take care of the brat." He said. She rose an eyebrow. "I heard you two. I think you should go to that party. You never know who you might befriend."

"No thanks Benny." She said enjoying her last bite. She quickly got up, setting the dishes in the sink, and walked around. "I'll see you tonight. Add anything else we need to the list for groceries."

"Whatever Hails, just know that you are off babysitting." He reminded her. She nodded before stepping out of the kitchen. She grabbed her old black Jansport backpack and began her walk to school.

-

She looked up from her book as a commotion started in the cafeteria. A bunch of jocks were standing in the center, tossing a football. She sighed. They were pathetic and could not wait to get out of there. Hopefully those in college are way more mature then this bunch.

"Listen up! We have our rivalry game tonight against the Lions. After we beat their ass, party at Zac's." One of the jocks shouted. The whole cafeteria cheered as the the three main jocks smirked. She felt disgusted as she stared at them. Girls hung from their sides like leeches.

She stared at the shortest of the three: Evan Green. He had short brown hair and hazel eyes. He was pretty tall, but not compared to his two best friends. He's the sweeter of the two, or so she heard. His twin sister Bella is the one to blame.

The next in line for the throne was Nate Price. His chiseled cheekbones look like they could cut anyone that got into his way. His brown eyes and black hair only added to his bad boy attire. It's rumored that he's in a gang. He gets away with everything, considering his dad is the senator. It must be nice to not have any punishments or regrets.

Lastly, there's Zac Logan. Zac's shaggy brown hair and light brown eyes scream attractive. His body definitely does not disappoint with his bulging biceps and toned stomach. He's also the tallest of the three, being 6 foot 4. He's captain of the football team and he's supposed to be valedictorian.

He has the looks, the smarts, and the athleticism. He's the total package, especially with his wallet. His parents own one of the wealthiest companies in the country. He legit does whatever he pleases and that includes girls.

"Zachary Logan, get off of that girl." She heard a teacher shout. She turned and saw the bad boy with his tongue down Sasha Nelson's throat. Sasha was the reigning queen of Freedom High School. Bleach blond hair and bright blue eyes, and fake tanned skin screamed bitch. Being captain of the cheer squad only added to her title. She made sure everyone knew she was in charge.

"Call me Zac-ey." Sasha said in a gross tone which she could only assume meant to be seductive. She scrunched up her face at the diva and shut her book. She slipped it into her bag before getting up. Picking up her uneaten food, she tossed it in the trash. The queen bee managed to ruin her appetite.

She made the small walk to her next class, wanting the day to be over with. She didn't really have any friends and no social life. She lost them all when she was forced to move cities. Her brother couldn't take care of them in their previous town, causing them to have to leave. She thought people would be nice in the city, but her hope quickly shut down.

She was too shy to approach anyone and too poor to fit in. So, she stuck to herself. School and her family came first, even if that meant giving up friendship. Sometimes she wished she was more of an extrovert like her younger brother, Luke but decided that it was the only way to get what she wanted.

She wanted nothing more than to be a nurse. She wanted to help people just like her mom. Her father lost his life taking her mother to the hospital. There had been a horrible accident and she had been called into work. Her father drove her and that's when a drunk driver hit their side of the car.

They died upon impact. She wanted to remember her mother and being a nurse was the only way she knew how to do that.

She slipped into her classroom, smiling at her teacher. She took out her phone, having a couple of minutes before students began to walk in. She opened a text from Josh, seeing the grocery list. She chuckled fo herself upon reading it. Condoms was at the top of the list. She quickly erased it and shut her phone off. She was sure that Luke asked for those. He was always asking for some. It's not like he'd actually have a use for them.

"Dude! I cannot wait for this game." She heard someone say. She turned her head slightly, seeing Nate and Evan. It was one of the classes she shared with the pair.

"Zac's party is going to be epic. Who are you taking?" Evan asked. She watched as Nate smirked. His eyes roamed the classroom, landing on her own. She quickly whipped her head to look at the teacher. She was writing today's assignment on the board.

"Not sure yet, but I promise you that it's going to be a great night." She heard Nate say. She could picture his perfect smirk. She was disgusted that she even thought he was attractive. She wished that he would disappear, being the worse of the two.

He had hit on her numerous times. She denied every one of his advances. She thought he was done since Luke confronted him. She wasn't even sure why the two were friends but she was grateful that her brother cared. Although, it seemed like Nate was back to pestering her.

"Just don't hit on my sister." Evan groaned. Nate chuckled. She quickly turned around and saw that the boy was staring right at her. She quickly turned back. She tried to keep her heart rate from sky rocketing, but failed.

Nate scared her. If the rumors were true, Nate had the ability to kill someone with his pinky. She also heard he carries a gun and has killed a guy.

He's also said to be one of the best drug dealers in the state. She wouldn't doubt it. His cheekbones cannot be natural.

"Alright class, today we will be reviewing your midterm essay. Please take out a sheet of paper and write down the notes." Her teacher said. She felt her inside calm down as she found the needed materials. She faced forward, not wanting to see the bad boy again.

-

She took the list and proceeded to walk into the store. She was hit with the wonderful smell from the bakery. She wanted nothing more than to enjoy one of the delicacies, but knew she couldn't. She could only buy what was needed. Any extra money would go into her savings account. She needed to get into college.

She ventured off down the first aisle. It was full of cereals and coffee. She chose Cinnamon Toast Crunch for Luke, Raisin Bran for Josh, Honey Nut Cheerios for Ben, and Lucky Charms for Trinity. Seth still had Cocoa Puffs in the pantry. Her, she would eat whatever. She then bought a container of coffee beans. It was the only thing that motivated her in the morning.

Walking out of the aisle, she noticed the fruit was on sale. She quickly pushed the grocery cart in that direction. Fruit was her favorite food group. She could live off it if she had to. Mangoes, kiwis, berries, bananas, and watermelon were her most favorite. Whenever she saw that one was on sale, she was sure to pick it up. She chose to enjoy her share of the grocery list in fruit instead of candy or condoms like her brothers.

Filling up the car with her desired fruits, she pushed the cart further down the store. She noticed that the next thing on the list was the drinks. She needed to get Gatorades and water bottles. She noticed the aisle full of drinks and made her way there. She turned the corner into the next aisle, hearing glass hit the floor. She gasped. She could not afford to pay for whatever she broke. She quickly looked and saw that she did indeed hit something, well someone.

Zac Logan stood there stunned. He wasn't sure what had just occurred. One moment he was picking up a bottle of Smirnoff Vodka, the next he was hit and the bottle was shattered on the ground. He looked up from the clear liquid and saw a girl. The grocery cart was in her hands as she stared at the mess she caused. She seemed familiar but he didn't know from where. He could only assume they had a class together. He's sure he hadn't slept with her.

"I'm so sorry." Hailey said. Her voice came out a few notches higher than usual. She felt her cheeks heat up as the attractive boy stared back at her. She felt even more embarrassed than before.

"It's alright. I'm blocking the whole aisle. It was my fault." Zac said. Hailey shook her head.

"No, it's okay. I'll pay for the damage." She said already thinking of how much she'd have to pay. She was sure the fruit would all have to be put back. She might even have to skip the coffee beans. She's sure that she can just drink iced cold water in the morning.

"No, I got it. My dad won't care about the price." Zac told her honestly. His dad didn't care what he did. He only cared about the inheritance from his grandparents.

"Are you sure?" Hailey asked. Zac nodded. She let out a sigh of relief. Josh would be pissed if she came home without their groceries. She was glad that he wouldn't have to know about her clumsiness.

"I'm Zac by the way." He said. He put his hand in front of his body, smiling down at her. She stared up, not sure what to do. It's not every day one bumps into the hottest guy in town.

~~~~~~~Updates will begin July 23rd. Until then,xoxo,Liv814
~~~~~~~

Chapter 2 | Party in the USA

Z ac stared at the brunette. She was stunning and unlike any girl he had seen before. She continued to stare at his hand. He had just introduced himself to her.

Hailey was in shock. Zac Logan was in front of her, talking to her. She was no one compared to him. Why was he talking to her? Oh yeah, she broke the bottle of Vodka. She took his hand, shaking it. She noticed a weird shock flow through her body. She ignored him and gave him a timid smile.

"I'm Hailey." She said. Zac grinned at her. He was breaking through this girl's shell. He had a feeling like he was going to be seeing her a lot more and for once, he was glad.

"I'm having a party tonight. You should come. You can bring your friends or your boyfriend." He told her. She watched her stare back at him. He wanted to know if she was taken while Hailey wanted to know why he was inviting her. Was this the universe telling her to have some fun for once? Her brother was going to his party and Ben encouraged her to go too.

"Maybe." She found herself saying. She needed to think it through. Did she want to go to a party full of wild, unsupervised teenagers? She was sure alcohol was going to be present. Zac Logan was here buying it. Wait, how can he purchase it? She was sure he wasn't twenty-one.

"You need to come. It's supposed to be legendary." He stated, breaking through her thoughts. He knew it was true. All his parties were amazing, thanks to his parents' wealth.

"Maybe. I'm supposed to babysit my little sister tonight." She told him. Although she knew it wasn't true. She just didn't know if she wanted to become friends with the school's most popular guy. He's known for sleeping with girls and then forgetting them. She didn't want to be a number to add to his list.

"I promise it'll be fun." Zac said before slipping his phone out of his pocket. He unlocked it and clicked on the messages app. "Give me your number and i'll text you the address."

"Okay." She whispered. She took his iPhone X and typed in her number. She could feel his intimidating gaze on her as she typed. She soon saved it and handed him the expensive phone.

"I'll see you tonight babe." He said. He plastered on his signature smirk and gave her a once over. She was definitely different. He then grabbed his cart and pushed it out of the aisle. He needed to buy chips. He was sure Nate and Evan could get the rest of the alcohol. He wanted to leave without her backing out of coming. He just hoped she'd show up.

Hailey watched his retreating figure. She didn't know what just happened. Did she really just bump into the Zac Logan? All her life she had steered clear of him and his friends. Well, she tried to. His best friend Nate Price doesn't seem to leave her alone. It's like he has this obsession with her. She didn't like it. She didn't like him at all.

The thought of Nate made her want to forget about the party. She wanted nothing to do with him. He was worse than Zac. He was the real bad boy. She was sure he'd rule the school if it wasn't for Zac Logan being practically perfect. Every girl wants a smart, athletic, hot guy. Zac Logan was that while Nate Price was only hot and a troublemaker. Don't get her wrong, they are both insanely attractive. She just rather have the one with more qualities.

She felt her phone buzz in her pocket. She slid it out, assuming it was only Josh. He keeps tabs on her, more so that she's officially an adult now. She doesn't understand why he's so protective, but didn't really care to ever ask.

As she unlocked her phone, her eyes widened upon realization of who the text was from. She felt her heart began to race. Was she supposed to reply now?

Unknown: can't wait to see you tonight.

Unknown: party starts @ 9.

She reread his words, making her heart go into a frenzy. Maybe she should go to this party. She'd finally get Luke off her back for always being at home. She could even meet some people and learn to have some fun. Okay, that was a bit of a stretch, but going for an hour wouldn't cause any harm. Right? She shook away her doubts. She was going. She just hoped Josh would let her.

Looking down at her outfit, she felt out of place. Everyone else was dressed to impress. She was simply wearing a pair of dark wash ripped jeans and a white flowey tank top with a pair of black sandals. She at least had the decency of wearing light make up and curling her brown locks. She didn't have anything else to wear. This was her first party.

She gazed at the scene in front of her. It was like straight out of a movie. Kids were running around with red solo cups in their hands. Girls were wearing absolutely nothing while guys stared at them with hunger. It was definitely a high school party. Maybe she shouldn't have come. She was out of place and didn't know anyone. This only reminded her of her nonexistent social life.

Having grown up without her parents, left a hole in her heart. She tried to fill it up with school and work. She only ever focused on them and her family. One would imagine that she'd have a few friends or at least know a few people. She knew of people and had very few acquaintances that she made in class, but never enough to call them friends. She had just stuck to herself, helping her brothers take care of the rest.

She decided to stand near the door in case she needed an escape route. If she didn't find him in ten minutes, she was leaving. Luke could find his own way home. She glanced around, hearing laughter.

Hailey looked around and saw him. He was standing over by the balcony that over looked the city. She stood there unsure of whether to go up to him. She wanted to say hi. That's the decent thing to do since he invited her. She took a deep breath and walked up to me.

His back was turned to her, allowing her some time to breathe. His brown messy locks moved in the slight breeze. She was entranced, not noticing that they were now alone.

"Hi." She spoke. Zac turned around, a smirk plastered on his face. She admired his body encased by his signature black leather jacket. Yeah, he was definitely attractive.

"You made it." He said. She nodded. She was frozen, not knowing what to say. He had a weird effect on her. She didn't like that she felt powerless against him. "You look beautiful."

She opened her mouth before shutting it quickly. She only had met him hours before, yet she still couldn't believe it. Zac knew who she was and was complimenting her. He called her beautiful. She didn't even think she was dressed right. She knew she wasn't.

"Hi." She squeaked. He chuckled. She involuntary shivered upon hearing his laugh. The way his eyes gazed into hers made her heart do stupid flips in her chest.

"You already said that babe. Now come on. I want to introduce you to my friends." He told her. He wrapped his arm around her waist, pulling her deeper into the party. She ignored the weird sparks that flowed from his touch.

Her eyes began to dart from side to side. It was her first time ever at a party. She had only ever seen them in movies. They don't do them justice to the real live thing. She saw girls half naked, running around without a care in the world. Others had their tongues down guys throats, even down some girls. She scrunched her face in disgust upon seeing some jock chugging beer out of a keg. A group of guys surrounded him, cheering him on. She moved her gaze onto a group of people in the kitchen. They seemed like the normal people she wished she knew. The people she wished she was friends with.

"Hey guys." Zac said approaching them. The group turned to look at them. She knew who they were and one knew her. She gulped as his eyes made contact with his own.

"Wow. Hailey Foster at a party. I didn't know you knew what they were." Nate said with an arrogant smirk. She rolled her eyes. How could she forget about him being Zac's best friend.

Zac watched the scene unfold. He didn't like how Nate was treating her. He tightened his hold around Hailey's waist. He felt a gaze on him. He saw

Bella, Evan's twin sister smirking. He ignored it and focused on his best friend.

"Nate." Hailey stated. She didn't want to interact with him. She just wanted to be with Zac. Maybe with the girls and Evan, too. She just didn't want to be with Nate and his infuriating smirk.

Zac frowned as Nate's smirk deepened. What is Nate planning? Nate continued to stare down at Hailey. His hold only seemed to tighten on Hailey. He wasn't going to let Nate anywhere near her. Even if Nate was his best friend.

"Want to dance?" Nate asked. Zac's hold couldn't get any tighter on Hailey's waist. She didn't know what was causing him to do it but she didn't not like it. His arm continued to shoot little sparks up her body. It made her tingle inside.

"No thank you." Hailey told Nate with a blake face. The girls all laughed as Nate's smirk only seemed to grow bigger.

"You will one day." Nate said before taking a sip of his beer. "There's Sash. See you all later."

The boy then disappeared out of the kitchen. Hailey didn't bother to follow his figure. She never liked him and never would. He was an arrogant ass who always got what he wanted. She hated it.

"You are our new best friend." Bella said. Mariah nodded. She focused on the two girls. They were extremely different from each other, especially her. What's that saying? Opposites attract? "I'm Bella by the way."

"I'm Mariah. I love your top." The blond of the two said. She was slightly 5'6" with light blond hair and bright blue eyes. She was built, but in a good way. She definitely played sports.

Bella was a brunette and shorter than Mariah. She was around 5'4" and had an amazing body. Her brown eyes, almost hazel, shined in the light. She had similar figures to Evan. He was her twin brother.

Zac watched as the two girls he called sisters introduced themselves. He loosened his hold on Hailey, but maintained his arm around her body. It was as if she was a magnet and he needed to have his arm around her. He wasn't sure why, but he wasn't going to question it.

"Hey Zac, we're gonna go dance." Bella said as she reached for Hailey. His eyes widened as Bella's smirk deepened. He felt his cheeks heat up. "Could you let go over her now?" She teased.

He quickly unwrapped his arm, already missing her warmth. He watched as the three girls disappeared into the living room. He turned to Bella's twin, his best friend. He was studying him.

"What Ev?" He asked. He grabbed a new bottle of beer from a cooler and began to chug it. He never felt those weird spark things and it frightened him. He also never wanted a girl to be near him as much as he wanted Hailey in his arms. It was weird.

"You like her." Evan stated. Zac raised an eyebrow, not believing this. He had only met her hours before. That is not possible.

"No I don't. I only met her today. Meddle in someone else's love life." Zac said with annoyance. That only seemed to trigger Evan. He then began to laugh and loudly. "Shut up!"

"Dude, you know she's Luke's sister. Luke Foster? Who also happens to be Josh Foster's brother?" Evan said. He widened his eyes. Luke was on the football team with them. He was one of his close friends considering he was a year younger than him. Luke always talked about his protective older brother Josh who took the parental roll when they lost their parents.

He didn't know much about the family except that they're really close and don't let anyone in.

Zac also knew that Josh was once the best football player in the state. He heard stories about his plays and wins. He was definitely his role model when he was in junior high. He was saddened that he never got to see him action.

"So what if she's a Foster?" Zac defended. Evan smirked.

"Good luck getting on their good side. They already hate Nate." Evan chuckled. He rolled his eyes. He was different than Nate. Yeah, he was his best friend, but he's an idiot.

"Dude, we're just friends. Nothing is ever gonna happen." He told Evan. Evan shrugged but held his smirk. He sighed, turning to look at the girl of their conversation. She was dancing and seemed to be enjoying life. They were only friends, right?

Hailey felt uncomfortable all of a sudden. She felt as if someone watching her. She turned away from the two girls and saw Zac. He was staring right at her. He had an unreadable expression. She felt subconscious and stopped dancing. She then turned back to the girls. They both had smirks.

"So Zac?" Bella asked. Hailey felt her cheeks heat up. She didn't know why she suddenly felt embarrassed by the mention of his name.

"What about Zac?" She asked. She turned back and saw that Zac was still watching her. It made her heart flip.

"You like him." Mariah stated. Hailey shook her head. Impossible.

"I only met him at the grocery store today." Hailey told them. She then proceeded to retell the story about her clumsiness. "So, no. I don't like him."

"You find him attractive right?" Bella asked. Hailey sighed, nodding. "Zac is a great guy. Now if only he could settle down. Besides, I think he likes you."

"What? Why? What?" She asked with confusion. Mariah then nodded her head, causing Hailey to turn around. She ran into a hard wall. She stepped back, rubbing her nose. Thank god she didn't break it. She looked up and gulped. It was Zac.

"Can we dance?" Zac asked. Hailey nodded, not being able to find the words. Zac quickly wrapped his arms around her waist. She kept her arms at her sides. Was she supposed to place them on his shoulders? "Wrap your arms around my neck Hails. I promise I won't bite."

She felt her cheeks heat up. She did as she was told, feeling butterflies in her stomach. She only hoped they were from nerves. This was the first time she dances with a guy that isn't her brother.

There bodies began to sway. She let herself relax, enjoying being in his arms. It was different and she liked it. She didn't know what it meant but she just hoped something good will finally happen to her.

Zac looked down at her. She was definitely beautiful. He liked having her in his arms. Was Evan right? Did he like her? He had only met her hours before, yet he didn't want to be away from her. Was she the one he was looking for? Because if she was, he was glad he finally found her.

~~~~~~~~I am so excited to start. I know I said July 23rd but like Zac is hot & is urging me to continue his love story. So comment and vote!xoxo,Liv814
~~~~~~~~

Chapter 3 | Summer Shade

Hailey was still starstruck. She had no idea how her life could do a 180. She was used to being alone, with her siblings, trying to get through life. Now, she was walking down the hallway with friends. She actually had people to call friends.

She turned to look at the two girls walking with her. The whole school had their eyes on them. She was freaking walking with Mariah Carter and Bella Green. She always thought they were airheads and stuck up, but they weren't. They were intellectual, sweet, and most importantly, not snobby. She had judged them way too quick and vowed to never do it again.

"Hailey, do you want to come with us to Carl's later?" Mariah asked. Her blond locks bounced as they neared homeroom. The two girls were surprised to know that they shared multiple classes with Hailey. They even complained why they hadn't met before.

"Actually, I work there tonight." She told them, feeling embarrassed. They were all filthy rich and didn't have to help their family survive. She was envious, but knew that it kept her humble and appreciative of everything her brothers have done for her and her family.

"Wait, you work there? That's awesome! Are you guys hiring? I want to get a job so mom can stop complaining about me not doing anything. Just because my brother plays football, does not mean I have to be a cheerleader." Bella said with an eye roll. Bella was definitely not cheer material. This girl was somewhat badass, with a a snarky tongue and teasing tone. She rather be hanging with the boys then going dress shopping with the girls. Hailey admired Bella's acne free skin and bright hazel eyes. She was gorgeous and her personality was awesome.

"I can talk to Carl. I'm sure he'll love the help." She told her truthfully. Her boss was always complaining about the lack of help.

"That would be amazing. Thanks Hails." Bella said giving her a side hug. She gave her a small smile, still unaccustomed to their personality. They were witty, loud, and friendly, while she was shy and quiet, unsure of herself.

"Ugh." Mariah groaned as they neared their classroom. Hailey assumed it was because of their teacher. He was boring and mean. He was that teacher at the beginning of the year that had assigned seating. A few months in, and now he just glares at his students who don't follow the rules.

Hailey looked into their assigned room and she knew why Mariah had groaned. Zac and his friends were in this class. They weren't in here before, were they? Did they switch into her homeroom?

"Chill Mariah. I don't know why you complain about my brother and his friends." Bella said walking in. Hailey looked for an open seat near the front, finding one in the second row. She was about to sit when she heard her name.

"Hails, over here." She heard his melodic voice. She felt her cheeks blaze as eyes whipped towards her. She covered her face with her hair, making her way over to her new group of friends. "Why were you going to sit there?"

"I like sitting near the front." She whispered towards Zac. He rose an eyebrow, admiring her. He was attracted to this girl and it was more than just her looks. Her personality was something he knew he adored. She was different than anyone he had met and that only made him want to get to know her more.

"You won't believe what she just told us." Bella blabbed to her brother. Hailey felt uncomfortable being the center of the conversation. Thankfully, they had an open seat which she took. She looked down at the notebook in her hand. Closing her eyes, she felt her heart rate start to drop as her thoughts consumed her mind.

She was nervous. This year was her last try at getting a scholarship to be able to live her dream. She needed the grades to earn the money so she can become a nurse. She needed to put her focus in it. This was everything to her.

"Hails works at Carl's and is going to help me get a job." Bella told the group. Zac's gaze continued to stay on the girl. She continued to look down at the notebook. Zac subconsciously pulled a strand of hair away from her face, tucking it behind her ear. Hailey looked up, unsure of what had just occurred.

Her eyes connected with Zac's. He was studying her, wanting to remember every curve and angle her face held. She was beautiful any every way. Hailey felt her breath pick up speed and she stared into his eyes. It was as if she was stuck in a trance.

"Bells, mom will flip." Evan said with annoyance. He then turned to look at Zac. In a blink of an eye, Evan's hand found its way to the back of Zac's head, whacking him.

"What the fuck Evan?" Zac said breaking the eye contact to glare at his friend. Evan rolled his eyes before giving his twin sister his full attention.

Hailey chuckled at the scene. They reminded her of her siblings. They were always slapping each other.

"Good morning class. This is where you will be spending the next thirty minutes in silence. I have work to do. Now please settle down, I will be taking roll." The teacher said walking in. She looked forward, stifling a laugh upon seeing Zac glared at Evan. Evan rolled his eyes before slapping Zac again. She wanted to laugh but knew better than to call for attention. She just wanted the rest of senior year to be calm and smooth. She couldn't wait to live her dream.

-

Wrapping her apron around her waist, she felt all tingling. It had only been a few moments since Zac's arm was wrapped around her shoulder. She had no clue what it meant but she knew that she wanted it to happen again.

Zac and his friends were outside the diner, discussing their plans for the weekend. She hadn't noticed them when Ben dropped her off. She was focused on her idiotic brother belching some song by AC/DC. She knew his love for the rock group and let him enjoy himself.

It was weird seeing him so carefree. Josh and him were definitely the responsible ones, besides her. They knew that their family came first before anything else. The two boys had a nonexistent social life. Well Ben had friends from baseball, but she knew he wished for that special someone to share it all with. Plus, he was too focused on her own life.

"Hailey!" She heard Evan's voice. It cut through her thoughts of her annoying brother. She gave Ben a wave before seeing him drive off. He had to pick Seth up.

"Oh, hi." She said softly. Zac's arm wrapped around her as she neared them. His eyes focused on her, making her nervous. He seemed to pull her tight to his body, providing warmth.

"Hailey, is it weird if we stay and eat?" Mariah asked. She wanted to say yes, but she shook her head instead. She didn't want to scare off her new friends so soon.

"No, not at all." She said. She unwrapped herself from him, excusing herself. She couldn't be late. She stepped into the diner, glad to be surrounded by the air conditioning.

It was late September and the heat didn't seem to disintegrate. She loved that it was summer all year, but hated it too. She wished fall and winter to happen just once.

"Hailey, about time." She heard her boss Carl say. She gave him a tight lipped smile. He was a tall, lanky guy. He had a bald spot growing in between his brown hair. An uneven mustached sat on his top lip. He claimed he was handsome, but she knew that was untrue.

"Hey Carl." She called out. He turned around, awaiting her response. "Are we hiring?"

"Maybe. Why?" Carl asked. She turned to look at the door. Her new found friends had walked in. They were laughing at something. She found herself smiling. She finally had someone to call a friend.

"My friend Bella was wondering." She told him. Carl followed her gaze. He turned back.

"Let her fill out an application. I'll call her tomorrow." Carl said leaving her. She watched him disappear into his office. She took her notepad and walked over to her friends. It was a coincidence that they sat in her section.

"Hello, my name is Hailey. I will be your server. What can I get you all to drink?" She found herself repeating the script. She watched as the group stared at her. She suddenly felt subconscious.

"Hails, no need for that. We'll all have Coke." Mariah said. She nodded. She was about to leave when she heard one of them call her name.

"Since you're our server, does that mean you'll be at my beck and call?" She heard Nate say. She rolled her eyes at his comment. She ignored him and walked away. "What the fuck man!"

She turned and saw Nate rubbing the back of his head. Zac was smirking as the girls were laughing. I'm guessing somebody else whacked him for a change. She shook her head in silent laughter and made her way behind the counter.

She grabbed five glasses and filled them up with the desired drink. She then placed them on a tray and walked back to the table. She set a glass down in front of each person. They were all staring at the menu.

"So, what did your boss say? Did you ask?" Bella asked. She nodded. She tossed some straws at them before responding to the twin.

"He'll call you tomorrow." She told Bella. Bella screeched in happiness, making her giggle. She'd have a friend at work now too. Maybe life was finally looking up for her.

-

Hailey looked up at the sky. Seagulls flew around as the sea breeze shifted her brown locks. She always loved coming to the beach. Something about the ocean calmed her down. Memories of her last time with her parents flowed, causing a tear to fall.

Even after all these years, she still felt like they were with her. She could imagine her mom wrapping her in a hug, telling her everything is going to be alright. She used to never believe it, but after just a few days of knowing Zac, she started to believe it.

Speaking of the attractive brunette, Zac spotted Hailey near the shore. She was secluded from the screeching kids, looking out at the ocean. He jogged down, making his way towards her. He had texted her but got no response.

He wanted to see her, to just be with her. He didn't know why the sudden urge, but after spotting the elderly couple again in the streets, something in him stirred. So he texted her and frowned upon seeing an unread text. So he texted Bella.

Evan's twin was like his own little sister. She was his go to for girl troubles. He asked her about their new friend. Bella responded with an answer he didn't like. She didn't know where Hailey was. That frustrated him so he decided to jog near the peer. The saltiness of the ocean relaxed his senses. He was in his own world when he spotted her.

"Hey." Zac said startling her. She turned, seeing him standing a few feet away. She sighed. She came to the ocean to relax her brain over this boy, yet here he was.

"Hi." She found her voice. She turned back towards the ocean, breathing in its scent.

"What are you doing?" Zac asked. He watched her close her eyes.

"Reminiscing." She mumbled. She could picture her dad scolding her for talking to a guy. He always treated her like his little princess, even with Trinity around. She was sure he'd be even more protective now.

"I was looking for you." Zac said. He stuffed his hands in his front pockets, wanting to be near the girl. Earlier during the week, he subconsciously wrapped his arm around her shoulder. He didn't realize he was doing it until he caught Bella's eye. She smirked, gesturing to the arm. He looked down at it, widening his eyes. Hailey soon dismissed herself to work. He instantly missed her in his hold.

"What for?" Hailey asked. She looked at him, admiring him. He looked good in his jeans and black t-shirt. He could make anything look good.

"I just wanted to hang out. Can I sit?" He asked. Hailey nodded. He quickly sat next to her on the sand. He was a few inches from touching her, yet he felt the heat. That'd be enough for now.

"I used to come here with my parents." She found herself saying. No one really knew that they had died years back. She was glad for that. Whenever one found out, pity was given. She hated it, but she hated having lost her parents even more. She'd give anything for just one more day with them.

"Are they busy a lot?" Zac asked. He was curious as to the topic. The few days he had known her, he has discovered that she keeps to herself and only lets people know what she wants them to know. She's mysterious to him.

He knew that they were gone, but wasn't sure if she knew that he knew. He didn't even know if she knew that he was friends with her brother. He didn't want to overstep his way in her life so he chose to be clueless.

"No," she whispered. She continued to stare out into the ocean, collecting her thoughts. She didn't know why she stated it. But something about Zac made her want to tell him everything and anything. "They died about eight years ago."

"I'm so sorry Hails." Zac said wrapping an arm around her. Her head laid on his chest. She was stunned at the movement but appreciative. She didn't even realize she was crying until Zac wiped a few tears away. "You don't have to tell me anymore. We can discuss it another day, okay."

She nodded. She wiped the rest of her tears away and unraveled herself from his hold. She took a deep breath and faced him. Concern and worry flashed in his eyes. Her heart did a small flip.

"They died in an accident. My oldest brother Josh has taken care of us since." She told him. Zac nodded, missing her in his arms. "It's just the six of us."

"Six?" Zac asked. He was confused. He thought it was only Josh and Luke. He didn't know they had more siblings. No wonder Josh became the adult.

Hailey giggled, standing up. Everyone always reacted like that. Everyone assumed it was just Luke and her. Or that Josh was her only sibling. They don't seem to notice Ben, Seth, or Trinity.

"Come on. I'm sure Ben would love to meet you." She said stretching her arm out. Zac took it. She noticed how her hand fit perfectly in his own. Goosebumps rose as he kept his hand in hers. She made an attempt to pull away but Zac only tightened his hold.

"So who's Ben?" He asked cautiously. He needed to know if she had a boyfriend. He didn't want to intrude. He didn't want to start to fall for a girl that would only see him as a friend.

"My brother. He was the one that convinced me to go to your party." She stated. She wanted to see his reaction to her having four brothers, who are all protective of her. She knew it was too soon to develop feelings over a guy she just met, but she ignored it anyway. When is she ever going to be alone with Zac Logan again?

~~~~~~~~I want to clarify something. These are NOT the same characters as Defend Me. I like using the kids names to sort of excite my readers to read my new book. So, in The Rebel in Disguise, the kids names are Kristina and Annika. That's where Krissy's name came from. Annika was originally for another story as well, but I deleted that one. I hope this clarifies some things! xoxo,Liv814
~~~~~~~~

Chapter 4 | Friends

Walking into the Foster home, Zac didn't know what to expect. Were they going to be shy like her? Were they going to hate him instantly? He knew one sibling and knew of the other. He was just scared of those he didn't know.

Zac stared at Hailey's siblings. When she said they were six, she meant six. She had four brothers, two who are older than her. Zac was slightly intimidated by the look the eldest was giving him. He had heard of Josh Foster. His football coach talked very highly of him.

Josh was sixteen when he was forced to give everything up for his family. He quit football and began to build homes instead. He almost quit school, but pursued to finish his education. Zac's coach says that Josh was the greatest player he ever saw. Since that day, Josh had been his role model and now he was standing in front of him. He was kind of shocked but frightened.

"Joshie, this is Zac." Hailey said introducing the two. She watched as Josh glared at Zac. She gulped. Why did she bring him home so soon? They weren't even a couple. They were barely friends! What was she thinking?

"Zac Logan." Josh said narrowing his eyes. Zac felt highly uncomfortable. He didn't know what to say or do. Usually everyone loved him. "Captain of the football team."

"Yeah." He gulped. "Coach talks about you. He pushes me to be just like you."

"He does?" Josh asked. His intimidating glare vanished with surprise. Zac took that as a good sign.

"Yeah, I looked up to you when you still played. I told everyone I wanted to be as good as you." Zac told him honestly. Josh then smirked.

"Want me to sign something?" Josh teased. Hailey's eyes widened. Well that went better than she thought. Usually, Josh would go all psycho older brother before being comfortable around anyone she brought home.

"Maybe a picture sometime." Zac joked. Josh laughed, nodding. He felt like Josh liked him, which made him grin with happiness.

"Make yourself at home Zac. Welcome to the family. I'm going to go make burgers for dinner. Behave Hails." Josh said giving her a smirk. She felt her cheeks heat up. Josh would embarrass her.

"Alright, since Josh approves, I should too. I'm Ben." One of the guys said. He had blond hair and blue eyes. He was built like an athlete, but not a football player. He would have known him, or at least of him. He doesn't look much older than them.

"He plays baseball at the community college in town." Hailey told Zac. She could read Zac's calculating face. He was trying to figure out if he knew him. Zac wouldn't unless he watched baseball. She guessed Zac only knew of Josh because the entire state knew him. Josh was set to play professionally but gave it up to raise her and her siblings.

"Nice man. I played when I was in elementary school before I found football." Zac told Ben. Ben nodded. He could see that he was starting to accept him too. After all, Ben was the reason they were here.

"Not to burst your bubble, but Hailey prefers baseball over football." Ben said with a teasing tone. Hailey's eyes widened. Ben just had to go there.

When she had come home from the party, she felt amazing. The night had been great and Zac never left her side. She felt protected and wanted. She was starting to like the guy.

So Ben being Ben, asked how the party went. She explained how she didn't do anything illegal and danced the whole night. She even told him about her new friends. Ben then asked about Zac. She had given the answer through her cheeks. Ever since, Ben has teased her about her small crush on the boy.

"Ben, shut up." She said through gritted teeth. The two boys only laughed at her uncomfortableness.

"Oh don't worry. I'm sure i'll be able to persuade her." Zac said throwing an arm around her. He watched as her cheeks tinted even more. Zac caught on to her brother's words, feeling happy. Did that mean Hailey liked him back?

"Now could you persuade her to drive me to the library?" One of the other boys he was yet to meet asked. He was short and blond. He was different then the rest. He didn't look like someone that enjoyed being active. He had walked back into the living room.

"This is my last brother, Seth. He's a nerd." Hailey said with a cheeky grin. Seth rolled his eyes. Zac chuckled at their interaction.

"I'll take you if you want. I prefer to do my homework there." Zac told him. Seth's eyes widened causing him to continue speaking. "My house is always loud and no one else goes there."

"See Hailey! That's exactly why I want to go there." Seth said in exasperation. Hailey sighed. Zac only seemed to get more attractive in her eyes. He loved to study and his brothers already loved him.

"Can I watch my cartoons now?" Hailey heard her sister say. She saw the ten year old with a look that meant trouble. A cranky Trinity is a horrible Trinity.

"Oh yeah, sorry Trin." Hailey said pulling Zac. They had been standing in front of the tv the entire time. It was the only space they had in the living room. The rest of her siblings had gone to do their own thing. "That's my sister by the way."

"She's adorable." Zac said watching the young girl. She looked like a mini Hailey but with a lot more attitude.

"Come on, we can go hangout in my room if you want." Hailey said taking his hand. Those same sparks traveled up both their arms. She ignored them and continued their walk down the hallway and up the stairs.

They passed a few old family photos and a giant collage. Trinity had made it with pictures of them. They looked happy and carefree, but deep down they missed their parents. Even Trinity, who was only four when they died, remembers them.

"You guys only have three rooms?" Zac asked. He was amazed that they didn't have the same luxuries as him, yet they were happy with everything they had. He wished his parents were like them, not caring about money. He was slightly envious at that.

"Luke and Seth have bunk beds in their room. Josh and Ben take turns sleeping in their room. One takes the bed while the other takes the couch. Trinity and I share the master. Josh said we needed it since we were girls and Trinity has more toys." Hailey found herself explaining to him. She was jealous that Zac didn't have to share anything with anyone. He was an only child with very rich family members.

"I really thought this would have been more girly." Zac said when they walked into her room. She had a big bed with a desk in the corner. A mirror was placed on top. Toys littered the ground while a huge toy box sat in the corner. They had a medium sized closet and a dresser with a small tv on top. This was smaller than his own bedroom.

"Trinity and I agreed to white walls. We didn't agree on the rest of the decor. She enjoys barbies and make up, while I am more of a plain Jane." Hailey told him. Zac made a mental note of that. She liked simple and not extravagant things. "So, how's football?"

"Great! We win tomorrow and we're in the first place spot. A few more and then playoffs will begin." Zac found himself saying with so much excitement. He loved football more than anything in the world. It was his one shot of getting away from his messed up family.

"That's great! Ignore Ben's comment from earlier. I like football just as much." She told him with her cheeks ablaze. Zac smiled as her cheeks reddened. He seemed to like that look on her. He loved it even more if it was because of him.

"You're coming to the game tomorrow, right?" Zac asked. Hailey nodded. Zac smirked. Maybe he should get her a jersey with his name and number on the back. Would that be too soon? He hadn't even asked her out yet.

"Of course. Luke is playing too. Plus, I have to be there to cheer on my friends!" She said. She watched as Zac's smile faltered. What did she say?

Zac hated that word immediately. Friend. He finally found a girl he was seemingly interested in and she calls him a friend. He wanted to be more than a friend.

A week of knowing her and he wanted that. Dang. Was he that desperate to find the one or did he truly like her? He was confused now. Maybe they needed to be friends first? He wasn't sure how to start a relationship. He's never had one before.

"Of course! Evan and Nate would love to see you there." He said with a fake smile. He knew Nate would more than love to see her there. He wasn't sure why Nate had a small obsession with her. Ever since the party, Nate just seems to bring her up. He would have liked the topic if it weren't for his annoying remarks.

"Evan, totally! Nate, no thank you." She said sitting on her bed. Zac sat down too. She suddenly felt subconscious about everything. She had her freaking crush in her room, who just met her family and they're sitting on her bed.

"Nate is a jerk. Ignore him." Zac said. He found himself inching closer to her. He wanted nothing more than to kiss her. He needed to prove that he did have real feelings for this girl and it wasn't all in his mind. Maybe then, he'd ask her out. It would definitely get the twins off his back.

"Oh I know. Every day in class, he says something inappropriate." Hailey said standing up. She didn't like how close Zac was getting to her. She needed to breathe.

"I'll get him to back off." Zac said, suddenly feeling angry. Hailey shook her head.

"It's alright Zac. I learned to ignore him. Besides, Luke will hear and want to start another fight with him." Hailey said in annoyance. She hated that they were all so protective of her. She was more than capable of handling herself.

"That's why they got into a fight? Nate said that he was hooking up with the girl Luke was seeing." Zac told her. He could remember them in the locker room. If it weren't for coach, he was sure they'd have been bruised up and possibly suspended. Their school did not tolerate fights.

"Ew no. I was not hooking up with either of them. Nate is not my type." She found herself saying. She widened her eyes, not meeting Zac's gaze. She could feel it penetrating through her.

"Then what is your type?" She heard him say. His voice had deepened, making her heart race. She looked up and saw that he was now a few inches from her. She could feel his breath on her face, making her cheeks tingle.

"Um, well, um." She struggled to speak. His brown eyes were captivating her own. She felt herself start to go weak at the knees. Almost as if he knew, he wrapped an arm around her waist. Sparks flew as they touched, making her heart beat even faster.

Their bodies were now touching and they were yet to break eye contact. She found herself lost in his eyes. She could stare into them forever as the brown illuminated with yellow flecks in the light. His free hand suddenly cupped her cheek. Her heart was now racing at fast speeds.

Zac stared down at the girl. This was it. He could finally kiss her and prove that he did indeed like her. Her eyes stayed on his as he flicked his own down to her pink lips. They looked soft and he wanted to truly know if they were. He rubbed his thumb on her cheek, feeling her involuntarily shiver. He smirked. He shifted his face closer, only millimeters away. He wouldn't kiss her until she answered his question.

"Who is your type?" He whispered. Hailey went to speak, being caught off by a cough. They separated, seeing a smirking Ben at the door. Zac frowned. He was so close.

"Dinner is ready. Hails, next time, shut the door. You don't want Josh to catch you." Ben said before disappearing. Hailey nodded, feeling her heart still racing. She struggled to catch her breath. She was inches away from kissing Zac. She found herself wanting to do it. If only she had moved her head closer then maybe, just maybe she would have had her first kiss.

"Do you want to stay for dinner?" She asked after she found her voice. She saw Zac stiffen, as if he forgot he was still there. He then relaxed, giving her a smile.

"I'd love to Hails, but i'm going to Evan's. His mom makes some mean lasagna. I'll see you tomorrow." He said to her. She found herself saddened. She wanted him to stay. She liked being around him.

"Alright. Bye Zac." She said. She gave him a tight lipped smile. She wasn't really sure how to act now. They had almost freaking kissed! She almost kissed Zac Logan!

"Bye Hails. Enjoy the burger for me." He said. He was about to walk out of her room but stopped. He needed to do this before he chickend out. He walked back towards her and gave her a peck on her forehead. She stood their stunned at the movement. He then walked back out of her room and down the stairs.

His lips felt on fire. He hadn't even kissed her yet that intimate moment caused his heart to do weird shit in his chest. He ignored it and went into the kitchen. He had to say bye to her siblings. He wanted them to like him.

"Hey, thanks for letting me hangout." Zac said at the entry way of the kitchen. Ben, Luke and Josh were in there. Josh was carrying a tray of burgers while Ben was chopping up vegetables. Luke was sitting on his phone, mixing a pitcher of purple liquid. He assumed it was Kool-Aid.

"Hey, thanks for bring my sister home. She loves to wander off." Josh said. He then put the burgers down. "Stay for dinner."

"Yeah Zac. We'd love to hear about your feelings for my sister." Ben smirked. Zac's eyes widened as Luke's phone fell onto the counter. He gulped. Luke was now glaring at him. "Luke chill."

"Like hell. I can't have him and Nate going after her." Luke said. Rage was pooling out of his words. Zac suddenly felt scared to be on his bad side, but pushed that feeling away at the mention of Nate.

"Nate? What do you mean Nate?" Zac asked. Josh sighed.

"That's a conversation for another day. Will you be staying?" Josh asked. He wanted to, not only to hear about Nate, but also because he wanted to be around Hailey and her family. They actually cared for one another, unlike his own.

"No, I was invited to my friend's before I found Hailey at the pier. But thank you. I'd like to stay some other time if you guys will have me." He told them. Josh nodded. Ben smirked while Luke glared. Okay, those are three different emotions.

"Have a goodnight. See you soon." Josh said before disappearing out the door. Josh seemed to be going outside. Luke then picked up his phone and marched over to him. He was about four inches shorter but he was still as intimidating.

"I swear you hurt her and I will hurt you worse." Luke said in a very threatening tone. Zac nodded. That was the last thing he wanted to do.

"Luke, go wash up." Ben ordered. Luke sent Zac one last glare before leaving the room. That left him with Ben. "He's right though. Don't hurt her. She took the death of our parents the worst. She can't have anymore heartbreak."

"I don't want to hurt her. I'm not even sure what I want yet. I'm attracted to her but I don't know how to do any of the dating stuff. I never have." Zac found himself saying. Ben nodded in understanding. "I just like having her around."

"She likes you too, even if you guys did just meet a week ago. Just get to know her before you ask her out." Ben told him. He nodded. He was right. They needed to be friends before they could ever be more.

"Thanks Ben. I'll see you soon." He said. He was about to walk out of the house when Ben shouted.

"Well duh, you are my future brother-in-law." He said with a smirk. Zac's cheeks reddened. Ben sure knows how to tease people. He shook away his embarrassment and got into his car. He needed to figure everything out and the only way to do that was the twins.

Chapter 5 | She Looks So Perfect

Zac stepped outside into the cool night. The sun had set into the ocean and the sea breeze was lightly blowing. It was peaceful, yet his night was not. The twins were hot on his tail as he said those words to them. They wanted to know everything. That was one thing they for sure had in common: they loved gossip.

When he arrived, he walked right into the Green household. They lived on the beach, having their own private one in their backyard. They threw some of the best parties, aside from his own. They hardly threw them now because their mom was home more often.

Zac was envious of their relationship with their parents. He wanted to be close with them. He wanted to share how his day went and what classes he hated.; how football was going and that funny thing Evan did at lunch. There was nothing more that he wished for than for his parents to forget about the money and focus on him and his life. They were always engrossed in having everything but their son.

As Zac stepped into the Green's home, he heard laughter from upstairs. He jogged up the stairs and found the twins in their arcade room. They were sitting on beanbags as they stared at the big screen with remote controls in their hand. He could only guess they were playing Fortnite. Empty soda cans and chip bags littered the room as half eaten candy bags sat on the floor. He could only guessed they had been playing for hours.

"Yo." He said flopping onto an unoccupied bag. The twins let out a grunt, too focused on their game. Zac sighed. He knew what would cause them to forget about the game and pay attention to him. He let out a deep breath before speaking. "I met Hails family."

The controllers then dropped, making noise on the ground. He saw the pair had paused their game and were staring at him with wide hazel eyes. At least they were paying attention to him now. He waited as they gathered their thoughts. Bella was the first to speak.

"Did you just say you met Hailey's family?" She asked with disbelief. Zac nodded.

"What? How? Why? This early? You aren't even dating." Evan spoke next. Zac shrugged. It all happened too quick.

"I know. I found Hailey at the beach. She told me about her parents and then somehow that led to the conversation about her siblings and then we got to me coming over to meet them." Zac told them. The twins continued to stare with wide eyes. "They were awesome, by the way."

"So then why are you here, looking like you are about to shit your pants?" Bella asked. She was always a little vulgar, but she had grown up with him and Nate. It wasn't until high school where Bella met Mariah. Soon, the five were best friends, even if Mariah pretends to hate them. They all know she loves them and wouldn't trade them for anything in the world.

"Because," Zac said feeling his cheeks heat up. "We were going to kiss until one of her brothers interrupted."

"Oh my god. You guys kissed!" Bella screeched. Zac covered his ears before hearing the noise muffled. He saw Evan with a pillow in her face. He chuckled.

"Dude, you just met her and you already fallen for her. I told you that you liked her." Evan said with a smirk. Zac rolled his eyes. He didn't bother denying it. He did like her, but her brother Ben was right. They needed to be friends to see if they truly did get along. It had to be more than just physical attraction.

"I'm still confused. Why are you here and not there, if you like her?" Bella asked once Evan took the pillow off her face. Her eyes were calculating, trying to figure him out. He sighed.

"Because, I need to be friends with her first. We just met a week ago. Plus, I can't just jump into a relationship. I don't even know how to be in one." He found himself saying. Next thing he knew, pillows were being thrown at him. He got off the beanbag and ran out of the room. He heard a grunt from behind and saw the twins were right behind him. He took a sharp turn and ran down the stairs, being careful to not trip. He went straight to the sliding doors that led to the backyard. As he stepped outside, the ocean waves crashed, bringing a sense of tranquility that was soon cut off by the loud and obnoxious twins.

"What the fuck do you mean you need to be friends? You can't friendzone her!" Bella yelled. Evan nodded, agreeing with his twin. Zac turned away from the ocean and focused on them.

"Dude, if you like her make a move. It'll be too late if you wait." Evan added. He sighed, they were right, but he had to do it this way. He needed to make sure that she was the one he wanted to change for. They would only have a few months together before he'd leave. Besides, what's the point in dating her if they're going to break up in the end? Would it even be worth it?

"Can we just agree to disagree?" Zac asked. The twins groaned.

"Fine. But, that doesn't mean we are going to stop her from falling in love with you." Bella said with a smirk. Zac rolled his eyes at the teasing.

"Dude, just don't waste too much time." Evan said. Zac nodded. He didn't want to waste any of her time or his own. He wanted her in his life, he just wanted to make sure it was the way he thought.

"Now, who is up for a round of fortnite?" Bella asked. They all looked at each other before running back into the house.

-

Walking into her English class, Hailey felt his eyes on her. She frowned. Was he ever going to leave her be? She sat down at her usual spot, hearing him speak to Evan. At least she liked Evan. She'd hangout with him, Zac, and the girls at lunch. Nate would join sometimes but then disappear with some slut. She liked the days he chose to leave.

"Hi Hailey! Did you do the homework?" She heard Evan ask. She saw the teacher was occupied with notes on the board so she turned around.

"Hey, yeah. Why? Did you miss a question?" She asked. They had been assigned questions to a chapter they were supposed to read.

"No, but I think you missed mine." Nate spoke. She gave him a blank stare as he smirked. He was flirting and she didn't like it. Can't he take a hint?

"What question?" She asked with boredom evident in her response.

"Can I have your number?" He asked, teasing. She rolled her eyes and turned back around. The teacher then began her lecture. She tried to focus, being unable to with the flying pieces of paper. She looked back quickly to see Nate with his infuriating smirk. She wanted to slap it right off his face. He's such a jerk!

"Alright class, we will be working in groups for the rest of the day. Pick groups of three." She heard her teacher announce. Hailey quickly looked around the room. Moments like this, she hated that she didn't have any friends. Those she talked to in class weren't in this one. She sighed. Maybe she could work alone?

"Hey, join us." She heard Evan say. She turned around and sighed. At least she likes half her group. She was sure that Nate wouldn't cooperate. Maybe she'd be able to do the assignment alone.

"I promise i'll stop making jokes." Nate said in a serious tone. She sighed. Oh what the heck.

"Fine." She grumbled. She turned her body around, looking at the assigned worksheet. They were to answer more questions and read the next chapter. Alright, seemed easy enough. Although, it wasn't.

Nate spent the entire hour flirting with everyone. He especially would tease her and annoy her to no end. At least Evan seemed to actually want to get work done. She vowed to never partner with Nate again. She began to pack her things when the bell rang.

"Hails, thanks for working with me. I'm sure Nate wouldn't have contributed anything. He'd just copy my paper." Evan said as they walked out of the classroom. They began to walk down the hall, running into the Zac.

Her breath caught in her throat as she took in his appearance. She hadn't seen him since their almost kiss in her room the day before. The football players were allowed to ditch homeroom on game days and she wasn't at lunch with them. She was slightly avoiding him, but only because she didn't know how to act around him. They almost kissed!

"Hailey, hey." Zac said, scratching the back of his neck. She watched the biceps brachii contract before removing her eyes from his arm. She then stared up into his brown eyes before her gaze shifted down to his lips. She almost kissed him. She suddenly found herself wishing she had.

"Hi." She said in a whisper. Zac looked at the girl he couldn't keep off his mind. He tried distracting himself by thinking about the game. They were playing for the number one seed in the state tonight. He knew his team could earn it.

"How are these baboons treating you?" Zac asked. Evan scoffed.

"We, well I am treating her like a princess. Now, this dimwit," Evan said pointing at Nate, "is another story." Evan said. Zac turned and saw Nate leaning up against a random locker. He had a bored expression on his face. Zac couldn't read his best friends thoughts.

"Nate." Zac stated. Hailey watched the boys. She didn't want to interrupt. They seemed to be in their own little world, forgetting she existed.

"I'm not doing anything you wouldn't do." Nate said full of arrogance. Zac frowned. He would have done everything he was doing, but he didn't see the fun in that anymore. He wanted a serious relationship. He wanted what his parents didn't have.

"That's what i'm afraid of." Zac said. Nate rolled his eyes before separating himself from the locker.

"I have to go to class. See ya." Nate said walking off. Zac raised an eyebrow at his best friend's behavior. He was acting weirder than usual.

"I'm off too. I promised Bell's i'd give her the worksheet for math. See you at the game Hails!" Evan said. She gave him a small wave as his disappeared into the crowd. She turned to Zac. He was looking down at her, making her redden.

"You're coming to the game right?" Zac asked. He wanted her there.

"Of course. I wouldn't miss it. Plus Bella and Mariah had been pestering me all week to go. I can't ditch them now." She said with a giggle. Zac grinned, making her heart flip in her chest.

"Can you meet my outside the locker room about an hour before the game starts? I want to give you something." Zac asked. She nodded, unsure of what he wanted to give her.

"Yeah, i'll text you when i'm on my way." She told him. Zac nodded, feeling excited. He just hoped she appreciated his effort.

"Alright babe, i'll see you." He said. He gave her a quick hug before walking off. He couldn't be late to class. Coach would kill him. He walked further down the hall, feeling his smile widen. He was going to make this game a memorable one.

-

Standing outside the locker room, he felt nervous. Earlier, he felt like it was the right thing to do. Now, he wasn't sure. Hailey had texted him of her whereabouts and would be there in a few minutes. He held the old jersey in his hands, feeling his heart beat fast.

Not only was he going to play in a very important game, but he was also going to give Hailey his old team jersey. He wanted everyone to know she was his, even if they weren't dating. He wanted to be her friend first before asking her out. He just wanted no one else to notice her until then.

He heard footsteps around the corner. He ran a hand through his hair smiling as he took in her appearance. She was in ripped jeans and a plain white tee. She had a grey hoodie wrapped around her waist.

"Hey babe." He said getting her attention. Hailey looked up, stunned by him. He was dressed in his uniform. He had black lines on his cheek and his hair was its messy self. He looked really, really good.

"Hey Zac, what is it you wanted to give me?" She asked. Her heart was beating quickly as she noticed he was holding something.

"I wanted you to wear this. I notice you don't have a team shirt on, so it'll be perfect." Zac said. He handed the jersey to Hailey. She quickly unfolded it and gasped. It was one of Zac's old jerseys. It had his number, 4, and his last name on it.

"It's fine Zac. I can buy a shirt later." She told him. She tried handing the jersey back but Zac wouldn't take it.

"No. Wear it. I don't use it anymore. Besides, you'll look cute in it." He said. Hailey's cheeks reddened at his comment. Zac smiled. He loved making her blush.

"Alright. Thanks." She said. She then slipped on the blue and yellow jersey, watching in hang to her knees. She scrunched it in the back before tying it with an elastic. Her brown hair would have to stay loose for the night.

Zac stared at her, feeling his heart begin to race. She looked perfect standing there in his jersey. He was sure everyone would now know that she was his. And someday, that would be true, even if he did leave.

"Anytime. Now go and find a seat. I want you to be able to watch my muscles." He teased. Hailey felt her cheeks heat up even more. What is it with this boy and embarrassing her? It was even worse that he knew she was more there to admire his body than to watch the actual game.

"I do not come for that." She said trying to defend herself. Zac only chuckled.

"It's okay if you do. Now go." Zac said. She nodded. She did need to get going and so did he. She didn't want him to get into trouble for being out here and talking to her. He had a game to win. "I'll see you afterwards."

"Good luck." She said to him. He grinned.

"I don't need luck if I have you." He stated. He then pecked her forehead before jogging inside. Hailey stood there stunned. It was the second time he lays a kiss on her. She wasn't sure what it meant, but she knew she wanted the next one to be on her lips.

She looked down at her outfit and felt her heart skip a few beats. She was sure the moment the girls saw her, they'd want every detail. She tried fighting off her smile as she made her way to the stands. She had a game to watch.

-

Zac ended up winning. She watched as him and the guys threw their helmets in the air. The entire game was nerve racking. The scored continued to bounce back and forth. The fans were on the edge of their seats until the very end. Zac threw a winning pass to Nate in the in-zone. The crowd had gone wild. She felt so much energy and excitement.

"Girl, don't think that just because we didn't ask about that jersey, doesn't mean we aren't gonna ask now." Bella said as they made their way out of the stands. They were going to congratulate the boys on the field.

When she arrived from seeing Zac, the girls widened their eyes at her outfit but didn't say anything. The game was beginning in a matter of seconds and the girls did not want to lose any second of it. She was grateful for the distraction. It gave her time to think about everything. But, she really didn't have time because of the game. It was exhilarating and left no time to think.

"We're going shopping tomorrow." Mariah said. Hailey shook her head. She hate going clothes shopping, plus she didn't have the money to spend.

"No thanks." She found herself saying. The two girls raised an eyebrow before shaking their heads.

"Oh no you don't. We need to make you hot for the party tomorrow." Bella said. Hailey looked at them with confusion.

"What party?" She asked. Mariah laughed as Bella smirked.

"The one Evan and I are throwing." Bella said. Hailey nodded in understanding before shaking her head again. It was her turn to babysit Trinity.

"I can't. I have to babysit my little sister." She told them. Mariah shook her head.

"No. You are coming shopping and to the party. I'll ask one of your brother's to take her if I have to." Mariah said with determination. Hailey was about to reply but stopped. Zac was talking to the school slut, Sasha. She felt her stomach twist with disgust. What did boys see in her?

"Oh ignore that skank. He hates her." Bella said catching her gaze. Hailey shook her head. She couldn't get jealous. They weren't together and she was sure he didn't like her like that. "Besides, you're the one he likes. Now agree to come before I smack some sense into you."

"Fine, i'll go. I'm sure my brother Ben will take her. Now, i'll go shopping but i'm not buying anything." She told them. Mariah nodded but kept a smirk on her face. She felt frightened by her attitude but ignored it.

"We promise that Zac won't take his eyes off of you all night." Mariah said. Hailey felt uneasy but didn't reply. Maybe shopping with them would be fun.

Chapter 6 | Crush

F our hours in and she was exhausted. Hailey didn't know the mall had so many stores with so many things to purchase. The girls were going crazy over everything: sales, clearance, colors, styles, and sizes! It made her brain hurt.

Bella was obsessed with buying Hailey dresses while Mariah wanted to buy her cute pairs of skinny jeans and pretty tops. Hailey said no to both. She didn't have the money for any of the outfits. She had only brought enough cash for a drink at Starbucks and that was a splurge.

They were currently in the coffee and tea store, enjoying a much needed break. She had ordered a grande mango black tea lemonade. The girls had insisted on buying her the larger size, but she denied it. She didn't like other people paying for her stuff.

"Hailey, we need to go back and buy that dress." Mariah pleaded. Hailey shook her head. It was way out of her price range plus her brothers would kill her if she walked out of the house in something like that. It emphasized her nonexistent curves and barely covered anything.

"You would look killer in it!" Bella added. Hailey continued to shake her head.

"No thank you. I'll just wear jeans and a t-shirt again." She told them. The girls gave her blank looks, causing her to roll her eyes.

"You can just borrow something because we are not letting you show up in jeans." Mariah said as she sipped on her venti iced latte. Bella nodded. She had ordered a venti strawberry açaí with lemonade. She let Hailey try some and she found it tasty, but not as good as her own drink.

Soon, the girls got into a somewhat comfortable silence. They were lost in their own thoughts, Hailey thinking about her potential outfits for the night. Maybe she should look for a dress that was within her price range and not too showy. She was about to comment it when moments later Bella broke the silence with a smirk.

"So that jersey?" Bella asked with a teasing tone. Hailey's cheeks quickly reddened. She was surprised it took them this long to bring it up.

After the game, they congratulated the boys before Hailey had to leave. They had no time to really talk about anything. She simply said congrats to Zac and the boys before walking off to find her eldest sibling. Josh was there to pick her and Luke up. He had watched the game and commented on the jersey when she found him. She told him that had Zac lent it to her because she didn't have any football team shirts. Luke eyed her curiously while Josh said that was nice of him. She didn't run into Ben when she got home, which she was thankful for. She was sure he'd start with his teasing and say Zac claimed her. She was positive that Zac didn't give her the jersey for that.

"What about the jersey?" Hailey asked. She knew exactly what they meant. She just didn't want to admit it.

"Don't play dumb Hails. Zac gave you his jersey to wear. Guys only do that when they claim a girl as theirs." Bella said. Mariah nodded in agreement.

"But i'm not his girl." Hailey defended. She felt her heart race at that thought. That can't be the reason Zac gave her the jersey. He said it was because she had no school gear, which was partly true. But, was he claiming her as his? She found herself smiling at that possibility, even if it was a very faint one.

"Oh but you are. You're grinning from ear to ear. You like him." Bella stated. Her cheeks only seem to redden. "You do, don't you?"

"I think I might have a small, itty bitty crush on Zac." Hailey mumbled to the girls. They stared at her with their mouths open. Was it really that hard to believe? They were just teasing her about him. Did they know something she didn't?

"Oh my god." Mariah finally spoke after a complete minute. Hailey stared at the two girls. She didn't know what else to say.

"This is perfect." Bella said. Hailey stared at the brunette. What is she talking about? "You will definitely look hot tonight."

"What?" Hailey asked. Mariah let out a laugh that sounded slightly evil. She suddenly felt scared of her new friend.

"Just shut up Hails. Tonight will be a night you won't forget." Mariah said with a smirk. She nodded, sipping on her drink. Maybe if she stayed quiet, they'd forget she existed. She didn't know what the two had planned. She definitely didn't know if it was good, but there was only one way to find out.

-

No. No. No. And no. She was not going to come out of Bella's room looking like this. She was wearing a tight maroon dress. It was strapless with a thin strap that tied around her neck like a halter top. The skirt went barely passed her butt with cutouts underneath her cleavage. They gave her silver strappy heels to wear and did her makeup. Her hair was in a pony tail. Although, the girls had straightened it, she didn't want her hair in her face.

"Not happening." Hailey said as she stared in the mirror. She heard the girls groan for the thousandth time. Was she really complaining that much?

"No. You are going downstairs like this. We all look hot." Bella said. She chose to wear a high-waisted black leather skirt with a zipper down the front. She paired it with a see-through white top tucked in. It had the words 'Louis Vuitton' printed on it. Since it was sheer, she had on a black bikini on underneath. She paired her outfit with black booties. Her hair was in waves and her makeup was natural with a nude, pink lip.

Mariah was wearing a black leather jacket on top of a black body-con dress. It was short but emphasized her figure amazingly. Hailey was jealous of the curves Mariah got from playing endless hours of soccer. She put on black over the knee high boots. Her blond locks were curled while her makeup was full of silvers on the eyes. She looked gorgeous. Hailey was nothing compared to her two new friends.

"You all look way better than me." Hailey said. She looked exposed and unlike herself. She knew she should have denied Bella buying her this dress. She had joked about wearing it and was now regretting it.

"Oh shut up. You look hot and Zac is going to agree. I'm positive he won't be able to keep his eyes or hands off of you." Mariah stated. Her cheeks tinted red for the thousandth time. The girls had done nothing but tease her since she told them about her crush. She was never going to need blush again.

"Why did I tell you guys?" Hailey asked as she covered her face in embarrassment.

"Because we are your friends and we deserved to know. Plus, now we can leave you and Mr. Logan alone." Mariah teased. Hailey groaned again. Were they ever going to stop?

"Now come on, the party started." Bella said as she put away her makeup pallets. The party was downstairs and one could feel the music. Hailey only assumed the house was already packed with teenagers wanting to get wasted. The party had only started about twenty minutes ago. "I hope Evan put away mom's valuables."

"Of course he did. He's a total good boy." Mariah said. Bella rolled her eyes. For the few days Hailey has known him, Evan was definitely on the responsible side of things. The three boys were definitely different from each other, yet so alike.

"Now come on." Bella said. She grabbed Hailey's wrist, knowing that if she didn't, Hailey would try to escape. Maybe she could disappear when they left to dance. She was sure Ben would come pick her up if need be.

"You are going to have fun." Mariah ordered Hailey. Hailey nodded. She needed to have fun. She convinced Ben to take care of her sister again. She needed to at least enjoy this party or that would have gone to waste.

"Alright. Let's do this while I still have the confidence." Hailey said. The two girls smirked before walking out the door. The music blared as they began to walk down the hall. Bella locked her bedroom door before following them down the stairs.

Teens filled up the living room, dancing, drinking, and talking. Usually, they'd have to squeeze through the sweaty bodies, but it seemed as if everyone parted ways for them. It was like a scene in a movie. They walked through the party with all eyes on them. The music continued to play, but no one moved. Hailey felt subconscious, but continued to follow the two girls. They headed into the kitchen where they found the boys.

Evan was leaning up against the counter with a bottle in his hand. Nate had his arm around some random girl and Zac was sitting on the counter. He looked bored out of his mind. He was staring down at his phone, ignoring the party around him.

The clicking of the girls heels seem to draw the boys out of their mind. The first to see them was Evan. He looked up from his bottle. His eyes widened as he took in their appearance. He was in shock at the two girls, who weren't his twin.

Hailey noticed Nate next. He was whispering something in the random girl's ear as he looked up. He, too, widened his eyes. For some reason, they way her eyes met his caused a weird emotion to flow through her. She didn't like it all.

"Woah." She heard Zac's voice. She disconnected her eyes from Nate's and found herself blushing. Zac was staring her up and down, biting his lip. He was really attractive, even more so in his black leather jacket and plain white tee.

"Hey guys. How do we look?" Bella asked as she twirled. Hailey grabbed the end of her skirt and attempted to pull it down. It still felt way too short. It only seemed to get shorter. She really wished she was wearing jeans.

"Smokin'." Hailey heard Nate say. She looked at him as he stared at her with a smirk. His eyes began to roam her body, making her queasy. She needs a big hoodie or something.

"Hailey, want to dance?" Zac asked. He was suddenly standing in front of her. She couldn't see Nate and she let herself relax. She didn't trust that boy and she didn't like him. He was the known bad boy. Everyone knew what he was capable of.

"Um well um." Hailey began to stutter underneath Zac's gaze. Zac was looking down at her with a smirk. His brown eyes were shining as they stared into her own. She suddenly felt his hands on her hips. It sent shock-waves to her brain, alerting her that she still needed to say a response.

"Please?" Zac asked. He wanted to have this girl all to himself, but he knew it was too soon. He was pushing it with the jersey, but he couldn't help himself. He wanted everyone to back off.

When he'd look up from the field to the stands, he saw her with the two girls. She looked beautiful and having her in his jersey was the icing on the cake. Some of the guys on the field noticed her, but didn't say anything. As soon as they saw his jersey, they backed off. Hopefully, they would stop talking about her in the locker room. She was the guys' newest conquest since the girls befriended her.

He wanted to protect her and wasn't going to allow some idiot to play her. They all wanted to sleep with her and add her to the list. Zac for once, didn't want to be apart of it. He actually wanted to date the girl and not sleep with her. He wanted to be the boyfriend. He never thought he'd ever be thinking that. The word felt so foreign to him.

"Sure." Hailey found herself saying with a new found confidence. Zac's smirk changed into a grin. She noticed he had a dimple on one side. Zac took his hands off her hips and took one of her hands in his own. Sparks ignited as they intertwined their fingers together. Zac then pulled her out of the kitchen and into the living room.

People again parted ways as they made their way to the center of the dance floor. Everyone watched them. Zac didn't seem to notice anything while Hailey hated being their attention. Once everyone found out about her parents, no one would look at he the same. It was one of the reasons they moved.

Zac found the center of sweaty bodies where he pulled Hailey into his chest. Her hands flew up trying to stop her fall. She didn't trust herself in the heels. She then saw that she didn't fall and her hands were placed on or above his pecs, on his chest. His body tensed underneath her hands. She could feel Zac's heart under her palm. It was beating fast.

Zac liked the way Hailey was staring up at him. He wanted nothing more than to crash his lips onto hers. She looked beautiful in that dress which only made him want her more. He guided Hailey's hands around his neck, watching her cheeks redden. He chuckled. He loved making her blush.

"Sorry." Hailey whispered in his ear. She was sure he wouldn't have heard her from the blaring music. The whole room was thumping as teenagers danced on each other. They were grinding and practically having sex on the dance floor. It was a typical high school party.

"It's alright babe. Just move to the beat." Zac whispered back. She shivered as his breath met her ear. Zac smirked as he saw how she reacted to him. He placed his hands back on her hips and moved her side to side. Together they began to dance to whatever song was on the speakers.

After a few songs, Zac felt himself in a trance. He couldn't look away from the girl in his arms. She was enjoying herself and it was with him. Nothing could ruin the moment. Hailey giggled as Zac chuckled. They weren't dancing like other couples, but they were still having fun. She enjoyed being in his arms and never wanted to leave.

"Hey man, can I dance with her?" They heard someone say. Hailey looked away from Zac and saw Nate. Zac's smile turned into a frown.

"What?" Zac asked. Nate chuckled.

"I asked if I could dance with her." Nate repeated. Hailey tensed in Zac's arms. He could tell she didn't want to be with her.

"Hailey, would you like to dance with Nate?" Zac asked her. She looked up at Zac, hoping he could read her and say no for her. She didn't want to leave him for Nate. She didn't want to be anywhere near him.

"No, thank you." Hailey whispered. Nate's smirk morphed into a frown. That caused Zac to smirk.

"Go dance with Sasha." Zac said noticing the blond. She was wearing practically nothing in short shorts and a crop top. Her hair was curled in big waves as she wore sky high heels. Usually he would have been on top of that, but he didn't want that anymore. Gladly, Nate was into her.

"Come on babe, just one dance." Nate said to Hailey. Her stomach twisted as he called her babe. She didn't like the word when it came from him.

"She said no Nate." Zac said cutting in. He placed Hailey behind his back and looked at his best friend. Nate glared at him. The fight felt wrong but Zac didn't like the way he was bothering Hailey.

"Damn, fine. I'll go fuck Sasha then. Enjoy yourself." Nate said before stomping away. The brown haired boy with the sharp jaw line soon disappeared. Hailey felt herself let out a breath. Zac whipped around and pulled her into his chest. Her heart started to race again, but this time she liked it.

"Are you alright?" Zac asked. Hailey nodded as she laid her head on his chest. His hands were around her waist, hugging her tight. "I'm not sure what got into him."

"It's alright Zac. Nate has always been like that." She told him. Zac grimaced as she repeated those words from days earlier. He needed to know why Nate wouldn't leave her alone.

"How about we go get a drink?" Zac offered. Hailey nodded. He untangled himself from her and grabbed her hand once again. More sparks flowed through their bodies as he pulled her back towards the kitchen.

Hailey gasped as she saw her younger brother snogging a girl. She didn't know he'd be at the party, much less making out with a girl in the kitchen. Zac's head whipped around as he heard Hailey. His eyes soon found Luke which he smirked. It was about time the damn boy gets a girl. He felt Hailey tense beside him.

"Stop watching." Zac teased. Hailey's cheeks brightened making her smack his chest. He feigned hurt making her giggle. They both knew Hailey would never be able to hurt him. He was a wall of steel. Hailey wondered if he had a six pack.

"Can you just get me that drink? I think i'm going to be sick." Hailey said turning away from her brother. She saw Zac nod before pulling her further into the kitchen.

They were now in the corner with the girls. They smirked as Hailey walked in with her hand securely in Zac's. She felt her cheeks blaze once again. Zac then let go of her hand only to place them on her waist. In a matter of seconds, she found herself in the air before being placed on the counter.

"Stay here." Zac said. His hands were on her thighs, sending sparks up her leg. She nodded, not being able to find words. She saw Zac disappear before hearing the girls making kissing noises.

"Muah muah muah. I love you Zac." Bella said in a high pitched voice.

"Let's make so many babies tonight." Mariah added in the same tone. Hailey rolled her eyes.

"It's not like that." Hailey defended. The girls stared at her before bursting into laughter.

"Right and i'm not Evan's twin." Bella said. Hailey sighed. Maybe it was like that then.

Meanwhile, Zac fished through the coolers for water. He didn't want to have alcohol if he was going to be with Hailey all night. He wanted to make sure she was safe from any drunk idiot and still be able to remember the night with her.

"Damn bro, you got it bad." He heard Nate say. Zac found the water bottle before pulling it out. He then turned around to face his best friend.

"Nate, what the fuck is your problem?" Zac asked full of irritation. Nate scoffed.

"I don't have a problem. Why the fuck would you think I did?" Nate asked. Zac narrowed his eyes.

"Because you won't fucking leave Hailey alone." Zac told him. Nate matched his glare.

"There are things you don't know." Nate said through gritted teeth. It was Zac's turn to scoff.

"I'm your best friend. What don't I know?" Zac asked. Nate broke the staring contest. Zac noticed a small crowd of people surrounded them.

"Not here Zac. Not here." Nate said before walking away. Zac stood there confused. What was that? What was Nate hiding? Why did he suddenly feel like he couldn't trust his best friend?

Chapter 7 | A Million Dreams

It was beginning to feel like a routine to be sitting on the beach, admiring the blue ocean. Every Saturday morning, she found herself enjoying the sea breeze. She liked being on her own, imagining her mom with her. She had a cup full of hot chocolate and her fuzzy blanket wrapped around her body. It was as if her mom was there. She could almost feel her presence.

She closed her eyes to bask in the tranquility that the early morning provided, only to be interrupted by someone stepping on a branch. She turned around and saw Zac. He gave her an apologetic smile. She giggled.

"What are you doing here?" She asked him. Zac sat down beside her, stealing her warm beverage. "Hey! That's mine."

"Sorry babe, but it's cold. What are you even doing up so early?" Zac asked her. She ignored the butterflies that fluttered at the endearment. They were just friends. She had to keep reminding herself of that.

"Thinking." She stated. Zac nodded. He admired the girl beside him. She was wearing a soft blue top with what he assumed were jeans. He couldn't tell from the blanket laid around her body. "Did you call Seth?"

"Maybe." He teased. Her youngest brother was helping keep tabs on her. He didn't want anyone else discovering her. He didn't want to share her with anyone else. She was amazing in every way. Plus, he enjoyed the company at the library.

When Hailey and the girls were off shopping the day before, he found himself at the Foster residence. Ben had opened the door. He had pink lipstick and a matching pink tutu on. Zac struggled to keep himself from laughing.

"Shut it." Ben said with a frown. That's when Zac lost it. He let out a bark of laughter, earning daggers from Ben. "Logan."

"Okay. Okay, i'm done." Zac said as he tried to end his fit. A minute later, he was able to keep a straight face, well as straight as possible while still staring at Ben.

"My sister isn't here." Ben said still annoyed. Zac nodded.

"I know. She's off with the girls. I actually came to see if Seth wanted to come with me to the library." Zac said. Ben's eyes widened at his words. He then allowed him in. Zac stepped into the living room, seeing Trinity on the ground. She seemed to be picking up colorful objects. "Hi Trinity."

The little girl looked up. She had a confused face. Did he not remember her? It had only been a few days since he was last here. Seconds later, she got off the floor and ran to him. Her small body hugged his left knee, taking him by surprise.

"You're Hailey's boyfriend!" Trinity said squeezing him tight. He chuckled.

"Not yet." He said through a grin. Ben chuckled, sliding off the tutu. "How are you princess?"

"I'm awesome. Benny let me do his makeup. Isn't he pretty?" Trinity asked with a cheeky smile. Ben looked at Zac with a blank stare. Zac burst out laughing again.

"He looks beautiful. So, where's your brother Seth?" Zac asked her. She shrugged, detangling herself from him.

"Seth!" Trinity shouted. Ben chuckled as he wiped off the sparkles. Footsteps were heard before a clumsy Seth ran into the room.

"I was summoned?" Seth asked. He was out a breath. He looked at Trinity before he looked at Zac. "Zac, hey."

"Hey Seth. I was wondering if you wanted to come to the library with me?" Zac asked. Seth's eyes almost popped our of their sockets before he was nodding his head.

"Let me just grab my stuff." Seth said with excitement seeping from his words. Zac nodded, chuckling. Seth then ran back up the stairs.

"Seth has been bugging me to take him. I was supposed to take him today, but Hailey asked me to babysit Trin." Ben told him. Zac nodded in understanding. The girls kept bringing it up at lunch, trying to convince her to go shopping with them. "She also wanted to go to that party tonight. Be careful. She hasn't done anything."

"I know. It's one of the things I like about her. I'll take care of her." Zac told him. Ben nodded. Moments later, Seth ran into the room again.

"Alright. I'm ready." Seth said. He had his backpack slung over his shoulder. "I'll see you later Ben."

"Be careful Seth. Take care of my brother Zac." Ben said. You could here the authority in his tone. It surprised Zac how in seconds he changed from the goofy brother to the protective guardian.

"I'll drop him off in a few hours." Zac said. Soon, the two were out the door. Seth gasped when he noticed Zac's car. He had an all black 2018 Dodge Challenger. It was his 18th birthday present from his dad. One of his 'i'm sorry i don't care about you' gifts.

"This is beautiful." Seth said in awe. Zac chuckled, unlocking the car. "You are my new best friend."

"I'm glad you think that man. Now come on, let's go to the library." Zac said shifting the car into drive. The two spent the entire drive talking about cars. Zac even managed to convince him to tell him things about Hailey. After spending a few hours with him, and dropping him off before the party, he found out that he not only enjoyed the afternoon with Hailey's brother, but that Hailey is the girl he's meant to be with.

Zac smiled at the memories he made with Hailey's youngest brother the day before. He then turned to look at the girl. She was looking at him with a goofy grin.

"So, what are you doing up so early?" Hailey asked. Zac handed her the cup back. She took a sip of it, glad for its warmth. It was only eight in the morning and the sea breeze was still slightly cold on this Sunday morning. She liked to wake up before dawn to enjoy the early morning. It was her favorite time of day. The sun was rising and the world around her was peaceful. It also gave her time time to sit and think about everything.

"I couldn't really sleep." Zac told her. It was true. He had been restless with thoughts of Nate flooding his mind. He was confused as to why he was so rude and mean to Hailey. He didn't want to continue to ask him, knowing Nate wasn't one to talk about his feelings.

After finally giving up on sleep, he chose to get out of bed. He showered and changed, finding himself texting Hailey. He knew it was early, but was hopeful that she was an early bird. When he received no text back, he called

Seth. He had woken him up, not being very helpful. Seth then agreed to check her room, not finding her. He then mentioned that she sometimes goes to watch the sunrise. He knew where she was immediately.

"This is my favorite time of day." Hailey said. She looked out at the ocean. The sun was slightly in the sky, creating oranges within blues. It was beautiful.

"Let me guess, it's quiet?" Zac joked. Hailey shook her head, laughing.

"Because it is quiet and peaceful. It signifies a new day and that whatever was bothering you before is in the past. One must focus on the future, making the next day even better. My mom told me that once." Hailey said. A random seagull flew by before landing a few feet away. It picked something up before disappearing. She took a sip of her drink, finding it empty. She frowned. Zac drank it all.

"I like that. Your mom seemed like an awesome person." Zach said. Hailey smiled.

"She was. I would spend every moment possible with her. When she wasn't at home or my brothers' games, she was at the hospital, helping others. She always wanted to be there for everyone. It's the thing I loved most about her." Hailey said with a small smile. She felt tears start to prick her eyes. "It's also the thing I hated most."

"What do you mean?" Zac asked. She closed her eyes, trying to control the tears threatening to fall. Talking about her mom always made her cry.

"There was a terrible accident one day. She got called into work because they were short on nurses. My dad was driving her when their car collided with a drunk driver. They were killed instantly." Hailey said. The tears began to slip down her face. She quickly wiped them away. She didn't want to cry today.

"I'm sorry Hails." Zac said. He scooted closer to her, wrapping his arm around her. She inhaled his scent, feeling better instantly.

"I want to help people like her." Hailey told him. She wiped away her remaining tears, getting out of his hold. Her heart was beating fast, already missing his warmth. She needed some distance from the boy if she wanted to last. She was sure her heart would explode.

"Like volunteering?" Zac asked. She shook her head.

"I want to be a nurse like her." She told him. She felt a sense of pride. She knew her mom would have been ecstatic from the news. Her mom always made it important that one has to be selfless to be able to be selfish.

"That's awesome Hails. So then, what are your plans after college?" Zac asked her. Hailey sighed.

"Nursing school. I want to go really bad, but I don't know if i'll be able to." She stated. Zac raised an eyebrow.

"What do you mean?" He asked.

"We don't have the funds for me to go. Ben goes to college because of his baseball scholarship. I'm working to help pay for the things at home, but also to save money. Although, I don't think i'll be able to pay for it all on my own. Plus, I don't think Josh can take out anymore loans. He had to when our parents died." Hailey told him. Zac nodded in understanding.

"I'm sure you'll get a scholarship to the school you want." Zac told her. He wanted to be optimistic for her. She deserved to go and leave her dream.

"I'm hoping, but I don't think academics will be enough." She told him. The only ones that ever seem to get a full ride are those with athletic abilities, like him.

"Apply for outside scholarships. My mom works with some foundation that works with kids in need. I'm sure she has some connections that can help." He found himself saying. He didn't like talking about his parents' work, but if it meant helping Hailey, he'd attend their work parties and dinners.

"Zac, that's sweet of you. But, no. I don't want you to go to that trouble. I'll figure something out." She told him. Her heart was squeezing at the thought of him doing whatever he could to help. It made her like him more. He was being selfless and thinking of her. "So what are your plans after high school?"

"I don't know yet. I want to get as far away as possible from here." Zac told her. Hailey's heart stopped squeezing, cracking instead. He wanted to leave this town, while she wanted to stay close to home. She didn't want to leave her siblings.

"What's so bad about here?" She asked. Zac looked at her. Sadness was in her eyes. He didn't want her to think it was because of her. It was the total opposite. She might be the only reason he'd ever stay.

"My parents. They don't care about me or anyone else. They aren't even together anymore. They haven't been since I was 9. All they care about is themselves, their image, and the amount of money they have. The only reason they haven't officially split is because my grandparents will take away their fortune." Zac told her. He suddenly felt like a weight had been lifted off his shoulder's. He had never told anyone those feelings before. Nate was the only one that new about his parents façade. With Hailey, it just felt easy to tell her everything, including him wanting to leave everything behind.

Hailey sat there stunned at his words. She assumed he wanted to leave to meet new girls or something. What he said, was what she'd never expect. Zac seemed to have everything, which he did, all except love. He didn't have the same relationship with his parents she had with her siblings. She wouldn't be able to survive if it weren't for them.

"I'm sorry Zac." Hailey whispered. Zac turned to look at Hailey. The sadness that was on her face was now replaced with pity. He shook his head.

"It's fine. I have my friends. That's all that matters. Besides, I have you now in my life." He found himself saying. Hailey's eyes lit up, making her cheeks redden as well. "So, besides being a nurse, what other dreams do you have?"

"A million dreams of helping others and my family." Hailey smiled. Zac chuckled.

"Where do you see yourself in five years?" Zac asked. Hailey thought about the question.

"I would be graduating from college. I hopefully will have a job at a hospital helping others." Hailey told him. Zac nodded.

"What about the rest of your life? Friends? Family? Love?" Zac asked. Hailey's eyes widened at the L word. Her heart was racing as thoughts of Zac filled her brain. She quickly shook them away, feeling her cheeks heat up, again.

"I hope that my family is better and not worrying about money. They are the most important people in my life. Josh sacrificed everything for us and I want him to be happy too." Hailey said. Josh sacrificed his entire life for them and she was beyond grateful. She hopes to be able to repay him someday, even if its with just naming her son after him.

"Will all your siblings be graduated?" Zac asked. Hailey shook her head.

"Trinity will be a freshman I think. What about you? Where do you see yourself? What are your dreams?" Hailey asked. Zac shrugged.

"I haven't really thought about the future. I just know that I want to be happy. I want to be away from my parents, but still near the people I love." Zac said. He looked at Hailey. She was looking out at the ocean, listening to him. They had different ideas of the future, yet they both came back to hoping they were happy.

"Speaking of your friends, what happened to Nate last night?" Hailey asked. She saw Nate leave during the party and never came back. When Zac came back from grabbing them water bottles, he seemed slightly angry and frustrated. She didn't ask, not wanting to but into his life.

They had just hung out with Mariah and the twins. Evan spent the entire night flirting with Mariah who just brushed his comments off. Bella was slightly tipsy and dancing in the kitchen. She enjoyed the rest of the night with them, but was still worried about Zac. He didn't seem to be as happy as before.

He later took her home with a word. He did manage to say goodbye and gave her a small hug, which caused her heart to do flips. It was one of the reasons she had woken up early. She wanted to think about the boy causing a whirlwind of emotions, while talking to her mom about him.

"I don't know. I haven't heard from him." Zac told her. He didn't want to talk about him. "Do you want to go get breakfast?"

"Sure." Hailey said. She ignored the topic of Nate. She could sense that he wasn't ready to talk about it.

"Come on," Zac said getting up. He offered his hand which she gladly took. She slipped the blanket off and stood up. Zac tightened his hold on her, not wanting to let go. Those same cliché sparks were flying as they walked towards the parking lot.

Hailey had walked to the beach, enjoying the coolness of the ocean while Zac had driven his car. He opened the door for her which she giggled at.

He chuckled at her reaction before walking to the driver's side. He quickly got in and drove to the diner.

Hailey rolled her eyes as Zac sang along to the radio. He was singing horribly after he found her recording him. She giggled as Zac's voice changed. She decided to stop recording the cute boy and paid attention to their surroundings. She saw Carl's diner which made her whip her head to him. He had a smirk on his face.

"Zac, out of all places we could have gotten breakfast, you chose my work?" She asked. Zac shrugged but kept the smirk on his face. He pulled into the parking lot as his phone vibrated. He made sure the car was parked before taking it out.

Hailey watched as Zac's smirk widened. He shut the car off after slipping his phone back into his pocket. She was curious as to who texted him but brushed it off. They both got out of the car and made their way inside. The little bell rang which caused the guests to turn to look at her.

"Hailey? What are you doing here on your day off?" Carl, her boss asked when he noticed her.

"Zac wanted your amazing breakfast." She said sweet talking him. He chuckled.

"I'm glad someone thinks that. Now, go ahead and find a spot. I'll be over in a sec." Carl said. She nodded, turning to look at Zac. He was facing his phone. Zac had received a text from Evan asking if he wanted to come over for breakfast. Zac had replied that he was getting some food with Hailey if he and Bella wanted to join.

"Zac?" Hailey said. Zac looked up and saw a confused Hailey.

"Yeah?" Zac asked. Hailey raised an eyebrow. He could sense she was curious about who he was texting.

"Where do you want to sit?" She asked him. Zac looked around and found a booth big enough to fit six. He began to walk over and slid in. "Not that this isn't fine, but why such a big one?"

Zac was about to reply but stopped when he heard the diner door open. The bell rung and he heard his best friends walk in. Bella was fighting with Evan as Mariah looked annoyed. He hoped Nate would have come, but there was no sign of him.

"Hey guys!" Mariah said when they reached them. Hailey was surprised to see them.

"What are you two fighting about?" Zac asked the twins. Bella grumbled.

"Mom caught us last night. She grounded us." Evan explained. Zac burst our laughing. Mrs. Green was always so strict. It was why the twins hardly threw parties.

"This dimwit blamed me for the party." Bella said with narrowed eyes. Hailey quirked in eyebrow.

"I panicked. I'm sorry Bella." Evan said. Bella scoffed.

"Okay, shut it. I've had enough. You both are going to get grounded any-way." Mariah said as she flipped through the menu. A few moments later, Carl came up to their table. They ordered, leaving them alone once again.

"How did you guys know we were here?" Hailey asked. Bella smirked while Evan chuckled. Mariah just looked plain annoyed.

"Your boyfriend here texted us to come join." Bella said. Hailey's cheeks rose in warmth as her heart skipped a beat.

"I was peacefully sleeping when they made me get out of bed. I don't understand how you guys aren't hungover." Mariah stated. Evan laughed.

"Oh Mariah, Mariah. It comes with practice." Evan said. Mariah tossed her straw wrapped at him. "Any way, Bella is the only one that actually drank."

"I was not drunk." Bella interjected. Zac scoffed.

"Bell, you were dancing by yourself in the kitchen. We all knew you were drunk." Zac told her. Bella crossed her arms across her chest.

"Either way, i'm not hungover. Mariah is just mad I woke her up from her dream." Bella said. Mariah's eyes widened before she began to glare daggers at her best friend.

"Shut. Up. Bella." Mariah said through gritted teeth. Everyone watched the scene unfold. Both Zac and Hailey were confused why Evan seemed to want to be anywhere but there.

"I'm going to get some fresh air." Evan said sliding out of the booth. Zac followed him.

"We'll be right back." Zac told the girls. They nodded, engrossed in their own thoughts. The two walked out of the diner and into the late summer heat.

"Is that Nate?" Evan asked. He was pointing out the window. Zac focused in and saw Nate in the alley with some guy. Zac frowned. He knew exactly what he was doing.

"He told me he stopped." Zac told Evan. Evan shrugged.

"Nate won't give it up until it's too late." Evan said. They turned backed towards the windows of the diner. They focused on the girls. They were laughing at something. Well that little fight stopped.

"I hope it isn't." Zac said seeing as Hailey blushed. He smiled.

"You've got it bad my dude." Evan said changing the subject. Zac shook his head, trying to deny it.

"I can't. She has a million dreams while my only wish is to be as far away as possible from this place." Zac told him.

"Dude, chill. I know you hate your parents for who the hell knows how long, but you can't just leave. Besides, I can tell Hailey wants to stay close to her family." Evan said. Zac nodded. "Who knows man, maybe you'll have a million dreams soon."

His sight stayed on the brunette, finding himself imagining his life here, close to home. Slowly it was beginning to not look as bad. Maybe with the right person at his side, he won't want to leave.

Chapter 8 | Same Girl

- -

Have you ever had one of those days where everything seemed too perfect to be true? Where everything was going right and one was just waiting for the other shoe to drop? Being at an ultimate high, only to be dropped all the way down? Zac never expected the other shoe.

Zac was on a high from happiness and excitement. He had hung out with Hailey for hours yesterday. They talked about everything and anything. He was in awe at what he found out about the girl. He was now more enticed by her than he thought. He had it bad, like really bad.

It was now Monday morning. He was avoiding his best friend, not that Nate was even looking for him. He hadn't heard from him since the party. Zac was kind of glad because he needed time to think about everything. He was still confused about his vague answers and why he didn't want to talk about it. He needed to know what he was hiding.

Walking into homeroom, his eyes were instantly drawn to Hailey. She was laughing at something Evan had said. She looked beautiful and carefree. He wished she was his, but they needed time. He wanted to know her inside and out; thankfully, the day before he learned more about her. Now, he just wanted to be around her. He was going to make her his soon.

Walking up to his best friends, he noticed that Nate wasn't there. His shoulders relaxed and he sat down next to Hailey. She turned away from Evan and grinned at him. He smiled back, forgetting his previous thoughts of his best friend and focusing on the gorgeous girl beside him.

"Hi Zac." Hailey said. She smiled. She had curled her hair and managed to look even more beautiful than usual. Zac didn't even think that was possible. She was also wearing a tank top and jeans. It was different than her usual outfit. He hoped she dressed up for him.

"Hi babe. Ready to be back at school?" He joked. Hailey rolled her eyes before turning to look at Mariah, who scoffed.

"Why would anyone be happy to be back at school? It's school." Mariah asked with sass. Zac rolled his eyes. When is this girl not dramatic?

"It was a joke Mar." Zac told her. She stared back at him, unimpressed. Why was he friends with her again?

"Any way, it's my first day at Carl's!" Bella said changing the subject. Hailey felt herself become nervous. Carl had called her last night and told her the news. She was excited to have Bella working with her, but nervous too. She was supposed to help train her around the diner but that also meant that the boys, specifically Zac would be coming in more. She was nervous enough being near him and now she had to serve him. She was barely able to survive the first time!

"How do you feel about my twin intervening in your work life?" Evan asked with a raised eyebrow. Hailey giggled at his professional tone. Evan was definitely the jokester of the group.

"I just hope I don't mess up when i'm training her." Hailey joked. The group of them laughed as their homeroom teacher entered. Soon they were focused on school and wishing it was lunch.

Later that day, Hailey looked in the bathroom mirror, pleased with her lipgloss. She had woken up early that morning with the need of spicing up her look. She had chosen dark blue skinny jeans and a white lace tank top. She pulled on a light beige cardigan on top to prevent being dress coded. She even wore a pair of sandals instead of sneakers. She was definitely dressed out of her comfort zone.

"Girl, I am impressed. Your outfit is really cute." Bella said from beside her. They had math together previously and had made a pit stop in the restroom before heading to the cafeteria. Bella wanted to check her hair and pee.

"Thanks. I'm not sure what came over me, but I felt like wearing a cute outfit." Hailey told Bella. Bella smirked before replying.

"I think it has to do with a certain brown haired bad boy." Bella teased. Hailey saw her cheeks becoming enflamed in the mirror.

"You two better not be talking about Zac Logan." They heard someone say. Sasha, the queen bee, emerged herself from one of the stalls.

She was wearing her typical mini dress with sky high heels. Hailey didn't understand why she wasn't sent home for her very provocative outfit. Not to mention the amount of makeup she wore could be a mask of her real face. Why was makeup even a thing?

"What's it to you Sasha?" Bella asked, annoyance and irritation in her tone. She turned away from the mirror and was staring at the blond. Her hip was cocked to one side as Bella placed her hands on her hips. She screamed attitude.

Hailey focused on their reflections, not wanting to meet her eye. She was scared of what Sasha was capable of doing. She was rich and manipulative. She also knew how crazy she was, especially when it came to Zac.

"Zac Logan is mine." Sasha said as she narrowed her eyes at Hailey. Hailey gulped. "Stay away from him slut."

"If anyone here is a slut, it's you, bitch." Bella said exaggerating the last word. Sasha balled her fists as imaginary smoke came out from her ears. Hailey needed to get them out of there before Bella started a real fight. She could not afford detention or even suspension!

"I am warning you." Sasha directed towards Hailey. Hailey nodded, not knowing what else to say. She didn't want to be her target.

"Since this conversation was pointless," Bella said as she gathered her things. She then grabbed Hailey's hand. "Bye skank."

Bella pulled her out of the bathroom. She pulled her down the hall and straight into the cafeteria. She could feel Bella fuming. Hailey widened her eyes as Bella made her way towards the beginning of the food line.

Bella didn't even seem to care that they were skipping the line. Hailey was even more surprised that people didn't seem to care either. Being popular had its perks she guessed. Bella then let go of her hand and grabbed a lunch tray. She began to fill it with food. Hailey knew it was wrong of them to cut, but filled her tray up too. She did not want to mess with Bella. She was frightening when angry.

They quickly paid for their food, Hailey grabbing pizza and a container of grapes. She also grabbed a water bottle and followed Bella to their table. They set their trays down, earning curious looks from their friends.

"What took you guys so long?" Evan asked. He reached for a grape from Hailey's plate. She frowned. This was her food.

"We ran into Sasha." Hailey told him in a small voice. Zac's head snapped to hers. He hadn't said anything at first to not seem clingy but now he wanted to know everything.

"What did she want?" Zac asked. Zac felt himself become angry. He told Sasha that they were done. It had been weeks since he heard from her but that was only because Nate was screwing her. He guessed word got out that Sasha wasn't the one in his life anymore.

It was only a matter of time until Sasha found out about Zac wanting Hailey. He was surprised it took her this long. Sasha was manipulative, stubborn, selfish, snobby, and a total bitch. She hates sharing, but she mostly hates losing. Zac knows what Sasha is capable of doing to get what she wants.

"That slut threatened her." Bella said stabbing her pasta. Hailey looked down at her food. Suddenly, her pepperoni pizza didn't seem as good.

"I swear I hate her. Who does she even think she is? She doesn't run this school." Mariah said while munching on her salad. Hailey wrapped her cardigan tight to her body. She felt Zac shift closer to her, slightly relaxing her beating heart before she remembered she was near Zac. It started to race again but this time, it was a good thing.

"Dude, what did you ever see in her?" Evan asked Zac with disgust. Hailey stared at her pizza, feeling disgusted at the thought. She almost forgot that he was involved with her. It seems so long ago, when truthfully, it had only been a few weeks.

"She was a good fuck." Zac said from beside her. Her eyes widened as he said those words. She knew Zac was a player but she never really believed it. It was weird to hear him talk about a girl like that. He was always so sweet to her. "But I never want to fuck her again."

"Damn, such a gentleman." Bella sassed. Zac rolled his eyes at her before focusing them on Hailey. She somehow made herself small. He knew Sasha had frightened her but he wanted to make sure she knew that he would never return to that slut.

"I'm done with fucking random girls." Zac told Bella, but it was more for Hailey. He wanted her to hear this. He watched as she took a sip of her water. "I'm looking for the one."

Hailey then spat her water out, somehow landing on Evan. Evan, who was across from her, stopped moving, stunned at the sudden shower. Zac burst into laughter. The girls soon followed. He stayed still as water dripped from his chin onto his white t-shirt and onto the table. He was soaked.

"What the hell just happened?" Evan asked perplexed. Hailey quickly found napkins and placed them on his face, attemtping to dry him. "Hails, I can do it myself. Unless, you want to get handsy, i'm all for it."

"Oh shut it Evan. I was going to apologize for showering you with my spit, but maybe you deserved it." Hailey said dropping the damped napkins on the table. She sat back down, frowning. Evan chuckled, wiping his own face. That atmosphere returned to being light, but seconds later the topic returned to Sasha.

"What the hell is Nate doing with Sasha?" Mariah asked. The group all turned their heads to see Nate talking awfully close to Sasha. She was nodding her head as if Nate was telling her to do something. It was the first they saw him since the party.

"That boy needs to learn to stop going after sluts." Bella said. Zac turned his head back and saw disappointment flash in her eyes. Well that was weird.

"One day Bells." Evan said as he took a bite of his pizza. Somehow, Hailey's water had missed wetting it too. Evan watched as Nate gave something to Sasha. He was now curious about their conversation but even more curious as to what Nate was hiding. He needed to find out, and soon.

"So, did anyone do the English homework?" Mariah asked.

-

Throwing his gear in his locker, Zac finally had the chance to talk to Nate. They had been avoiding each other the last two days and Zac just wanted an answer. Why was Nate such a jerk to Hailey? What did Hailey even have to do with Nate?

He saw Nate with a frown as he slid off his own gear. He shoved it in the locker before pulling on a grey shirt and his black jeans. Zac did the same, sliding on grey jeans and a navy blue shirt. He slid on his combat boots and black leather jacket.

"Nate." Zac said. Nate stiffened upon hearing his voice. He let out a sigh before turning towards him. The atmosphere instantly thickened.

"Zac." Nate spoke. Zac raised an eyebrow. Looks like Nate isn't going to ignore him. Zac tried to talk to him on the field but he wouldn't listen. The only time Nate would was for the plays on the field.

"We need to talk." Zac told him. Nate pulled on his white Vans and sat down. He let out an irritated sigh.

"About?" Nate asked. Zac scoffed. He had to be joking. Zac was about to open his mouth when multiple lockers were slammed shut. Their team-mates' voices began to disappear, leaving them in silence. It was better that they did this alone. No one needed to know that they weren't talking.

"Why the fuck are you such a jerk to Hailey?" Zac asked. He crossed his arms across his chest. They weren't leaving here until he knew the truth.

He was done with his best friend's bullshit. He wanted his old best friend back.

"Can you just drop it?" Nate asked, irritated. He grabbed his bag turning to look at him. Zac narrowed his eyes.

"No! Now tell me what the fuck your problem is." Zac ordered. Nate rolled his eyes. He was one of the guys on the team that didn't like Zac's authority. Nate then looked him straight in the eyes. Zac wasn't prepared for his next words.

"You want to know what my problem is? Then fine. I have fucking liked Hailey since she first moved here. She'd never date me because of my stupid reputation so I teased her in class. I still wanted her in my life. I didn't know what else to do. But now, knowing that you like her, I feel like ripping you to shreds. No one else noticed her and the second I am about to finally ask her out, you come into her fucking life." Nate told him. His eyes were filled with rage and jealousy.

Zac didn't know what to say. He never thought Nate would ever actually like a girl, much less one like Hailey. He usually went for the blond bimbos who only cared about themselves and their appearance. Hailey was the total opposite of those girls. She cared about everyone else but herself. She was smart and caring. She was too sweet for her own good and full of goals and determination. Her beauty was just an added bonus Zac liked.

Zac didn't know what to respond to his best friend. He wasn't meeting his eye. It felt off. Nate wasn't being Nate. What did he expect him to say? That he would stop liking Hailey so he could date her? That he'd give him his blessing? Hailey didn't trust Nate and Zac knew how much she disliked him. He also didn't want to tell him that because Nate would think he wanted her all to himself, which he did. But, he wasn't going to be selfish. Not right now.

"Nate." Zac sighed. Nate scoffed. He finally looked up with narrowed eyes. Zac was taken back by his sudden increase in attitude. Nate was angry before but now he looked deadly.

"What Zac? Are you going to take something else away from me? I finally like a girl and she fucking likes you. Even if you say you'll back off, she wants you. She's fucking terrified of me and my stupid reputation. Nothing you say Zachary will make this situation any better." Nate yelled with anger laced in every word. Zac stayed quiet. He was right, but that didn't mean Nate had to taken out his anger on him.

"Nate, listen to me. It is not my fault that she's scared of you. How about you try being friendly and make a friend out of her? Who knows Nathanial, you might find love in someone else." Zac told him. He emphasized his best friend's name, knowing he'd listen.

"Shut up. Just leave me the fuck alone." Nate said with rage dripping from every word. He then shot him one more death glare before slamming his locker shut. He could feel Nate's anger radiating onto him. It only made him angrier.

Nate was being a complete jerk. It wasn't his fault that he had begun to like Hailey. If he would have said something, their lives would be completely different. Nate can't blame this all on him. Besides, Hailey doesn't like Nate. He has been a dick to her since the beginning. Did he really think that being mean to her would make her fall in love with him? He's so pathetic! Nate was better than that.

Zac slammed his own locker shut, seething. He was pissed at his best friend and didn't know where to get rid of his pent up anger. Football practice had just ended and he knew his parents were home. They would only add fuel to the ever burning fire.

His parents were home for some charity event Nate's dad was throwing. They had been begging him to go with them. He hadn't responded, but he knew it was mandatory. The only reason he ever did go was because Nate was also forced to go. But now, he wasn't sure. He didn't want to see Nate. He knew they'd get into an argument that would end up with punches being thrown. They would definitely be in the paper the next day.

He didn't want to get yelled at by his parents for coming home angry. So, Zac went to the one place he knew he'd be able to forget everything. He went to the bar on the outskirts of town. As he walked in, he instantly recognized the man behind the bar. It was an old, chubby man with tattoos up his arms. He had a permanent scowl on his face and Zac was yet to ever see his mouth form into anything other than a frown.

"Hey Bones." Zac said as he sat down. The bartender turned to look at him before grimacing. No matter how evil the guy looked, he'd try to convince Zac to stop his underage drinking. Zac didn't even bother to deny his age. He had enough cash for a fake i.d. and a shit load of booze.

"Logan. I thought I saw the last of you." Bones said as he poured him a glass of whiskey. Zac tipped the glass back, feeling his throat burn. Zac placed the glass back down which Bones filled up again.

"Never." Zac stated. He tipped the glass back, making Bones raise an eyebrow.

"What are we celebrating?" Bones asked. Zac let our a humorless laugh. If only.

"How I finally find a girl worth liking and my best friend tells me he's in love with the same girl." Zac told him with disgust. Bones' eyebrows shot up. Zach chuckled. He definitely wasn't expecting that. "I swear my life continues to get even more fucked up."

"Logan, there are other fish in the sea." Bones told him. Zac rolled his eyes at the stupid saying, tipping back the glass for the fourth time. He knew that by the sixth drink, he'd be under the influence, but he didn't care. It was better than beating up his best friend. Maybe he could forget about their conversation.

"Tell that to him. I am not moving out of the way for him. He had his shot. He was too much of an idiot to change and now he's blaming me." He told him. Bones nodded. He liked coming here because Bones would listen and give him advice. He was almost like the dad he never had. Zac grabbed the fifth glass full and tipped it back. He felt his breath start to get heavy and his words start to slur. "Can you give me a beer now?"

"I swear Logan, no driving." Bones scolded as he placed the bottle of whiskey down. He then went over to the fridge where he grabbed a beer bottle. He unscrewed the lid, handing it over. Zac took a sip, looking around.

The bar was small with a few tables around the room. A small jukebox sat in the corner while booths lined up the wall. It was dark and quiet. It was kind of like a rest stop to the city. Zac liked it because no one knew him or judged him. He was just another lonely soul wanting to forget.

"Mind if I sit?" Zac turned and saw a blond that looked rather familiar. He tried to remember where he knew her from but failed. His brain was fuzzy and focused on forgetting.

"Go ahead." Zac said. He took a drink of his beer and focused on the girl. She was wearing a low riding top and a short, black skirt. She had on heels that looked too expensive to belong here. She looked out of place.

"So, what's got you downing your sorrows away?" The blond asked. Zac shrugged. Why had he come here again? Right, his best friend loves the girl he likes. Ironic. The one time he wants to believe in love and fate throws this curveball.

"Wanted to forget. What about you?" He asked. The girl seemed to be deep in thought before shifting her face closer to his. She smelt like cotton candy, a scent that was way too familiar.

"Fun. I wanted to have some fun." She said in a low voice. It was slightly seductive, making him instantly forget everything. He took a drink from his beer, almost finishing it.

"What did you have in mind?" Zac asked. He tipped the bottle back, staring at the smirking blond.

"Want to get out of here?" The blond asked. Zac began to feel his eyes get heavy. He got up, slightly stumbling. Maybe he should leave the bar. Maybe he's had enough for the night. Fresh air wouldn't kill him.

"Sure." Zac said. His words were slurring but he didn't care anymore. He looked at the blond and saw her smirk. She still seemed familiar but he pushed that thought as far away as possible. He wanted to forget everything he knew. He wanted his previous life back.

"Come on." The girl said. She grabbed his hand and pulled him towards the exit. He made sure to leave a couple hundred dollar bills before focusing on the blond. Hopefully he'd be able to forget the brunette that clouded his mind since they met.

Chapter 9 | M. I. A.

Walking into class late, Zac knew his coach would make him suffer for it later. He just didn't care anymore. Zac didn't find it in him to show up on time. He didn't want to run into Hailey either. He wanted to rewind time and pretend that he didn't make a mistake. One that he truly regrets.

It had been about a month since he last talked to Hailey. She's called him a few times but he ignores her. He doesn't know how to face her after knowing what he did. He blames Nate. It was all his fault.

Speaking of him, he's been in and out of town. Nate was off with his dad doing business most of the time which allowed Zac to slightly breath. He didn't want to deal with drama of liking the same girl. But, he did know that he needed to apologize to Hailey for ignoring her but he just couldn't do it.

As he walked in late, he gave his teacher a excuse pass, and turned to see Hailey with the girls. Evan was beside them, looking bored. It was only homeroom but Evan clearly seemed to hate being the only guy. Zac had been ignoring all of them. They had no clue what happened between him and Nate. He wasn't sure what he was supposed to tell them. Evan has tried to talk to him during football, but Zac doesn't let him. He doesn't want Evan to know of his mistake.

"Alright class, I know this is only homeroom, but we have a small project. Chose a partner that you don't know." Their teacher said giving them an eye. She knew who everyone was friends with. Zac's eyes instantly flicked to Hailey's. She was scanning the room when her eyes landed on him.

Hailey hadn't heard from Zac since their morning on the beach. She had called him multiple times but he's never reached out to her. She didn't know what she did wrong. She continued to hangout with the girls and Evan. Nate had also been ignoring them all. She heard Bella mention something about him flying to New York. She was kind of glad he was gone. He wasn't pestering her anymore. Although, she did kind of miss his teasing.

As her eyes landed on Zac, she saw dark circles under his eyes while his hair was disheveled. He looked handsome, yet the light he always had was out. She wanted to know what was wrong. She assumed it had to do with his family, hoping it wasn't about her.

She continued to look around the room, seeing multiple people had already found a partner. She sighed. Thanks to her nonsocial life, she was partnerless again. She saw Mariah team up with some girl while Bella was with one of the other football players in class. Evan ended up with a cheerleader.

She saw Zac turn away from her and talk to some girl in the front of class. She felt her heart crack at the sight. She knew he wouldn't want to be her partner but it still hurt her to see him act normal with everyone else. What happened to him?

"Hailey right?" She heard a male voice. She turned and saw a boy with dark skin and pretty brown eyes. It was one of the school's basketball players.

"Um, hi." Hailey said softly. He smiled which showed cute dimples. He was attractive.

"Hi, i'm Jordan. Do you want to be partners?" He asked. She nodded. "Awesome."

He sat down next to her which made her feel nervous. She focused on the board. Her teacher had written up the assignment which was to create a small presentation about interesting facts about your partner. It was so that the senior class could get to know everyone before the school year ended. It was the school's way to make sure everyone was friends.

"When do you want to meet up and do this?" Hailey asked. Jordan looked down at her. He was over six foot. He had to be in order to play basketball.

"After school for sure. I have basketball practice at six, so it has to be before then." Jordan told her. She nodded. She could do that. "Can I get your number, by the way?"

"Sure." She said handing her phone to him. He quickly typed in his number as the bell rang. He handed it back to her as they got up.

"Cool. I'll text you later." He said to her. She smiled at him as they exited their class. Maybe he wouldn't be so bad.

-

Walking into English, Hailey felt like something was off. She hugged her books closer to her chest as she saw him. Nate was back in his usual seat. He had earphones in and was looking down at his phone. He looked paler, having spent time in New York instead of sunny California. She sat down and hoped he wouldn't see her.

She wasn't very lucky, feeling him tap her shoulder. She adjusted her things on her desk before turning around. His brown eyes were boring into hers and he smiled. It looked genuine and it made her feel uneasy. It was weird to see him not smirking.

"Hi Hailey." Nate said. Hailey gave him a small smile. "How are you? What have I missed?"

"We are about to finish the book." Hailey told him. She waved her copy which caused him to chuckle.

"Maybe you could help me catch up sometime? I promise it'll be all work and no play." He told her. She widened her eyes. Nate wanted her to tutor him. Usually she would have said no to spending time with him, but maybe volunteering will look good on her transcripts. Plus, she can find out what happened between him and Zac.

"Sure. Why not." She told him. Nate's eyes widened, not expecting her answer.

"Wow. Okay. Can I have your phone so I can give you my number?" Nate asked. She nodded. She quickly unlocked it before passing it to him. He began to type, stopping when it buzzed. "Who's Jordan?"

"The basketball player in our homeroom. Which by the way, you missed a group project. He's my partner for it." Hailey told him. Nate passed her phone back. She looked at the text. He wanted to meet up after school at the diner. She chuckled to herself.

"Are you guys a thing or something?" Nate asked. She looked up and saw he had narrowed eyes. Okay, that was weird.

"We just met." She said with an eye roll. Nate was about to reply when Evan's voice was heard.

"About time you come back to class." Evan said sitting down. Nate frowned.

"I'm leaving tomorrow." Nate said glaring at Evan. Evan stared at him, trying to analyze his friend. Hailey quickly turned around. Whatever drama that boy was in, she didn't want to be involved. Their English teacher then started the lesson, allowing her to focus on that instead of the two boys behind her.

-

"What the fuck has been going on with you?" Evan asked after football practice. Zac shrugged, earning a glare from Evan. "Ever since we found Nate with Sasha at lunch, you've been sketch."

"It's nothing." Zac said as he changed out of his gear.

"What do you mean it's nothing? What the fuck did you do?" Evan demanded. Zac scoffed.

"What makes you think I did something?" Zac asked. Evan gave him a blank stare. He could read him like a book. He sighed. "I messed up."

"What did you do?" Evan repeated. Evan was usually patient unless someone was dodging his questions. His temper flares up quick. It's one of the things him and Bella have in common.

"So I confronted Nate about him being mean to Hailey." Zac began. Evan nodded, urging him to continue. "He told me he likes her."

"Nate likes Hailey? That's what he said?" Evan asked. Zac nodded.

"He told me that he has liked her for a while and he was mean to her because of it. Then he got all mad because right when he was going to ask her out, I came into the picture." Zac told him. He rolled his eyes at how pathetic Nate sounded. If he really liked her, he could have asked her out since the beginning.

"So what did you do wrong?" Evan asked. Zac sighed. This was the part he most regretted.

"I was angry at Nate for blaming me so I went out and got drunk. I somehow ended up waking up in Sasha's bed." Zac said feeling disgusted at the thoughts. It happened a month ago and he still felt like he needed to shower a hundred more times.

"Is that why you've been avoiding Hailey?" He asked. Zac nodded.

"I feel like I cheated on her." He replied to Evan. He felt like he betrayed her.

"Dude, you guys aren't together so it doesn't even matter." Evan told him. Zac shook his head.

"I had just gotten done telling her that I was done sleeping around, especially with Sasha, and then I go and do it. I'm an idiot." Zac told Evan. Evan sighed.

"Nate just dropped a bomb on you and you only knew one way to react. Just talk to her. I'm sure she'll understand." Evan said. Zac sighed. He was right. He needed to confront his mistakes.

"Fine. I'll go over to her house later." Zac said. Evan nodded, satisfied with his answer.

"Don't forget icecream and flowers." Evan said. Zac chuckled. He hoped everything would be alright.

-

Hailey was beginning to wonder why she always found herself at Carl's even when she wasn't working. Jordan had texted her during class, asking if she wanted to meet today. She replied yes. She hated procrastinating projects.

They decided to meet here since it was in the middle of their homes. He lived near the twins while she lived a few blocks away. She found a booth in the back of the diner and took out her notebook. She had written down a few questions to ask him. She had also ordered two Dr. Peppers and some french fries.

"Hey!" She heard Jordan's voice. She looked up from her notebook and smiled.

"Hey." She replied back. He slid into the booth, across from her. She sipped on her drink before returning her gaze on him. He was dressed in his basketball attire instead of his jeans and plaid shirt from earlier. "So, I took the liberty of making an outline."

"Awesome. This way we won't veer off topic or forget anything. We'll be done with this project in no time. When is it due by the way?" Jordan spoke. Hailey looked down at their assignment worksheet.

"In two weeks. Our presentation can be whatever we want as long as we manage to meet the criteria." Hailey said. Jordan nodded, taking out his own things.

"What should we do for our presentation then?" Jordan asked. Hailey shrugged. She wasn't very creative. Not only did she lack in the athletic department, but she also lacked in the creative one. She was a plain Jane.

"I have no idea. I hate designing things." She told him honestly. He chuckled.

"What if we do like an interview from a movie and record it. We can be like on the news or something." Jordan suggested. She was impressed with his skills already. This project was definitely not going to be a waste of time. She'd actually enjoy doing homework for once.

"Let's do it." Hailey said. Jordan nodded, writing the idea down. "Now, tell me about yourself Jordan Fitzgerald."

"Well Hailey Foster, I am eighteen years old. I play point guard on our school's basketball team. I am a senior and my favorite subject is biology. I haven't figured out my plan in life but I know that I want something to do with the human body. I am the youngest of three and love Raising Cane's." Jordan told her. She wrote everything down.

"I wish we had a Cane's nearby." She said. She loved the chicken fingers and the cane's sauce. It was delicious. Too bad the closest one was over an hour away.

"I know. Whenever we go up north for basketball, I make sure to get some. Now, tell me about yourself." Jordan replied. He was looking at her intently, as if studying her. She squirmed in her seat before speaking.

"I am the middle child of six. Four are boys. Even though they are torture, I loved them. I also want to be a nurse in a hospital. So, my favorite subject has to be human anatomy. I am in love with the cardiovascular system. Get it." She said joking. Jordan's smile widened as he silently laughed. "I am yet to get my license and my favorite sport to watch is baseball." Hailey said. Jordan chuckled louder, making her raise an eyebrow. She didn't make a lame joke this time.

"You don't have your license? You're eighteen right?" Jordan asked. She nodded.

"I just don't have the need to drive around. My brothers do that for me. Plus, we only have two cars. It'd be pointless." She said. Jordan nodded, understanding her answer.

"So, five siblings?" Jordan asked. She chuckled. She knew he was going to ask about them. Everyone is always so surprised to find out how many there are, especially when she mentions no parents.

"Yup. I have two older brothers who are extremely protective but still cuddly teddy bears at heart." She said with a smile. Jordan matched it. She saw his dimples pop out again. This boy was really attractive. Not as much as the boy currently ignoring her, but still attractive.

"When should we film this?" Jordan asked. He was writing things down in his notebook. She looked down at hers. She had bulleted everything he said. She still had a few random questions she wanted to ask, but nothing that couldn't wait another day.

"I work tomorrow so maybe Thursday?" Hailey suggested. Jordan shook his head.

"I have basketball practice tomorrow, Thursday and Sunday. Maybe Friday?" Jordan asked. She thought about it.

"Aren't you going to the football game?" She asked. She still went with the girls, even if Zac had been M.I.A. in her life. She at least got to see him play the sport he loved.

"Oh yeah. We're in the playoffs right? That means Thanksgiving is soon." Jordan said with excitement. Hailey giggled. She loved the holiday for all the food Josh made.

"We can film it Saturday." Hailey said. Jordan nodded.

"That works! I should get going. Do you need a ride home since you don't drive?" Jordan teased. Hailey rolled her eyes but nodded. She would have had to call Ben, who would just tease her about the boy she was hanging out with.

"Yes please." Hailey said. They quickly gathered their stuff and walked out of the diner. She gave Carl a small wave who only chuckled. She then followed Jordan to a white truck. It seemed slightly older than the expensive ones around but still brand new.

She was slightly jealous of the fact that he had his one car and his license, but shook that though away. She was grateful for everything she had. Josh worked hard for their things.

Jordan unlocked the car. They both got in, the air conditioning blasting. Hailey pulled on her seatbelt as Jordan pulled out of the parking lot. She looked out the window, turning when she heard Jordan's voice.

"So where do you live?" Jordan asked. Hailey quickly gave him the directions, only being a few blocks away. "Your brothers aren't going to kill me right?"

"Why would they?" Hailey asked with a chuckle. Jordan smiled, turning into her neighborhood.

"For bringing home their sister. You said they were protective. I assume it's over you." Jordan said. They were nearing her home.

"As long as you don't hurt me. We're good." Hailey told him. She pointed at her house which Jordan stopped in front of. "Thank you for the ride. Have fun at practice!"

"I'll see you tomorrow in class." He told her. She smiled before slamming the door shut. She waved as he drove off. She quickly went inside with a grin on her face. No thoughts of the bad boy in her mind.

-

Zac stared up at the small house. It was so different than his own. It was a two-story with small windows and old brown shutters. The front door was a dark brown with a small window beside it. They had a small porch with a smaller dying plant sitting beside the door. They had a small garage fit for one car and a driveway fit for two. It seemed as if no one was home. The cars were missing and all the lights were off, all besides one.

The window that overlooked the quiet street was shining bright. He knew that was the master. That meant Hailey was home. He made the walk across the nonexistent grass with mostly dirt, and up the three steps to the door. He readjusted the melting icecream in his hand before ringing the doorbell.

He shifted from foot to foot, seeing Hailey open the door moments later. She stared back at him, surprise in her eyes. What was he doing here? She hadn't heard from him in weeks and now he was standing on her porch with flowers.

"Hi Hails." Zac said. Her name felt foreign on his lips. He hadn't realized how much he's missed her. He was such an idiot.

"Zac, what are you doing here?" She asked. She opened the door and let him inside. She was grateful that she was home alone. Josh took Trinity to Peter Piper Pizza. She had received an A on her math quiz, so he was spoiling her for the night. Seth was at a friend's doing homework. Ben was at baseball practice till late, while Luke was off being Luke. She never had a clue what he did in his spare time.

"These are for you." Zac said handing her the flowers and the bag of icecream. Hailey quickly took them and walked into the kitchen. Zac was on her heels. She placed the icecream in the freezer. It was cookie dough.

"I'm sorry i've been M. I. A. lately." He told her. She gave him a small smile.

"I figured you were going through stuff. I'm here if you ever need to talk." Hailey said to him. She placed the red roses in a vase. Her heart was beating fast. She knew what red roses meant. She just hoped that's what Zac meant.

She had been racking her brain for weeks, trying to figure out what she did wrong and she always came up empty. She just tried to continue to live her life without him as he continued to ignore her and his friends. She even thought maybe Zac found out about her crush and was letting her down easy. With the red roses he had brought, now she was confused. Why had Zac ignored her?

"That's why i'm here." Zac said shifting in his spot. Hailey glanced at him. He seemed worried and scared. What happened to the carefree, happy guy she met?

"Is everything alright?" Hailey asked him. He shook his head.

"I made a mistake." Zac said. Hailey nodded. She was confused at what he was trying to explain, but listened anyway. "You know that day we found Nate talking to Sasha in the cafeteria, well later that day, I asked him why he was so mean to you. That's why we got into an argument."

"Zac, I told you to leave it alone." She said frowning. She hated being the reason the two weren't talking. They were best friends and here she comes ruining it. Zac shook his head.

"I couldn't just leave it alone. You didn't deserve to be treated the way he treated you." Zac said with a matching frown. Hailey's heart skipped a beat. "Any way, he told me why. I got really angry."

"What did he say?" Hailey asked. She was curious as to why Nate was always a jerk. He had seemed to stop, never really talking to her anymore. She did feel his gaze on her during class which felt worse than his teasing. He didn't speak after their conversation.

"It's unimportant now. He's going to stop being a dick to you. But I was angry and there were only three ways I knew how to control my anger. One was with football but we had just gotten done with practice. Two was to get into a fight. I couldn't risk being suspended, no matter how much I was urging to bash someone's face in. So I went with option three: getting drunk and sleeping with random girls." He told her. Hailey's eyes widened. He could see the sadness, disappointment and rejection in her eyes. This was why he didn't want to tell her.

He didn't want her to feel like he chose Sasha. He would chose Hailey every single time. Hailey is a hundred times better than her. She actually had qualities he liked. He could hold a conversation with her and he loved every second they did. He liked Hailey, a lot. Too much to have ruined whatever he chance with her by being a complete idiot.

"Is everything better now?" Hailey asked. She felt betrayed and rejected. She knew they weren't together but he had told her he was done being a player. She assumed it was for her but she thought wrong.

"No, well i'm not angry at Nate anymore. I'm angry at myself. I feel like I lied to you Hails. I regret sleeping with Sasha. I couldn't face you knowing I did that. That's why I have been ignoring you. I didn't want you to find out about me being stupid." Zac told her. Hailey stared back at him. He couldn't figure out what she was thinking.

Hailey didn't know what to say. Was she supposed to be happy that Zac felt like he cheated on her because that meant he liked her too? Was she supposed to be angry that he slept with Sasha, out of all girls? She was confused about everything. What did this all even mean?

"Hailey, I promise you that this will never happen again. I feel terrible that I did it and I feel even worse that I did it with her. I feel disgusted." Zac told her. Hailey nodded.

"It's okay Zac. You don't have to explain yourself. We aren't together." Hailey said the last part joking. She felt Zac tense up before quickly shaking his head. "Come on. Let's go outside. The stars are out tonight."

Together, they walked out to the porch. She sat down on the steps with Zac beside her. She felt warm with him near. She knew that she liked Zac, a lot and she couldn't really be mad at him. They weren't together, yet he felt the need to be sorry. She found it sweet, but that didn't stop her from being disappointed.

He was capable of stopping himself from sleeping with her, but he still didn't. He let it happen. She just hoped that it wouldn't happen again. She wasn't sure her heart would accept it the second time around.

Zac and Hailey stared up at the sky. The stars were twinkling as crickets chirped. It was peaceful and beautiful. She loved the sunrise more, but the stars at night were just as amazing. They told unshared stories that made Hailey wonder what life was like all those years back.

"Thank you." Hailey whispered. She took her gaze of the bright stars, feeling Zac's eyes land on hers. She felt an uncomfortable feeling stir in her stomach. She didn't know what it meant, but she didn't want to get rid of the feeling. Especially, with the way Zac was looking down at her.

"For what?" He asked her. He was confused, unsure of what she thanked him for. Was she saying thank you for being polite? For apologizing? She didn't have to respond to any of that. He just wanted her to know that he wasn't choosing Sasha.

"I know it's only been a few weeks since we met, and a few more of you ignoring me, but my life has changed for the better. I'm glad I bumped into you." She told him honestly. His eyes blazed an unknown emotion she couldn't decipher. She was never a fan of reading people. She hated that people could read her.

"No, thank you Hails." He said meaning it. This girl had given his life meaning, even though he messed up. He planned on keeping her for as long as he could. Even if that meant losing his best friend.

~~~~~It's edited but not? I'm too lazy to reread, so point out mistakes please.xoxo,Liv814ps, if y'all haven't noticed, i'm trying to update every other day & want to finish this book by august 23rd.!
~~~~~

Chapter 10 | Treat You Better

Being the only girl at home, besides Trinity, Hailey found it weird to hear giggling in her house. It was rather early; too early for visitors. She slipped out of bed, stretching her limbs.

She had gotten home late after the football game. The boys and the test of the football team had won. Zac had played really well, turning to look at her after each touchdown. She had worn his jersey, curling her hair too. She could feel the curious eyes on her throughout the game. She ignored them and focused on the attractive boy. She was definitely glad they were talking again.

Hailey shook away her thoughts of the previous night and focused on the task at hand. She pulled on one of Ben's baseball hoodies over her tank top. It reached her thighs, slightly covering her running shorts. She ran a hand through her hair and stepped out of her room.

The laughter was louder in the hall. Hailey saw her siblings' doors closed. Now she was really confused. She walked down the stairs and heard Luke's voice. She turned and saw him on the couch, with a girl.

"Luke, stop." The girl said giggling. Hailey stopped moving, confused and surprised at the entire situation. Luke was smiling at the girl. She had dark hair and bright blue, almost green eyes. She looked familiar but Hailey was sure she'd never met her.

"Hails, you're up." Luke said flipping his gaze to her. Hailey nodded, staring at the girl. Why did she seem so familiar?

"Yeah, what are you doing up?" Hailey asked him, flipping her eyes to the girl for a second.

"Hails, this is Tasha. We're doing a project. She had to come over early." Luke told her. Hailey nodded. That made some sense.

"Hi, nice to meet you. I'm sorry if my laughter woke you up. Your brother is just really funny." Tasha said gazing at Luke. Luke smiled back at her. Hailey was confused. Did this girl actually like her brother?

"If you excuse us Hails, we have work to do. We can go finish in the backyard." Luke said getting up. Tasha grabbed her things and followed Luke out of the room. Hailey watched as they disappeared.

Hailey continued to rack her brain. Tasha seemed very familiar. She had the same bright blue eyes as someone. She just couldn't figure out who. Her outfit was also very cute, with shorts and cute blouse. She had on sandals with that Tori Burch sign. Hailey shook her head. It didn't matter if Tasha seemed familiar. She had other things to focus on.

Hailey walked into the kitchen and saw Ben at the counter. He had a bowl of cereal sitting in front of him as his head was placed in the palm of his hand. He was slightly snoring, making Hailey giggle.

"Shut up. I'm trying to sleep Hails." Ben mumbled. Hailey laughed even louder.

"Go to your room." Hailey said. She walked around the island and pulled her own bowl out. She filled it with Fruit Loops and sat next to Ben.

"I wish. It's Josh's turn and he's still asleep. Luke woke me up and got me to leave the living room. I swear if it wasn't for homework, i'd still be asleep." Ben grumbled. Hailey began to eat her cereal when she heard Ben move. "So, how was the game?"

"Great! The guys won." Hailey told him. Ben nodded. His eyes were still very full of sleep but he seemed to be fighting it. "You can go sleep in my room if you want. I have some homework to do before Jordan comes over, but I can just do it in here."

"Who is Jordan?" Ben asked. He was now fully awake, studying her.

"My partner for this project in homeroom." Hailey said. She spooned more cereal into her mouth. "He should be here around 3."

"So it's a guy." Ben stated. Hailey nodded. Why is he being so weird? "Does Zac know?"

"Does Zac know what? What does Zac have to do with this?" Hailey asked. She was now really confused.

"It's looks like he has some competition now." Ben said. Hailey rolled her eyes.

"No he doesn't. He doesn't even like me like that. Besides, I just met Jordan in class on Wednesday. He doesn't like me like that either." Hailey said. She ate the rest of her cereal before getting up. She placed the empty, dirty bowl in the sink. "Since you will not be sleeping in my bed, I am going to go do homework."

"One, if not both, of those boys likes you Hails." Ben shouted as she walked out the kitchen. She shook her head, silently laughing. Ben was ridiculous. No boy liked her.

-

Loud, obnoxious pounding caused Zac to turn in bed. His muscles were aching and his brain was begging him for more sleep. The knocking on his bedroom door continued, making him groan in annoyance. He slid out from the covers and made the walk to his door. He swung it open, revealing his mother.

"Zachary, what are you doing in bed so late?" She asked. She was a tall blonde with bangs and bright blue eyes. She was scary when angry.

"I got home late from the game mom." Zac said. He ran his hand through his hair, noticing that his mom wasn't dressed in her typical blazer and heels. She was wearing jeans and a blouse. "No work?"

"No. I actually have the day off. I was wondering if you wanted to get some breakfast." His mom said. His eyes widened. It was the first time she had ever had a day off. He was even more surprised that she wanted to spend the day with him.

"Sure! Let me get ready." Zac said fully waking up. His mom nodded, walking out. She shut the door behind her. Zac made his way to his connecting bathroom and walked in. He saw his large shower and turned on the hot water. He then undressed, slipping in.

Once clean, he wrapped a towel around his waist. He then took a spare towel and ruffled his hair. Satisfied with the outcome, he brushed his teeth before walking back into his room.

He walked over to his black dresser and pulled out a pair of jeans and a t-shirt. He slid them on, along with a pair of boxers, and grabbed his phone.

He had the sudden urge to invite the brunette but shook his head. It was his first real day with his mom. He wanted to enjoy it. Hailey can meet her some other time.

Zac then pulled on his black boots and stuffed his phone and wallet into his pockets. Walking out of his room, he walked down the large staircase and found his mom in the living room. She was flipping through channels on their flatscreen.

"Ready?" She asked. Zac nodded. She then shut the tv off and got up. She grabbed one of her designer purses and walked out the front door. "Is it alright if I drive?"

"Sure mom." Zac said. He followed her to her silver BMW. Getting into the car, Zac was trying to fight of the grin. He was extremely happy with the way life was working out. Not only did he finally have Hailey back in his life, but his mom was making an effort too. He just hoped things would start looking up for him.

"Zac, what's on your mind that has you grinning?" He heard his mom's voice cut through his thoughts. Zac turned and saw her with a smile. It had been a long time since her ever saw her show emotion other than frowning.

"Mom, I-" Zac stopped talking. What did he want to tell her? Would if be weird if he talked about the girl he liked? Isn't that supposed to be a topic one avoids with their parents? He didn't know how to act with her. It was unfamiliar territory.

"Zac, I know we don't have the best relationship, but I am here for you. I still am your mom." She said. She now had a small smile on her face. He could sense that she regrets not being more apart of his life.

"Hailey. That's her name." Zac stated. His mom nodded. He saw that she turned into Carl's. Zac chuckled.

"What's so funny?" She asked as she shut off the engine. They both got out, walking into the warm air. It was nearing the end of October and California was still warm. Zac hoped fall would soon approach, but that was nothing more than a wish. It was only get slightly cooler, but never cold enough for snow.

"Carl's. This is where Bella and Hails works." Zac said. He opened the door and was met with the familiar chime.

"Hey Zac! Hailey isn't here today." Zac heard Carl say. Zac laughed.

"I know. It's her day off. I'm actually here to enjoy some food with my mom." Zac told Carl. Carl's eyes shifted to his mother. She had a warm smile on her face as Carl's eyes roamed. "Mom, this is Carl. He owns the diner. Carl, this is my married mother."

"Nice to meet you ma'am. Your son here spends way too much time ogling my best employee." Carl said in a teasing tone. Zac's eyes bulged out of their sockets.

"Does my son have a crush on said girl?" His mom asked. He could hear the teasing in her tone. Zac frowned.

"Carl, we want pancakes and iced coffee." Zac said trying to change the subject. Carl ignored him, leading his mom to a booth. Zac sighed, following behind.

"Oh yeah, Hailey is awesome. Zac believes that too, don't you?" Carl asked. Zac frowned with annoyance as he slid into the booth. "Alright, i'll stop. I'll go get you that food."

"Thank you Carl." Zac said irritated. He watched as the lanky man walked over to the counter. Zac then turned to see a grinning mom. "Mom?"

"So Hailey, there is a girl?" She asked. Zac turned away, feeling his cheeks redden. Why was he embarrassed? Hailey is an amazing girl. "What's she like?"

"She's perfect mom." Zac said letting the words tumble out. He was sure his cheeks were a bright red now.

"Can I meet her?" His mom asked. Zac shrugged.

"Maybe. She's nothing like any of the other girls I-" Zac cut himself off. How did he explain to his mom his sleeping around without actually saying those words.

"I know about your lifestyle. You're just like your daddy. Hopefully you can turn that around before it's too late." His mom said. Zac was more than surprised. He didn't know she knew and he especially didn't know his dad was like him.

"I hope mom. Hailey, she's beautiful and smart. She's sassy with an attitude, but sweet and caring. She has so much determination that she makes you want to work hard as well." Zac said looking out the window. He could imagine her smiling up at him with those gorgeous brown eyes. He wanted nothing more than to set his lips on top of hers.

"Don't let her go Zac. Hold onto her for as long as you can. True love only comes once." His mom said. Carl then came over with the delicious smelling food. The two dug in, enjoying each other's presence.

-

Running a hand through her brown locks, Hailey felt satisfied with her look. She was wearing a plain black tee with shorts. She didn't want too be to dressed up for Jordan, but she didn't want to look ugly either.

"Hailey! Some guy who isn't your boyfriend is here!" She heard Trinity's voice. Hailey's eyes widened as she slipped on her black sandals. She then ran out of her room. She could hear Trinity's voice as she neared the living room.

"Hailey, hey." She heard as she stepped down the stairs. She saw Jordan standing in the living room. He was dressed in black jeans and a red plain tee.

"Hey, sorry for her. She's, well, crazy." Hailey said. Jordan chuckled.

"I am not crazy." Trinity said with a pout.

"Go to our room. We have homework." Hailey told her sister. Trinity frowned before stomping up the stairs. Once her sister was out of view, she turned to look at Jordan. He had an amused smile on his face.

"So, you have a boyfriend?" Jordan asked. Her cheeks shined from embarrassment.

"No, she thinks Zac is. My brother Ben got that idea into her mind." Hailey said. She led Jordan into the backyard. She knew that was where she'd get the least amount of noise from her rowdy siblings. Why did they all chose to stay home today?

"So you're single?" Jordan asked. Hailey nodded, sitting on one of the lawn chairs they had.

"As a pringle, now shall we film?" Hailey asked. Jordan nodded, smiling brighter.

-

Clicking the save button, Hailey was exhausted. They had been filming and editing for the last few hours. Josh had come out and brought refreshments and snacks. Hailey was grateful, having skipped lunch. Now she just wanted a juicy burger.

"Can't believe we actually finished that." Jordan said munching on the remaining chips. Hailey saved the video again before powering her laptop off.

"I know. We're going to get an A." Hailey said. Jordan nodded. She began cleaning up their area, hearing Jordan clear up his throat.

"Can I ask you something?" He asked. She nodded, confused by his sudden change in attitude. "I know that we only met a couple of days ago, but I was wondering if maybe you wanted to go see a movie sometime?"

"Like a date?" Hailey asked. She didn't know what to say. She didn't think Jordan even thought of her like that, yet here he was asking her out.

"Yeah. What do you say?" He asked. Hailey blinked a few times. One side of her brain said no because of the boy she had met but the other said to go for it. Zac hadn't shown any real feelings towards her. Maybe a date with Jordan would be a good thing.

"Sure. Sounds like fun!" She told him honestly. Jordan grinned.

"Cool! I'll text you the details. See you on Monday." Jordan said as he finished gathering his things. She watched as he walked through the door into the house. She felt herself smiling like a goof. She had a date. She was going to have her first date.

"What about Zac?" She turned her head to Luke. She hadn't seen him since the mystery girl.

"What about Zac?" She asked. She grabbed her laptop and walked inside. Luke was on her tail.

"What is he going to say to you going on a date?" Luke asked. Hailey shrugged.

"Nothing. He shouldn't care. We're just friends." Hailey said in a sadden tone. She turned to corner and saw the boy. He had a frown on his face. "Zac? What are you doing here?"

"Luke let me in." Zac said. His frown stayed on as Hailey's gaze shifted to her brother. She frowned. That's why Luke was asking her about him.

"We can go to my room. Luke has chores to do." Hailey said glaring at her brother.

"Whatever mom." Luke said stomping off. Hailey let out a sigh. She wished her mom was still there to tell them to clean. But she knew that wasn't possible. She turned towards Zac.

"Come on." She said. She walked up the steps with Zac in tow. The atmosphere was thick and she was confused why.

"So you have a date." Zac said once they were in her room. She nodded, not wanting to make eye contact. She set her laptop on her desk and sat down. Zac was standing near the door, leaning on the wall.

"You heard that?" She asked. Zac nodded. She sighed. Just great. "You know that guy Jordan, the basketball player?"

"Yeah. He's quieter than the rest of the guys on the team." Zac stated. Hailey shifted in her seat, not wanting to look at him.

"We're partners and I guess we've been getting along. He asked me out on a date." Hailey said. She felt Zac take in a breath. She looked up and saw a flash of emotions in his eyes.

Zac stared back at the girl. That was great news. Note the sarcasm. Just as he was about to ask her out, here came that doofus. It seems like fate has funny ways of working out. It was just like him with Nate.

His mom had convinced him to come ask her out. He was against the idea. Yeah he liked her, but what if she didn't like him back. He didn't want to ruin their friendship. After a lot of arguing, he finally agreed. He had been a nervous wreck the entire drive over. Even after he saw the boy leave, he didn't think much of him. He knew Jordan and Hailey were partners. He just never thought they'd be more than that.

"That's great." Zac said in a monotone voice. He then stood up straight. "I have to go."

He turned around and walked down the stairs. He felt out of place. He walked straight towards the front door. He was about to reach for the door handle when he heard Ben.

"It's not too late." Ben said. Zac scoffed.

"She said yes. There's nothing more I can do." Zac said in defeat. Ben chuckled.

"So you're saying he's the better choice?" Ben asked. Zac frowned.

"I can treat her better, better than he can." Zac argued. Ben nodded.

"Then prove it. She'll see that she doesn't like him like that after the date. She won't even let him kiss her." Ben said. Zac felt his heart drop at his words. He imagined Jordan kissing Hailey which made him boil over in anger. "Settle down there. No need to be angry."

"I am not going to take that chance." He said through gritted teeth. He didn't want to give Jordan the chance to steal her first kiss away from him.

"Relax Zac. Go home. I'll talk to her. Now, relax and go." Ben said. Zac sighed.

"Fine, but help her discover that i'm the one." Zac said. Ben nodded. "Thanks man. I'll see you."

"Control the temp." Ben said before disappearing around the corner. Zac sighed, reaching for the door handle. Ben was right. If they were meant to be, Hailey would make the right choice. He just hoped it was at the right time.

-

If you would have told Hailey that she'd be hanging out with Nate Price, willingly, she'd tell you that you're crazy and on drugs. Yet, she was at Starbucks with him, actually somewhat enjoying herself. Nate was smiling at her as she sipped on her vanilla latte.

"Stop watching me you creep." She told him. He only chuckled before looking back down at his notebook. They had only been at the coffee shop for fifteen minutes and Hailey was slightly annoyed, yet intrigued. He hadn't made any inappropriate comments or flirtatious remarks. It was weird. She wasn't sure she didn't like it.

She was still cautious of his every move. She still didn't trust him, but was going to give him the benefit of the doubt. Maybe Nate had changed and was really focused on catching up in class.

"I'm sorry. So what does foreshadow me?" Nate asked. Hailey put her coffee down and focused on Nate. He had a sharp jaw line with dark brown eyes that were incased be long, thick lashes. His lips were a light pink and his teeth a bright white. He had the perfect face with the perfect bone structure . His brown locks were wild, needing a slight trim which only added to his handsome face. He was definitely eye candy.

"To foreshadow is to hint at something that will happen later in the story." Hailey told him. Nate nodded, looking back and down at his notes.

"Can we take a break? My brain hurts." Nate said shutting his notebook. Hailey sighed.

"It's been like ten minutes Nate." She stated. Nate shrugged. He sipped on his caramel frap. "So, how was New York?"

"Alright. Way cooler in temperature. I had to wear a coat while I was there. I loved it." Nate answered with a bright smile. Hailey nodded. "Have you been there?"

"No. I've never left California before." She told him. He stared back at her with surprise. She chuckled. "There's a lot I haven't done."

"Like what?" He asked. A smirk was plastered on his face. Hailey rolled her eyes. Of course inappropriate thoughts would stir in his brain.

"Wouldn't you like to know." Hailey said with an eye roll. She bit into the cookie he had bought her.

"Name five things you haven't done." Nate said. His brown eyes showed amusement. Hailey laughed.

"Alright, let's see. I have never left California." Hailey said. Nate narrowed his eyes. She prevented herself from laughing at the grim line his face had made and thought carefully. "I have never failed a test."

"Alright four more." Nate said raising his hand. He had put his thumb down, leaving the rest of his fingers up.

"I haven't gotten my license." She told him. Nate's eyes widened. Why was everyone so surprised by that? There are lots of people who don't have their license.

"Why don't you have it?" Nate asked.

"I don't need it. My two older brothers drive me everywhere, plus if I did have it, I don't have a car to drive." She explained to him. Nate seemed interested in that.

"So, maybe I can teach you how to drive sometime?" Nate offered. Hailey was stunned. Why was Nate being so friendly? What the heck happened between him and Zac?

"Maybe. So, what else do we need to review?" Hailey asked, changing the subject. Nate sighed.

"Name three more." Nate said. Hailey shook her head.

"We have to finish this." Hailey said pointing at his homework. Nate frowned.

"Come on Hails. We can finish this some other time. I think I have enough stuff to be able to do the first few assignments I missed." Nate said. Hailey shook her head. He said this was all work and no play.

"Nate." Hailey stated. Nate smirked. That was the Nate she knew.

"Hailey, come on. Three more things and we can call it a day. I can even drop you off." Nate suggested. Hailey contemplated his offer. She had to take it. Ben was at baseball and Josh was at work. She had walked here.

"Fine. Come on." Hailey said putting her things in her backpack. Nate did the same. She tossed her empty cup into the garbage, following Nate out to the parking lot. "So where's your car?"

"I don't have one." Nate said with a smirk. She watched as he walked over to a motorbike.

"Oh no. Not happening." Hailey said with a shake of her head. Nate chuckled.

"Come on. Have you ever even been on one?" Nate asked. He pulled out two helmets, slipping one onto his head. He handed the other to her. She stared at the black helmet.

"No. I don't want to." Hailey said shoving the helmet back into his chest. Nate rolled his eyes, handing it back to her.

"Add this to the list of things you haven't done. Now you just need to tell me two more." Nate said starting the bike. Hailey thought about it. Maybe he was right. She had never been on a motorcycle before. She only lived a few miles away. The ride couldn't be that bad. Plus, he at least had a helmet.

"Alright fine. But, you need to go slow Nate." She said slipping the helmet on. She made sure it was secure as she sat behind him. She left about a foot of space between them.

"Hails, you need to hug me or you are going to fall off." Nate said. He was looking over his shoulder at her. She sighed in defeat, causing his smirk to increase. She shifted closer and wrapped her arms around his torso. She felt him tense before relaxing. Nate then revved his engine before pulling out of the parking spot. She felt him gain speed as they drove through the streets.

Hailey squeezed her eyes shut. The wind was ripping at her face as he sped up. She tightened her hold, not wanting to fall off. She felt the bike lean to one side, causing her eyes to open. She saw the whole city go by in a blur. Colors and shapes blended together as they rode.

She suddenly wasn't scared of the potential harm. She focused on her surroundings and began to enjoy herself. She laughed as she continued to feel Nate increase speed. Adrenaline was coursing through her veins. She felt like she was flying.

Soon, the ride came to an end. She felt the bike come to a halt and saw her home. She let out a breath she didn't know she was holding. She unwrapped her arms from Nate, sliding off the bike. She turned to look at Nate.

"Oh my god. That was exhilarating!" She said with excitement. Nate chuckled, watching her as she bounced in her spot.

"I told you. Now you can say you've been on a motorcycle." Nate said with triumphant. Hailey rolled her eyes, a smile playing on her lips. "So, two more things Hails."

"I have never enjoyed spending time with you." Hailey said as her cheeks flamed with embarrassment. Nate's eyes widened. He didn't say anything as he stared at her. Hailey began to feel nervous.

"There's a first time for everything babe." Nate said with smirk. Hailey groaned. The old Nate was back.

"And this is why that was something I had never done." Hailey said. She hoisted her backpack up her shoulder and walked up the steps to her house. She stopped walking when she was at her front door. She turned and saw Nate. He was watching her with a smile. "How did you know where I lived?"

"Luke, i've dropped him off a few times." Nate said nonchalantly. Hailey nodded. She searched for her keys in her backpack. She didn't even hear Nate approach her. "Hails."

"Yeah?" She asked turning around. Her eyes widened as she took in their proximity. He was inches away from her. She looked up at him and felt her heart start to race.

"Thanks for today. I had fun too." Nate said. He reached for her face, tucking a strand behind her. She felt her breath caught in her throat.

Alarms were going off in her head as his face decreased the distance between them. She stared up at him. She saw a weird emotion in his brown eyes as he looked down at her lips.

"Hailey!" She heard her brother say. Nate quickly stepped back. He masked his face with a blank emotion. Hailey blinked a few times, seeing Luke in the corner of her eye. He was glaring at Nate.

"Hey Luke. Nate was just dropping me off. Thanks Nate. I'll see you at school tomorrow." Hailey said with a tight smile, feeling awkward. Nate nodded, walking down the driveway. He didn't spare her another glance as he drove away.

She felt her heart rate start to settle as a mixture of emotions flooded her brain. Was she about to kiss the bad boy Nate Price? Was he about to steal her first kiss? She was so confused. That boy was bipolar as can be. She just didn't understand him. One thing was for sure: this was the first time she actually felt something for Nate.

~~~~~~~~~~~Guys, I think this is my best chapter so far. Let me know what y'all think! xoxo,Liv814
~~~~~~~~~~~

Chapter 11 | My Dilemma

A s Hailey stepped into her home, she felt Luke's glare start to increase. She ignored him as she stepped deeper inside. She went up the stairs towards her room. She saw Trinity playing with her toys, not acknowledging her presence. She slid off her sneakers and dropped her backpack by the door.

"Oh hey Hailey!" Trinity said finally hearing her. Hailey smiled, not quite meeting her eyes.

"Hey Trin." Hailey said to her sister. Trinity went back to playing with her toys, letting Hailey take in some air. A million thoughts were running around as she heard someone clear their throat.

"Hailey." Luke said. Hailey turned to see her brother glaring.

"What is your problem?" She asked him. She walked out of the room, leaving Trinity. Luke was right behind her as she made her way downstairs. She went into the kitchen, seeing Seth. "Hey Seth!"

"Hey! When is Zac coming over? I want him to take me to the library." Seth asked. He looked up from whatever textbook he was reading. Hailey shrugged. Thoughts of Zac only made her even more confused.

"I'm not sure. He's been super busy lately." Hailey said being vague. Her family didn't know that they had just started speaking again. She went towards the fridge and reached for a water bottle. She noticed she needed to go grocery shopping again.

"Hey Seth, can you go hangout in our room? I want to talk to Hailey." Luke said. Seth raised an eyebrow, gathering his things. He soon disappeared without a second glance. Luke turned to face her. The frown was back onto his face, confusing the heck out of her.

"Luke, can you stop looking at me like that? Why are you angry? What did I do?" She asked him. She sat down at the kitchen island on a bar stool. Luke crossed his arms over his chest, letting out a groan of annoyance.

"You were about to kiss that scumbag." Luke said with disgust dripping from his words. Hailey closed her eyes. She was very well aware of that.

"What I do in my free time is none of your business Luke." She said. Even if Luke hated him, he had no right to tell her what she can and can't do. She's older than him! Luke rolled his eyes.

"Don't you have a date with that one guy Jackson?" Luke asked with a raised eyebrow. She rolled her eyes. Of course he'd get the name wrong.

"His name is Jordan." She said politely. Luke stared at her, unfazed.

"My point being, you can't string along every boy you meet." He said. She stared at him, confused. What was he talking about?

"Huh?" She said.

"Jordan asked you out. Nate was about to kiss you. And Zac, well that boy claimed you as his. You need to fucking choose Hails." Luke said before he marched out of the room. She felt her mouth drop open in bewilderment. She did not have three guys pining for her.

Jordan barely knew her and just asked her out. She was being polite, since they had just met. For all she knows, there could be potential for them. She's never had a boyfriend so she isn't sure how dating even works.

Now for Nate, she was confused. That boy had been cold and mean to her for years. She still remembers meeting him at the end of Sophomore year when she transferred. He had been a flirt since the start, which she quickly denied his advances. His teasing tone only added to her annoyance about him.

Now a year later, she was actually enjoying her time with him. Ever since he came back from New York, he seemed happier. He had stopped being rude and vulgar, but still kept his teasing. She actually seemed to like talking to him in class. She definitely enjoyed their outing today. But that wasn't what confused her. What confused her was that he had been sweet to her. His bad boy demeanor had vanished.

He had leaned in to kiss her at the end of their hangout as if it were a date. She was sure she might have kissed him if it weren't for Luke. She felt that weird sensation of butterflies in her stomach as her heart raced. If Luke hadn't come out, she was sure she'd kiss him back. She never thought she'd ever be thinking that, much less hoping for it.

Did she actually like Nate? That would be too cliché. For the good girl to fall for the bad boy? No, it can't be. Besides, she has a date with Jordan. Plus there's Zac. She groaned at the thought of him.

She liked Zac, a lot. He was sweet, smart, and everything else a girl would want. He was perfect and it made her heart beat fast when he looked at her. The moment they met at the grocery store, she was starstruck. They way his lips curled into a smirk as his beautiful brown eyes roamed her body. She felt things for him she has never felt before. She loved hanging out with him. They've never really done much except talk, but she enjoys every second of it. It doesn't help that her siblings seem to like him too.

Don't get her started on that jersey. She still doesn't know what it means, or if it even has any meaning. For all she knows, Zac was truly just being considerate over the fact that she doesn't have any team football gear. But, she still has that small hope in her heart that it meant something to him. Was he actually claiming her as his? Why can't he just come out and say he likes her. She'd jump into any chance she has at being with him.

She groaned as she let her head drops into her hands. She was confused about everything. She didn't know what to do. She liked all three, one more than the other. Regardless of the fact that only one hasn't shown any reciprocated feelings, she doesn't know what to do. How could her life get so complicated?

-

Friday rolled around and Hailey found herself nervous. Jordan had asked her out during class, asking if it was alright if they went to dinner and then the football game. The boys were in the quarterfinals, moving closer to the championship. She had agreed, knowing she'd have the girls with her at the game.

As she looked in her closet for something to wear, she felt a presence at her door. She turned and saw her brothers. They were watching her with curious glances. She rolled her eyes as she flopped onto her bed. She could save her outfit for later.

"One of you speak." She said staring at the ceiling. There were stick on glow-in-the-dark stars for Trinity. They were actually pretty cute.

"So, you have your date tonight." Josh said first. She didn't bother to look at them. She was sure they were watching her every move.

"Yup." She said reaching for her cellphone. Jordan had texted her and asked if they wanted to meet there. She quickly typed yes. It's better that he didn't run into her siblings, especially Luke. He had been rude since the whole day with Nate.

"With Jordan? So you chose." Luke said next. She locked her phone and looked at the boys. Ben was analyzing her. She hated when he did that. He could read her like an open book. He knew everything she thought and felt.

"What about Zac?" Ben asked. Hailey sighed. Of course she'd be having this conversation with her three brothers. Shouldn't this be something she'd be having with Bella and Mariah?

"What about him?" Hailey asked. Ben sat down on her bed beside her. Luke took her desk chair as Josh stayed by the door, leaning against the frame.

"You don't like him?" Josh asked. Hailey sighed.

"Of course I do, but he doesn't like me. This whole thing about him 'claiming' me is bologna. We're just friends. Plus, would it really be bad for me to go out with Jordan? He's sweet and smart." She said defending her actions. Luke narrowed his eyes while Josh only stared back with a neutral expression. Ben was the only one still deep in thought.

"Yes." Luke stated. She rolled her eyes.

"Just because he's nice to you, doesn't mean you have to go out with him?" Ben stated. She sighed. There was a small part of her that wanted to prove her brothers wrong. Maybe, Jordan and her did have a future. She would never know if she didn't try.

"Hailey," she heard Josh's voice say. She looked him as he analyzed her. She felt awkward underneath his gaze. Times like this, she felt as if Josh was her father. She'd imagine that her dad would be acting just like the boys, wanting to know about threatening boys. "Why is Luke angry at you?"

"I don't know." She stated in a soft voice. She didn't want to tell him that there was a third boy. A boy who confused the heck out her. Monday, in class, he acted as if nothing happened. He continued his usual teasing but never brought up the kiss. He wasn't even that sweet guy she met for a brief second. It only made her even more confused. Not to mention that she got a headache after class.

The only one that seems to know what he wants is Jordan. He had been really sweet in homeroom. He walks her to first period and gives her a hug goodbye. It's really nice of him, but she doesn't feel anything towards him. Everything is platonic and she hates it. She wishes that she could fall for the good boy who cares about school and is really kind to her.

"Hailey." Luke said through narrowed eyes. She sighed. There was no way she was getting out of this conversation without telling her brothers about Nate.

"I almost kissed this other guy." Hailey mumbled. She felt all their gazes.

"You kissed Zac?" Ben asked. She could feel his excitement which she shut down with a shake of her head. "Then who?"

"Nate." Luke said through his teeth. One was able to sense the anger that radiated off of him.

"Nate? As in Nate Price?" Josh asked.

"That's the dickhead." Luke grimaced. She looked up and saw Josh with a neutral expression. Ben, on the other hand, was frowning, almost glaring.

"Hails, do you like Nate?" Ben asked. She shrugged. She didn't know and that's was angered her. She needs a sign. She doesn't know what to do or what to say.

"I don't know anymore. I just want to enjoy this date. I mean it is my first one." She said in a small voice. She heard Luke sigh. Ben gave her a small smile, while Josh stayed neutral. Her eldest brother was always in control, never letting anyone in.

"Hailey, you'll know who to pick." Ben said with confidence. She nodded, feeling a little bit better about his words. She stood up and went back into her closet. She decided she'd wear the jersey, just like every Friday. She also chose a pair of dark was skinny jeans with rips around the knees. She's pair it with her Converse.

"Can one of you drop me off at the diner?" She asked as she turned away from her closet. The three boys looked at each other, nodding, before all standing up. She groaned. Here they go in overprotective mode.

-

Her nerves were going crazy. As they pulled into the parking lot, her heart began to race and her palms began to sweat. This was her very first date. She didn't know what to expect. How was she supposed to act? What was going to happen? It was nerve racking and confusing. She had only talked to Jordan a few times, yet here she was. This meant that he liked as more than a friend, right?

"Hails, breathe." She heard Ben say underneath his breath. She rapidly blinked, realizing her lungs weren't getting oxygen. She needed to relax or she wasn't even going to make it inside. "If you like this boy, there's nothing to be afraid of."

"She's afraid because she doesn't like him." She heard Luke say in an irritated tone. She rolled her eyes. She opened the car door, slamming it. She heard the window roll down. She ran a hand through her hair and turned to her oldest sibling.

"Be careful Hails. We trust you, but that doesn't mean we trust him. Ben and I are on standby if you need anything. We'll see you after the game." Josh said in a deep voice. He was oozing authority. Hailey nodded.

"Thank you. Good luck tonight Lukey." Hailey said. She heard Luke groan as the others chuckled. She smiled. The butterflies in her stomach were subsiding. Ben was right. She had nothing to worry about. She began to walk towards the diner, hearing the annoying bell.

She looked around for her date and saw Jordan in a booth. She chuckled as she thought about their last time here. It was only a week ago, yet she still found herself at the diner. She put on a smile and made her way towards him.

Jordan was sitting in the same booth as last time. He was wearing a white t-shirt underneath a black leather jacket. He looked good, but not as good as Zac. She found herself frowning at comparing the two boys.

Jordan looked up as she approached him. He quickly smiled, which faltered as he looked at her. He then gave her a wide grin, which she sensed was suddenly fake. She slid into the booth across from the table and found the nerves dissolved.

"Hey Hails," he said to her. "You look," his eyes looked down at her football jersey. "-great."

"Thanks." She said with a small smile. She grabbed a menu from the table and began to flip through it. The atmosphere around them was beginning to get thick and awkward. Was this how all dates are?

"So, what's good here?" Jordan asked. She looked up from the menu.

"Do you want my biased or unbiased opinion?" She asked. Jordan laughed, making her loosen up. She had nothing to worry about.

"Unbiased." He stated.

"Everything." She replied. Jordan stared back at her.

"Biased?" He asked.

"I'm told to say the grilled cheese because my boss loves them. But, even though I do work here, I prefer the burgers or the chicken tenders." She told him. He nodded, impressed. She smiled, looking back down at the menu. She read a few things before putting it down. "I don't know why I read this. I know all the food."

"How is it working here?" He asked. She was about to answer when she saw one of her coworkers come into view.

"Hi, i'm Mel. I'll be your server for the night." Mel said. Hailey smiled. Mel was one of the sweetest girls here, being a year older than her. She tried setting Ben up with her, but Mel just enjoys being casual at the moment. "Oh, hey Hails."

"Hey Mel. I didn't know you were working tonight." Hailey told her. Mel chuckled.

"Bella had me switch with her so she could go to her brother's game. How come you aren't going?" Mel asked. Hailey's eyes flicked to Jordan. Mel gasped. "Sorry, i'm rude. You're on a date. But this isn't that hottie who comes in every shift."

"This is Jordan." Hailey said, feeling her cheeks heat up from her comment. She knew who Mel was talking about.

"What guy?" Jordan asked. Mel smirked.

"What's his name Hailey? Ash? Dan? Zac?" She said emphasizing his name. Hailey narrowed her eyes. Bella must have told her.

"Zac? As in Zac Logan? He comes in here?" Jordan asked. Mel nodded.

"That dude is practically in love with her. He freaking gave her his jersey, which by the way, she is wearing." Mel said pointing to it. Hailey frowned. Way to ruin her first date.

"Mel, can you bring us some waters?" Hailey asked, hoping to change the subject. Mel nodded, bouncing away. Hailey sighed. "I'm sorry about her."

"It's alright. I didn't know Bella worked here. Or that Zac came in all the time." Jordan said. He tensed as he said Zac's name.

"Mariah and Evan come in when we work." She said hoping to relax him. This might be her first date, but she knew not to talk about exes, even if you've never dated one.

"You're close to them." Jordan stated. She shrugged. She had only known them for about two, almost three months, yet she found herself with them all the time. She liked having a friendship with the girls.

"I met Zac one day and he invited me to hangout with them. The rest is history." She said. She looked down at her hands in her lap. She felt her heart race as she remembered bumping into him. She silently chuckled as she remembered she was going to pay for the bottle of alcohol. She was stupid to think she'd be able to pay for it, only being 18. Plus, she didn't have that kind of money.

"Here you go. What do you guys want for dinner?" Mel asked when she came back with the glasses of water. The two quickly ordered, leaving them in silence. She looked around and saw a few other people in the restaurant. She assumed everyone else was at the game. It'd be starting soon.

"So when is you first basketball game?" She asked Jordan. She saw that he was looking down at his phone. She found it slightly rude, then realizing it could be an emergency. She dropped the scowl. Jordan looked up, still typing away.

"In a few weeks. You should come." He said. He glanced at her before going back to his phone. She sighed. This night was not going how she planned.

-

"Girl, who is that?" Bella asked as they sat on the bleachers. Mariah was beside her. They were staring out at the field as the players ran out. Hailey sat next to Bella who was staring at her with wide eyes.

Hailey looked to her side and saw her date. She sighed. Jordan was engrossed in his phone, not looking up. He had been like that half the time. He was either into talking about himself or basketball. Usually she wouldn't mind talking sports, but she just didn't like nor understand basketball.

"Bella, Mariah, this is Jordan." Hailey said. Jordan looked up. He gave them a smile before looking back down at his phone.

"We know who he is." Mariah said in annoyance. "But why is he with you?"

"We were on a date." Jordan said answering. He slid his phone into his pocket. Hailey's eyebrows shot up in surprise. She thought he'd be spending the rest of the night on it. That's how it was at the diner.

"What the fuck happened to-" Mariah began to speak, only stopping when Bella shoved popcorn into her mouth. Hailey watched in amusement as Mariah spit the snack out. "What the fuck Bells?"

"Shut up Mariah. The game is about to start." Bella said through gritted teeth. Hailey was confused but ignored them. Those two had been best friends far too long for Hailey to understand them.

Hailey focused on the game, seeing Zac. Her heart began to thump in her chest as she saw him. He was running a hand through his hair, taking a drink. He looked handsome in his gear. She looked down at the jersey she was wearing, making her heart flutter.

Zac was taking a much needed water break, hoping to calm down his nerves. He ran a hand through his hair, frustrated. He had been trying for hours to forget Hailey. It irked him that Hailey was going out with Jordan. He didn't know when their date was, but it was happening soon. He knew that.

He was annoyed that he couldn't do anything about it. It seemed as if she chose Jordan and not him. He didn't know what to do to forget about her. During homeroom, the only class he shares with her, he'd sit next to his partner Paula. He'd try to focus on their project, but his eyes would wander, landing on Hailey. She was always laughing and smiling at Jordan. He was disgusted.

Zac looked up at the stands, instantly recognizing Hailey. She was sitting next to Bella and Jordan. He frowned upon seeing him but it disappeared when he was she was wearing his jersey. It fit her big and engulfed her small body. He loved it. He loved seeing her in it.

"Stop staring." He heard Evan say. He frowned. He was not staring. He looked back up and saw Hailey looking at him. He smirked at her. He knew her cheeks were red. He turned away and jogged towards Evan. He knew he was supposed to be angry at her for going out with Jordan, but he couldn't be. Hailey made him happy and he wished nothing more than to make her his.

"Where's Nate?" He asked Evan. He shrugged, slipping his helmet on. He sighed. Nate had been practicing, but still ignoring him. Zac didn't know what to say to him. He knew they liked the same girl, but neither would want to back down. He just hoped Nate would find someone else.

"Alright guys! On the field!" He heard his coach say. Zac's thoughts disappeared as he slid his helmet on. They had the ball on the fortieth yard line. He jogged to his spot, focusing on the game.

Hailey watched as Zac slid on his helmet. He looked incredible in his uniform, making her sigh from content. She hadn't really spoken to him since he came over Saturday. She knew she had to talk to him. She didn't know why he reacted that way to her going out with Jordan. She only hoped it was because he liked her. It gave her a small sliver of hope.

"Hailey, want to go get snacks?" Bella asked. She nodded. "We'll be back Jordan."

"Mhm." Jordan said. He was back on his phone. Hailey sighed. This date was a bust. Bella and her squeezed by, walking down the bleachers. They were in the front row, not really blocking anyone's view.

"Why didn't you tell us you were going out with him?" Bella asked. Hailey shrugged.

"Not really important." Hailey mumbled. Bella scoffed.

"Pretty sure it is." Bella said as they approached the concession stand. They ordered a Gatorade each and a pack of M&M's. "It's a big deal when we both clearly know you don't like him like that."

"What makes you think I don't?" Hailey asked. They began to walk back towards their seats.

"The jersey you're wearing. You wouldn't have it on if you weren't head over heels for Zac." Bella said. Bella squeezed in and sat down. Hailey did the same.

Her thoughts were overflowing with confusion. Was she right? Did she only like Zac? She groaned, earning her curious glances. She felt her cheeks heat up as she looked onto the field.

Her eyes instantly connected to Zac. He was laughing on the sidelines, not having a care in the world. She sighed. She had a real dilemma. Half of her wants him and the other half wants to forget.

-

Every time Hailey found herself at the Green's, she was astonished. Their house was a mansion. Money oozed from the corners. She gazed at the lavish items within the home as Bella pulled her up the stairs.

The girls had insisted on a sleepover. Hailey declined, earning protests. She knew her brothers would never allow her to sleepover at a guy's house, even if it was to have a sleepover with Bella. But, they weren't taking no for an answer.

Bella even marched over to Josh after the game. He was surprised to know that Hailey had friends, who were girls. He had assumed the only people in her life were the three boys messing with her head. Somehow, she managed to convince him to allow her to come over the next day.

Now, it was Saturday and Hailey found herself in Bella's room. It was dark purple. She had a queen bed with a black bed spread and purple pillows. A flatscreen hung on the wall above a dresser. She had a desk in the corner with a giant Mac. She even managed to have a vanity inside a walk in closet. She had pictures along the wall and a giant poster of Niall Horan.

"Finally!" Mariah said as she looked up. She was on her phone, laying on Bella's bed. She was dressed in shorts and a crop top. Her blond locks in a fishtail braid.

"Hey Mariah." She said. Bella closed her bedroom door. She had a serious face. She was getting down to business.

"So boy talk." Bella said. Hailey knew that was coming. She didn't give them a chance to ask their dying question after the game. "No more Zac?"

"I don't know. He doesn't seem interested." Hailey said with sadness. It was one of the reasons she gave Jordan a chance. She laid down on the bed.

"So Jordan then?" Mariah asked. Hailey groaned. "So no Jordan?"

"I don't know. He was great and all, but he was too into his phone half the night. And then there's freaking Nate." Hailey said. She stared at the ceiling, feeling their gazes on her.

"What about Nate?" Bella said in a clipped tone. Hailey sat up and stared at Bella. She had narrowed eyes, awaiting her answer.

"That's the thing! I don't know. One day he's an idiot. Then the next, he's sweet and giving me a ride home. Not to mention we almost kissed." Hailey said groaning at the end. She grabbed a pillow and covered her face. Why was her nonexistent love life now a mess?

"What?" Mariah screamed. Bella remained quiet as Hailey sighed. She then began to explain the entire study session to them. Maybe they'd be able to decode him. "So let me get this straight. Our Nate, likes you?"

"I don't know for sure. I mean don't you only try to kiss people you like?" Hailey asked. She knew she was new to the dating life, but she knew that much.

"I feel like you should dump Jordan." Mariah suggested. Hailey sighed.

"I know. I just didn't feel those cliché sparks with him. I was bored the whole night with him." Hailey sighed in defeat. She was really hoping she liked him. He seemed like a great guy.

"Do you feel them with Nate?" Bella asked. Hailey looked at Bella. She had a look of constipation on her face as she scrunched it up.

"Not really. I only ever feel them with Zac. But Bella, what's with all the questions about Nate?" She asked. Bella's eyes widened in alarm. She looked around the room as her cheeks grew red. Why was Bella embarrassed? Had she missed something?

"Bells, what are you hiding?" Mariah asked. She began to stutter.

"I-well, um you see, the thing is." Bella said. She seemed to be scared and worried.

"Bella, spit it out." Hailey found herself saying. Mariah nodded in agreement.

"I think I like Nate." She said quickly, but loud enough for them to hear. Hailey's eyes widened.

"You like Nate? As in the idiot who is your twin's best friend?" Mariah asked for clarification. Bella nodded, rolling her eyes.

"Do we know another Nate?" She asked full of sarcasm. Mariah rolled her eyes.

"So that's why you were getting all antsy about Nate liking Hailey." Mariah concluded. Bella sighed.

"Yeah. I've liked him for a while. He'll never like me back though. He only wants to hump and dump." Bella said in a low tone. Her eyes seemed to fill with tears. Hailey sat there stunned.

She never thought anyone would develop real feelings for him, yet she almost did. But knowing her friend liked him, she didn't want to develop anything. At most, friendship was as far as they'd get. She never really liked

Nate before. She didn't know why this was going to be different. Her brain was playing tricks on her.

"I feel left out." Mariah said. Bella and Hailey gave her a questioning look. "What? You both have guys. I have none."

"I mean you could date my brother. I see the way you look at him." Bella said with a smirk. Mariah widened her eyes. She seemed shocked. "Don't deny it. You think he's hot. I mean, I am his twin."

"Wait-what?" Mariah said, still shocked. Bella rolled her eyes.

"Any way, when are you going to make a move on Zac?" Bella asked. Hailey shrugged.

"He doesn't like me, so it doesn't matter. Either way, I need to break whatever it is off with Jordan. I don't want to string him along." Hailey said. Bella nodded, agreeing. "As for Nate, i'm shutting it down. Even if there is nothing, i'm making it clear that we're only friends."

"Thanks Hails. Now help me make him fall in love with me." Bella squealed. Hailey nodded. She wasn't even sure why she was confused. She knew it was Zac all along. Now, she just needs the boy to like her back.

Chapter 12 | Rewrite the Stars

T he moment Zac walked into homeroom, he could sense something was wrong. He looked around and saw the twins. They had their heads down on their desks, probably sleeping. He didn't see Hailey nor Mariah. He especially didn't see Nate.

That little fucker has been ignoring them all. He knew it was because of Hailey. It had been over a month since their talk, well argument, and it looked like Nate wasn't going to be around them again. It made him angry that he lost a friend over a girl, but it wasn't any girl. It was Hailey. She was special.

"Wake the fuck up twins." Zac said as he slid into his usual seat. He heard a groan as Bella sat up. Evan stayed down. His snores were becoming louder by the second. "What's up with him?"

"We stayed up late playing video games. I kicked him out of my room during the day because Hailey and Mariah were over." Bella said. She rubbed her eyes, yawning.

"Hailey came over?" He asked. Bella nodded, smirking. "What did you guys do?"

"She told us something. For one," she said before whacking the back of his head. "You are a jerk."

"What did I do?" He asked while rubbing his head.

"Why haven't you asked her out? You let Jordan do it!" She said in a loud whisper. The room was beginning to fill up with students. As much as he wants everyone to know he's crazy about Hailey, he needs to tell her first. Besides, everyone is stupid if they don't know what the jersey means.

"I was going to and that cunt beat me to it." He said with a grimace. Bella sighed.

"Well looks like Nate is going to beat you too." Bella mumbled. His eyes widened.

"What? What do you mean?" He asked. Bella sighed. Did Nate tell them he liked her? Did he tell them about their argument? What did he do to Hailey? He was going to beat his ass if he did.

"Hailey said she hung out with him Sunday last week. He almost kissed her." Bella said with a sad tone. Usually he'd ask about it, but Hailey was the only thing on his mind. Was Hailey going to kiss him back?

"Does she like him?" He found himself asking. Bella was about to reply when they both heard Evan groan.

"I do not suggest sleeping on a desk." Evan said rubbing his face. "It sucks. I need to invest in a pillow."

"Wake up Evan. Class is about to start." Bella said. Evan groaned again. Zac saw the last of their friends walk in as the bell rang.

"Hey guys!" Mariah said. She slid in her usual spot, followed by Hailey. She had a conflicted look in her eye. He was about to ask her what was wrong when Jordan walked over.

"Hey Hails." Jordan said with a bright grin. Zac frowned.

"Hey." She whispered. Hailey knew what she had to do, but she couldn't find herself doing it. She had never broken up with someone. She didn't want to hurt his feelings. He really did seem like an amazing guy. He just wasn't the one for her.

"Can you meet me after school in the courtyard?" Jordan asked. She nodded with confusion. She opened her mouth to ask why when their homeroom teacher began to speak. She focused on the notes on the board, ignoring the nagging feeling in the pit of the stomach.

She had woken up perplexed. She felt that something very bad was going to happen today. She assumed it was going to be her telling Jordan that she only wants to be friends, but she never expected what was actually to come.

-

That horrible feeling in her stomach only intensified when she saw Zac walk in. He looked angry, really angry. Sasha came in seconds later. Her stomach twisted in knots.

Hailey hadn't seen or heard from Sasha since the whole thing with Nate. She still didn't know why Nate wasn't really hanging out with them nor what he was talking to Sasha about. All she knew was that Nate argued with Zac which led to Zac sleeping with Sasha.

She felt the bile rise at the thought of them together. She pushed away her lunch tray and focused on Bella. She was busy writing her essay for English.

Mariah was off with her soccer friends. They had tryouts in a few days. Evan was next to his sister, sleeping.

"What's with that?" Hailey asked Bella. She pointed towards Zac who was glaring at Sasha. Bella looked up and raised an eyebrow, shrugging.

"She probably wants him back." She said bored. She went back to her essay. Hailey was glad she finished hers during the weekend.

"Hey." She heard someone say. She turned and saw Nate. She swallowed.

"Nate! About fucking time you join us." Bella said. She slid her notebook into her backpack, a huge smile on her face. Hailey laughed. Bella was making her crush very evident now.

"Can I talk to you?" Nate asked Hailey. She frowned. She looked at Bella. Her smile had erased and she was now glaring at her food. "Please."

"Alright." Hailey said. She left her things and followed Nate out of the cafeteria. She tried to ignore that horrible gut feeling and focused on their surroundings. They were in the hallway. No one was around. You were either in class or at lunch. The only thing there were the lockers.

"I'm sorry." Nate said with a sigh.

"For what?" Hailey asked.

"For kissing-for almost kissing you. I shouldn't have tried to do that. At least not without properly asking you out." Nate said. He scratched the back of his head as Hailey's mouth dropped open. The baddest guy in town was asking her out. Usually she'd be freaking out, but now she was annoyed.

"That's sweet and all, but what? No. I don't like you like that." She said being very blunt. Nate's hand dropped as he stared at her, dumbfounded.

"What? But you were going to kiss me." Nate asked. She shrugged.

"I know, but I realized that I don't like you like that. Plus, if you haven't heard, I went out with Jordan Friday night." She told him. His surprised eyes turned into narrow slits.

"That little fucker." He seethed.

"Woah, woah. Slow down. No need to be angry." She said, attempting to calm him down.

"I swear every time I try to make a move, someone gets in my way." He said with anger in every word. Hailey was about to remind him that she didn't like him like that when his words made her stop.

"Who else is there?" She asked. She was hoping he'd say Zac, but she instantly regretted that thought. She hated being the source of their arguments. They were best friends, yet now they weren't and it was because of her. Was that why they had their argument? Had Nate told Zac he liked her? She was about to ask when she heard a commotion from the janitor's closet.

Nate and her turned and saw Sasha walk out. She had a triumphant smile on her face. She ran a hand through her blond locks, taming the knots that had formed. That uncomfortable feeling was worming its way back into her stomach. Sasha smirked as she walked by.

A minute later, Zac came out of the same closet. Hailey's face became pail as she saw him. He was running a hand through his hair. A frustrated and angry look on his face. He turned towards her and Nate. Rage flamed in his eyes. She felt scared from the emotion directed towards them, but she also felt angry and betrayed. He did it again. He said he wouldn't, but he did it again.

She quickly turned on her heel, finding her way back into the cafeteria. She walked through the crowd of students. The bell was going to ring soon and she needed to grab her things. She walked over to the table and saw Bella shoving her things into her backpack. Evan was still sleeping.

"Hey Hails, what did Nate want?" Bella asked. Bella's eyes then widened, quickly standing up. "What did he do?"

"Nothing." Hailey answered with a quiver. She felt her tears start to fall. She quickly wiped them away, not wanting to cry over him. He wasn't worth it, yet it felt like her whole heart was breaking.

"Why are you crying?" Bella asked in a soft tone. Hailey kept a sob in as Evan woke up.

"What happened? Hails? What's wrong?" Evan asked. He quickly got up and wrapped his arms around her. Hailey then lost it. She wiped away the tears as she buried her head in Evan's chest. She felt a presence among her and she felt the heat he provided. She unwrapped herself from Evan, grabbing her things. She didn't want to be near him.

"Hails." Zac whispered. She ignored him as she walked off towards English. She knew she'd be sharing it with Nate, but it was better than Zac. She was never going to trust him again.

When Zac saw Hailey in the hallway with Nate. He felt anger course through his veins. He knew he had no right to be angry at his best friend because she wasn't his, but he still hated the fact that he liked her. What made him equally as angry, if not more, was Sasha.

She had been all over him the moment he stepped into first period. He had Spanish with her and she always made it a point to sit next to him. He managed to ignore her the last week, but it seems as she's back and worse than ever.

He had walked out of his math class to see her standing at his locker. He groaned in annoyance. Was she ever going to get the hint? He walked over with a huge glare on his face. Her, what used to be seductive, smirk slid off her face.

"Baby, what's wrong?" She asked running a hand down his chest. He grabbed her wrist, stopping her movements.

"I'm not your baby. I told you to leave me the fuck alone." Zac spat. That only encouraged Sasha more.

"I know you enjoyed our little late nights. Come on, we can have some fun during school too." She said. Zac frowned.

"Not going to happen." He said. He walked away, her on his tail. He sighed. She needs to fall in a ditch or something. He walked into the cafeteria, ready to make his way to the girl he would be with in the blink of a second. He only stopped when he heard Sasha's annoying voice again.

"Wouldn't want Hailey knowing she's the reason you and Nate aren't talking, now would you?" She said venomously. Zac turned, stepping forward. She smiled victoriously.

"Leave Hailey the fuck alone." He seethed. She laughed, humorlessly.

"Come with me or else I tell." She threatened. Zac's eyes narrowed even more. He knew she wasn't joking. She would tell her. He looked over at the table and saw that Hailey was talking to Bella. Evan was sleeping. Swear that boy can sleep anywhere.

"Fine. But this is the last fucking time." Zac said. Sasha smirked, grabbing his hand. She pulled him out of the cafeteria and into the nearest janitor's closet. She went straight to work.

Her lips were on his, making him feel more disgusted then ever. All he could think about was the brunette. He wished it was her with him. He wished he could hold her body in his own, as he placed kisses all over his face. He wanted nothing more to to feel the taste of her lips on his own.

Zac then pushed Sasha off. She stared at him with wide eyes. He wiped away her sticky, gross lipgloss off his lips with the back of his hand. He glared at her. Her annoying smirk didn't falter. That only added fuel to the fire. He was about ready to let it all out.

"Get the fuck out of here Sasha. I am done with you." He seethed. She only smirked. She knew she was going to tell Hailey, but not if he could stop it. "You tell Hailey about Nate and I will tell every single person in this school about your parents."

"You wouldn't dare." She said with narrowed eyes. It was his turn to smirk. Sasha didn't want anyone to know about her half sister. Everyone would then know that her perfect, rich daddy wasn't her sister's dad.

"Leave before I do." He threatened. Her jaw locked as she grabbed the door handle. She twisted it stepping out. She then smirked as she walked out. He didn't question that look, only groaning in frustration as the door closed.

How could he be so stupid! He somehow told her about Nate during his drunken mistake. Now, she was going to tell Hailey. He was sure she'd never want to be with him if she found out that was the real reason they weren't talking. He had assured her that it wasn't about her, when it really was. She wasn't going to forgive him. Sure surely wasn't if he ever found out about this. He'll just tell her had to print something for Math.

He ran a hand through his hair, feeling it stick up everywhere. Sasha had a tendency to pull on it. He shook away that thought in disgust and opened the door. He attempted to fix his hair as he walked down the hallway. He looked up and felt his anger increase.

Hailey was standing in the hallway with Nate. Confusion, anger, disgust and disappointment, but mostly sadness radiated off of her. As she stared at him, he saw the tears start to well up in her eyes. He was about to explain when she turned on her heel.

He groaned in frustration. He fucked up again! He stopped and punch the closest locker. He felt his knuckles start to bleed, but not even the pain could erased the look she gave him. He quickly followed behind, not wanting to talk to Nate. That would only anger him more.

He walked into the cafeteria and saw Hailey in Evan's arms. He was cradling her, confused about her emotions. He felt that feeling from the morning make its way back. He walked over to the table. He was a few feet away from her, but even then, he could see her tense. He hadn't said anything and she could feel him. It made him slightly smile that her body reacts to him but it diminished when he remembered why he was there. What he caused.

"Hails." He whispered. Hailey pushed Evan away, grabbing her stuff. She then walked away, tears falling down her face. His heart was breaking. He caused this. It was his fucked up self that's making her cry.

"What the fuck did you do?" Bella said. Anger was very evident as his nostrils flared. Evan had the same look. They were scary when they were mad, especially when it was at him. "What. The. Fuck. Did. You. Do!"

"I messed up!" He shouted. People turned towards them. He glared at each and everyone, making them whip their heads away. They all disappeared as the bell rang. He groaned. He'd have to wait until after football practice to talk to her now. He couldn't wait that long knowing she was hurting because of him.

"Zachary Logan! My office now!" He heard. He turned and saw the school's principal. He had a furious look in his eye. This day just kept getting better and better.

"Alright." Zac said. He turned to look at his best friends. "I messed up, but tell her it meant nothing."

Bella and Evan looked at each other. They were having a silent conversation. Bella was the first to open her mouth, being cut off by the warning bell. They both sighed before grabbing their stuff and disappearing.

Zac turned and saw the evil old man. He had white and grey hairs on his balding head. He was a few inches shorter than him, but just as scary. He used to play football for the school before he turned into a teacher, and then the principal.

"In my office!" He demanded. Zac nodded, feeling even more frustrated than anything. Sasha just had to come and ruin everything, again.

-

Hailey ignored everyone. They were all watching her with suspicious eyes. She sighed as she engrossed herself in her work. Evan had tried talking to her, but she didn't want to tell him. She felt pathetic. Why did she have to fall for Zac?

Nate wasn't in class, which she was glad about. She could only deal with so much drama in one day. She even made it to her last class of the day without speaking to anyone. Mariah was the only one that didn't seem to know what was wrong. She was even more grateful for the pop quiz that didn't allow them to talk.

As the bell rang, she gathered her things and made her way to her locker. She just wanted to be home with a tub of icecream. She then remembered she still had the one Zac gave her. She let out a humorless laugh. How funny that he gave her the icecream she was about to use to stop herself from crying over him.

She was about to shut her locker when she felt her phone vibrate. She placed her things back in the locker and pulled her phone out of pocket. She saw that it was a text from Jordan. She sighed. She had forgotten that she promised to meet him in the courtyard. He said he was waiting for her. She shoved her things in her bag and shut the locker.

As she walked down the hall, in the opposite direction of freedom, she saw a crowd of people. She tried to see Jordan but it was no use. There were even people with their phones out. They seemed to be recording something. She looked around and was finally able to see Jordan.

He was in the center of the courtyard with a teddy bear and a rose. Her heart stopped. He had a huge grin on his face when he saw her. She walked towards him as her heart began to beat erratically. She hated being the center of attention.

"Hey Hailey." He said. She heard people awe around her. She saw a few guys from the basketball team holding signs. They each had a letter. She tried to piece the letters together but they seemed to be in the wrong order.

"Lomafr?" She tried pronouncing. Jordan scrunched his face up in confusion. He turned around and saw his teammates

"You idiots are in the wrong order." He shouted. They quickly scrambled before she was able to read the word.

"Formal?" She tried again. Her eyes then widened. Oh no. This cannot be happening!

"Will you go to winter formal with me?" Jordan asked. She couldn't move. She was going to break things off with him, yet here he was. He was asking her to the dance.

He had a hopeful gleam in his eyes. She couldn't say no. The entire school was here. She was sure this would be put on social media as well. She didn't know what to do. She knew she didn't like him, but she didn't want to embarrass him either.

She saw movement in the corner of her eye and saw Zac. She felt bile start to rise. That attractive jerk face needs to disappear! She saw as a frowned formed onto his face. She smirked. She turned back towards Jordan. He was waiting for his answer.

"I'd love to." She found the words coming out. Jordan's grin widened as everyone around clapped. She saw Zac disappear into the crowd. She turned towards Jordan.

"This is awesome babe!" He shouted as he wrapped his arms around her. She faked a smile. Grimacing at his words and feeling nothing for him. "I'll drop you off at home."

He reached for her hand and pulled her away from the crowd. He gave her the bear and rose. She stared at the sweet gestures as his hand squeezed her own. She felt nothing towards him. No sparks. No fireworks. No butterflies. Nothing and she hated it.

Jordan was sweet, smart, kind, and charming. She wanted to feel everything for him, but she didn't. There was only one guy she did and he didn't like her back.

She wished she could rewrite the stars and have Jordan be her happily ever after. She sighed. There was nothing she could do but hope she developed feelings for Jordan.

-

Zac punched another hole into the wall. At least this one was in his bedroom. After seeing Jordan ask Hailey to the winter formal, he came straight home. He couldn't risk damaging school property. He was already on probation with a week of lunch detention for putting a hole in the locker at lunch.

He explained everything to his principal, saying he got angry and needed to release his anger. It was better than injuring a student. The principal only frowned and told him his punishment. Zac was sure he wouldn't be suspended, especially with the championship game around the corner.

That was the only thing keeping him sane. He needed to lead his team to victory to be able to get out of this town. He couldn't stand being there anymore. His parents would flip when they heard what he did today. At least his mom would be semi-understanding. He'd explain to her that he saw Nate with Hailey and he got jealous. It was partly the truth.

Zac turned around and punched the wall again. He let out a yell in frustration. How could the girl he's crazy about be attracted so some other guy? He's stupid to think that time would let them become closer when it only allowed them to get farther apart. He should have made a move when he first met her. He should have asked her out after that party. He should have told her how he felt after the argument with Nate. He should have told her! He needs to tell her!

"Zachary! What is going on?" He heard his mom's voice yell. He turned around and saw her peeking into his room. "Why is there a hole in the wall?"

"Because I punched the wall." Zac said through gritted teeth. He didn't want to deal with her right now. His mom only narrowed her eyes at him. She was glaring at him with deadly eyes.

"Zac, tell me what's wrong." She demanded in a softer tone. He scoffed. His anger hadn't diminished since Sasha and every thing around him was only adding fuel. He was about ready to let all hell rang loose on his mom.

He took a deep breath, seeing her face scowl even more as she waited for an answer.

"Leave me the fuck alone!" He shouted. His mom gasped at his outburst. He turned around and grabbed his jacket. He slid his phone in his pocket and marched out of his room without a glance back.

"Zachary Xavier Logan!" His mom shouted. He ignored his mom as he ran down the stairs. He didn't even want to retaliate against her for using his middle name. With a new found anger, he stomped out of the house and towards his car. He pulled his door open and jumped in.

Seconds later, he found himself driving at fast speeds out of his neighborhood. He didn't even care that he was being reckless and dangerous. He had one thought in his mind and that was getting Hailey. He needed to explain everything to her, once and for all.

He took a sharp turn into her neighborhood. He was going to make her his. He slammed on the breaks as his car stopped in front of her house. He took a deep breath, trying to calm his anger. He couldn't be mad. He would only lash out on her. He needed to be calm to explain everything to her.

He looked out his window saw her brothers' vehicles. He suddenly felt nervous. It had been over three months and she never mentioned liking him. Was he just overreacting? Did Hailey truly like Jordan? He slammed his hand on his steering wheel, making his car horn go off. He groaned.

What was wrong with him? He's the most wanted guy, yet the girl he wants the most doesn't want him. He isn't supposed to feel nervous around a girl. He isn't supposed to be freaking out about telling a girl he likes her. He shouldn't be like this.

"Zac?" He heard. His head whipped towards the side and saw Hailey. She had her hair in a messy bun and a baggy t-shirt. It looked like her brother's.

Her face was red and puffy. She had tear stains running down her cheeks. He suddenly felt nauseous. This was all his fault. "Zac?"

He sighed. He needed to confront her and tell her everything. He needed to do it. He quickly undid his seat belt and opened his door. He made his way around his car. She was hugging her body tight, quivering. She looked like she was about to fall apart.

"Hailey." He whispered. Her body then began to fall as sob left her. He quickly engulfed her in his hold. Her tears began to fall. "I'm so sorry."

"Zac, stop." She said through her sobs. She looked up at him. She didn't want him to see her breaking. She didn't want him to see her hurting because of him.

The moment she got home, her tears would not stop. She hated that she lost Zac before ever actually having him. She drowned herself in the ice cream he bought her, only crying even more. She was glad no one was home, being able to let it all out.

After an hour or two, her pity party became a party for 6. All her siblings came home, rushing to her side. Josh watched from a far while Ben cradled her. Luke only glared at the wall, lost in his own thoughts. Seth and Trinity brought her chocolate and more ice cream. She thanked them, her tears finally beginning to dry.

"Hails, what happened?" Ben asked her cautiously. She let out a humorlessly laugh.

"Zac is back with Sasha and i'm going to formal with Jordan." She said wiping away her tears. She then turned towards Luke. "I told Nate I don't like him. Oh, and i'm crying over a guy that doesn't like me."

"So, no more Nate?" Luke asked. Hailey shrugged.

"I want to be friends with him. I mean Bella likes him." Hailey said with a giggle. Luke only rolled his eyes, fighting a smile.

"Hailey cakes, are you crying over Zac?" Ben asked. Hailey sighed.

"I'm crying because he doesn't like me. He came out of the janitor's closet with Sasha." She said with disgust. That moment was engraved into her brain, taunting her.

"Is that why Zac was angry during football?" Luke asked. Hailey turned to look at him.

"What?" She asked. Her eyes were wide.

"Evan was ignoring him while Nate only seemed to glare from afar. The whole team just thought they got into another fight. But, I still don't understand why he's mad." Luke said. Hailey shrugged.

"Probably angry he got caught." She spat. Ben sighed, hugging her close. "I'm fine Benny."

"No you aren't. You're crying because you saw him with another girl. But Hails, that doesn't seem like him." Ben said defending him. She got out of her brother's grasp.

"Why the fuck are you defending him? You aren't the one that messed up." She growled. Her head was fuming.

"Language Hailey." She heard Josh say. She ignored him. She had a right to be angry at her brother.

"Because Hails! Zac is crazy about you. I highly doubt he'd be seeing another girl." Ben said annoyed.

"Well then he has a funny way of showing that." She said in a sarcastic tone. She then glared at her brother. "You wanna know why he didn't come around for a month, he got into a fight with Nate and then slept with that slut. He was so embarrassed and ignored me."

"You're an idiot Hails." Ben said exasperated.

"Ben." Josh said slowly. Ben had his hands in fists, glaring at her. She was well aware of the argument they were having in front of the rest of their siblings.

"He was ignoring you because he thought that the moment he told you he messed up, he was going to lose you before he even had you." Ben shouted. Hailey stopped moving. Her mouth dropped open.

Zac liked her? Is that what Ben just said? So, the whole claiming her with his jersey was real? What? No. It can't be. Zac doesn't like her. He only thinks of her as a friend. Ben is lying. He's just trying to make her feel better.

"Speaking of the devil." Luke mumbled.

"What are you talking about Luke?" Josh asked. Luke then pointed out the window. Hailey walked over and saw Zac's car on the street. She saw him slamming his hand on the steering wheel before a honk left his car.

She quickly slid on some shoes and ran out there. She wanted answers and she wasn't going to let him leave without them. She said his name, getting Zac to turn towards her. She saw how angry and frustrated he looked. She said his name again, feeling her whole body want to give up.

"Hails." He whispered when he got out of the car. That's when she lost it. He caught her before she hit the ground. She let the sobs leave her body as the stupid cliché fireworks erupted in her belly. Even through anger and disgust, she still had feelings for Zac. "I'm sorry."

"Zac, stop." She said. She wanted to stop crying over him, but she couldn't. She liked the boy too much and no matter what she tries to do, fate keeps changing her plans. The moment she wants to tell Zac she likes him, Nate comes and then Sasha shows up. Don't even get her started on Jordan. She just wants her old life back, or at least to go back to the very first time she met him.

"I wish I could rewrite the stars. I wish I could go back in time and change it all. I should have told you everything from the start." He said. Her sobs only got louder. He hugged her even tighter.

There was nothing in the world he could do. No amount of apologizing was going to fix what he had done. He broke the girl because of his stupidity. He lost her because he was scared. He was frightened about what love was like and that's what drove him towards her. He wanted to feel it. He wanted to be in love and now, he was sure he was the farthest from it he had ever been.

"Hailey, I am so sorry. I never meant to hurt you." Zac said. Hailey wiped her eyes. She needed to stop. She needed to know why.

"Zac," she let out a breath. "Why were you with Sasha?"

"Because i'm an idiot. She threatened to tell you why Nate and I aren't talking. I didn't want you to know so she said she'd be quiet if I was with her one more time. But during it all, I just kept seeing your face. I couldn't go through with it. But by then, it was too late. You saw me leave after Sasha. You wouldn't let me explain that nothing happened. We just kissed before I pushed her away." Zac told her.

She closed her eyes and looked up at the sky. Her heart was beating fast from the different emotions she was feelings. She wanted to be angry at him for allowing Sasha to control him. She wanted to be disappointed that whatever Nate and him are mad at each other for was far more important than her. She needed to know what that was.

"Zac, why didn't you want me to find out about why you and Nate are fighting?" She asked. She looked at him. He looked away, not meeting her stare. He let out a loud breath before replying.

"Because Nate and I are fighting over you."

~~~~~~So, whatcha think? Comment, Vote, Follow.xoxo,Liv814
~~~~~~

Chapter 13 | 10,000 Hours

{ A/N: There's a lot of multimedia within this chapter. Hope you enjoy!!!}~~As Hailey laid in bed, she tried really hard not to move from restlessness. Trinity was fast asleep next to her. She wished she was too, but thoughts of Zac filled her mind, not allowing her to fall asleep. She kept replaying the moment they had. It was intimate and heart racing. She wished she could go back and change the ending.

She didn't even care that she was the reason for the guys' fight. What happened afterwards was what was keeping her awake. She wished she would have closed the space between them. She was sure Zac was about to, if it weren't for her annoying brothers.

Josh was the first one out of the house. He had a look of hatred, frightening not only Hailey, but Zac as well. Hailey had never seen her brother so angry. She didn't know why he was. She had just found out the real reason the two boys were ignoring each other. She was the one that was supposed to be mad, not Josh.

"Because Nate and I are fighting over you." Zac said in a low voice. She gasped.

"What? Me? Why?" She asked with confusion. So, Zac did like her. That didn't really explain why the two began to ignore her. What else was he hiding?

"Nate likes you and he's mad that I like you too." He said in frustration. He ran a hand through his hair. Hailey stared back at him, stunned. Had she really just heard Zac Logan confess his feelings for her? Ben was right? Zac likes her? Wait, Nate likes her? They were fighting over her? This made no sense.

"I-I don't-ugh!" She shouted. Zac stepped back, surprised at her outburst. "I just hate being in the middle of this. I feel like ever since we met, our lives have taken a different route. Nothing good comes from us being friends."

"That's the thing Hails." Zac said. He grabbed her hand and pulled her into his chest. She let out a gasp of surprise. She was caught off guard. She stared up at him as his hands made their way to her waist. His hands gripped her sides as he stared into her eyes. Her heart raced and fireworks began to fly as their bodies touched. She felt all those cliché sparks with him, but now they seemed to burn even brighter.

As she stared into his brown eyes, she saw emotions she thought she'd never see from him: desire, want, need. His eyes seemed to sparkle as he gazed into her own. Only one thought flooded her mind.

She wanted to know what it was like to kiss Zac Logan. No, she needed to what it was like to kiss Zac Logan. She saw his gaze flick down to her lips. Her breath hitched as his face grew closer. This was it. It was going to happen.

"Hailey," he whispered. "I don't want to be just friends. I want be more than that."

They began to lean in, urging to close whatever space was left between them. Hailey let her eyes flutter close as Zac's breath mingled with her own.

She could feel his lips just millimeters away. All she had to do was lean in just a fraction more.

"Hailey, inside. Now!" Josh's voice demanded, interrupting them. She opened her eyes wide, at the authority. Hailey didn't have time to think about Zac's words. She pushed herself away from Zac and turned to look at her brother. He was glaring at both, frightening her. Her brother wasn't someone who got angry a lot. Hell freezes over before he even shows one bit of it.

"Josh, stop. Wants wrong?" Hailey asked. Josh only narrowed his eyes at her. She let out a squeak before fully unwrapping herself from Zac. He was looking just as confused as her. She whispered goodbye before going inside.

She still wasn't sure what had happened. She tried to ignore the thoughts and feelings Zac has caused her and got ready for bed. She still had school the next day, even after the most dramatic day of her life.

As she thought about what she had to face, Jordan and Nate came to mind. She wanted to groan in frustration, but she couldn't. She didn't want to wake up her little sister. She didn't want to be the target of her attitude if she did.

Hailey turned, slowly, being careful not to wake her sister, and reached for her phone. She saw she had notifications. She had a handful of texts. She unlocked her phone before clicking on the app. She opened the first message.

Her heart began to flutter as she read the messages from Zac. Even after everything that had occured today, he still manages to make her smile. She shut her phone off and set it back on her night stand. She was finally able to let her mind shut off. She fell asleep, dreaming of the boy she bumped into while grocery shopping.

Waking up, Zac had one thing on his mind. He was going to make Hailey officially his. He couldn't wait any longer, especially with the almost kiss they had. He couldn't wait to finally know what her lips felt like.

When he told her the entire truth, it felt like a weight had been lifted off his shoulders. He hated telling her that she was the reason him and Nate weren't speaking, but if he wanted her to know he liked her, the truth had to come out.

He found himself smiling at the thought of Hailey being his. She finally knew he was crazy about her. If she didn't know it, he made it clear in the text he sent her last night. He wanted to know if she was alright after receiving wrath from Josh. Zac wasn't entirely sure why her brother was angry but decided not to but in. She'd tell him when she was ready.

As he got ready for school, that goal of seeing Hailey suddenly disappeared. He ran into his father in the kitchen. He was dressed in his work attire, looking expensive. He tried to get out of the house without being seen, but it was impossible. It was like he saw everything.

"Zachary, we need to talk." His deep voice said. His father then turned around, glaring at him. Zac sighed. There was no way he'd get out of this one.

"Alright." Zac replied. He stayed quiet and waited to hear whatever his father had to say. He watched as he let out a breath of annoyance.

"What is this detention your principal called about?" His dad asked. A scowl was permanently plastered onto his face. Zac couldn't remember the last time his father smiled.

"I punched a locker because I couldn't punch Nate." Zac told him. His dad's scowl deepened. Zac shrugged. He wanted the truth.

"Why were you fighting with Nathanial?" He asked. His tone was full of worry. Zac scoffed. Why does he care now? He's never around. He just sends his assistant to deal with him. At least his mom came home every once in a while and actually took the time to get to know him. "Actually, don't tell me. I'm late for work. I'll see you at the game Friday. Don't get into anymore trouble Zachary."

His dad then stepped beside him, going towards the garage. Zac watched his father's figure disappear, allowing him to breathe. Did his dad just say he was going to his game? Why did he suddenly care about him and football? Why is his dad even back in town? His parents are never in the same place unless it was for business. His phone then began to ring. He shook away any thoughts of his dad and answered.

"Dude, where are you?" He heard Evan say. Zac was surprised to hear his voice. He thought he'd still be mad over yesterday.

"At home, my dad wanted to talk." Zac said with a frown. It's ridiculous how much his father affects him. He was in such a good mood too.

"Get to school, now! Coach is looking for you. Plus, you're late to homeroom." Evan said. Zac groaned. Can his life just get any more worse? "Hurry up Zac."

Evan hung up, leaving a frustrated Zac. He let out a groan. He then slipped his phone into his back pocket and made his way out of the house. Well looks like Hailey is going to have to wait until tonight.

-

Hailey looked around the cafeteria for Zac. He hadn't shown up to homeroom. She couldn't ask Evan about him because he wasn't there either. She asked Bella about both and only told her that Evan was called in to see his coach. Hailey hadn't seen any of the boys all day. She was glad she hadn't seen Nate. She didn't want him confessing his feelings again when Bella is crazy about him.

Hailey explained to Bella and Mariah why she had been crying yesterday. She also told them about Zac coming over and apologizing for Sasha. She left out the part of Zac and her almost kissing. She couldn't think about it without her heart wanting to explode from her chest. She only hoped that it would be happening very soon.

She also told them about why the boys were fighting. Bella looked sad at the mention of Nate, but pushed those thoughts away. She said she'd deal with that later. Mariah and Bella threatened to kill Sasha, which Hailey wanted, but declined their offer. Bella mentioned that said she'd castrate Zac but wouldn't because she wants Hailey and him to have kids. That made Hailey bright red.

Mariah was the only one who was thinking about everything and not talking. Since she wasn't there to witness any of it, she thought everything logically. She told Hailey that she needs to tell Jordan about not going with him to formal.

Speaking of him, he sat next to her in homeroom. He took Zac's empty spot, ending the conversation she was having with them. Hailey wanted to tell him that she didn't want to go to formal with him, but she didn't.

She felt bad that she was stringing him along. That she didn't really like him as more than a friend. He was a great guy, but she had no feelings for him. They were simply platonic. She didn't want to ruin formal for him by not going as his date. He seemed extremely happy. Plus, the entire school knew about them. She didn't want to embarrass him or herself. She just plastered a faux smile and listened to him as class ended.

As usual, he walked her to class. The only difference today was the kiss on her cheek. When embarrassing things happened, her cheeks would turn bright red, but she didn't feel that heat. She just felt sad and irritated with herself. She watched him disappear, feeling nothing but disappointment. That kiss on her cheek only confirmed her feelings for Zac.

"Girl, stop searching." Mariah said with annoyance. Hailey huffed. She looked down at the salad she had chosen. She was too busy searching for said guy to pay attention to her lunch picking skills. At least it had chicken.

"I haven't seen Zac." She mumbled. She stabbed a tomato and plopped it into her mouth.

"At least that boy finally manned up and told you how he felt. Now we just need Nate to like me." Bella said with a look of determination in her eye. Hailey giggled.

"Ugh, you two are going to have dates for the dance and i'll have to go stag." Mariah groaned.

"Take Evan." They heard a man's voice suggest. The girls whipped their heads and saw Nate. Hailey gulped. Great, he decides to show up now. "He's too nice to ask some random girl out without her thinking he likes her."

"Thanks for your input Nate." Mariah said groaning again. He chuckled. Bella stared up at Nate. She was gazing up at him in adoration. Hailey coughed, getting Bella's attention. Hailey gestured towards Nate. Bella scrunched up her face in confusion before her eyes widened in understanding. Bella had to tell him how she felt, before he wanted to talk about his feelings towards Hailey.

"Hey, can we talk?" Bella asked Nate. He nodded, confusion in his eyes. Bella then grabbed her things and walked away. Nate followed behind, unsure of what was happening. They disappeared out the door when Mariah got up.

"Where are you going?" Hailey asked. She picked at her salad, not really feeling it anymore.

"To see what happens. Come on." Mariah said as if it were the most obvious thing. Hailey nodded in understanding. She, too, wanted to know how things would end for them.

They quickly got up and followed them. They could hear groans and scoffs from the hallway. As they rounded the corner, they saw Bella with fists. They widened their eyes. What were they saying? Why was she angry? They got closer, finally hearing.

"Bella, what the fuck is going on? What are you saying?" Nate asked. He got closer to Bella. He had a cautious step which only seemed to anger Bella more.

"I like you, you jerk!" Bella screamed. Nate stared back at her stunned, before crashing his lips on hers. Mariah and Hailey stared at them. Bella quickly pushed him away. "What are you doing? I thought you like Hailey?"

"I do. I did. Hailey was the closest person I met that reminded me of you Izzy. Evan said I couldn't like you, so I started sleeping with girls to forget you. I then met Hailey and she reminded me of you. I thought that by liking her, i'd be able to forget you." Nate said in a soft voice. Hailey wanted to awe, but remained quiet. She didn't want to ruin their moment. Mariah then grabbed her hand and led her back inside the cafeteria.

"Well that went better than expected." Mariah said. Hailey laughed.

"Now we just need Evan to ask you out." Hailey teased. Mariah rolled her eyes. "I have to go to class. See you later."

"Bye Hails!" Mariah shouted, going in the opposite direction. Hailey smiled. She got rid of one boy, now she just needs to figure out what she's going to do about Jordan.

-

Sliding on his helmet, he finally felt like he was able to relax. He'd have the opportunity to release his anger and stress. He needed to tackle some guys. He grabbed his water bottle and followed his teammates onto the field. He spotted Nate and Evan. He frowned. When did they become close again? Zac jogged over to them, glaring at Nate. Evan only smiled. Zac pulled off his helmet.

"Nate." He spoke first. Nate turned towards him and smirked.

"Zac." He replied. Zac frowned.

"Zac, chill. Nate is apologizing." Evan defended. Zac narrowed his eyes at his two friends.

"He's right. Sorry for being a jerk man. I realized that I don't really like Hails like that. I was trying to forget about Bella." Nate told him. Zac felt his scowl disperse. He grinned.

"Fucking shithead. We stopped talking for a month because you liked the wrong girl?" Zac asked rhetorically. Nate nodded, chuckling. Zac felt all his stress leave his body for good. He didn't need to tackle anyone anymore. He just needed to talk to Hailey. He couldn't wait to go see her after practice.

"Wait, Bella?" Evan asked, very frazzled. Zac smirked.

"Right, about that." Nate said scratching the back of his head. It was Evan's turn to glare.

"What the fuck are you talking about?" Evan said. His arms were crossed across his chest. He was giving Nate a menacing glare.

"Bella and I are dating." Nate said. Evan's mouth dropped open. Zac stepped back, not wanting to be in the punch zone. He watched as Evan's face turned red from anger.

"I thought I told you to not date her." Evan said in a threatening tone. His body was prepared to launch on him. Nate stepped back. His eyes darting in caution.

"I know, but man. Your sister is perfect. She's smart, sassy, sarcastic, sweet, and insanely gorgeous. How could I not fall for her?" Nate defended himself. Evan stopped moving, observing their friend. Nate seemed sincere, which was weird because Nate never talked about a girl like that. It was usually 'she has a nice ass or a nice rack.'

"So you actually like my sister?" Evan asked. His anger diminishing. Nate nodded, a small grin on his face. Zac chuckled. He felt good to not be on that end anymore.

"Damn Evan. You're the only single one now." Zac joked. Nate laughed.

"You aren't dating Hailey yet." Evan replied with a smirk. Zac frowned.

"Thanks for reminding me dipshit." Zac said glaring at his friend.

"Dude, she likes you." Nate said with a grin. Zac sighed.

"I told her about us fighting over her." Zac told Nate.

"Good. She needed to know before someone else told her." Nate said.

"I also told her I wanted to be more than friends." Zac added. He felt his friends' gazes on him.

"About time you grow some balls. But what about Jordan?" Evan asked. Zac narrowed his eyes. Way to bring that up. "Sorry, i'm being realistic here."

"I'm going to go see her tonight. I want to ask her out on a date. Hopefully she says she'll tell Jordan they're over. That way i'll be able to take her to formal." Zac said. A grin slid onto his face as he thought about her. He could only imagine how beautiful she'd look at the dance.

"Logan!" Zac heard his coach shout. The three of them turned and saw him with a clipboard in his hands. He was ready to get down to business.

"Yes coach?" Zac asked.

"Time to practice. We have a championship to win!" His coach said before blowing his whistle. The three of them turned. Smirks on their faces. There was no way in hell they'd lose the semifinals game. No way at all. They were going to bring home the 'ship.

-

As Hailey made her way to her favorite spot in the sand, she felt her phone vibrate. She slid it out, hoping it was Zac. She felt her goofy grin slide off her face. It was Jordan. She opened the text and saw that he was asking what color dress she'd wear. She responded that she didn't know and she'd get back to him. She let out a sigh as she plopped onto the sand.

During English and Economics, she spent the entire time thinking of ways to let Jordan down easy. She came up with nothing. She had no clue what to do about him. So upon coming home, she told Seth she'd be on the beach. She hoped the calming ocean would help sort out her problems.

The oceans waves crashed. The seagulls squawked by, not really ruining the tranquility. Hailey loves the peacefulness. She loved it even more with it being the spot her and her parents would come to. She wished she could ask her mom for advice. She didn't know how to deal with this mess she was in. She grabbed a pebble from the sand and threw it. It landed a few feet from the ocean. She sighed. She sucked at sports.

"Quite an arm there Foster." She whipped her head around and saw Zac. He was dressed in board shorts and a blue t-shirt. It hugged his muscles in all the right places.

"Hey." She replied. She turned away, not wanting to be caught ogling him.

"What are you doing?" Zac asked. He plopped himself on the sand beside her. The ocean breeze was chilly, but with Zac so close in proximity, all she felt was heat.

"Thinking. Showing off my amazing canon of an arm." She joked. Zac chuckled. She looked out at the ocean. The silence around them was comfortable, but that didn't stop her heart from racing. All she could think of was of that kiss they almost shared.

"Well Hailey Foster, I think you've got a chance of going pro. You want my quarterback position?" He teased. Hailey rolled her eyes. "But really babe, what are you doing out here?"

"Thinking about everything. When did my life get so complicated?" She asked, not really asking for an answer. She sighed. She not only found an amazing group of friends, but she found three boys that all wanted her. Luckily, one didn't anymore. She just never thought she'd be caught up in all this drama. All her life she spent worrying about her family and becoming a nurse. Now she is actually feeling like a teen.

"When you bumped into me. What can I say Hails, it was a lucky bump." He joked. Hailey let out a giggle before it turned into a sigh. She wanted everything with this guy. He had made it clear he liked her, yet they weren't together. She didn't know if she was ready for that. He'd be her first and that terrified her.

"Hailey, can we give us a chance?" Zac asked. He had a hopeful gleam in his eyes. She sighed. That's was what she was afraid of. She racked had her brain for hours on how to let Jordan down but none of the outcomes were right. She wanted to be with Zac, but couldn't until she broke up with Jordan.

"Can we just wait until after formal?" Hailey asked. Zac stared at her. Was she serious? After everything they had been through? She still didn't want to be with him. He thought she liked him as more than a friend.

When football was over, he drove home for a quick shower and changed into a t-shirt and his swim trunks. He had a feeling she was at the beach. He then drove to the Foster residence. He couldn't wait to see Hailey. He managed to go through the entire day without seeing her and it was making him go crazy. He just wanted her to be officially his.

When he arrived, Seth opened the door. He was more than eager to let him in. Seth asked about the library which made Zac chuckle, before agreeing to hangout with him soon. Zac then asked about his older sister. Seth informed him that she had changed and gone to the beach. Zac than excused himself and drove to the spot. Zac wasn't even sure why he didn't immediately come looking for her here.

"I told Jordan i'd go with him. I just can't back out now." Hailey said. She saw the look of disappointment on his face before he masked it with anger. She knew it wasn't at her but towards Jordan.

"You're too kind princess. But fine. That jerk better not try anything." He threatened. Hailey giggled. Her heart finally felt normal. As she looked out at the water, thoughts of her parents came to mind. Would they be happy she's happy? Would they approve of the boy next to her? Would they like him as much as she did? "What's going on in that pretty brain of yours?"

"I'm just thinking of my parents. How are yours?" She told him. Zac stiffened beside her. She knew he didn't have a great relationship with them.

"My dad is home for the semi game. I was nervous before, but now, i'm terrified. He has never come to a game before. This is my last one in high school before the championship. I don't want to disappoint. I want to bring the team that victory." He told her honestly. He felt her hand find his. She gave him a squeeze. He looked down at her. He grinned. Yeah he was scared, but with this girl on his side, he'd get through anything.

"Zac, you are an amazing guy. You are even better at football. I've never seen someone with the skills you have. It's phenomenal. It's your dad's loss if he's never seen you in action. You look so happy on the field. It's like you're in your own little world when you're out there." Hailey told him. As she finished her little speech, she felt the heat rise to her cheeks.

"Thanks Hails. You're right. As long as you're there, I will be fine. I don't need his approval." Zac said. Hailey bit her lip, fighting off a smile. Even through this, Zac managed to make her heart flutter.

"You don't need anyone." She told him.

"I just need you." He said with a cheesy smile. Hailey laughed. Zac watched as she enjoyed herself with him. They weren't really doing anything, yet he loved every second of it. He loved being near her and making her laugh. He could hear it all day and he'd never get tired of hearing her laugh.

"So, what's the plan for after your big win? Party and party and yeah?" Hailey giggled. Zac chuckled.

"Maybe. I'm not sure. But as long as i'm with you, i'll be happy." Zac said. Hailey giggled.

"Stop being so cheesy, but really. Are you throwing a party?" She asked. Her cheeks were a bright red from his words.

"Do you want me to throw one?" Zac asked. Hailey shrugged.

"I feel like the whole school expects you to." She told him truthfully. He sighed. He knew that too. There was usually a party after every win. He would have to throw one after this one. They'd be on their way to the championship.

"Only if you come." Zac said. Hailey let out a laugh.

"I'm sure the girls wouldn't let me miss it." She said truthfully.

"You could spend the entire night with me by my side." He said. Hailey bit her lip. He was so tempting.

"You'd get bored, quick." She joked. Zac shook his head.

"I'd spend 10,000 hours with you Hails. I'd spend so much more." Zac replied. Her mouth dropped open. He was gazing down at her. His eyes held so much emotion. She just wanted to feel his lips on hers. His lips were eye level with hers. She could see how plump they were. She was sure they'd be soft too. "Hails."

"Yeah?" She asked. She blinked a few times, trying to get out of the daze she was in.

"Mariah is on FaceTime." Zac said. Hailey looked at her phone and saw the call. She sighed. She was never going to kiss him. She grabbed her phone and answered it.

"Hey, where are you?" Mariah asked. Hailey flipped the camera and showed her the calming ocean. She then put it on the front camera again. "What are you doing there?"

"Talking." Hailey replied. Mariah smirked.

"With who?" She teased. Hailey rolled her eyes. She pointed the camera at Zac. He gave Mariah a cheesy smile. "Hey Logan, mind dropping this girl off at the Green's?"

"Sure." Zac said getting up. He offered his hand to Hailey. She gladly took it.

"Why am I being taken to Bella's?" She asked. She followed Zac to his car and got in. Zac turned on the car, feeling the engine roar to life. They then began their drive.

"Girl talk. So, Zac, sorry but you'll have to be away from Hails for another night." Morgan informed them. Zac chuckled as Hailey's cheeks brightened.

"It's alright Hails. I think she deserves that talk. She needs to gush about how perfect I am." Zac teased. Hailey's eyes widened before she smacked his arm. "Hails, i'm driving babe."

"Hurry up Zac, we do have school tomorrow." Mariah said in an irritated tone. Zac rolled his eyes. Why are the girls so dramatic? "See you in a bit."

Mariah then hung up. Hailey placed the phone in her lap. She faced the boy beside her. His hand was on top of the gear shift. Hailey felt a few butterflies start to flutter as she placed her hand on top of his.

Zac looked to his right and saw Hailey with a timid smile. He chuckled. He loved making her nervous. But, he loved making her blush even more. He removed his hand from the gear and grabbed her hand. He intertwined their fingers together.

"This next week is going to be tough." He said. Hailey sighed. She knew that hiding her feelings for Zac, after practically confessing them to each other, was going to be hard. But after the dance, she'd cut everything off with Jordan. She liked Zac and only Zac.

"It'll be fine. What's another week going to do?" She asked. Zac nodded. She was right. It'll only intensify their feelings for each other.

"Just don't do anything I would, with him." Zac said with a scowl. Hailey gave him a blank look.

"That's literally everything!" She shouted. Zac chuckled. That was the point. He didn't want to see his hands anywhere inappropriate nor his lips anywhere near hers. Hailey was his and only his.

"Just let him know you guys are only friends." He said. Hailey nodded. She saw the Green mansion come into view. Zac stopped the car. She unbuckled her seatbelt and turned to look at him.

"Alright. Thanks for dropping me off." She said. She grabbed her bag and went to open the door. Zac's hand circled her wrist. She turned around, feeling his lips on her forehead. Shocks sparked throughout her entire body.

"Have fun princess." He said. He gave her a big grin, making her heart race. She giggled as she exited his car. She walked up towards the door, being able to feel his gaze on her.

The front door then opened. Bella had a huge grin on her face. She pulled her in, shutting the door behind her. Bella didn't say a word as they made their way upstairs. Hailey was curious as to the reason she was here, but waited to be told.

"About time. Zac drives slow." Mariah said when they entered Bella's room. She was looking at herself in the mirror. She was wearing a white mid sleeve romper with red detailing. She paired it with black booties and a high pony with lots of volume. Her style was so girly and cute. Hailey was jealous.

Bella was wearing black joggers with a matching black crop top. Her midriff on full display as she paired it with a black bomber jacket with white lines down the sleeves. She also had a black flannel tied around her waist. Her brown hair was down in its messy waves. She looked amazing. Even with all black and many layers, Hailey was envious of her looks.

"So, why was I summoned?" Hailey asked. She felt slightly underdressed with them. She was wearing a plain white tee and black workout leggings with her black Nikes. Her hair was in a high pony.

"We are going to buy you a dress that makes you so hot, Zac won't know what hit him." Bella smirked. Hailey quickly shook her head.

"Why not?" Mariah asked. Hailey sighed.

"I didn't break up with Jordan. I'm still going to the dance with him." Hailey told them. Their jaws dropped open.

"Why? You don't like him like that." Bella stated. Hailey could tell they were confused.

"The whole school and their moms know Jordan asked me to formal. I can't just say no, never mind. I don't want to go with you anymore. Everyone is expecting us to show up together." Hailey told them. Bella frowned.

"I hate people sometimes." Bella mumbled. Hailey nodded. If he hadn't asked in front of the whole school and their cellphones, she would have apologized and said no thank you. He practically forced her to agree. Did he not see they didn't click on their date?

"I have a great idea!" Mariah chirped. The two girls looked at their blond friend. "We are going to make you look so hot, Zac won't have a choice but to fight for you. At least that way, Jordan won't know it was you who didn't like him. I mean, you can last a few more days with that boy."

"I like it Mariah. Zac will get insanely jealous and make a move!" Bella clapped. Hailey didn't like how excited they were getting. They also didn't know that Zac had made a move. "Come on Hails, don't you want to see Zac get all jelly because you aren't his."

Hailey thought about it. She hated that she had to spend time with Jordan, but she had already told Zac they had to wait until formal. Plus, it wouldn't be that bad to have a guy fighting over you. What's the worst that can happen? Jordan backs off and she gets to live happily ever after.

"Alright, i'm in." Hailey smirked.

~~~~~~Part of the dance is next(;xoxo,Liv814
~~~~~~

Chapter 14 | You Belong with Me

The crowd roared as Nate caught the ball Zac had thrown. Zac smirked. They were one kick away from winning it all. He jogged off the field, ripping his helmet off. He looked up at the stands and saw the girls. They were jumping with excitement. Huge grins on their faces. He focused on one in particular. The one that made his heart race.

Hailey screamed as Nate ran to make a touchdown. When they scored, her and the girls found themselves jumping up and down. She didn't even care how ridiculous she looked. She looked out onto the field and saw Zac looking at her. He was smiling at her, making her stomach do flips.

Her and Zac managed to steer clear of each other for the last week. It was driving her insane. They'd only talk when their friends were near. She wasn't sure she'd be able to control herself around him. All she could think of was kissing the life out of him.

Being away from Zac, only made her spend time with Jordan. He wasn't that bad, but she just didn't enjoy her time with him. He was always on his phone, doing god knows what. She just didn't feel intrigued by him.

He would never be more than a friend. They did show the class their presentation.

Everyone was surprised to know they had paired up and caused them to go to the winter formal together. Everyone assumed they were also together, together. She tried to deny it but Jordan only encouraged them when he wrapped his arm around her waist. She felt disgusted and humiliated. She couldn't wait for the dance to be over. Hailey just hoped that Zac didn't find out. She didn't want to distract him with that. He had the championship game that night and everyone was buzzing about it.

After their amazing win the previous week, no one could wait for this game. Sadly, Zac's father was still home, so Zac didn't have the chance to throw a party in celebration. Everyone was assuming he'd throw one after this win, but he said no. They had the dance and that would be enough.

Thinking about the dance made her heart plummet. She wasn't looking forward to it and spending even more time with Jordan. She was excited to wear her new dress, courtesy of Bella and Mariah, and finally be able to be with Zac. She couldn't wait to be his.

"Girl, I can feel the sexual tension between the two of you." Bella teased. Hailey whacked her arm earning a glare from the twin. She rolled her eyes. She looked back at Zac and saw he had a smirk on his face. She rose an eyebrow causing him to nod his head in her direction. Hailey turned and saw Jordan.

"So you did come to the game." Jordan stated. Hailey gave him a tight lip smile. She had told him that she wasn't feeling well and wouldn't be going. "And, you're wearing his jersey, again."

"Hey, yeah. I went home and laid down for a bit. I wasn't going to come but Bella and Mariah dragged me here." Hailey told him. It was partly the truth. The girls did come pick her up for the game.

"Yeah, sorry. She couldn't miss this game! We made her put on the jersey too." Bella said agreeing. Hailey let out a sigh in relief, thankful for the girl.

"Oh, can I drive you home then?" Jordan asked. Mariah was the one to answer.

"Actually, she's sleeping over. We're going to get ready for the dance at my house." Mariah told him. Jordan nodded, a deflated look on his face. "You're alright with her meeting you at the dance, right?"

Hailey turned to look at her friend. That was not a part of the plan. She turned back to look at Jordan. He was staring at her. Hailey only gave him a sheepish smile. The less time she spent with him, the better. Jordan then sighed.

"I guess that's alright." He told them. Mariah screeched, earning a huff of annoyance from him. "What now?"

"We won!" Mariah said pointing at the score. Hailey looked and saw that the kick was good. They had won. Their school won the championship. The boys brought the trophy home. They were going to be over the moon!

"Oh my god!" Bella shouted with equal excitement. The girls quickly swung themselves over the ledge before dropping onto the field. Hailey was surprised they didn't break anything. They were up at least four feet in the air. "Come on Hails!"

"I don't know guys. That drop is high." Hailey said fidgety in her spot. She turned and saw Jordan. His eyes were on her. She looked back down, realizing she rather be with them than him. "I'll see you tomorrow."

She took a deep breath before swinging her legs over. She looked down and took a big breath of air. Here goes nothing. She let herself drop, waiting for the impact of the ground to hit her feet. It never came. She opened her eyes, which she subconsciously closed and saw big brown eyes.

"Couldn't let my princess drop on to the crowd." Zac whispered in a teasing tone. His breath fanned against her face, making her cheeks heat up. She noticed he was cradling her to his chest. She liked this position. "Better put you down before we cause a scene."

Hailey nodded, feeling sad. She loved being in Zac's arms. As Zac placed her down, she felt Jordan's glare. She turned her head and saw that he was watching them. Anger was fuming from him. She looked away. She could deal with that later.

"Congratulations guys! This was the best game yet!" Mariah yelled. Evan and Nate were with them now. Other people had stormed the field to congratulate the players.

"I agree. Who would have thought we'd be here." Evan said. He wrapped his arm around his sister, squishing her into his side.

"I love you Ev, but let me go." Bella said in a muffled voice. She was attempting to push herself away. Evan sighed and unwrapped his arm. Bella huffed before wrapping herself around Nate.

It was still weird seeing them together. Ever since they confessed to each other, they have been inseparable. It was annoyingly cute. Evan is the only one not really on bored with the whole thing.

"So, party?" Mariah asked Zac. Zac chuckled.

"I thought you guys had a bunch of stuff to do before the dance tomorrow?" Zac asked. Mariah shrugged.

"Are you sleeping over?" Mariah asked Hailey. Hailey turned and saw her brothers make their way over. Perfect timing.

"Congrats guys!" Ben was the first to say. Zac smiled. "That was like the best winning play i've ever seen."

"Thanks Ben." Zac said to him. They did the bro hug thing, before Ben pulled away. Zac smiled as she saw them interact. It made her heart grow that they got along.

"Oh my god. You're Josh Foster." Evan asked with wide eyes. Hailey rolled her eyes as he stared at her older brother.

"In deed I am. Nice to meet you." Josh said sticking out his hand. Evan gladly shook it. Josh then turned to the other boy in the group. "Nate."

"Hello Josh." Nate replied. The atmosphere around them began to thicken. Hailey knew why. She had pestered her brother about why he interrupted Zac and her. Josh finally caved and said he didn't want her kissing anyone until she made up her mind on who she wanted to be with. That's when she told him about Zac and that Nate really only liked Bella. Josh was much happier afterwards.

"Hey, is it alright if Hailey sleeps over?" Mariah asked. Josh's smile slid off his face. Hailey sighed. She knew he'd say no.

"She either sleeps over tonight or tomorrow after the dance. You guys can decide. Either way, we'll be going now. Congratulations boys. Bask in the glory." Josh said. Everyone waved goodbye. Hailey watched as the two disappeared, probably to congratulate Luke. Well she wasn't expecting that answer.

"Tomorrow for sure then." Bella said. Hailey nodded. That was probably better. "Do you need a ride home then?"

"No, i'll drop her off." Zac said. Hailey felt goosebumps on her arms. It would be the first time they were alone in days. It excited her, yet scared her. She wasn't sure what would happen between them.

"Well, we have to go take pictures and shower. See you all in a bit." Evan said excusing themselves. Hailey and the girls watched them disappear into the crowd.

"Oh my god. Zac couldn't take his eyes off you. This plan is going to be a success." Bella smirked. Hailey rolled her eyes, letting the grin slip on.

"I still can't believe i'm going alone." Mariah pouted. Bella scoffed.

"I told you to ask my brother." Bella said. Mariah rolled her eyes.

"Wouldn't it be weird?" Mariah asked. Bella shook her head. "But he doesn't like me like that."

"Who says he doesn't? Plus, you are only going as friends. It shouldn't matter if - wait. No. No. No. Mariah!" Bella yelled. They earned a few weird glances from people but the girls ignored them. They had been walking back towards the locker room to wait for the guys. Bella was going home with Evan and Hailey with Zac. Mariah had her own car and Nate probably had his bike.

"What Bella!" Mariah screamed. Bella huffed in annoyance. They finally reached the locker rooms. There were a few girls mingling around, probably to talk to the guys. Sometimes Hailey forgot that the three are the most popular boys in school. It was still surreal for her to be hanging out with them.

"You like my brother. That's why you won't ask him. You want him to like you." Bella stated. Mariah rolled her eyes.

"No, I do not." Mariah defended. Bella was about to reply when giggles were sounded nearby. The three turned and saw the most of the football team was now showered and out of their gear. Hailey subconsciously began to look for Zac. She had goosebumps trailing her arms and butterflies flying in the pit of her stomach.

When Zac and the boys left the girls, Zac had a one track mind. He was to go into the locker room, shower and change. He wanted to do it as quickly as possible. He didn't want to keep Hailey waiting. The boys joked about Zac being whipped, but he didn't care. He liked Hailey, a lot.

"Zachary!" He heard his Coach shout. He had just finished putting on his shoes and was about ready to exit. He didn't even care that that was his very last football game of high school. He only wanted to be with Hailey.

"Yes Coach?" Zac asked. His coach gestured for him to follow into the office. He did just that, letting his annoyance radiate off him. He didn't know what his coach wanted, but he wondered why it couldn't wait until Monday.

"I have a few things to tell you son. One, thank you for being on this team. With you as captain, we were able to accomplish many things we hadn't in years. You brought us to the championship game and led us to a win. Two, you are damn good. The best I had seen since Josh Foster. I wished I could have coached him, but you filled up that need. I am damn proud of you Logan. Now the last thing I want to tell you is that tonight, there were college and university scouts all over those stands. I just received word that not one, but five are interested in you. There hasn't been an official offer, but they're coming. Congrats Zac. You deserve this." His coach finished saying.

Zac didn't know what to say. He knew he was supposed to be thinking of college and life after high school. He knew since day one that he wanted to get out of this town, away from his parents. But now that he may have that chance, he wasn't sure. All he knew was that he wanted to focus on the now and enjoy his life with Hailey.

"Thank you coach. This is amazing news." Zac told him. He had a grin on his face, but he knew it wasn't meeting his eyes. He had a lot to think about now.

"Don't let a girl come between you and this amazing chance. Now go out there and enjoy the rest of the night." His coach said. Zac nodded, exiting his office. He saw that most of the guys on the team were long gone. He exhaled a loud breath. That was definitely not how he wished to be feeling after that win.

He slid on his leather jacket and walked out of the locker room. He was met with a few screams and giggles. Girls were literally throwing themselves on him. He politely declined and began to make his way through the sea of people. He searched for his friends and for Hailey. He wasn't able to spy them until he heard Mariah's scream of annoyance.

He then found them by the end of the crowd talking. Nate had his arm wrapped around Bella as she leaned into him. Hailey had a small smile on her face as Evan seemed to be doing the talking. Mariah had her hands on her hips.

"Hey guys!" Zac said. They all turned their heads to him.

"Dude, what did coach want?" Nate asked. Zac looked away from Hailey. She was staring at him, studying him.

"He wanted to congratulate me on the win. Said I was the damn best player he's ever had." Zac said in a cocky attitude with a smirk. "And, that I will be receiving offers very soon."

Hailey's mouth dropped open upon hearing Zac. She knew that Zac had the chance of being scouted to play in college. Even if he didn't, he had the money to go to college. It made her slightly sick that she was jealous of his fortune. She wants to be able to keep studying and become a nurse. She knows that it'll be difficult to achieve, but she wants it more than anything.

"Damn, Zac Logan is going pro!" Nate shouted. People nearby began to clap which soon turned into the entire crowd cheering. Zac chuckled. He hadn't received any offers yet and they were this happy. Now imagine the offers he does get. He hoped to get one from Michigan State. It was far enough from California, but still had an amazing football team.

"So, are we getting drunk?" Someone nearby asked. Zac chuckled. Of course that was what everyone cared about. He quickly shook his head.

"Go home. We have the winter dance tomorrow." Zac shouted. The crowd groaned. He knew that a lot of people were only going because there was usually after parties. Zac hadn't heard of any, but he knew someone would have one. It just wouldn't be Freedom High School without one.

"Nate, throw the after party." Bella said. The crowd began to disperse, sending out congrats.

"Maybe, I think my dad might be home. He's organizing some charity thing for next week." Nate replied with a shrug.

"We'd throw it, but mom is home. She wants to take pictures of us before the dance." Evan said with an eye roll. They all looked around, their eyes landing on Hailey.

"Don't even look at me. I'm not even sure what the first thing about throwing a party is." Hailey said. They all laughed, making her cheeks tint. Zac loved seeing her blush.

"My evil dad is home." Zac said with an eye roll. "That leaves Mariah."

"Woah, woah, woah. How was I roped into throwing a party. I'm having the sleepover after the dance." Mariah said. Bella scoffed.

"It's not like we can't have the party and the sleepover. It'll just mean we can get black out drunk and not drive." Bella stated. Mariah frowned before groaning.

"Fine, but you three," Mariah said pointing at the boys. "Are coming over and setting up. Nate, buy the alcohol."

"Yes ma'am." Nate smirked. Mariah rolled her eyes.

"Party at Carter's then." Zac said. Mariah nodded, a small smile on her face. Zac then turned and saw Hailey. "Ready to go babe?"

"Yeah." Hailey stated. She felt her heart skip a beat when he called her babe. She still wasn't used to that and they weren't even together yet.

"We'll see you all tomorrow." Zac said. He grabbed Hailey's hand and began to pull her towards the parking lot. "So, did you enjoy the game?"

"Yeah. You were amazing." Hailey said. She felt her cheeks heat up. Her hand was still securely in his hold. She liked her hand being in his. It felt like they were made for each other.

"You're amazing." Zac said. She rolled her eyes. A giant grin plastered onto his face. "So, what color is your dress?"

"Not telling you." Hailey said. Zac let go of her hand when the reached his car. She opened the door and got in. Zac quickly did the same.

"Why not?" He asked once they were in the car. He placed one hand on the steering wheel as the other wrapped around the back of Hailey's seat. He then began to pull out of the parking spot.

"Because, you'll want to match. I'm sadly going with Jordan." She said. She felt her happiness dissipate at that thought.

"Don't worry. Just twenty-four more hours." Zac said. She sighed. Music from his radio began to fill his car. She looked out the window, admiring the night sky. Stars were out, sparkling in the moonlight. It was beautiful. "So, after the epic party Mariah throws, we'll go on a date."

Hailey whipped her head towards Zac. He had a grin on his face. He was looking at the stoplight in front of him before stealing a glance at her. Her jaw was open in surprise. He chuckled.

"A date?" She asked. Zac nodded. She was not expecting those words to come out of his mouth.

"I want to do this properly Hails." Zac said. He turned into her neighborhood. She felt her gaze on his. As he came to a halt in front of her own, he felt those weird flying things in his stomach. Whenever he was alone with Hailey, he felt them.

"Thank you for the ride Zac." Hailey said softly. She opened the car door, unbuckling her seatbelt. She was about to step out when she felt Zac's hand on her wrist. She turned her head and saw a grin on his face.

"I'll see you tomorrow." He said. He then leaned forward and pecked her cheek. Her cheek then blazed. He chuckled. He loved it.

"Bye." Hailey said getting out. She walked up the steps and walked in. Her brothers were already home. She closed the door behind her and let out a content sigh. She wasn't sure what she did to find Zac. He made her feel special. He was really sweet and understanding. She couldn't wait until this whole scheme with Jordan was over.

-

Teen Wolf couldn't even mask the annoyance Hailey was feeling. The boys were to arrive in a few hours and they weren't ready. Bella kept complaining about the eye shadow while Mariah ignored her. She was somewhere in the bathroom, doing who knows. Hailey had, thankfully, gone with straight hair. Bella just had to do her makeup.

"Guys, what time are they going to get here?" Hailey asked. She heard a muffled shout from the bathroom. She paused Liam and Theo's fight. "What?"

"In about an hour!" Mariah screamed. Hailey nodded. Maybe she should get changed into her dress.

"Sit." Bella said, dropping a brush onto the vanity. She had stood up. Her makeup was done beautifully. "Let's get you hot now."

"Alright." Hailey said. She got up, pulling down her shorts. She un-paused the tv and sat down in front of Bella's vanity.

"When i'm done, Zac will be begging you to be his." Bella smirked. Hailey rolled her eyes, hoping she'd be right.

After a painful thirty minutes, not even Scott McCall could fill up the silent room. Bella was quiet as she concentrated on doing her makeup. Mariah had come out once, saying she needed an eyebrow pencil.

"Alright. Now go and put on your dress." Bella said. She out down the setting spray. Hailey nodded, grabbing it from the door where it was hung. She took it into Bella's walk in closet and slipped off her baggy shirt and shorts. She was careful to not ruin her makeup and hair. She smoothed it down and exited the closet.

"Damn!" Mariah shouted. Hailey felt the blush in her cheeks. She felt gorgeous in the dress. Something she didn't always feel. "Zac will not be able to keep his hands off of you."

"I agree. I'm glad we went with this dress. It's long, yet short. Formal is more for short, casual dresses. It's perfect. Even it's not really summery. For prom, you are definitely going for a long dress. I already have ideas!" Bella shared. Hailey chuckled. Of course she did.

Hailey looked in the mirror. She was wearing a halter top dress with a cut down the middle of the skirt. It was kind of a romper style with shorts, but it had fabric that flowed all the way down. She paired it with black pumps.

"Okay, how do I look?" Mariah asked twirling. She had her hair in beautiful bun with hairs framing her face. Her makeup was done naturally. Her dress was a simple body hugging black dress with a V neck. It showed just the amount of cleavage and went down to the middle of her thighs.

"Great! Now, you're going with my brother." Bella said. She put on some lipgloss.

"You did not." Mariah frowned. Bella shrugged.

"He's down. He didn't want to go alone either." Bella said. She then waltzed into her closet.

"This girl." Mariah muttered. Hailey chuckled. She reached for her phone and took a selfie in the mirror. She posted it on snapchat. Her brothers wanted to see her in the dress.

"So," Bella said emerging herself from the closet. "How do I look?"

"Fabulous." Mariah stated. Bella was wearing a white, strapless dress. It had a cut down the middle, showing off her tan legs. She paired it with blue pumps that matched the blue eyeliner she wore.

"We are going to be the eye of the crowd." Bella gushed. She then walked out of her room, grabbing a small black clutch. "Come on."

Mariah and Hailey grabbed their own things and followed behind. They were careful to not trip down the stairs. They heard laughter from the foyer. Hailey suddenly felt nervous. This was her first dance. She barely even knew how to dance.

"You guys look amazing." Evan said. He was the first to see them. He was usually the one to boast about their appearance. Bella smirked as she walked over to Nate. Evan walked over to Mariah. "You look beautiful."

"Thank you Evan." Mariah said. Her cheeks were blushed as she let out a giggle. Hailey stopped staring at the future couple, feeling Zac's gaze on her. She turned and saw him. Hailey felt her cheeks heat up as she took in Zac. His hair was combed and his usual smirk was off his face. He was dressed in a black suit with a matching bowtie.

Zac knew that Hailey was going to look beautiful in whatever she wore. She could wear one of her brother's shirts and leggings, and she'd still be the most beautiful girl in the room. But when Hailey walked down the stairs, he wasn't expecting to be blown away. She looked perfect.

As he took in her appearance, his eyes stayed on her legs. He didn't like the amount she was showing, knowing every other guy would be staring at them. He hated that he couldn't officially make her his until after this dance. He was already counting down the hours. He just had to survive watching her with Jordan.

"You look gorgeous Hails." Zac said. Hailey giggled. He always made her feel beautiful. "I'm not sure i'll be able to survive tonight."

"It'll be fine. Just dance with your fans." Hailey teased. She felt her heart race as his brown eyes stayed on hers. She felt excited knowing Zac couldn't keep his eyes off her.

"Not a chance. You're the only one I want to be with." Zac whispered. He wrapped an arm around her waist, pulling him against his chest. He looked down at her lips. They looked deliciously inviting.

"Stop you two. We have to take pictures." Bella said. Zac sighed, resting his forehead on hers. He was so close. He just wanted to kiss her and show her how much she means to him.

Hailey pushed on Zac's chest, feeling his defined muscles contract. She felt nervous being so close to him. She knew he wanted to kiss her as much as she wanted to kiss him. But they couldn't yet. She was sure she wouldn't be with Jordan if they did.

"Alright. Group pictures first." Bella directed. Hailey turned and saw Mrs. Green in the room. She was holding up a professional camera. Hailey giggled. She could only imagine what prom will be like. Her heart skipped a beat, imagining being with Zac. She couldn't wait.

-

Walking into the dance, Hailey felt goosebumps. The gym was decorated in silver balloons. Streamers were strung and twinkling lights lit up the room. There was tables spread out to the sides with a refreshments table in the corner. A DJ in the back with the center clear for dancing. It was pretty to see how much work the student council put into the dance.

"What was the theme?" Bella asked. Hailey shrugged.

"It's winter theme. Instead of doing homecoming last month, they waited until after football was over. I don't really understand the whole winter theme, since we don't really have winter here. It's only 75 degrees and it's the end of November." Mariah said. They all nodded. Hailey looked around and spotted Jordan. He was with his basketball team. A few girls lingered around them. She hoped one would catch his attention before she caught his.

"I'm going to go get some punch." Bella said dragging Nate away. Mariah then turned and stared at Hailey.

"Are you going to go over there?" She asked. Hailey turned and saw that Jordan still hadn't seen her. She shrugged.

"I don't want to." She said honestly. Mariah glared at Jordan before turning her eyes to Hailey.

"Then don't. Spend the dance with me." Zac pleaded. He hated knowing that she would be whisked off by that jerk any minute.

"Let's go dance. Maybe the crowd of people will hide you." Mariah said grabbing her hand. She led them to the center of the dance floor.

An upbeat song was playing. Hailey let her body relax. She swayed to the music, enjoying herself. Zac and Evan were also with them, laughing. Evan was doing some weird skipping thing. Hailey giggled as his hands swung in the air. Evan did not know how to dance.

"There you are."

Hailey turned and saw Jordan. He was smiling at her. She gave him a tight lipped smile as she took in his appearance. He was in a white button up and slacks. Jordan looked around and frowned. She knew why without having to turn. Jordan had been glaring at Zac every chance he got.

"Hey. I didn't see you." Hailey said lying through her teeth. She hoped Jordan would just let her be.

"I was with the guys. Come on." Jordan said. He reached for her hand. She sighed, letting him take it. He then walked them off the dance floor. He was going back to his friends. Hailey sighed. This was a dance. They were meant to dance. "Hey, this Hailey. My girlfriend."

"Hey!" Most of the guys said. She tried to smile, but couldn't. He had just called her his girlfriend. That was far from what they were. They had gone on one date. They hadn't even kissed!

"Hi." She said in a monotone voice. She turned and saw her friends looking at her. Bella and Nate had returned. She sighed.

"You look hot." One of the guys said. She grimaced. No one should call a girl hot. It's rude and takes away from a girl's personality.

"So, then you're Jordan's girlfriend." One of the other guys stated. She turned and shook her head.

"We aren't dating." She told them. Jordan glared at her.

"Yes we are. We went out and now we're together." Jordan said. He then wrapped his arm around her waist, pulling her against his side. Hailey instantly felt uncomfortable. She wanted to be anywhere but there.

"No. We went out once. That does not mean we're dating." She said with an eye roll. She felt him begin to squeeze her side in a hurtful matter. She gasped. She quickly pushed him away and walked off. She didn't not want to deal with that. She went straight to the punch bowl. Maybe that would make her feel better.

Zac didn't move as he saw Jordan take Hailey away. He wanted to call out for her, to beg her to stay, but he couldn't. She had told Jordan she'd come with him. He watched as he introduced him to all his friends. He envied them. They didn't deserve to know a girl as amazing as Hailey. He watched as Hailey stiffened. He was ready to pounce. His eyes stayed in slits as he saw Jordan wrapped his arm around her.

"Dude, stop. I'm sure if you had lasers in your eyes, he would be scalding." He heard Nate say. Zac quickly turned away to stare at his best friend. He frowned. Bella was tucked into his side. That's how Hailey should be with him.

"I can't. She's supposed to be with me." Zac said. He then turned back to her. His eyes went wide as he saw that she wasn't near him. He began to search for her. What did Jordan do to her.

He finally found her by the punch bowl. He chuckled as she quickly spit the drink into her cup. She didn't know that Nate spiked it. She then placed the cup on the table. Zac saw Jordan approach her again. He sighed. Hailey nodded and they made their way onto the dance floor. Hailey placed her arms on his shoulders. She stayed back a few inches from him. Jordan then pulled her into his body.

"That's it." Zac said through gritted teeth. He left Nate and his friends. He made his way through the crowd towards them. He was going to get her once and for all.

"Hails," she heard Zac say. She quickly turned and found herself grinning. He looked amazing in his suit and the jealous vibes she got from him only added to his charm. She separated from Jordan, who had gotten too close for her liking. Jordan frowned at her movement then glared at Zac.

"What do you want Logan?" Jordan spat. Zac frowned. His eyes in narrowed slits.

"Hailey, want to dance?" Zac asked. She was about to answer when Jordan replied for her.

"No she doesn't. She's here with me." Jordan said. His arms were now crossed across his chest. His eyes full of anger.

"I wasn't talking to you. I was talking to her." Zac said with so much venom in his voice. Hailey had never heard Zac so angry and intimidating. If she didn't trust Zac with her life, she would have been terrified of him. "Hailey, you belong with me."

"She's my girlfriend." Jordan argued. Hailey scoffed. Jordan then turned to her. "What!"

"I am not your girlfriend! We went out on a date once! We aren't together! I only said yes to coming with you to the dance because the entire school was watching us." She screamed. She earned glances from some people but she ignored them. She had enough. "I don't even like you!"

"Don't be such a bitch." Jordan said. Zac was only able to see red after that. He swung his hand back, aiming for his ugly ass face, but felt a soft hand on his.

"He's not worth it Zac." Hailey said softly. Hailey knew she should have been afraid, but she wasn't. She felt honored that Zac was going to fight for her. "Come on."

She grabbed Zac's hand and intertwined her fingers with his. Those same sparks flowed through her as she dragged them away from Jordan. She should have never agreed to come with him. He was such a jerk and was glad he had finally shown his true colors.

"I'm sorry." Zac told her once they were away from him. She sighed.

"It's not your fault. It's his." Hailey said glancing behind her. Jordan was staring at them with rage in his eyes. She knew he wouldn't try anything. He wouldn't risk getting in trouble and be kicked off the basketball team. She was just glad this was over.

"I know it's that dick's fault. But, i'm saying sorry for not interrupting sooner. I saw how uncomfortable he made you." Zac said. She smiled. Her heart beating erratically at his words.

"Well thank you. His hands were definitely traveling lower than needed." Hailey said joking. She tried to lighten the mood but that only made Zac scowl. "Come on."

"To where?" Zac asked. He let her pull him towards the dance floor. He nodded in understanding. She pushed past people until she was able to find their friends. Nate and Bella were swaying, looking at each other. Mariah and Evan were laughing. Hailey definitely saw sparks fly between them.

"Finally! I thought Zac was going to shit his pants if he saw you getting cosy with Fitzgerald." Nate teased. Zac frowned. Hailey only giggled.

"Come on, let's dance." Bella said detaching herself from Nate. Hailey nodded, feeling light and happy. This night was finally going in the right direction.

Chapter 15 | Last First Kiss

Love can happen at any moment. Some don't wait for it to happen, while others just wait till it hits them. It's something you can't really plan. Either way, love is one of the most magical things one can experience. It gives you happiness, adrenaline, and desire. The need to explore with your significant other. Learning more and more about that person and still falling for them every day. Love is amazing and Hailey way quickly finding that out.

Hailey giggled as she twirled in Zac's hold. She felt herself becoming lighter and happier than she's ever been. She didn't have to deal with Jordan anymore and she was in the arms of the boy she liked. Nothing could ruin the way she was feeling.

"Have I told you how gorgeous you look in this dress?" Zac asked with a grin. The moment Zac got Hailey to himself, he was over the moon. Everyone could finally know that she was his and only his. The desire to kiss her only intensified with the way she bit the bottom lip to keep herself from grinning. It was damn mesmerizing.

"No." Hailey giggled. She wrapped her arms around his neck as his gripped her hips. When Jordan did that, she felt uncomfortable. Under Zac's hold, she felt sparks from his touch, winding up the butterflies in her stomach.

"Well then Foster, you are breathtaking! You are hands down the most gorgeous girl in this entire room, if not the world." Zac said it casually. Hailey couldn't stop the heat that was creeping onto her face. Zac knew how to make her blush and she was sure that he enjoyed every second of it.

They continued to sway, staring into each other's eyes. The slow song that had been playing change to an upbeat one. Even during the junping from their surroundings classmates, they stayed in each other's arms. They talked about everything and anything.

Hailey couldn't get enough of this boy. She was addicted. He was like a drug. No rehab can fix it. He was perfect, even with his flaws. She was noticing that she may be falling for him. She only hoped he'd be there to catch her.

"Zac! I have been looking everywhere for you." Zac heard her annoying voice purr. He groaned. He slightly pushed Hailey back who was resting her head on his chest.

"Sasha, I fucking told you that I wasn't coming to the dance with you. How many times do I have to tell you that we are done? I don't want you anymore." Zac told Sasha. Her blue eyes began to well with tears. Zac felt bad about his outburst, but she needed to get it through that thick skull of hers. They were never, ever getting back together.

"But Zac!" Sasha screamed. Everyone nearby was now watching them like a hawk. Hailey didn't like it. Zac and her were in such a great mood. Sasha Nelson just had to ruin it.

"Sasha, just go." Zac said. He narrowed his eyes, testing her. She looked at Hailey and began to glare.

"This is all your fault bitch!" Sasha shouted. Zac let out an exasperated sigh. He was done with her and her drama, too.

"Sasha, just go before you make an even bigger fool of yourself." Zac said. He looked around and saw that they indeed had drawn a crowd. Some even had their phones out. He was sure Sasha would be publicly humiliated all over social media.

"This isn't over." She huffed. She took a turn and walked off. Sac wasn't even sure what he was attracted to when it came to her. It must have been purely his yanno doing most of the thinking. Because now that he had Hailey, no one would ever he able to compare to her. She was damn right beautiful, inside and out.

"I'm sorry about her." Zac cooed. He wrapped his arms around Hailey and laid her head back onto his chest. That's where she belonged. They rocked side to side as Hailey hugged his body. She felt secure in his arms.

"She's a nut job. I'd hate to be related to her." Hailey joked. Zac chuckled, making his chest vibrate.

"Alright Freedom High School, this is the last song of the dance." The DJ said into a microphone. Hailey smiled as they swayed to the slow song. She paid no attention to her surroundings and focused on the boy in front of her.

He was perfect in every way, shape or form. Zac had climbed his way into her heart. He was sweet and caring. He paid attention to the little things, like the fact that she loved cookies and cream icecream. His laugh made her weak at the knees. She loved the way his eyes sparkle when he talks about the sport he loved. Hailey could listen to him all day and never get bored. His intelligence was his biggest quality, not that his attractiveness isn't. Hailey couldn't complain about that either. He was built in the most perfect way, like he was a god. His jaw structure and perfect lips.

Hailey groaned at that thought. She still hadn't kissed him. She looked up and saw that he was watching her with a curious look. She felt her cheeks heat up. She was glad he couldn't read her mine because she was sure he'd tease her about. She just couldn't help herself.

"Everything okay in that pretty little brain of yours?" Zac asked. He could see the internal battle going on in her eyes. There was something on her mind.

"Nothing." Hailey said too quickly. Zac chuckled.

"There's something definitely on your mind babe." Zac said. He could hear the song beginning to end.

"It's just - well you see the thing is." Hailey began to explain. She felt herself becoming flabbergasted at the thought of telling him she wants him to be her first kiss. She should already have had this experience. She's a senior in high school.

"Hailey, what's wrong?" He asked softly. Hailey let her eyes land on his lips. They were right there. She just had to plant her own on his. It wouldn't be that hard.

Zac watched as her eyes traveled to his lips. Hailey's cheeks were subconsciously heating up. He wanted to chuckle at the reaction, but didn't. He couldn't stop focusing on the girl staring at his lips. Did she have the same desire be had about wanting to kiss her? She began to bite her lip, preventing herself from talking.

"Hailey?" He whispered. Hailey stopped staring at his lips and looked into those big brown orbs. Why couldn't she just come out and say it? She just had to spit it out. What was the worst that could happen?

"I want you to be my first kiss." Hailey whispered. It wasn't meant to be so quiet, but she didn't want anyone else knowing she hadn't reached that milestone in life. "I haven't had my first kiss yet."

Hailey looked down, embarrassed. She knew she shouldn't have been, considering that Zac was very understanding. She just didn't want to see the surprise in his eyes. She suddenly didn't feel good enough.

Zac was known to be with girls left and right. He had one night stands and shameless hook ups. He was experienced in it all while the most she had ever been were hugs and the forehead kisses he gave her. What if she wasn't good at it? She didn't want to disappoint him. She then felt his hand on her chin. He tipped it upwards, causing her to look into his eyes. They were a darker shade, filled with desire. She gulped.

As Hailey said those words, Zac's heart rate began to quicken up. He knew that she hadn't shared that part of her life yet. He was going to be her first boyfriend. His heart skipped a beat at that thought. But he was even more intrigued by this girl with her asking him to kiss her.

He was planning on doing it anyway, but the tone in her voice as she asked him to be her first kiss, he couldn't contain the want he had for her. He was overjoyed, over the moon, to be her first kiss. That meant no one else had the privilege to do what he was about to do. It excited him more than it ever should.

"Hailey," Zac said softly. His hand was still on her chin. He slid it up and rested it on her cheek. He could feel the heat in them. He looked down at her lips. They were full and plush. He couldn't wait to feel them against his. "I want to be your last. Baby, let me be your last first kiss."

Hailey was shocked at his words, but that didn't give her enough time to register them into her brain. She quickly felt his lips on hers. She didn't know how to respond. She was still in shock. Zac Logan was kissing her. She was having her first kiss. He was her first kiss! Her brain then shut off.

She felt his hands grip her waist, pulling her in to his body. She wrapped her arms tight around his neck, moving her lips against his. They were soft and tasted like red vines and vanilla. His cologne filled her nose as she struggled to catch her breath. She had to pull away, needing air.

Zac laid his forehead against hers, breathing hard. That was the best kiss he had ever felt. He had imagined kissing this girl since the day he met her and actually doing it, was nothing like he imagined. It was better!

"Woah." Hailey whispered. Her eyes were still closed. She had to take in the entire movement. She didn't want to forget it. She just had her first kiss and it was with someone amazing. It was amazing.

"I have been waiting so long to do that." Zac said. Hailey's eyes widened. She was staring into his eyes. Her heart rate began to relax as she saw no regret in his eyes. She was afraid that he wouldn't want to ever do it again, because she did. She loved the way his lips moved against hers. The way his hands grip her hips, bring her body flush against his. The way he took control. She loved every second of it.

"I never thought that's what kissing felt like. I'm kind of mad I hadn't been doing that sooner." Hailey said, letting the words tumble out. She opened her eyes wide. Zac's eyes darkened.

"I'm glad you haven't. I love the fact that i'm your first kiss. No one else knows how your lips taste." Zac said. He leaned in and connected his lips to hers. Hailey kissed back instantly. He felt himself smiling as their lips moved in sync. He wanted to deepen it, but they were still in the gym. It would have to wait until they were alone.

"About time!" They heard. They broke away, both of them breathing hard. Hailey felt the sparks still on her lips. She touched her lips, smiling. Her first kiss was better than she could have ever imagined.

"Come on. You have to help the boys set up." Mariah said. She was the one to interrupt them. Zac was kind of glad because he wanted to continue with Hailey, but in private. "And, we have to get you into another outfit. Now come on."

Zac rolled his eyes at her dramatics. He reached for Hailey's hand and pulled her into his hold. Hailey gasped at the sudden movement. He then began to follow Mariah. Hailey at his side. He glanced at her as the exited the building. She looked beautiful, even more than before. She was glowing as she bit her bottom lip, trying to contain the smile that was threatening to escape. He loved being the reason for that grin.

"So Nate and Bella left to get the alcohol. Evan is waiting for you, so that you can get started with the setup. Hailey and I are going to spread the word. The dance is about to end anyway." Mariah said. Zac nodded. He didn't want to leave Hailey, but he knew he'd have plenty of time with her.

"Alright. See you guys at the house." Zac said. He let go of Hailey's hand, bringing his face close to hers. He heard her breath hitch, making him grin. He then gave her a chaste kiss, walking away with a smirk. He loved making her feel nervous. He took a glance back and saw that she was fighting the grin again. He smiled. This night was beginning to be perfect.

"Not that i'm not happy and all, but damn, you can't keep him off you. I swear that boy has been whipped since the day he met you. Remember the last party he had, he wouldn't leave your side. Who knew it was love at first sight." Hailey heard Mariah rant. Hailey smiled at the distant memories. Her heart skipped a beat at the word love.

Could this really be love? She didn't know what it felt like or what it would be like. She just knew that she liked being around Zac. She couldn't see herself without him in her life. He had wormed his way into it and she never wanted him to leave.

"Alright, now, how was it? The kiss!" Mariah asked. Hailey's cheeks heated up. "Actually, let's wait for Bella. She'd kill me if you discussed it without her. Now come on."

Mariah began to walk back towards the gym. Students were beginning to leave. Mariah then took her phone out of her clutch and began to type. Students everywhere were on their phones.

"Party at my house at 10!" Mariah shouted. Everyone began to buzz with excitement. "Nothing a little text couldn't do. Now come on."

Mariah began to walk back towards the parking lot. They had all come in separate vehicles so that they could each do their own task for the party. Mariah had her Range Rover parked. She quickly got in. Hailey doing the same.

When they got to the Carter mansion, Hailey was not expecting that. It was huge! It was this big like white box type house. It had many windows, that overlooked the beach and the backyard. It was gorgeous! Hailey could only imagine the sunsets.

"This is amazing." Hailey gushed. Mariah chuckled.

"It's awesome alright. Sometimes I wish my dad would have bought a house a little simpler. But, I do love these windows. And the pool!" Mariah said. They walked further into the house.

Hailey couldn't believe that she was here. It had this open floor plan that let everything be seen. It was surely going to help keep the party under control. The windows allowed the backyard to be seen as well. The pool looked magnificent in the moonlight. The beach was just icing on the cake.

"About time Mar, these couches are heavy." Evan said. He wiped his hands, seeing Hailey. "Oh hey. Zac is outside."

"That's cool. But, we need to go get changed." Mariah said full of sass. Evan rolled his eyes and walked into the direction of the kitchen. Mariah then grabbed Hailey's hand and dragged her up the stairs. Hailey was in awe with the view from the second floor. "My room is this way."

They walked down the hall, passing rooms like a in-home gym, a movie room, a music room, and a room that only had pillows. Hailey questioned what rich people did to have these ridiculous things.

Mariah then opened the door to her bedroom. It was white with splashes of pink. She had a king size bed with white and pink throw plows. She had windows all on one side, over looking the pool. A white chandelier hung on one side, above a pink round futon. She had a white vanity with a pink plush chair. The whole room screamed Mariah.

"Your room is amazing." Hailey said. Mariah chuckled.

"Thanks, but let's find you a new outfit." She answered, waving off the compliment. She walked into a closet which seemed bigger than Hailey's room at home. It was full of shoes, shirts, skirts, dresses, handbags, and belts. "Found it!"

Mariah gave Hailey a hanger. It had a sparkly silver material hanging from it. Mariah then handed her a pair of nude pumps. Hailey inspected it. Unsure of what she had in her hands.

"What is this?" Hailey asked. She couldn't find its form. Was it a jacket? A top? A skirt? This certainly couldn't be an outfit.

"A dress. Now slide it on. Your makeup and hair will be fine." Mariah said walking back in. Hailey sighed. There was no use in arguing with this girl. She found another door and walked in.

An extremely extravagant bathroom filled with a four person shower and bath. It had a Jack and Jill sink and another grand window. The view just kept getting better the more they explored. Oh, and a toilet with a pink cover. Hailey chuckled. Of course the bathroom would also be amazing.

Hailey slid off her dress and slid on the new one. It had a deep cut, only covering her breasts. The straps wrapped around her neck, almost like a choker. It went past her butt and only her butt. It was short. Like really short.

"Mariah, I don't think I can wear this!" Hailey shouted. The bathroom door opened, revealing Mariah and Bella. Bella gasped.

"This look amazing! Zac won't keep his hands off you. Which by the way, congrats on finally being together!" Bella said with so much excitement. Hailey felt her cheeks heat up. Hailey took the time to see their outfits.

Bella was wearing a strapless black, body con dress. It went barely past her butt. She paired it with a black leather jacket and black stilettos. She also added some purple into her makeup instead of the blue.

Mariah was wearing a t-shirt style dress with many designs. It flowed to the top of her thighs which she paired with black over the knee boots.

"Um, okay. I feel somewhat better about my over revealing outfit." Hailey said tugging at the fabric. She meant it in a teasing tone, but was still very unsure. She had never been this daring before.

"Girl, chill." Bella said. That was easier said than done. "Now come on. I can already hear the party."

Hailey sighed. She wouldn't be able to change their mind, plus she thought she looked kind of hot in this outfit. She instantly began to wonder what Zac would think. Would he like it? Or would he hate it because it reminded him of all the bimbos? She began to hyperventilate.

"Oh my god. Are you okay?" Mariah asked. They were at the top of the stairs, ready to make their entrance.

"Nervous." Hailey said through her breaths. She focused on her breathing, wanting to calm down. She couldn't have a panic attack just because her outfit was slightly revealing. She had to get it together. At least her brothers wouldn't be here. She stared at her friends. Worry etched onto their gazes. Hailey closed her eyes and took a deep breath. "Alright. I'm good now."

"You sure?" Bella asked. Hailey nodded. "Good, because Zac keeps darting his eyes everywhere. I'm pretty sure that boy is looking for you."

The butterflies in her stomach began to flutter. She was nervous to see Zac while she was so, well sexy. She didn't know if he'd like it. She was excited about being so daring. This wasn't like her. She kind of like doing everything she wouldn't normally do.

"Come on! I love this song." Mariah said walking down the stairs. Bella was behind her. Hailey took a deep breath and followed behind.

Everything happened in slow motion. As Mariah descended, everyone's eyes traveled to her. She radiated confidence. Bella was next. She had a smirk on her face. She walked like she owned the place and didn't have a care in the world. Nate was definitely rubbing off on her.

As Hailey stepped down, she felt goosebumps travel up her arms. She looked around and saw her classmates' expressions. They were stunned and full of surprise. She searched the crowd for Zac. She wanted to be in his arms, away from the wandering eyes.

She gasped as she felt a pair of arms circle her waist. She felt the heat he gave off as well as the intoxicating smell. She loved his cologne. He quickly turned her in his grasp, causing her to squeal. She stared up into his brown eyes. He had the same look on his face from earlier, right before they kissed. She felt her cheeks blush as those thoughts. She wanted to kiss him over and over again.

Zac was mingling with his friends. Someone was talking about the game. Everyone was butting in with the same excitement as the previous day. It was still surreal that they brought home the trophy. Zac knew he'd be able to do it. He just had to focus on the game and not the girl in the stands.

Just knowing that Hailey would be going to the dance with Jordan made his blood pulse with rage. He wanted to go up to that guy and tell him that Hailey didn't like him. But, he stopped himself. He knew Hailey wanted to be polite. He had to trust that nothing would happen to her.

"Hey man, is that Hailey?" He heard one of his teammates ask. Zac's head whipped around and saw Mariah walking down the stairs. She sauntered over to them. Zac slid off the counter and walked into the living room. The music was still blaring but everyone's eyes were on a girl.

He got closer, not really recognizing her at first. Bella smirked as she walked by. Zac got closer and saw Hailey in a skimpy silver dress. He was surprised to see her so exposed. His other head began to excite as he got closer. The dress hugged her body right, clinging to her like a second skin. He saw that Hailey was slowly turning her head, no doubt looking for him.

He wrapped his arms around her, causing her to gasp. She stiffened in his hold before relaxing on instinct. He smirked. He turned her around, placing his hands on her hips. She squealed. She looked up at him.

He felt like he was in a trance. He couldn't look away. She just kept pulling him in. Her cheeks began to blaze as he continued to look at her. She looked hot and beautiful. But, mostly sexy. He had never seen her like this before. He hated that everyone else was seeing her too.

"This dress is really short babe." He spoke. Hailey bit her lip, still staring at his eyes. She knew if she broke contact, she'd be putty in his hands.

"I know." She said in a high tone. His thumbs began to massage her hips, making her stomach twist. He was causing her body to react to his touch.

"I want you so bad. I want you so badly, Hails." Zac said in a husky tone. She felt her heart explode out of her chest. She could see his eyes coat was lust and desire. It made her gulp. She didn't know she could make him feel that way.

"What the fuck?" Hailey heard her brother's voice. She looked away from Zac and saw Luke. He had his arm around Tasha, the girl she met a few weeks ago.

"Luke? What are you doing here?" She asked him. She got out of Zac's hold and was staring at her brother. Luke's eyes kept roaming her body with disgust. She crossed her arms over her chest, trying to gain some modesty in front of her younger brother.

"I'm at a party? Ben thinks this is at Tasha's house." Luke said. Hailey frowned. She hadn't lied to her brothers about sleeping over at Mariah's. She just hadn't told them they were having a party too.

"Why would it be at Tasha's?" She asked. She turned to the brunette. Her bright blue eyes screamed familiarity but she still wasn't sure from where. "Hi by the way."

"Hi Hailey. I love this dress! I saw the rose gold one and was debating on purchasing it. It looks amazing on you!" Tasha said. Hailey smiled. She was really nice and pretty. She could see herself getting along with her.

"Anyway, why wouldn't it be at hers? Tasha's older sister throws parties all the time. She's captain of the cheer team, so she kind of has to." Luke said. Hailey was about to reply when she felt the blood drain from her face. Tasha's older sister was- Oh no, this cannot be real.

"Please tell me your last name isn't Nelson." Hailey asked. She felt Zac stiffen beside her. "Did you know?"

"No. I never actually met her. She would just talk about her. There parents are divorced." Zac said. Luke's eyes were narrowed. Tasha shifted uncomfortably. "Your Sasha's sister."

"Umm well yeah. She doesn't want anyone to know. So, could you possibly keep that quiet?" Tasha asked. Hailey nodded. As much as she despised the queen bee, she wouldn't ruin Tasha's life too.

"Your secret is safe with us." Hailey said. Zac nodded in agreement. Tasha smiled.

"Now that that is cleared up, can we go back to our previous topic. Ben, and especially Josh, will kill you f they saw you dressed like that." Luke said full of distaste. Hailey rolled her eyes.

"Luke, this isn't even that bad. I'm honestly wearing more than most of these girls are." Hailey said looking around. On cue, some girl walked by in a bikini. They were near the end of their 'fall'. Why was she in a bikini? Oh right, it was still 75 degrees out.

"Just put on a jacket or something. Borrow a different dress." Luke said covering his eyes. Hailey rolled her eyes.

"Fine. I'll see you tomorrow Luke." She said before grabbing Zac's hand. She pulled him up the steps into the direction of Mariah's room. She turned the knob, grateful that it was unlocked. She let go of Zac's hand and locked the door behind them.

"Not that I don't like how hot this dress makes you, but I agree with your brother. I hate knowing that people are eye fucking you." Zac said with a frown. Zac hated that no one was able to keep their eyes off of her. She was his and only his.

"Oh my god." She groaned before letting out a huff of annoyance. "Fine."

She stomped into Mariah's closet. She was in awe once again. She had so many different outfits and styles. She wasn't sure which one she wanted to choose. She pushed the clothes around until her eyes landed on a much better dress. She quickly slipped out of the silver one into that one.

It was a black two piece dress. The top covered her cleavage, being sleeveless. The skirt was black with fringe. It was all made of leather material. Her belly button was exposed, but still very decent. She then changed into black strappy heels and pulled her hair into a ponytail. She felt more like herself, but still very cute.

"Woah." Zac said when she stepped out. She gave him a little twirl which made him let out a growl. Her cheeks tinted a bright pink. "You look phenomenal and much more like yourself. Not that I didn't like the exposed skin, which I wanted to lay my mouth on, but this is what you're comfortable in."

Hailey's mouth dropped open at his sexual remark. It made her insides all gooey. Even when he's being the sweetest guy, he manages to make her warm inside. She quickly closed her mouth and grinned.

"Come on. Let's go back downstairs. I'm sure the girls are looking for us. Besides, the longer we stay in here, the less likely we'll leave." Zac said. His tone was playful but turned in a husky one at the end. She felt goosebumps graze her skin. She was more than tempted to stay in the confined room with him, but she knew they couldn't. Plus, it was too soon. They had only kissed. She wanted to take things slow and see how everything turns out.

As they made their way downstairs, Hailey was able to see the drunken teens. People were dancing, making out, giggling and just having fun. Hailey wanted to be like that. So, she must up the courage she didn't know she had and stopped Zac as he dragged them into the kitchen. He turned, a face full of worry.

"What's wrong?" Zac asked. She bit her lip, feeling her face heat up again.

"Would-I, well um, can I get a drink?" She asked. Zac's eyebrows shot up, but nodded. He continued to pull them into the kitchen. He stopped when they found their friends. The boys had bottles of beer in their hands. Bella had a cup while Mariah simply had a water bottle.

"What the fuck! You looked so hot!" Bella screamed as she took in Hailey's appearance. She was sitting on the counter with Nate by her side. Mariah was beside her. Evan was near the drinks.

"She did. That's why I had her change." Zac said with narrowed eyes. Bella rolled her eyes.

"You idiot. That was the purpose of the dress." Bella defended. Zac scoffed. His scowl deepening.

"For what? So the entire school can know how hot my girl is? I don't need guys ogling her." Zac said with as much venom as he could muster. He hated the fact that there were guys that wanted her. He knew they only wanted her for one thing, while he wanted her for everything.

Hailey's heart was thumping as she listened to Zac. He was jealous of all the guys here, but they didn't compare to him. She didn't want any of them. She placed a hand on Zac's bicep, feeling goosebumps as she touched his skin. His head quickly turned. The scowl on his face morphed into a grin.

"Right, so what do you want drink babe?" Zac asked. He waited for her to respond. She didn't know what she wanted. She looked at the bottles beside Evan. Evan's eyes followed hers before a smirk was placed onto his face.

"Hailey Foster, what kind of alcohol do you want to try?" Evan asked. He grabbed two bottles. One had clear liquid while the other had a golden one. "Vodka? Or Tequila? We also have bourbon and whiskey."

"What's the difference?" Hailey asked. She suddenly felt very nervous. They had been drinking for years. This was only her first time. She turned to look at Zac, who shrugged.

"The Vodka! Smirnoff is amazing." Bella said with a giggle. She drank whatever was in her cup before passing it to her brother. "Fill me up twin."

Evan took the red cup from her and opened up the bottle with clear liquid. He began to pour it. Hailey contemplated her choices before reaching for an empty cup. She passed it to Evan, who filled it up with the same liquid. He passed it back. Hailey looked at it before taking a deep breath. She placed it by her lips, tipping some of it back. It had a weird taste, but wasn't horrible. It had a slightly fruity flavor. Almost like blackberry or raspberry. She kind of liked it. She took another sip.

"So?" Bella asked. Hailey giggled.

"It's awesome." She said. She sipped some more, earning a chuckle from Zac. "Why haven't I tried this before?"

"Because you, babe, are not supposed to suppress to peer pressure. These idiots do." Zac said taking away her cup. She frowned. She only had one. She wasn't even drunk yet, not that she wanted to. She did not want to know what a hangover was like.

"Zac!" She whined. "I'm trying to have fun." She pouted. Zac placed the empty cup beside Bella. He then placed his hands on Hailey, lifting her up onto the counter.

"If you want to have fun, you can do it without liquid courage. This stuff is stupid and makes you different. I like you just the way you are." Zac said. His hands were still on her hips, creating a different wave of emotions.

"Zac, stop being a sap." Nate said. Zac turned around to glare at his best friend. Nate only smirked, drinking his beer. He sighed.

"Fine. But, the moment you become too intoxicated, I am stopping you." Zac said. Hailey nodded. She felt herself become excited at the idea of being possibly drunk. She just hoped she woke up fine.

"This calls for celebratory shots!" Evan shouted. Zac rolled his eyes. Of course it would. He took the plastic shot glasses and lined them up as Evan filled them.

Hailey was intrigued. She knew tequila was usually for shots. She watched as the boys got everything ready. Nate brought over a bowl of limes, passing one to everyone. Zac then passed the small cups around. Hailey felt the bubble of excitement ready to pop.

"Alright Hails, you take the shot. Lick this salt," Zac said as he poured some onto the back of her hand. The lime was in that hand while the shot in the other. "And then you suck on the lime. Okay."

"Mhm." She said. Shot, salt, suck. Okay, that shouldn't be hard.

"Alright. On the count of three." Mariah shouted. "One."

"Two!" Bella yelled.

"Three!" Nate said last. Hailey tipped the shot back. Her mouth grimacing as the liquid burned down her throat. She then licked the salt before popping the lime into her mouth. She sucked on it, the sourness soothing her throat.

"Oh my god. Why does one do that?" Hailey said taking out the lime rind.

"It's gets you drunk faster. Now come on, round two." Bella said giggling. Hailey chuckled. Alcohol wasn't that bad. She gratefully took another shot with her friends. She giggled as Nate and Bella disappeared. Evan stayed with Mariah as Zac wormed his way in between her thighs. He was looking at her.

"What?" She asked. She wiped her facing. Maybe she had something on it. Zac shook his head.

"Nothing. I just like looking at you." Zac said. He grinned at the girl in front of him. He liked seeing this carefree side to her. She was trying to enjoy herself like the rest of their friends. He was very tempted to grab another beer, but knew he shouldn't. He wanted to make sure this girl was safe.

"Thanks for letting me drink." Hailey giggled. Zac chuckled.

"Anything for your princess. Anything for you." He said. And he meant it.

-

It had been a couple of weeks since the Winter Formal. Hailey had been in awe with Zac. He knew how to cheer her up when she didn't get the grade she wanted and he made her smile. He was contagious and she couldn't get enough. With school, they barely saw each other, but when they did, Hailey cherished every moment. It was the little things that count.

Thanksgiving had passed and went. She had fun with her siblings. Josh made an amazing dinner which consisted of grilled chicken, rice, and steamed vegetables. It wasn't the traditional turkey and stuffing, but it was delicious nonetheless. They watched a few movies, some consisting of Christmas. They even began to talk about this year's plans.

Hailey was more than excited for the new season. She loved everything about it: the presents, the decor, the cold, the peppermint, and especially the vacation. She loved being off from school for two weeks to enjoy life. She still had to work, the holiday season being the busiest, but she enjoyed it. She was even more excited to share her holiday cheer with her friends. She just hoped they'd be in town.

"Hey girl." Mariah said placing the lunch tray she was holding down. She had yet another salad with a banana.

"So, excited for your first soccer game of senior year?" Hailey asked. Mariah was team captain and more than ready to bring home a win.

"Duh. Our first game is against the Lions. They are so going down." Mariah answered with a smirk. The Lions were their rival high school from across town.

"Oh no. Why did you get her talking about soccer?" Evan asked as he slid into the spot next to Mariah. Mariah gave him a playful glare before pecking his cheek.

At the party, drunk Evan found himself confessing his feelings Mariah. Mariah was more than shocked, especially because he was intoxicated. She only said okay before shoving him into one of the guest rooms. The next morning, Evan asked about his confession. Mariah then told him she liked him too. They've been together since. Surprisingly, Bella was okay with their relationship, but that didn't stop her from being disgusted when their tongues were down each other's throats.

"Shut up." Mariah said. Evan gave her a cheesy grin. "So, where's your boyfriend?"

Hailey shrugged, not wanting to tell her that they weren't together. At least they weren't officially. He walked her to class and pecked her cheek. He'd hold her hand and wrap his arm around her waist. But as far as she knew, they weren't a couple. It made her slightly sad, but then again, she didn't know much about dating and she didn't want to ask.

"There he is." Mariah said with a smirk. Hailey turned around and saw Zac in a grey v-neck and his black leather jacket. His hair was a mess but that only made him ever more attractive.

"Hey there pretty brown eyes. Whatcha doing later tonight? Mind if I spend some time with you?" Zac asked as he approached their table. Hailey rolled her eyes at his cheesiness, but still liked the way he made her feel.

"Hey Zac, I am just going to be doing some homework. Why?" She asked. She drank the soda she had purchased for lunch. She also had a ham sandwich and some chips.

"We're going on our first date. Pick you up at 7."

~~~~~~~~First person to mention all five songs used in this chapter, gets a cameo in the next one.xoxo,Liv814

Songs Used in Order:1. 2. 3. Last First Kiss by 1D4. 5.
~~~~~~~~

Chapter 16 | Better With You

Hailey's leg bounced up and down as English class went on. She couldn't find herself to focus on whatever they were learning. Her brain flooded with thoughts of the date. She didn't know what to wear or how to act. Her last one was a bust. What if the date went terribly and she had to stop talking to Zac. She didn't want that to happen.

"Hailey, what the fuck is going on? Stop bouncing your leg. It's fucking annoying." Nate said with a glare. She had turned around when she heard his voice. She glared back at him, chewing on her lip. She stopped moving her leg.

"I'm sorry. I'm just nervous." She mumbled.

"For what? We don't even have an exam." Nate said, still very irritated. Evan sighed.

"Zac told her they're going on their first date today." Evan clued him in. Nate nodded in understanding. Him and Bella were off doing god knows what during lunch and hadn't joined them.

"But why are you nervous? You like Zac. Shouldn't be freaking out." Nate said in an obvious tone. Hailey rolled her eyes. How sympathetic.

"It's my first real date." She whisper screamed. She looked around, not wanting her classmates to hear. She turned back to the pair.

"What about the one with Jack?" Nate asked. Hailey rolled her eyes. Did any of the boys remember his name? They share homeroom with him.

"Jordan, and that one was terrible so i'm not counting it." She said. She turned around and saw their classmates busy. Had their teacher assigned class work?

"Well alright then. But relax, your bouncing leg is driving me nuts. Just focus on Shakespeare or who ever this book is from." Nate said picking up the textbook. Hailey let out a giggle, focusing on the board. Nate was right. She had nothing to worry about. She liked Zac and that was enough.

-

Hailey threw another article of clothing behind her in frustration. She had no idea what to wear! She had no clue where they were going or what they were doing. How was she supposed to know what to wear? She let out a groan. This was useless.

"Why did a fashion tornado come through here?" Ben asked, pushing open her bedroom door. She let out a scream. He had startled her. "Sorry, but what's wrong?"

"I have my first date with Zac!" She screamed in frustration. Ben chuckled, flopping onto her bed. She glared at her brother. Trinity had made it earlier. Now it was going to be all messy.

"That boy is crazy about you. Show up in sweats and he'd be happy." Ben said. He was now on his phone, earning yet another glare from Hailey. "Hails, chill. Just wear whatever. It honestly doesn't matter."

"But I don't know what we're doing. Do I need a dress? Should I wear sneakers? Is it going to be cold? I don't know what to wear." She said in even more frustration than before. She wanted to ask Zac again , but he kept saying it was a surprise. He was no help.

"Fine Hails. Wear," Ben said getting up. He started going through her pile of clothes. She watched in confusion as he chose an outfit. "This."

"What if it isn't right?" She asked, studying the clothes he picked out. Ben smiled smugly. She then gasped. "You know where he's taking me, don't you!"

"Secret safe with me. Now get ready. He'll be here soon." Ben said, leaving her room with a smirk. She glared at his figure, shutting the door behind him. Of course Zac would tell her siblings where he was taking her. She was sure Josh wouldn't let her go without that information. She huffed before sliding on the outfit.

She was wearing a pair of distressed jeans with rips, a black tank top with a black leather jacket on top. She didn't know where that jacket came from, but wasn't going to oppose. It was cute.

She decided on wearing her hair natural with only mascara and lipgloss. She didn't know how to do eyeshadow nor contour. Plus, she didn't know how done up she hd to be. Better to be natural then over the top. She lastly pulled on black ankle boots. They were cute and comfortable. Perfect for whatever Zac had planned.

"Hailey!" She heard her little sister's voice yell. She quickly grabbed her phone and keys. She had her debit card in her phone case. She then left the comfort of her room, walking down the stairs. She heard Zac's laugh as she stepped on the bottom step.

Her heart began to beat at a very fast pace. She rounded the corner and saw Zac. He was wearing a black leather jacket on top of a black shirt with white lines. His black jeans hung dangerously low. He looked even more attractive than he usual attire.

But, what caught Hailey's attention, was the haircut he had gotten. His shaggy brown hair was now shorter, but still long enough to tug on the ends.

"Woah, you look amazing babe." Zac said first. His grin brightened when he saw her enter. She was wearing the jacket he had bought her. He wanted to be cliché and match. Ben was very helpful, but that didn't stop the teasing he got from him. Zac just ignored him, feeling those stupid butterflies in his stomach. He wondered if Hailey felt them too.

"You got a haircut!" Hailey said. She went up to him and ran her fingers through it. It was still soft. She smiled, looking at Zac. He had a smirk on his face. "Sorry."

"I love it Hails, but I think Joshy over there doesn't." Zac whispered. Hailey turned around and saw Josh with narrowed eyes. She chuckled, feeling her blush intensify.

"Alright, I want Hailey back by one o'clock." Josh said in his responsible adult voice. Zac nodded, wrapping his arm around Hailey's waist.

"Wait, my curfew is eleven though?" Hailey asked with confusion. Ben answered.

"Usually, Hails, people want their curfew extended even longer. But, where you and Logan are going, you need to be there past midnight. Now, be a good girl and shut up." Ben said with a chuckle. Hailey rolled her eyes, sticking her tongue out at her brother. She was still annoyed that he knew where she was going and she didn't.

"I promise that she'll be home by then." Zac said. He was looking forward to his date with this girl. He was more than surprised that Josh and Ben were okay with him taking her. Josh was hesitant, but agreed when Ben persuaded him. Zac was more than lucky to have received their blessing to be with Hailey. He couldn't wait to make it official.

"I'm trusting you Zac." Josh said with narrowed eyes. Hailey watched as Zac nodded, securing his hold on her.

"I promise that she'll be happy and back, in one piece. Thank you for letting me take her out tonight." Zac said with sincerity. Josh nodded, a smile making its way onto his face.

"As long as Hailey is happy." Josh said looking at her. Hailey bit her lip, looking up at Zac. She felt her heart skip a beat as he gazed down at her.

"I am." She said softly. Zac's smile formed into a grin that she quickly matched with her own.

"I am too babe. Now, let's get going." Zac said. He unwrapped his arm from her waist and took one of her hands in his. "See you all later."

"Bye!" Hailey said as she walked out the door. She followed Zac to his car, becoming more excited by the second. Zac opened the car door for her, making her giggle. He gave her a cheesy grin, sliding in. Soon, they were off to their surprise journey.

-

Her eyes widened. Her surroundings made her heart beat fast. Had Zac really brought her here? She saw the ears on kids as they ran towards the entrance. She felt her mouth go dry.

"Disneyland?" She asked in disbelief. Zac chuckled, wrapping his arm around her waist. He wanted their first date to be perfect, so why not at the most magical place on Earth. "You brought me here? To Disneyland?"

"Yes babe." Zac said chuckling. Hailey's eyes remained wide in surprise.

"Oh my god Zac! Thank you." She said wrapping her arms around his neck. Zac smiled, encasing the girl in his own arms. He would do anything to make this girl happy.

"Come on babe. We have lots to see." He said. She let go of him and grabbed his hand, pulling him towards the entrance. She was more than excited to see everything. It had been one of her dreams to come, with it being nearby, but she had never had the chance. She was still in shock that she was there and with the boy she was crazy about.

Zac took the lead and led her to the entrance. He gave the ticket operator their tickets before she handed it back to them. Hailey was going to treasure it forever. She should start a shadow box and place them in there! Hailey then saw the Disneyland sign in the grass. She wanted to take a picture with it. She saw others post them on Instagram. She couldn't wait to show everyone that she's at Disneyland!

"Can we take a picture?" She asked. Zac nodded, smiling. She was cute when she was excited. Zac slid his phone out of his back pocket and took a picture of her in front of it. She was grinning. "I want one with you too!"

Zac nodded. He stopped the next person he saw and asked if they could take a picture of them. They agreed, so he made his way next to her. He wrapped his arm around her shoulder, bringing Hailey into his chest. They both smiled at the phone.

"This is amazing!" Hailey said looking down at the pictures. She was going to post those and more on her social media accounts. "Trin is going to be so mad I came without her."

"This was actually her idea. She mentioned how it was one of your life goals to come. So, I thought i'd be the perfect boyfriend and bring you here on our first date." Zac said. Hailey's heart was beating erratically as he said the word boyfriend. Did that mean they were official?

"Well thank you." She said with tinted cheeks. She would ask him later, not wanting to jump ahead. Maybe he'd ask her to be his girlfriend later on. For now, she was just going to enjoy everything.

"Come on. We have much to explore." Zac said. Hailey nodded, still not believing her eyes. This was by far going to be the best first date ever.

-

Zac loved seeing Hailey laugh and enjoy everything. She had been nonstop smiling at everything. She snapped photos of every ride and character. She claimed she wanted a picture of everything to be able to remember everything. Zac didn't protest. If it made her happy, than so be it.

It was nearing nine, which meant the firework show was about to begin. They had just gotten off the "It's a Small World" ride. It had been the one where Hailey took the most pictures and videos.

"Come on. I have a surprise." Zac said. Hailey's eyes widened.

"Another one?" She asked. She was more than amazed that Zac had brought her to such an incredible place. What more could he have planned?

Zac grabbed her hand and pulled her towards the castle. That's where the fireworks show was the best, or so he googled. They squeezed through other parks visitors. All wanted the best spot. Hailey's patience was running thin as Zac pushed though people. She excused them as Zac continued to pull them. She followed with a frown from his rudeness. What did he have to show her that he was disregarding his manners?

Zac checked the time on his phone. They had about five more minutes before they went off. He continued his pursuit until he reached a spot where he knew they'd be able to see them light up behind the castle. He stopped, pulling Hailey into his chest.

"What's the surprise?" Hailey asked. Zac smirked. She claimed to be patient, but she really wasn't. She wanted to be in the know for everything. He liked that about her.

"Just wait Hails." Zac whispered in her ear. She involuntarily shivered. Zac smirked. Hailey rolled her eyes and looked around. Other people were standing around. What were they waiting for?

Soon, the crowd began to chant. Hailey's anxiousness was beginning to rise. What was going on? Zac gestured for her to look at the castle. It was lit up in the night, making it even more gorgeous.

"I have had the best time with you." Zac spoke. Hailey gave him a shy smile. Zac had a way with words that made her stomach full of butterflies.

"This has been amazing Zac. Thank you. We could have just gone to dinner." She said. Zac chuckled.

"I didn't want this to be just an ordinary date. I wanted it to be fun and surprising. But either way, I just wanted to spend time with you. Everything is better with you Hails." Zac said. He began to lean in, feeling her breath on his face. Her eyes were dilated as they stared into his. He took in a deep breath before connecting his lips with hers. She let out a small gasp as the fireworks went off. She quickly separated from him, seeing the beautiful colors light up the sky.

"This is by far my favorite day ever. It's all thanks to you." She said, looking into his eyes. They were brown and full of life. He was happier than he had ever been and it was all thanks to this girl. He started to lean in again, wanting to feel her lips against his.

She closed her eyes, connecting their lips once again. She started moving her lips against his. Zac smiled as they moved in sync. His hands gripped her waist, causing her to moan. She grasped onto his chin, trying to express everything she was feeling into the kiss.

As they moved in sync, the butterflies in her stomach fluttered at high speeds. The fireworks she was feeling matched the ones going off around them. It was perfect and by far the best kiss they had shared. They didn't want it to end.

They separated, needing air. Zac placed his forehead on hers. Their breathing matched, both gasping for much needed oxygen. Hailey looked into Zac's eyes, giggling. Zac raised an eyebrow, pulling away from her.

"What's so funny?" Zac asked. He let go of her waist and pulled her into his chest. They both looked up at the bright sky. The fireworks were still going off. The crowd ooing at the show. It was phenomenal.

"How the fireworks went off as we kissed. You planned that, didn't you?" She asked. Zac shook his head.

"They have fireworks every night." He said. She rolled her eyes.

"I meant you kissing me as they went off." She said lightly slapping his bicep. She felt sparks as her skin grazed his.

"No, but I don't think that wasn't fate. Anyway, come on. While people are enjoying the sky show, the lines are shorter. Let's go ride Space Mountain again!" Zac said grabbing her hand. She nodded enthusiastically, wanting to go on every ride possible. She didn't know when she'd be back again.

-

Riding home, Hailey was exhausted. They had managed to go on over twenty rides in the few hours they were there. Since it was colder at night, there were less guests than during the day. Plus, it was a school night. She didn't even care that she hadn't done her homework. It was worth it.

"Zac, thank you." She said again. Zac squeezed her hand. He was holding it the entire ride, wanting to be touching her. He had grown so much closer to this girl. He never wanted to be away from her.

"I'm glad you had fun." He said. He looked over at her. She was grinning.

"I had more than fun. This was the best day ever! I knew Disneyland had so much to do, but there were so many things we didn't get to see." She said with a small pout. She suddenly let out a yawn. It was past midnight. Way beyond her bedtime.

"I promise you that we'll go back. That will not be the last time we visit." Zac said. He meant the words that came out of his mouth. He liked making this girl happy. He liked seeing her smile and enjoy herself in the simple things. He liked this girl, a lot.

"Zac, you have no idea how much this meant." She said through another yawn. He chuckled. She had been fighting her sleep for the last hour. She was being stubborn and determined to stay awake until they made their way back to her home.

"Hailey, close your eyes. We'll be back at your house soon." He said softly. She shook her head, rubbing her eyes. She wanted to enjoy every single second of their date, even if they were simply in the car.

"Tell me something I don't know about yourself?" She asked. Zac glanced at her. She had closed her eyes.

"I received a few offers from schools." He said. He had been waiting for the right time to tell her. He got letters from schools in state, as well as out of state. He was still waiting for one from Michigan State.

"That's awesome Zac. I'm proud of you." She said. She knew Zac was capable of reaching greatness. She also knew that it was a real possibility that he'd be moving away for college. She didn't try to dwell on the future, but mostly because she wasn't sure she had one.

She had sent in applications to the nearby community colleges and a few of the big universities. She was yet to receive any acceptance, but she was determined to make the most of whatever life had planned for her.

"I know that whatever I end up doing after high school, will have to have football in it. I don't think i'd be able to major in anything without it. It's my de-stressor." He said. Hailey let out a small giggle before it was covered up by a yawn. "Hailey, just close your eyes."

"No." She said snapping them open. She saw Carl's as they drove by. They'd be at her home in a few minutes. She'd be able to last till then.

"Hailey." He stated.

"Zachary." She said in the same tone. He rolled his eyes. This girl was definitely full of surprises.

"You are so stubborn, you know that." He mentioned. She chuckled, nodding. He turned into her neighborhood. It was peaceful and quiet. He was sure everyone around them was asleep.

"I don't care." She said. He drove down the street, slowly coming to a stop. He had parked in front of her home. He shut the engine off. He had ten minutes left to spare. He sighed. At least Josh wouldn't be angry with him.

He unclipped his seatbelt, opening his door. He jogged to her side and opened the door for her. She frowned. She was more than capable of doing it herself. She stepped out of the car, ignoring the previous thought. Zac grabbed her hand, intertwining their fingers together. He led them up to her porch.

"I have probably said this enough tonight, but thank you Zac. You have no idea how much this meant to me." She said. She was looking up at him. Their hands still together as they stood in front of each other. She didn't want to say goodbye.

"I'd do anything for you Hails. I like you, a lot." He said. He stepped closer to her until their bodies were flushed against one another. Hailey's cheeks flamed.

"I like you too." She said in a soft voice. She felt her heart rate accelerate. His free hand made his way up to her face. His thumb grazing her cheek as she leaned into his palm. The electric sparks coursed through their bodies.

"Can I kiss you goodnight?" Zac asked. Hailey nodded, biting her bottom lip. Zac leaned in, pecking her lips softly. It was almost a chaste kiss, but with so much meaning. "I'll see you tomorrow."

"Bye Zac." She said. He took his hand off her face, leaving warmth across her skin. She bit her bottom lip again, trying to prevent a giant grin. She turned around, opening her front door. She took a glance back and walked in. Shutting the door, she exhaled in awe. It was by far the best day ever.

As Zac watched her close the door, he smiled. He knew this girl was special the moment they had bumped into each other. He was glad fate had brought them together because he was happier than he had ever been.

He stepped off her porch and made his way to his car. He got in, still thinking about Hailey. She was perfect in every way, shape and form. He was extremely lucky to have met her. He didn't know that she'd mean so much to him.

When she asked for him to tell her something she did not know, he wasn't planning on talking about the future. His plan had always been to move across the country to Michigan State University to play football, but meeting her, he wasn't so sure. He wanted to include her in his future, but they had different paths they wanted to follow.

Was he crazy to be falling for a girl, knowing he had to leave soon? He shook away that thought as his grin morphed into a frown. He had just had the best time with her and he was depressing himself with talk of the future. He needed to focus on the now and enjoy whatever time he had with her. He didn't know when it'd be the last. So with thoughts of their date, he drove home with a small smile.

-

The holiday season only seemed to get better and better. Things with Zac were going great and her siblings were ecstatic. Luke was even grinning. Well, that was because he had a girlfriend.

Hailey still found it weird to know that Tasha was Sasha's younger sister. Sasha was such a, well a bitch. Tasha was actually sweet and caring, nothing at all like her sister. Hailey had spoken to Tasha a few times when she had came over. Luke, surprisingly, is clinging and protective of her. Hailey knew he'd be a good boyfriend to Tasha.

As Hailey browsed through this season's fashion, you found a cute blouse that she was sure Tasha would love. She quickly chose the right size and color, going over to Luke. They were currently doing some last minute Christmas shopping, with the day being a week away.

"Luke, what about this one?" Hailey asked. Luke looked up from the pair of jeans he had been staring at. Hailey chuckled as his focus registered on the top.

"Do you think she'll like that?" He asked. He was inspecting every corner and string of the fabric. Hailey assumed Luke was scared to disappoint. It was his very first time with a girlfriend, that her and her siblings knew of, so she assumed he wanted to impress her. Plus, the Nelson siblings were kind of loaded.

"I believe so. She doesn't seem like the type to hate anything that isn't designer. It's cute." Hailey said waving the shirt on the hanger. Luke nodded, reaching for it. "What else do you need to buy?"

She looked down at the jeans Luke was staring at. She was intrigued with the style. Maybe she should buy a pair or two. Or should she get some for the girls. She mentally groaned. She had no clue what to get them. They, like the Nelson's, had money. They could buy whatever they wanted to. So, Hailey had to think of something sentimental because they could buy everything.

Her brain instantly flipped to Zac. He could buy whatever too. What does one get for Christmas when they can purchase whatever in the world they want? She only had a few dollars she could spend on them and her siblings.

"Hey Luke," she called out. He was now staring at sunglasses. Did he not have enough things for Tasha? "What should I get Zac, Nate and Evan?"

"Well Nate doesn't need a present." Luke said with a frown. Hailey rolled her eyes. He needed to get over that silly grudge. "Evan I think would be happy with food. For Zac, well I mean you could give him something that's not materialistic."

"Like?" She asked very confused. Luke had a smirk on his face before it morphed into disgust.

"Oh god. Why did I just say that? I do not need to be thinking about my sister and her boyfriend's sex life." He said in horror. Hailey's eyes widened, matching his face.

"As much as your idea is," Hailey thought of a word. "Intriguing, I guess that's a good word. No, thank you. Zac and I aren't even official."

"What do you mean you aren't? You went out. He's been all over you since the winter formal. It's practically been a month and he hasn't asked you to be his girlfriend?" Luke asked in astonishment. Hailey nodded, biting her bottom lip. She was so used to having these kind of conversations with Ben. At least Ben wouldn't judge, but only tease. She didn't know how Luke would react.

"Luke, he just hasn't asked me." She said timidly. It did make her very confused, matching his face. Luke was right. They kissed, a lot. They went on a date, at freaking Disneyland. He walks her to class. The whole school knows they're 'together', so they why hasn't he asked her?

"I swear he better ask you soon or my fist is going to need to do some talking." Luke threatened. She rolled her eyes. She knew he had a bad temper, but Zac would win in a fight. He was not only taller, but stronger as well. He is the team captain.

"Just help me find presents for them." She said. Luke nodded, a scowl still on his face. Hailey began to search the rest of Hollister, hoping to find something.

She managed to find some cute off the shoulder tops for Mariah. They were girly enough for her. Hailey would need to go to a different store for Bella. This one wasn't her kind of fashion.

Hailey went towards the men's side. She saw multiple shirts and bottoms, none screaming out for the guys. She rounded the corner and saw a button up with pineapples on it. She chuckled to herself. This was a shirt Evan would wear. She quickly picked one out, relatively in his size, and continued her search.

Like Bella, she'd have to go to a different store for Nate. Hailey never realized how alike those two were when it came to their outfits. Bella mostly wears black, kind of like a bad ass, while Nate was just a bad ass with a bad reputation. They were kind of a match made in heaven. How cliché.

"Done yet?" Luke asked. He had a bag with the purchase for Tasha. Hailey nodded, going towards the register. She quickly paid before following Luke out into the mall. "Where should we go next?"

"I got things for Mariah and Evan. We already bought Seth and Trinity things. We can go to the sports store for Ben. Maybe I can find something for Zac there. I don't know what to get Josh. And, I think we need to go to Tilly's for Nate and Bella." She told Luke, mentally checking off her list of people to shop for.

"Let's go to Tilly's. It's around the corner." Luke said. She nodded. Together they walked through the mall into said store. Hailey instantly went to the girl's side. She found a black t-shirt dress that she was sure Bella would wear. She quickly picked out her size. She browsed some more, having the possibility to find more things.

She then went to men's side. She found, surprisingly, a few plain t-shirts that Nate would wear. She didn't think Nate would wear anything with a print. She racked her brain for previous moments where he has, coming up short. She shrugged and bought the items. She found Luke in the shoes section. He was staring at a pair of Vans. Hailey observed them. She'd come back later and purchase them for him.

"On we go." She said with a giggle. Luke nodded, breaking his gaze. "To the sports store!"

"So cheery." Luke mumbled. She giggled. How could she not be. It was Christmas. The happiest time of year. She contained her happy smile as she made their way to the giant store for sports.

Hailey strolled towards the baseball section. She browsed all the items, finally choosing a baseball t-shirt, like the one Troy Bolton wears, that's white with a colored border and sleeves. She chose a blue one and a green one. Both colors of his college. She also bought him some eye black. His games would be starting after the holiday season.

"Good choice Hails." Luke said. She nodded, a grin on her face. She then walked over to the football section. Maybe she'd be able to find something for Zac.

She saw the endless row of cleats, deciding not to buy him shoes. They were darn expensive and she didn't know his size. She walked over to the helmets, also deciding no. Where ever he went to continue playing would provide one. She saw the footballs, also shaking her head. She had no clue what to get Zac. Was Luke right? Should she just give him that?

No, she wouldn't and she couldn't. She wasn't ready for that. Besides, she was sure Zac cared about something more meaningful than that. Not that that isn't special, it's just that she could give him something more meaningful that an action. She groaned. Why was she even thinking of this?

"Hey, Hailey." She whipped her heads towards the voice. A frown was now on her face.

"Hi Jordan." She said in a bored tone. His smile faltered.

"What are you doing here?" Jordan asked, gesturing towards the footballs.

"Shopping for Zac." She said, crossing her arms over her chest. Jordan's smile disappeared.

"I see you are still with him." He said. Hailey nodded. Even if she wasn't officially with him, she still liked him and wanted to be with him. Plus, what Jordan didn't know, wouldn't kill him.

"So then there's no chance of us starting over?" Jordan asked. Hailey shook her head, biting her bottom lip.

"If you are talking about being a couple, then no. But, we can try to be friends." She said. Jordan shrugged. "It's up to you. Now if you'll excuse me, I have to find my brother. See you."

She walked off, leaving Jordan in the aisle. She was lightly fuming. How did he even think that he still had a chance, especially with the way he treated her. He was a jerk! She rounded the corner and saw Luke. He was looking at the Hydroflasks.

"I'm going to pay for these and then we can leave." She said gesturing to the things in her hand. Luke nodded. "Should I get one of these for Josh?"

"I was thinking that too." Luke said picking up one of the bigger sizes. It was a plain black one. "What if I get him a large one and you get him a smaller one and the straw lids?"

"Yeah, that works. He can use one for work and the other when he's running errands." Hailey said picking the lids. She then chose a navy bottle in a smaller size. "Let's go pay."

The two of them made their way over to the register. She quickly paid for their things, exiting the store. Hailey now only needed to purchase something for Zac. She had no clue what to get him. He seemed content with his life, never mentioning that anything was missing, except his parents. As much as she wished she could get them back together for him, she couldn't. She'd have to think of something else.

"Come on Luke, let's go home. We can come back another time." She said. Luke nodded. Exhaustion was suddenly making its way into her bones. She still had a week to think of something. Plus, she'd have to come back for Luke's shoes. She left the mall with a smile on her face.

Sliding out of his car, Zac was grinning. It was their last day of the semester and he had loads of fun. Note the sarcasm. He had taken multiple exams and was now mentally exhausted. But, now he had the chance to enjoy break with those he loved.

He was excited to be spending the season with his friends and Hailey. He was planning on asking the girl to be officially his this Christmas. He knew he should have asked sooner, but he wanted to go all out. He did on their first date, so why not when he asked to be official. He had something grand and was sure she'd say yes.

Walking into his house, he dropped his bag by the door. He'd pick it up later. He strolled into the kitchen, seeing a glass of water. He frowned. No one should be here. He didn't see his parents' cars in the driveway.

He walked back out of the kitchen and towards his father's study. His dad only used it whenever his mother was out of town. Those two never in the same place. Zac wasn't even sure how they were ever in love. He knew they were mostly just together for the money. Zac hated that.

There's was nothing more that he wished for than to be loved by his parents. He wanted to have the happy family, where everyone got along. At least his mother made an effort with him. His dad only scolded him when he did something wrong. But, never praised him when he did something right.

His father had gone to the Championship game, but didn't even congratulate him on the win. He was on the jet the next morning, flying to God knows where. He was sure he wouldn't see him again until the next year.

So walking into his father's study, he was surprised to find the man sitting there. He had a permanent scowl etched onto his face as he stared at the Mac screen. Zac cleared his throat, getting his father's attention.

"Zachary, you're home." His father stated. Zac nodded. He just wanted to know why he was here. He only came back for business and to yell at him. He was sure he hadn't done anything wrong. He passed his tests and would still be at the top of his class. He was on the path to become Valedictorian.

"Do you have a charity event this weekend?" Zac asked, trying to be polite. He couldn't just come out and ask what he was doing home. His father would scold him and threaten to take something away for being disrespectful.

"No, I am actually in town to talk to you, son." His father said. He stood up and walked around his desk. He gestured for Zac to come further in. Zac walked with caution. He had no idea where this conversation would be going. "I saw the mail today. You have been given many offers."

"Did you open them?" Zac asked. He was trying to maintain a calm tone. He didn't want to blow up. That would not end well with him.

"Of course. I wanted to see what schools were even worth your time. I still believe you should go to Harvard for business, so you can take over the family empire." His father stated. Zac frowned. He didn't want to go there and he didn't want to be in charge of any business. He wanted to be normal and continue playing football.

"Father," Zac said cautiously, "I do not want to pursue a career in business. I am going to continue playing football until my time is up."

"You can go to Harvard and do just that." His dad stated. His shook his head.

"It wouldn't be the same. I can even go to Stanford and study business, while playing football." He scoffed. His temper was rising and he wasn't about to stop it. He hated that his father tried to control his life. He wanted to make his own choices.

"You will not be going there." His dad's voice rose. Zac exhaled.

"I am going to go where I chose, father. If I want to stay close to home, I will. If I want to go to Michigan State, I will. It is my choice." He snarled. His father's eyes widened at his outburst.

"Zachary, you need to focus on the future. Forget about that girl." His dad said. Zac's anger began to diffuse. How did he know about Hailey? That had never met. He was sure his mother didn't tell him. He didn't even know if they were on speaking terms.

"What girl?" Zac tried playing dumb. His father chuckled. The sound being humorless.

"I know all about Hailey Foster. Did you really think I wasn't watching over you? That's the reason why you and Nathanial weren't speaking. Now, do forget about her. She does not fit to our standards and is not fit for this family." His father ordered. Zac stood there stunned. He didn't know his father was keeping tabs on him. He thought he just forget he had a son and didn't care about anything that occurred to him. Did his father actually care?

Wait, he didn't. He only cares about himself. He just stated that Hailey wouldn't be good enough for this family. Well he was right. Hailey was above this family. She didn't deserve to know a man like his father. She was sweet and caring. She wasn't roped into the materialistic things. She wanted meaningful items that showed that one actually cared. Which she did, a lot! She wants to be a nurse and care for those who cannot care for themselves. She's the most selfless person he knows! He was about to let his father disrespect her like that.

"Father, if I want to give up on Michigan State to be with Hailey, than I will. It's my choice." Zac pushed. His anger had risen once again. He needed to get out of there before he punched his dad.

"You need to focus on your future Zac. Forget about the girl or you'll regret giving up this chance." His dad said. Zac continued to glare as he thought about his father's words. Was he right? Would he regret giving up Michigan State for the chance of being in love? Was he willing to take that chance? Zac didn't know what to think. He just knew he had to make a choice and it had to be soon, before it was too late.

~~~~~~~~~Songs from Previous Chapter, in Order:1. All I Ever Need by Ameezy{ Austin Mahone }2. We Are Never Getting Back Together by TSwizzle{ Taylor Swift }3. Last First Kiss by 1D{ One Direction }4. How Badly by IRL{ In Real Life }5. Pretty Brown Eyes by The Aussie { Cody Simpson }
~~~~~~~~~

Chapter 17 | He Could Be the One

Hailey sighed with content. Life only seemed to get better and better. The one thing that would make it all perfect would be getting into a university with a full ride. That was her ultimate goal. That way Josh didn't have to worry about her expenses nor how to pay for her education. She'd get to kill two birds with one stone.

Hailey rolled over on her bed and saw Ben watching her from the door. She let out a scream. How long had he been there? It couldn't have been that long? He was still wearing his baseball gear. He must of had an early practice. It was around at eleven in the morning.

"About time you notice me. I thought you were never going to leave your little fantasy." Ben said walking in. He went towards her desk and sat down on the swivel chair. Hailey didn't bother to sit up right. It was her room and she was in her bed.

"I wasn't daydreaming." She defended. Usually, she would be, but she was just thinking about life and everything good about it.

"Either way, what were you thinking about?" Ben asked as he twisted around in the chair. Sometimes Hailey didn't understand how this was her older brother. He acted younger than Trinity at times.

"Life." She stated vaguely. She heard Ben scoff.

"Life with Zac." He teased. Her cheeks subconsciously tinted pink at the mention of the boy. She couldn't stop thinking about him. He had taken her to Disneyland! Who takes someone to Disneyland as their first date? Either way, she was in awe at how sweet and caring that boy was. He was so selfless and understanding. She was crazy about him and she sensed he was crazy about her.

"Maybe, I guess. Life with Zac. I kind of like the sound of that." She said, not really thinking about her brother in the room. She suddenly began to imagine what life with Zac would be like if they did last. She smiled, thinking of what the future would hold for them. She knew that life would be great as long as she had him by her side.

"So you want a future with him. You must really like him Hails." Ben said. Hailey nodded, sitting up. Her cheeks were already pink from the words that were about to leave her mouth.

"I think he could be the one." She said, biting her bottom lip. Ben gasped. "Is that crazy?"

"No Hails." He said with a shake of his head. "If you are to be with anyone, i'm glad it's Zac."

"Thanks Ben." She replied. She then let out a giggle. She's thinking about being with Zac and she wasn't even officially with Zac. How ironic.

"What's with the giggle?" Ben asked. She shook her head.

"Nothing. Now, tell me what you want for Christmas." She said changing the subject. If she wanted to further along her list of things to do for the holiday season, she would have to stop thinking about the dreamy boy and focus on her wonderful family.

-

Snow grazed the ground as the holiday cheer filled their hearts. Chimneys were lit as snowman filled the streets. It was a beautiful sight to see. Just kidding. They lived in California, where it was still sunny and warm. Snow did not exist nor were there hot chocolates brewing. Plus, Zac wasn't feeling so cheery.

It had been a week since he had spoken to his father. He had hung out with Nate and Evan. They'd play video games and go out drinking. He was yet to see Hailey. He wanted to be with her, but he also wanted to live his dream. Was his father right? Was love not worth it? His heart began to beat fast as he thought about love. He knew he was falling for Hailey, to the point where he could be in love with her. He still didn't know what it really felt like. For all he knew, he could just be infatuated with her.

He groaned. Why did this have to be so complicated? Why did his dad have to come and butt into his life? He was going to ask Hailey to be his, now he didn't know. Should he just let her down now before they became attached? Who was he kidding? He was already attached to her.

He hadn't seen her since school ended. It was physically hurting him to not be with her. He wanted to see her smile. Her eyes twinkled when she laughed. God, that laugh made him weak. He loved hearing it. He wanted to hold her in his arms. He wanted to kiss her. He loved kissing her. He loved making her blush. God, he loved everything about her.

Zac quickly stood up. No, no, no. Is he? Could he? Was this real? Zac began to pace his room. Was it too late? Did he already? He groaned. The moment he feels like maybe he could still be friends with her, even though he'd be leaving at the end of school, this comes up.

Did he want to get rid of this chance? Did he not want to know what it felt like to love? Would giving it up be worth it, for the chance to play football? Was his dad right? Should he just stay in California and go to Stanford? He could play football and study business. Plus, he would be near Hailey.

Hailey.

He needed to see her. He needed to include her in this choice. She needed to know what he felt. He needed her.

He quickly slid on his shoes. He ran out of his room and down the stairs. He pulled on his leather jacket and out of the house. Remote starting his car, he got in and pulled out of the driveway. He needed to tell her how he felt before he made this choice.

-

Putting up the last of the decorations, Hailey felt content. Christmas was always her favorite holiday. Even more that she didn't have her parents to enjoy the season with. She used to love baking with her mom and helping her dad put up the lights. She missed them even more during this month, but was grateful to be spending it with her siblings. As long as she had her family, she'd enjoy the cheer.

"Hails, can you check on the cookies?" Josh called. He was upstairs, doing God knows what. He had disappeared once the cookies were in the oven.

"Sure!" She called out. She walked over to the kitchen and opened the oven door. The kitchen filled with the aroma of the sugar cookies. It was tradition for them to bake some so Trinity could decorate them for Santa. She put on oven mitts, sliding out the delicious smelling treats. She placed them on the counter top, letting them cool. They'd decorate them later tonight. They'd watch How the Grinch Stole Christmas while doing it.

She skipped out of the kitchen, going back into the living room. She had to finish wrapping the remaining presents. They'd be opening them in the morning. She was reaching for a roll of wrapping paper when the doorbell rang. She made a sound of confusion, opening the door.

"Zac? Hey." She said. She hadn't seen the boy in a week. She assumed it had to be with something about his parents. That's at least what Nate said when she asked. Nate also mentioned that his father was in town, so Hailey left Zac alone. She knew he didn't get along with him.

"Hails, can we talk?" Zac asked. Hailey nodded, letting him into her home. They sat down on the couch. Hailey watched him with curiosity. He looked to be struggling with something.

"Zac, what's wrong?" She asked. She hated seeing him like this. She hated it even more since she discovered her feelings for him. She wanted the bright and smiling Zac.

"My dad, he's home." Zac began. He didn't know how to explain everything to Hailey. He wanted her opinion on him leaving without telling her he loved her. He was sure that if she said those words back, he wouldn't leave.

"I'm sorry Zac." She said softly. She scooted closer to him. She just wanted to be near him. To let him know she was hear for him.

"He told me that he wants me to pursue business to take over the family business. He wants me to go to Harvard." He said. Hailey gasped. That was one of the most prestigious schools in the country! She knew Zac had the ability of getting into such an elite school.

"That's amazing." Hailey said. She was proud of Zac. He had the ability to follow his dream and go to the best school possible. Zac shook his head, making her frown.

"I don't want to go there. I want to go to Michigan State. I'm not sure what I want to major in, but since I was a young boy, I wanted to become a Spartan. It's far enough to be away from my parents and i'd still be playing the sport I love." Zac told her. Hailey nodded, in understanding. She knew how much he disliked the relationship he had with his parents. He also had told her that his mom was opening up and trying to be a better mother. She was happy for him.

"So, what's the problem? If you have the chance of going to your dream school, you should go for it." Hailey said. She wished she had the chance, but she didn't. She didn't want to think about life as if's. She had to focus on what she did have and make do. Her brother had worked so hard for them that she couldn't think like that. She'd pursue her dream one way or another. She wouldn't give it up, even if it meant postponing it for some time.

"Hails, the problem is that I don't know if I want to go there anymore." He said. He wanted her to tell him to stay and be near her. He knew that Hailey didn't have the same options as him. She might even have to give up nursing school until she had the money. He wished he could help her in that department. But, Hailey would accept it. She'd want to work for it on her own and not be a charity case. It was one of the things he loved about her.

"Why wouldn't you want to go there?" She asked. Zac closed his eyes, exhaling rather loudly. She was confused.

"I don't know if I can move across the state, knowing you're still here in California, not living your own dream." Zac said. Hailey gasped. She could see the sincerity in his eyes. It made her sick to think that Zac would give up this awesome opportunity, just to stay near her. She wouldn't let him do that.

"Zac, no. I can't let you do that. The only way you should ever give up that dream is if that isn't your dream anymore. You need to chose what's best for you. Do not put me in that plan. I wouldn't be able to live with myself if you give it up for me. You can't." She said to him. Her heart was cracking. She didn't want him to leave but she wouldn't be able to sleep, knowing she took his dream away from him. She couldn't let that happen.

"Alright. I'll think about all my options for school, without making my decision of being near you. I'll chose the best one for me and only me." Zac said. He felt his heart rate increase. This girl was so selfless, it made him fall even more in love with her. He just wanted to come out and tell her. Maybe then she'd ask him to stay.

"Good, now go home Zac. I still need to wrap your present." She giggled. She was glad that they had this conversation. It meant that Zac really cared for her, enough to include her in his future. She wanted to have one with him, but not if it meant he'd give everything up.

She had to put her feelings aside and think of what is best for him. He needed to make this decision on his own. If he really is the one, they'd find their way back to each other. For now, she just needed to enjoy whatever time she has left with him.

"Can I stay?" Zac asked. Hailey's eyes widened. She bit her bottom lip. She didn't know if he could. It had always been her and her siblings.

"He can." Hailey and Zac moved their heads towards Josh, who was walking down the stairs. "You are welcome to stay."

"Is that okay?" Zac asked Hailey. Hailey looked at Josh, who was nodding.

"I'd love that." She said with a grin. Zac matched it with his own. If she thought she was happy before, now she was on cloud nine.

"So, what do you guys do on Christmas Eve?" Zac asked. He was looking around the room. They had boxes of decorations in the corner with a tree fully lit. The only thing that seemed to be missing with the presents under the tree.

"We decorate cookies for Santa and watch movies. Trinity still believes in him, so we go along with the charade. She should be back with the boys soon." Josh said. Josh sat down on the sofa, flipping the channel on the tv. Hailey had a Hallmark movie playing as she finished putting the ornaments on the tree.

"Where are they?" Zac asked.

"Ben took her and Seth to take pictures with Santa at the mall. Seth wasn't too happy, but went anyway since Trin asked him too." Hailey replied.

"Luke should be back any minute too. He was off with the girlfriend." Josh said. He was hardly paying attention to them and more to the characters on the screen.

"So him and Tasha are official?" Zac asked. Hailey nodded. She was jealous that he was in a relationship and she wasn't. She wasn't really sure what her and Zac were, but it had to be something if he was thinking of a future with her.

"When are you and her going to be official?" Josh asked. Hailey's eyes widened so much, the eyeballs almost fell out of her sockets. Zac only stared back at him stunned. "So?"

"Soon." Zac said with a smirk. He had something special planned for her. He wanted to have this conversation first before deciding what was next for them. Zac looked at Hailey. Her cheeks were bright red. He loved it. "So, what movie are we going to watch?"

The front door opened, revealing the rest of the Foster clan. Trinity bounced in, going over to Josh. Seth was next, wearing a smile. Ben chuckled as he closed the door. He smiled victoriously as he locked the door. Seconds later, Luke walked in with a glare.

"Ben, really?" Luke asked, shutting the door behind him.

"I told you last one in is a rotten egg." Ben said laughing. Luke only glared. "Oh, hey Zac."

"Zac!" Trinity shouted. She let go of Josh and ran to Zac. She engulfed him in a hug which he returned. Hailey smiled, seeing how Zac fit in perfectly with her family. It would definitely be hard to say goodbye to him, but she wouldn't think of that now. She had to think about the present.

"Hey, is it alright if I join in your guys' tradition?" Zac asked. He only would stay if they were okay with him.

"Anything for Hailey's boyfriend." Ben said sitting in between them.

"They still aren't together." Luke shouted. Hailey saw him mingling in the kitchen. She was trying to get rid of the blush that was permanently etched onto her face whenever Zac was around.

"Zac said soon!" Josh shouted back. Hailey wanted to hide her face in a pillow but Ben was holding them all in his chest. It was as if he knew what she wanted to do.

"I'm fine with him staying." Seth said. He was on the floor with a book in his hand.

"I love Zac. You can help me decorate cookies for Santa!" Trinity said. She was bouncing with excitement.

"Alright, looks like Hailey's soon to be boyfriend is staying. Now, can we decorate?" Luke asked. He came in, talking with a mouth full. Hailey frowned.

"Stop eating the cookies!" She shouted. He put his hands up in defense.

"I only ate the ugly ones." He said. Hailey narrowed her eyes at him.

"Calm down. Now come on. We have much to do." Josh said standing up. They all followed him into the kitchen. They quickly took out everything needed and got to work.

Hailey smiled as she saw Zac help Trinity. She was in awe at how well his fit in. She loved seeing him get along. She giggled when Trinity placed frosting on his nose. Zac quickly returned the favor. Hailey knew this season was going to be different, but she never imagined she'd be sharing it with him. She couldn't wait to see what else the future had in store.

-

"Wake up! It's Christmas!" Trinity shouted. Hailey rolled over. She let out a groan, seeing it was only eight in the morning.

"Can you not wake up before ten?" Hailey asked with a mumble. Trinity scoffed.

"It's Christmas!" She shouted. Hailey groaned, digging deeper into her covers. "Hailey! Zac is here!"

Hailey sprung out of her bed and into the bathroom. She quickly brushed her teeth and jumped into the shower. She managed to clean her body in record time, shuffling out of the bathroom. She quickly found an outfit to wear and pulled it on. She was wearing ripped jeans with black knee high boots and a red Christmas sweater. Her hair was in a high ponytail and she didn't bother to do makeup.

"That was quick. Too bad he isn't here." Trinity said walking back into the room. Hailey frowned. Her sister tricked her to get what she wanted. "Now come!"

Trinity disappeared again. Hailey sighed, grabbing her phone. She walked downstairs to hear her brothers already up. They were sitting around the tree, bouncing with excitement.

"Good morning sleeping beauty. Took you long enough." Ben said. He was still in his pajama bottoms and an old tee. He had a mug of probably coffee in his hand.

"Trinity lied to me." Hailey stated. She sat down in a free spot on the couch. Trinity shook her head.

"No I didn't." She defended. Hailey frowned.

"You told me Zac was here." Hailey pouted. Josh laughed.

"Actually," Ben began to speak. There was suddenly a loud commotion in the kitchen. They all turned and saw white smoke. "Really? You better not be burning them!"

"Do not burn my kitchen Logan!" Josh scolded. Hailey's eyes widened. She quickly got up and saw Zac in the kitchen, covered in flour. She burst out laughing.

"Oh shut it." Zac grumbled. He had been making pancakes for them when he reached for the flour. He didn't know it wasn't sealed and poof, the flour went flying as it landed on the counter top.

"What are you doing here?" Hailey asked, waving the white clouds away. She wanted to giggle.

"Josh invited me to open presents." Zac said. He began to clean up the mess he created. He'd have to buy them a new bag of flour.

"But, why is there flour everywhere?" Hailey asked.

"I thought i'd say thank you for allowing me to stay last night by making pancakes. I reached for the flour and it fell." Zac said. He grabbed the now almost empty bag and placed it bag onto the shelf. He made sure to close the bag.

"Do we even have flour for them now?" Hailey said through giggles. She went towards the fridge and took out eggs and bacon. Pancakes would have to wait for another day. "Let's just make bacon."

"I'm sorry for making a mess." Zac chuckled. He wiped the last bit of flour off the floor and tossed the paper towel into the trash.

"It's fine. You look cute with flour in your hair." Hailey mumbled. She widened her eyes, realizing what she had said. She felt her cheeks flame in embarrassment.

"I like this side of you." Zac said in a low voice. He made his way over to her. His heart raced as he looked at the girl he loved. He wanted to tell her and badly. He wanted to show her how much she meant to him. He wrapped his arms around her back, pulling her into his body. She gazed up at him with pink cheeks. He loved that blush of hers.

"Separate." Zac turned and saw Josh with a frown as he crossed his arms over his chest. Zac let go of Hailey and leaned against the counter. "I love that you are all lovey dovey and crap, but I do not want to see it nor do I want to be an uncle."

"I want to be an uncle." Ben said walking in. He went over to the coffee machine and poured himself yet another cup. Hailey couldn't moved. Had she really just heard Ben say for her to get pregnant? She couldn't be pregnant right now. She wasn't even Zac's girlfriend.

"She's only eighteen Benjamin." Josh's voice was full of authority. Moments like that scared Zac. He was still impressed at how selfless Josh has been. He was given custody of five kids when he was still a kid. He took responsibility and cared for them. He gave up his life to be there for them and love them. Josh was his overall role model. He strived to be like him. He rather not be a father, like Ben hopes, but he wants to take care of those he loves.

"So, she'll have a bunch of energy to be a mom." Ben said in an obvious tone. Hailey couldn't find herself to speak. Why were they speaking like she was already a mom, choosing to keep the fetus.

"She can't take care of a child. She is not going to be pregnant." Josh said in a menacing voice. Hailey nodded. Josh was right. She didn't know how to care for a baby. She barely knows how to care for herself.

"Can I have a say in this?" Zac butted in. Hailey whipped her head to him. What is he about to do?

"No!" Ben and Josh shouted in unison. Hailey finally found her words.

"I am not going to be pregnant any time soon. So, can we please stop talking about this?" Hailey asked. She was uncomfortable in her own home. That was a first. Usually it was just embarrassing teasing, but now she just can't stand to be here.

"Good." Josh said with a frown. Ben only rolled his eyes as Zac scoffed. He wanted to explain that as much as he would love to have a kid with Hailey, he would wait years for that. They were both too young to be parents, especially when he didn't have parents that cared for him.

"Alright, now that we have gone through a very awkward morning. How about we open presents?" Luke asked, breaking the awkward atmosphere. When did he walk in? Everyone in the room nodded, agreeing that conversation should end. They walked out of the kitchen and back into the living room. Seth and Trinity were going through the pile of presents.

"What are you two doing?" Josh asked. Seth and Trinity froze, slowly turning around.

"Trin, said that I got a big box." Seth said sheepishly. Ben chuckled.

"If you got a big sized present, it would not be under the tree. You would snoop for it." Ben answered. He plopped himself onto the couch. Everyone else followed suit and sat down. Zac sat beside her, creating an unmistakable warmth within her. "Alright. Since you two seem to be impatient, open your presents first."

"Yay!" Trinity said. She began to search under the tree. Hailey wiggled into Zac's side. She sighed with content as he wrapped his arm around her shoulder. "Oh my god!"

"What did you get?" Seth asked. Everyone turned and saw Trinity pulling out a bunch of girly things from a box. "Okay, seriously. What did you get?"

"I got her a few dresses, some dolls, and some kids makeup." Ben said. Hailey was impressed with her older brother, but he had been spending more time with her. She kept giving up her babysitting time. Hailey needs to start hanging out with her little sister again.

"Thanks Benny! I cannot wait to try these out." Trinity said opening the makeup packages.

"Alright, Seth, you can open your giant present." Josh said. He had gotten up and brought out a big box. It was almost bigger than Trinity.

"Okay, I am real excited. What did you get him?" Luke asked. Seth began to shred the wrapping paper. He gasped as he unveiled the present. "What the fuck is this?"

"Luke." Josh said in a low voice. Luke rolled his eyes.

"So, what is it?" Trinity asked. Hailey examined the box. She widened her eyes. She knew how much Seth had been wanting one. He had been obsessed with astronomy lately.

"It's a telescope. Josh, thank you! This is amazing." Seth said with awe and appreciation in his voice. Hailey smiled. Her brothers deserved the world and more. Josh deserved everything. He had been so hardworking and understanding. He put his own life on hold to take care of them. She wished she could show Josh how much that meant for her, for all of them.

"No problem Seth. Just take great care of it." Josh said smiling.

"Alright Lucas." Hailey said in a teasing tone. Luke rolled his eyes. "Go find yours."

"Did you guys do secret Santa?" Zac asked. He had been wondering how they decided who opened what present.

"Kind of. We all know who was giving who a present." Ben answered. Zac nodded. That made more sense. He watched as Luke picked up a rectangular box. He unwrapped it, revealing a Vans shoe box.

"These are the ones I was looking at the other day. Thanks Hailey!" Luke said taking out a pair of black checkered print, slip on Vans.

"Welcome Lukey!" Hailey said. She loved seeing her brothers happy. One of the many reasons she loved Christmas.

"Alright. Trinity, give Hailey her present." Seth said. Trinity looked up from her makeup products. She had already plastered most of it onto her face. Hailey covered her mouth to prevent herself from laughing. She was sure Trinity would not appreciate that.

"Here you go Hailey." Trinity said. She passed her a small box with glitter paper. Of course this would be from Trinity. She pulled the paper off and saw a stethoscope. She gasped. She was extremely amazed.

"Trin, thank you." Hailey said. It just got her one step closer to her dream.

"Hails, those were mom's." Ben said softly. Hailey turned to see Josh. He was nodding. He had a sad smile on his face. She felt her eyes brim with tears.

She wondered if her mom would be proud of her. Would she have loved the fact that Hailey wanted to be just like her? Would she encourage her to become a nurse? Hailey wanted nothing more than to be able to cherish this moment with her mom, her parents. But, she knew she'd have to rely on the memories. Being with her siblings, and Zac, would be enough.

"Thank you. Thank you so much." Hailey said wiping away her tears. She closed her eyes and pictured her mom. She smiled, imaging that she was grinning back at her with a proud smile.

"Mom would be so proud Hails." Josh said softly. She closed her eyes tight and nodded.

"I hope so." She said softly. She placed them back into the box, setting it on the side table. She'd cherish that as her most prized possession. "Alright, so who is next?"

"I believe Seth needs to go." Zac said. Hailey softly gasped. She had forgotten that he was there. She quickly wiped away her remaining tears, glad she hadn't worn makeup. The mascara would definitely caused raccoon eyes.

"Here's yours from me." Seth said to Ben. He passed a medium sized box with baseball wrapping paper. Zac chuckled. "I hope you like it. If not, we can exchange it."

"Seth, this is amazing! I am keeping." Ben said. He had unwrapped a box containing a first basemen's glove. It was brown with white detailing. "I didn't think you were listening when I mentioned Coach putting me at first."

"How could I not be?" Seth said with an eyeroll. "You kept complaining about how you are meant to be at shortstop. Apparently all the "babes" loves shortstops."

"Glad to see your education is paying off." Josh teased. Ben rolled his eyes, slipping on the mitt. He pounded his fist into it. "Alright. I guess out gifting is over. Everyone else can open whatever."

"Josh, you still need yours." Luke said. He was staring at his brother with a annoyed expression.

"I'm guessing that by your ugly face, you are giving me a gift." Josh stated. Luke narrowed his eyes. Josh chuckled, sitting back. Hailey readjusted herself as Zac's arm brought her closer to his chest. She smiled. This felt like home.

"Lastly, to the best older brother and mentor anyone could ever ask for." Luke said in a mocking tone. Hailey chuckled at his description. Luke really did believe that. Josh was their overall role model, even if he can be a pain sometimes. Luke handed a bag to Josh. He took out pieces of tissue paper before revealing his present.

"This is so going to come in handy at work. Thanks Luke." Josh said inspecting the Hydroflask.

"It says it keeps you water cold all day. Let me know if it's true." Luke said. Josh nodded, placing the water bottle back into the bag.

"Alright, now you are free to open whatever it is you'd like." Josh said. Trinity quickly invaded the tree.

"Is it alright if I give out my presents?" Zac asked. Everyone was surprised by his words, but agreed. Zac got up; Hailey instantly missing his warmth. Zac picked up a few boxes from underneath the tree. "This is for you Trinity."

"Oh my god. Thank you." Trinity said. She quickly unwrapped the small box, revealing a tiara. It was made out of finer material but still childproof. Zac had envisioned Ben when purchasing it.

"For Seth." Zac said handing a card to him. Seth pulled it out, revealing an large amount of money on a Barnes and Nobles gift card.

"Zac, this is way too generous of you. I cannot accept it." Seth said. He attempted to give it back. Zac shook his head.

"I know how much you love books. Go ham and buy whatever you'd like." Zac said. Seth should his head again, not wanting to keep it. "Seth, if you don't keep it, i'll just buy whatever books and come hand them to you. At least this way, you get to chose what you'd like."

"I don't want to, but thank you Zac. I greatly appreciate your kindness towards me." Seth said. He was looking at Zac with a grin.

"You're one of my best friends Seth. I'd do anything for you." Zac said. Seth's grin only seemed to widen. Hailey found her heart growing as she saw the affection Zac had for her brother. He had no idea how much that meant to her and to Seth. "Alright, for Luke."

"What?" Luke asked. He took the box from Zac. He opened it and got a football jersey. "Not to burst your bubble Zac, but why would I want this?"

"It's yours." Zac said. It had Luke's last name and number on it.

"I can see that, but it's not football season." Luke asked. He left the jersey in the box. Hailey watched in confusion.

"After a ling talk with coach, we have decided to make you captain of next season." Zac said. Luke's eyes widened. His eyeball practically falling out of its socket. Hailey waved her hand in front of his face, trying to get his focus.

"Are you serious?" Luke asked. He pulled the jersey out and saw the letter C in the upper left corner. "Woah."

"You deserve it man." Zac said. It took come convincing, but coach had agreed that Luke was next in line to run the team. Not only had he been starting in a few games, but he had Logan blood. Coach thought that meant Luke was going to be just like Josh. He wasn't wrong, but they were different in every way. Josh was calm and collected, while Luke was temperamental and obnoxious.

"Thank you Zac." Luke said placing the jersey back in its box.

"For Ben." Zac said. He handed him an envelope. Ben opened it and dropped the card, in shock.

"Ben? Are you okay?" Hailey asked. Seth waved his hand in front of his face. Ben stayed still with wide eyes. "Ben? Benny? Benjamin!"

"Is he okay?" Trinirty asked. Josh picked up the contents of the card. He, too, dropped them in shock. He was frozen in place. Hailey was very curious as to what it had in it. She was about to pick them up when Luke grabbed it.

"Okay, what did you give him?" Luke asked. He looked down and dropped his jaw open.

"What?" Hailey asked. She ripped it out of Luke's hands. She quickly skimmed its contents, wanting to scream. "Oh my god. This is front row! What the actual heck!"

"Are you all alright?" Zac asked. He was beginning to worry. The present wasn't even such a big deal. He got them Yankees tickets in New York for next summer. They were right behind the third base dugout. They'd be able to see and possibly talk to amazing players like Aaron Judge, Brett Gardner, and Giancarlo Stanton.

"Zac, no. I cannot accept those." Ben said. He was shaking his head, still not believing what he had read.

"You can and you will. All of your are invited to the game. We can take my parents' jet and stay for the weekend." Zac said. He was already excited for the trip and he had to wait months for it. Either way, he was content with his ability to spoil the kids and spent time with Hailey. He also has a chance to learn what normality has become. Hailey loved every second of it.

"I-Zac, no, I can't-oh my god. I'll be in New York. I wonder if I can talk to Judge." Ben began to ramble.

"Alright, I got this for you Josh." Zac said. Josh raised his eyebrows in surprise. Zac struggled to get Josh a gift he knew he'd love. After speaking to his mom, he finally made a choice. It would not only benefit Josh but the family too.

"Wow Zac. This is just too much." Josh said in astonishment. Zac shook his head.

"You deserve it. You have done so much for this family, I thought i'd repay you." Zac said. Josh handed it back to Zac. "Take it Josh."

"Is that a car key? Oh my god Zac. You did not." Hailey said. She quickly got up and went towards the window. Everyone followed suit. In the driveway sat a black truck.

"If it makes it any better, it's not brand new. But at least this way, you'll have a third vehicle and you can use it for construction." Zac said.

"Zac, no. I cannot accept this." Josh said sternly.

"My mom was more than happy to gift it to you. I told her about you and everyone. She wants to meet you." Zac said.

"Your mom wants to meet him?" Ben asked. Zac nodded.

"She didn't raise me like she wished she had. She just wants to tell you how proud she is of you for stepping up in a time of need." Zac explained. Josh blinked. "Just take it. If you don't, it'll just be a car stowed in the depth of my dad's car garage."

"I want to pay you for this." Josh said. Zac scoffed.

"It's a gift. Now go and take it for a test drive." Zac said. Josh shook his head.

"After we are done with this. I believe you have one more present in your hand." Josh said with a smirk. Zac's cheeks increased in heat. His heart was racing as he looked down at it. He hoped and prayed this went right.

"This is from me." Zac said handing Haileh a small box. She unwrapped it and revealed a smaller black, rectangle shaped, box.

"What's this?" Hailey asked. She took out a heart shaped necklace with crystals. Her eyes fell out of the sockets as she saw the word "girlfriend" on it. She looked up at Zac.

"Hails, I am crazy about you. The moment we bumped into each other at the store a few months back, I knew that you'd mean something to me. And you do! We went through some ups and many downs to get to where we are now. I know I want you in my life and I know that I love you." Zac said. Hailey gasped. Had he really just said he loved me? Zac was smiling at her. She felt her grin match his. "So, Hailey, will you be my girlfriend?"

"Yes." Hailey shouted. She wrapped her arms around his neck. His grasped her hips as she buried her face in the crook of his neck. He kiss her head. She was finally his.

"About damn time." Ben said. Hailey pulled away, looking up at the man that loved her. That's when she knew she loved him too. Everything she had ever felt for him has led her to fall in love with him. He was such an amazing guy and she was crazy about him. She bit her bottom lip. Should she tell him now or wait until later?

"Now, can we finish opening presents?" Seth asked. He was watching them with a look of disgust. Hailey giggled. He probably was not enjoying their little show of affection and they hadn't even kissed.

"Yes!" Trinity shouted. She went back to the tree and picked up another present. "This is for you."

Zac widened his eyes but took the present. He slowly began to unwrap it. He gasped when he saw it. Hailey shifted in her seat as she watched him. She was nervous for it. She didn't know if he'd like it.

"Hails, you didn't have to do that." Zac said as he looked at the picture. Hailey had gifted him a semi-big picture frame with a picture of all their friends at formal. They were doing silly faces, enjoying each other's company and friendship. She had put the word 'Family' on it.

"I know how much our friendship means to you and everyone else." Hailey said. She wanted to hide her face in embarrassment. He had given her such an amazing present and she felt like she couldn't even compete. She had no clue what to get him since he could afford whatever he wanted.

"Hailey, this means more to me than you think. I love it." Zac said. He turned towards her and grinned. She was the most perfect human being he had ever met. He was so glad he had the chance of bumping into her and now he has the chance to make her happy. He wants to show her how much he loves her. "I love you Hailey."

"I love you Zac." She said with a giggle. Zac's eyes widened. She said it back. She loves him. He wanted to lean in and show her just how much he loved her, but he'd have to safe that for later. For when they were alone. Instead, he leaned in and placed his lips on hers, softly and fast. It was a chaste kiss, considering her entire family was watching them. But even then, Hailey finally felt whole. She looked up at her new boyfriend, who was smiling down at her. He loved her and she loved him. He was the one. She could feel it. She just hoped he felt it too.

Chapter 18 | Nobody But You

With sunny skies and clear days, nothing seemed to be able to go wrong. Only it was, for Zac. Zac paced his room. He had no clue what to do. How was he supposed to decide where he wanted to go to college? He barely could choose what shirt he wore.

Decision day was right around the corner. He had to sign with someone. He had so many options and none seem like the right one. Even his dream school was in the cards. Michigan State had offered a full athletic and academic ride. He had talked to the coaches and was excited to join the team. But then, he also received offers from Stanford University. That coach was also wanting him on the team. He promised to make him a starter. He, too, was offering a full ride.

Zac also got offers from Harvard, Yale, Texas A & M, Ohio State, Michigan, Oregon, Arizona State, USC, and Dartmouth. Zac couldn't believe his eyes. He assumed all the schools wanted him because of who his parents were, but also because of his abilities on the field. He knew he had to make a choice and it had to be quick. He only had a few daya left to decide.

He grabbed his car keys and left his house. The real reason he couldn't decide was because of Hailey. It had been a little over two months since they became official. Zac was overjoyed. He knew he loved Hailey but knowing that she was his and only his, made his heart grow. He felt all those cliché things with her and loved it. He loved how she reacted to him. How she cuddled into his side when they're watching a movie with her siblings. He loves how she chews on her bottom lip when she's thinking really hard. He loved how her eyes twinkle when he compliments her and don't even get him started on her blush. The most beautiful thing he has ever seen. He loves every single thing about her.

Zac had taken her out on a few dates. They went to dinner, where Zac discovered she hates cheesecake. They went to the movies. He purposely chose horror. They had even gone on group dates with their friends. They were excited to know that he had finally asked her to be his.

Nate was the only one that was on the fence. Zac tried to push away the thoughts of Nate liking Hailey, but it was difficult for him when Nate wasn't sure if Zac should make it official. Nate kept reminding him that he was leaving soon. Zac assured him that he loved Hailey and would find a way to make it work. Nate back down and only restated that he'd be able to find love again but he will not be able to go to his dream school.

That was one of the many reasons he couldn't decide what he wanted to do. His dad and Nate kept telling him to pursue his dream. If Hailey and him were really meant to be, they'd find their way back to each other later on. Zac didn't want to test that theory. What if Hailey found someone better and stopped loving him? He was scared of what the future holds.

He parked his car on the side of the street. He noticed that he wasn't the only one at the Foster House. He quickly got out, instantly recognizing the cars. He jogged up to the front door and walked in. Josh had made it very clear that he's family now and didn't need to knock. It made his choice that much harder.

"Zac!" He heard Trinity's voice scream. He stumbled back as she stuck herself to his side. He picked her up and hugged her tight.

"Hi princess." He said to her as he put her back onto solid ground. She giggled before smiling up at him.

"Are you here to see Hailey? She's in my room with Mariah and Bella." Trinity said. She was moving her hips side to side. Zac noticed she was wearing another tutu. It was one of the ones she had received for Christmas.

"Are you playing dress up with Ben?" Zac smirked. Trinity shook her head, giggling. "With who?"

"With me." He heard Josh's voice grumble. He turned and saw Josh walk out of the kitchen. He had makeup all over his eyes and face. He had butterfly clips in his hair as he sported a matching tutu.

"You look beautiful." Zac said. He covered his mouth to keep himself from laughing.

"Oh shut it." Josh said with a glare. Zac nodded, attempting to stop himself from laughing. "Hails is in her room."

"Thanks pretty lady." Zac teased as he jogged up the stairs. He walked down the hall towards Hailey's room, stopping when he heard his name.

Hailey had invited the girls over for a sleepover. She was supposed to be watching Trinity, but Josh was home. So, she asked and he agreed. She quickly called them and they were at her home in minutes. She was desperate for some girl time.

"It's been so long since we've hung out." Bella said as she laid down on her bed. Hailey sat at her desk chair. Mariah joined Bella.

"You are so in looooooove with your boyfriend." Mariah teased. She dragged the O in love for emphasis.

"Okay, yes. I am in love with Zac." Hailey said softly. Her blush was visible as she thought about it. It was one of the first days they weren't together. He had mentioned at school having to choose what he was doing for college. She quickly stepped back and let him be. As much as she wanted to be with Zac, she knew she had to let him decide on his own.

"Zac has been freaking crazy about you since he had invited you to his party back in September." Bella mentioned. Hailey nodded. She knew that day had changed their lives.

"Okay, enough about him. What are we going to do tonight?" Mariah asked. She got up and started going through Hailey's closet. "I heard there's a party."

"No." Hailey said with a shake of her head. She had planned a movie night with all the junk food Josh doesn't allow in the house.

"Oh come on. It'll be fun!" Bella offered. Hailey shook her head.

"It'll just be us three. It'll still be a girl's night." Mariah offered. She twirled one of her blond locks, waiting for Hailey to decide. Hailey turned to Bella who was getting off her bed.

"Just say yes." Bella insisted. She began to go through Hailey's closet.

"I have just the perfect outfit." Mariah said. She was searching through Hailey's closet again. Hailey groaned. She needed to find a way out.

"Say yes." Bella said in a singing voice. Mariah quickly followed suit. Hailey rolled her eyes. She hated when they teamed up against her. One of the many reasons she now liked pineapple on pizza.

"Promise you won't regret this." Mariah said. Hailey ignored them. Maybe they'd leave her alone. She turned around on her desk and looked in the mirror.

"This dress is amazing. Thanks Hails." Bella said. Hailey looked at her through the reflection. She had slipped on the dress Hailey had given her for Christmas. She really had chosen a great dress for her.

"You need to wear this." Mariah said handing her clothes. Hailey sighed. There was no way she'd convince them to stay home. She might as well give up now. Maybe they'd come back from the party sooner. She took the outfit in the bathroom and put it on. It was a black off the shoulder, long sleeve shirt with a black leather mini skirt. She tucked in the top into the skirt which had studs on the end of it.

Zac stayed quiet as he heard the girls decide about their plans. Maybe Mariah was right. They should all go out and have some fun. It would definitely help him stop thinking about his future. It had been in his brain for months now and he was nowhere near a solution. Getting drunk was what he needed.

He knocked on the door with one hand as he texted the guys with the other. He heard commotion from the other side before hearing the door swing open. Bella stood there in a black dress with her hair in a messy bun. A look of confusion on her face.

"What are you doing here?" Bella asked. Hailey and Mariah then came into view.

"I told you this boy cannot stay away from you." Mariah said in a teasing tone. Hailey rolled her eyes, smiling at her boyfriend. That word still felt so foreign to her. Being with him for two months was still not enough time to get used to it.

"The guys will be here soon." Zac said looking back down at his phone. He slid it back into his pocket, widening his eyes as he stared at Hailey. Hailey looked- "Woah."

"Doesn't she look hot?" Bella smirked. Zac's eyes stayed wide as he roamed her body. Her legs were on full display and her curves even more evident than usual.

"You look-woah." Zac said still tongue tied.

"Alright, go away. We need to finish getting ready." Mariah said shutting the door. Zac stood there, still stunned. He loved Hailey and her usual jeans and a t-shirt, but when she dressed like that, he couldn't help but think of everything he wanted to do to her. He quickly shook his head. He made his way back downstairs, attempting to squash away those thoughts.

As Mariah shut the door, Hailey let herself exhale. The way Zac's eyes raked over her body had her tingling. She had never seen that look before. Usually his eyes would dilate slightly, but they darkened as his eyes stayed on her legs. She shivered when his eyes met hers.

"I told you that boy is crazy about you. He was practically eye raping you." Bella said. She took her hair out of a bun and began to tease the top. She then applied a maroon lip.

"If you guys haven't done it, I am sure he's thinking about it right now." Mariah said in a knowing tone. Hailey felt her voice get stuck in her throat. Is that what that look meant? She felt her insides squirm. She wasn't ready for that yet.

"Anyway, we need to fix your makeup." Bella said. She pulled Hailey down and began to apply liner.

"Hails, I am so glad we convinced you to let us leave our presents here. I knew they'd come in handy." Mariah said slipping on a white loose blouse and black and white printed shorts. She tucked the shirt in and pulled on her black leather jacket. She was already wearing that earlier.

"So you need black pumps." Bella said once she was done with Hailey's makeup. "And you can just wear the strappy heels you came with."

"So demanding." Mariah teased. Bella rolled her eyes. "Come on. The party is about to begin."

"Let's go!" Bella said grabbing her bag. Hailey did the same. Reality finally hit her.

"I haven't asked Josh for permission." She said. The girls were halfway out the door. They stopped and looked at her.

"You have not, but you can go. Just be safe and someone be responsible to not drink. Be home by one." Josh said walking by. Hailey sighed as she registered his words. She had been slightly hoping he'd disagree with their plan. Channing Tatum and Alex Pettyfer were calling her name. Either way, she was going to have fun. She needed to have fun.

Her mind had been on over drive since Zac had practically asked her to ask him to stay. She focused on school and work. Carl was fine with her working extra hours. She still hung out with Zac, but it was usually with people around. She wanted to avoid the talk of college as much as possible. She just didn't want to be the reason he'd give up Michigan State for her. She loved him, but not enough to ruin his life time dream.

"Thanks Joshy! I promise i'll be careful." Hailey said hugging him. He chuckled, pushing her away.

"Go before I change my mind." He joked. Hailey nodded, following the girls downstairs.

"Was he wearing eyeshadow?" Mariah asked. Hailey shrugged. It was probably Trinity's doing. She had been obsessed with it since she got it for Christmas. She bet Ben was regretting it.

"You guys take so fucking long." Nate said as they stepped into the living room. Evan, Nate, and Zac were lounging on the couch. Some football highlights on the screen. The Super Bowl was in two days.

"I can go and take longer if you'd like." Bella offered. Nate rolled his eyes, pulling her into his chest.

"Hey guys!" Hailey turned around and saw Luke. He had walked out of the kitchen. Tasha was right behind him. Those two were pretty cosy with each other and Hailey was happy to see her brother happy. "Are you guys going to Max Shepard's?"

"Yeah, want to come?" Evan replied. Luke turned to Tasha who was nodding her head. She didn't seem opposed to the idea.

"If that's alright." Luke said. Everyone nodded. Hailey shrugged. She couldn't say no. Luke was friends with the guys because of football.

"Let's go. I'm being the DD, not only because I don't feel like being hungover, but mostly because we are taking my car." Evan said. He was twirling his keys around his finger. He was wearing a white shirt and jeans. He was sporting a brown jacket.

"Whatever you say babe. Let's go." Mariah said grabbing his hand and pulling him out the door. Bella followed behind. Nate raised an eyebrow at Zac. He, too, followed behind.

"I'm going to go get in the car. I can feel Zac's glares." Luke said. Hailey turned and saw Zac. He was blinking rapidly, as if he was trying to mask that he got caught. "Come on Tasha."

"Were you glaring at my brother?" Hailey asked once they were alone. Zac shrugged. He looked down at her outfit again. He bit his bottom lip as his previous thoughts wormed their way back into his brain. She was so beautiful.

"You look amazing." Zac said. Hailey's cheeks flamed.

"Thanks, but come on. They're waiting." She said with a giggle. Zac chuckled.

"Alright." He grabbed her hand and pulled her out the door. They walked over to Evan's black Suburban and piled in.

-

Hailey will never get used to the luxurious mansions and extravagant homes. It seemed like all her classmates were loaded. They had flashy cars and expensive items. Everyone knew they had money. As they walked deeper into the house full of drunk teens, Hailey decided that she would let loose. She would enjoy herself, even if that meant taking part in underage drinking. You only live once, right.

"Who's house is this again?" Bella asked. They walked through the sea of people until they were in the kitchen. They somehow always found themselves there. It was kind of like their spot.

"Max Shepard's." Evan replied. He looked around, surveying the current scene.

"That's some douche on the basketball team." Bella asked, although it sounded more like a statement. Everyone nodded in agreement. It seemed that since Hailey and Jordan weren't together, the basketball team has made it their life's mission to be total assholes to them. Zac couldn't stand it, especially when it was towards Hailey.

They have glared at her from a far and cut her in line at lunch. They even laugh at her when she walks by. If it wasn't for him wanting to have a future, he would have already bashed everyone's face in. He would wait until he could show them a piece of his mind.

"Let's go dance." Mariah said pulling Evan away. Evan waved bye as they disappeared. Hailey giggled as she saw the happy couple leave. They were so clingy, it was perfect.

"I'm down. Come on Hails. You can dance with me." Bella said pulling her away. Zac saw Bella give Nate a look as she disappeared into the crowd. Zac sighed. What did they have up their sleeve?

"Did you decide?" Nate asked once they were alone. Zac shook his head. It was the reason he was here, with a bottle of Jack. He just couldn't figure out what was more important. How he grew up is definitely affecting what his future will look like. He wants to make sure he chooses the best option, not only for him, but for Hailey too. Even if she says for him to forget about her, he's on the top of her list. He wants to be with her. He loves her!

"I don't know what to do." He said with a groan. He placed the lip of the bottle on his lips and took another gulp. It burned as it traveled down his throat.

"Choose what you think is the best option." Nate said. He took a sip of his own drink. He was holding a bottle of Bud Light.

"That's the thing Nate. I'm not sure what the best option is. I'm fucking in love with her. I don't want to just leave her here, but if I stay, i'm afraid that i'll regret not going to Michigan State. It has been my life long dream to be a Spartan. I don't know if i'm ready to just give that up because i'm in love. And damn it Nate, I fucking love being in love! She's perfect inside and out. I don't want to have to say bye to her." Zac told him. He slammed the rest of the bottle back in frustration. It was driving him nuts that he couldn't decide.

All his life, his parents always chose for him. Nate and him had been friends because of their parents. They both knew how much they despised being in the public eye, so they bonded. They have a real friendship because of it. He had someone he could actually rely on. When they met Evan, he was instantly a part of their group. It was one of the first times he had gone against his parents' wishes, but they soon approved the friendship because of his parents.

Zac was so used to his parents choosing what sport he played, what clothes he wore, what high school he went to, and what food he ate. He finally has an actual chance to choose his own school and he didn't know which one. He wished they'd chose for him. To chose between the sport he loved and the love of his life. He knew his dad wanted him to stay to run the family business. He knew his mom just wanted him to be happy. He knew Nate wanted him to go to Michigan State and he knew Hailey would tell him what to do. He had so many options that were just even more confusing. He wished there was some kind of sign to narrow down the options.

"I know you love her man. I love Izzy. It took me so damn long to finally come to terms with it. I regret not telling her from the start. Who knows man, maybe we would have been together since then, but I am happy with how things turned out. It made me realize that she really is the one for me. If I hadn't been an idiot, than I probably never would have realized how to make her truly happy." Nate said. Zac grimaced.

"Ew man." He said with disgust. Nate narrowed his eyes before whacking Zac's head. Zac glared.

"Not like that you idiot. I meant that I had the chance to get to know her and see what she loved and disliked. I was able to see what kind of person she truly is. I was able to see that it was true love." Nate said. Zac stared back at his best friend, stunned. He had never heard him talk about a girl like that.

"At least you guys will have a happy ending." Zac sighed. Nate shook his head. "You're staying here though."

"Bella is going to Princeton. She wants to follow in her mom's footsteps." Nate told him. Zac nodded. Mrs. Green was an alumni there. "Even Evan is going there. Those twins do not want to separate."

"Have you decided what you're majoring in?" Zac asked. He knew he was going to Berkley. His father was also an alumni there. One of the best schools for politics.

"No. I hate that. At least you know what you want to do with your life." Nate sighed. Zac shook his head. They were both in a difficult situation.

"It's not that simple. I wish Hailey could just come with me." Zac said. He reached for a beer and unscrewed the lid. He needed to get drunk to forget. He came to forget about his decision, not talk about it.

"Dude, the twins are both going to Princeton! I won't have my best friends or my girlfriend. I'm going to be miserable here. Even Mariah is going to NYU." Nate said. He too reached for another bottle.

"We're all going to East Coast schools." Zac joked. He let the beer slide down his throat.

"Dude, just go to MSU. Live your life. You can visit Hailey whenever you want and you can fly her out there. But, do not give up this chance because you finally found love." Nate told him. Zac was about to protest, but shut his mouth. He kept thinking about having to say goodbye but never thought of long distance. Could they do that? Did Nate believe in their relationship more than he did?

"Wait, how did you know I had been looking for love?" Zac asked. Nate laughed loudly.

"Dude, you have been wanting to be in love for as long as I can remember. You always stared at the Green's in fascination. You broke up with Sasha when you realized she didn't truly love you. Which by the way, sorry about her." Nate said. Zac shrugged it off.

"I never loved her." Zac said.

"That's one of the reasons you finally broke up with her. You realized that it was purely physical with her. You wanted the emotional part too. The moment I finally realized you wanted to know what it was like was that one day we were at Carl's. You were staring rather creepily at the old people sharing ice cream. You probably watched the Notebook the day before." Nate said. Zac rolled his eyes. The only reason they had seen it was because Bella forced them to watch it when they were younger. "All i'm saying Zac, is enjoy what you have now. Choose to go to MSU. If she really is your true love, she'll come back to you. It's that stupid saying."

"Who knew love would make you so philosophical." Zac joked. Nate rolled his eyes.

"Speaking of love." Nate whispered. Zac turned and saw their friends make their way back.

"What were y'all talking about?" Bella asked. She wrapped her arm around Nate's waist.

"Just about if you're a bird, than i'm a bird." Nate joked. Zac rolled his eyes.

"I knew you two loved that movie." Bella screeched.

"Wait, you two have seen the Notebook?" Mariah said through her laughter. Hailey was giggling. Who knew those two were truly romantics at heart.

"Bella forced us to watch it when we were younger." Nate explained. Bella shook her head.

"That was only the first time. I do recall you asking to watch it." Bella teased. Nate's cheeks tinted pink.

"Do you boys secretly have a thing for Ryan Gossling?" Mariah asked. Zac and Nate gave her a blank stare.

"Please, they love Ryan Reynolds. Wrong Ryan Mar." Evan said. The girls flipped their heard to him. "What? The Proposal is a pretty good movie."

"Are all you boys into romcoms?" Mariah asked.

"I say we ditched this party and have a move night." Hailey stated. They looked around their group. Hailey crossed her fingers behind her back. She hoped they'd agree. She was slightly having fun with them. They took a few jello shots and danced for an hour. They only came back to find Nate and Zac when they hadn't showed up. Bella kept reassuring her that she looked hot. When Zac didn't come to dance, she began to doubt that. As they made their way out of the dancing drunk teens, they saw that Nate and Zac were somewhat in a serious conversation. Bella being Bella, ruined it.

"I'm down. We can watch Clueless and 10 Things I Hate About You! Oh, and A Walk to Remember." Bella said. She was beginning to buzz with excitement.

"Can we watch Magic Mike? I saw the DVD on your desk." Mariah asked. Hailey was about to answer when one of the boys beat her to it.

"Hell no. We will watch the sappy romantic movies, but I will not sit through a movie about strippers." Nate argued. Bella began to pout.

"Come on. You loved Channing Tatum in 21 Jump Street." Mariah said. Nate narrowed her eyes.

"That wasn't a romantic comedy!" Nate argued. Mariah huffed.

"Can we at least watch a movie we want?" Zac asked. Bella pretended to contemplate before shaking her head.

"No, now come on. We do not have all night." Bella said. She grabbed Nate's hand and pulled him towards the front of the house.

"If it makes you feel better, i'll ask to watch The Hangover if you want." Mariah offered. Evan chuckled.

"What if we watch White House Down. It has Channing Tatum and killing in it." Even said. Mariah shrugged.

"As long as he's in it, fine by me. Sad to know him and Jenna Dewan aren't together anymore." Mariah replied. Hailey nodded. It was a tragic story. They were their OTP. What's next? Dylan O'brien and Britt Robertson split up? No thank you.

"Come on. My sister will flip if she finds out we weren't behind them." Evan said reaching for Mariah. He quickly pulled her away, leaving Zac and Hailey.

"So you love romcoms." Hailey teased. Zac rolled his eyes.

"Bella didn't have any girl friends growing up until she met Mariah in high school. She'd force us to watch them with her. What can I say? They aren't that bad. At least they taught me how to be an amazing boyfriend to you." Zac told her truthfully. He wrapped her arms around her in a hug. He placed his chin on the top of her head as she snaked her own arms around his body. She took a deep breath in. He smelled really good and he looked really good. He was just wearing a plain navy shirt and he looked like a million bucks.

"Thank you." Hailey whispered. She still couldn't get over the fact that the Zac Logan was in love with her.

"Thank you Hails for giving me a chance." He whispered. He kissed the top of her head, enjoying themselves in their arms.

"Hey, where did everyone go? I saw them walk out the door." Hailey heard her brother Luke say. She unwrapped her arms from Zac and turned to look at her brother. Tasha was holding his hand, looking just as confused.

"I forgot you came with us." Zac mumbled. Hailey had forgotten too.

"We're going back to the house to watch movies. You guys wanna come back with us?" Hailey asked. Luke looked at Tasha. She yawned. Luke chuckled.

"Yeah. Tasha looks ready to pass out." Luke said. Tasha frowned.

"Jerk." She said chuckling. Luke pulled her into his side, kissing her cheek.

"Come on. You can pass out during the movie." Luke said. He gestured for them to leave. Zac nodded, pulling Hailey along with him. Hailey admired her surroundings as they walked out of the house. Teens were still very much alive and enjoying their lives. They were dancing like no one was watching and drinking alcohol like their life depended on it. Hailey felt blessed to have a much better meaning of life, one that didn't involve getting black out drunk. That she was sure she was glad she didn't know what it felt like.

"About damn time. Thought you guys stayed to have a quickie." Mariah said when they reached them. Hailey rolled her eyes.

"Sorry, we found Luke and Tasha though." Zac apologized. The car began to move. Hailey finally began to feel calmer. She was away from that death zone.

"All good. Are you guys joining us?" Evan asked. Luke nodded.

"So what movie are we watching?" Luke asked. Haiely watched as Bella smirked.

"Care to tell them babe?" Bella asked Nate. Nate glared at his girlfriend.

"The Notebook." He spat. Bella let out a loud laugh.

"Why are we watching the bird people? Can't we at least watch a good movie?" Luke asked.

"So you've seen it too." Mariah said. Hailey saw her smirk in a teasing way.

"Everyone knows they are the ones in the canoe thing." Luke defended himself.

"Either way, get ready to enjoy a night full of romance." Mariah said

"God, we should have stayed at the party." Luke groaned.

-

The microwave and smoke detector began to go off in sync. Hailey jumped off the counter and saw black smoke rising from the heating device. She frowned. She opened the microwave door, coughing. More smoke was released as she reached for the now burnt to char popcorn. She took the bag and tossed it into the trash. She reached for another pack and placed it in for less time than before.

"You suck at making popcorn." Zac teased. She frowned.

"You distracted me." She said with arms crossed. Zac chuckled.

"You love me." He said. Hailey replaced her frown with a smile.

"I do love you." She said. He grinned back.

"And you love her. Now focus on the popcorn. We are waiting so we can start 13 Going on 30!" Mariah said interrupting them. They had already gone through four movies and were going on their fifth. Luke and Tasha had disappeared and Nate was passed out. Bella was still full of energy as well as Mariah. Evan and Zac were just bored.

"Let's go to your room Hails." Zac insisted. He wanted to spend quality time with his girlfriend without her girl friends.

"Trin is sleeping, plus Josh will kill you." Hailey said. She stopped the microwave and took out the bag. She opened it, releasing steam. It wasn't burnt this time. "Now come on."

"Fine, only cause I love you." Zac said following her back to the living room.

"Can we take a vote on what movie we are going to watch? Please." Evan asked. Bella shook her head.

"Hailey's house. She chooses." Bella answered. Evan looked at Hailey expectingly. Hailey shifted in his gaze. She didn't really want to watch any more movies, but she wasn't tired just yet. Or maybe she was in denial. She just didn't want the night to end.

"I say we call it a day. We're going to be back for the Super Bowl anyway." Zac offered. They looked at each other before sighing.

"Fine. But we are still sleeping over. I'm too tired to drive home." Mariah agreed. Bella nodded.

"Nate is half asleep anyway. It'll be one big sleepover. Now, where are there more pillows and blankets?" Bella asked. Hailey chuckled. Soon, she found herself in a mini fort with all her best friends. This was definitely the best distraction a girl could ask for.

-

"Wake the fuck up!" Someone shouted. Zac opened his eyes to see an annoyance.

"Bella, shut up." He grumbled. He turned and bumped heads with someone. "Ouch."

"What the hell Logan." He heard Nate groan. Zac flipped his eyes open. The Foster residence coming into view. Flashes of the previous day came to mind.

"Wakey wakey. Eggs and bacey. Actually, can you guys help us make food?" Bella asked. Mariah had a pleading look in her eyes. Zac groaned.

"Ask Evan." Nate grumbled too.

"He left to get us Starbucks." Mariah answered. Zac reopened his eyes and saw only the four of them. Hailey probably went to shower.

"Come on." Bella said. Nate and Zac sighed before following them into the kitchen. Bella and Mariah then began to take out items. They looked to know what they were doing, but Zac knew they didn't. They once almost burned the Carter Mansion while making cookies. Mariah was banned from her own kitchen for a month.

"Have you seen Hailey?" Zac asked after a while. Everyone shrugged. He sighed.

"Beach." Seth answered. Zac saw the youngest male Foster walk in. He looked tired but with a happy grin. He'd have to remind himself later to take him to the library. It had been a while since they had hung out.

"Thanks Seth." He told him. Seth waved as his face was stuffed in the fridge. He was probably looking for breakfast. "Make breakfast Bella. I'll be back."

He slid off the bar stool and turned out of the kitchen. He left his friends to make food, needing to speak to Hailey. He turned the corner, bumping into Ben and Josh. They seemed surprised to see him.

"Hello Logan." Josh stated. He still tried to act intimidating. Usually he was, but Zac needed to see Hailey. "What are you doing here?"

"Going to go get Hails." Zac said to them. He fished for his car keys in his pocket.

"What happened at the party and why are there so many teenagers in my house?" Josh asked. He was looking at the mess they had created in his living room. Pillows and blankets were thrown everywhere. Trash littered the floor and the curtains were still covering the morning sunshine.

"They slept over Josh. Now come on. We have to be great hosts and make food. I'm feeling bacon." Ben said. Josh gave Zac a pointed look before going into the kitchen with Ben. Zac quickly got his things and made his way out the door. He'd finally have time to talk to Hailey. He needed to figure it out once and for all.

-

Waking up with her friends in her home, she thought she'd feel refreshed and happy. She felt happy, but she still had that nagging feeling within her. They would all be leaving for college and she'd have to stay. She knew they were all going to big schools, with the Green twins going to an Ivy League one. She still felt jealous that they get to live their own dream while she'd be stuck at home, trying to figure out how to live her own.

The ocean waves began to splash as she stared out at them. She wished there was a sign that would tell her everything would be alright and everything would work out. She wanted to still be friends with them after high school. She still wanted to be with Zac, but she knew that would be impossible.

Zac would be moving to Michigan State and living his own dream. He'd become a starter on the football team and study biology. Zac would soon forget about her, which was what she feared the most. She was in love with him and wasn't ready to lose him after only six months. But, she knew she couldn't ask him to stay.

If she had the chance of going to the best school in Nursing, she'd go in an instant, even if that meant living Zac behind. She felt selfish as such thoughts, but she wanted to be like her mother. She wanted to help people who couldn't help themselves.

Her mother would tell her stories about those who would walk into the hospital. They all had hopes and dreams, while some were already living them. They'd explain how their life was and how they'd end up in the hospital. Sometimes it was because they were in the right place at the wrong time, while others it was simply because they ate a bad burrito.

Hailey laughed at that thought. She could still remember her mom telling her that story. They were here on the beach in the early morning. Hailey wrapped an arm around her body. The ocean breeze being rather chilly. She whipped her head around hearing a door slam. Her eyes widened as she saw her boyfriend. Was this that sign she asked for? Only, what does it mean?

"There you are Hails." Zac said walking over. He took off his shoes and let his toes sink into the sand.

"Hi." She replied back. She began to rack her brain for what this could mean. Does she ask Zac to stay with her or does she tell Zac to go follow his dream? She bit her bottom lip, unsure of everything.

"What is going on through that pretty brain of yours?" Zac asked as he sat down beside her. He noticed she was wearing a tank top and some leggings. He slid his jacket off and placed it on her shoulders. She had been hugging her body tight when he arrived.

"I know that you have been trying to talk about your decision Zac, but I can't. At least I can't until I decide to be selfless or selfish." Hailey told him. She had to tell him the truth. She couldn't keep hiding the fact that she wants him to stay. She wished his dream school was here in California. Then they wouldn't have to break up. Her heart broke just at that thought.

"Hailey, I want your opinion." Zac said with a frustrated groan. "If you weren't important to me or my future, I wouldn't be asking you for it."

"I know Zac, I just - I don't." She began to stutter. She didn't want to tell him her biggest fear. It was stuck in the back of her throat. She didn't want to place this on him only to veer him away from what he really wants, even if that's Michigan.

"Hails, tell me. Please." He pleaded. Hailey sighed. There was no way out of this. She had to tell him. She took another deep breath, closing her eyes.

"I'm afraid that I will lose you." Hailey said softly. She maintained her eyes closed. She felt Zac's hand grasp her own. She opened them and stared into his own. She saw the mixed feelings in his eyes. He loved her but he also loved his dream school. That's when she knew what she had to do.

"I want nobody but you Hails." Zac said. Hailey shook her head.

"You need to go to Michigan State. You'll regret it if you don't." Hailey said. Her tears were threatening to fall. He wanted her to make a decision for him, so she will. Even if it meant breaking her own heart.

"I don't want to leave you." Zac said. Hailey turned to look at him. Zac's own eyes were filled with unshed tears. She felt her heart begin to crack.

"You need to go Zac. You'll regret it if you don't." She said softly. Zac shook his head. He didn't want to leave her. His heart was torn between the two. Nate's words came to mind.

"Come with me then!" He offered. She gave him a sad smile.

"I would if I could." She said. She wanted to, but she couldn't afford it. She could have the best of both worlds. She'd have nursing and love.

"I'll pay. We can get an apartment and move in together. You wouldn't have to pay a thing." Zac said. She shook her head. She didn't want to have to diffuse the excitement he was creating.

"Zac, no. I can't keep letting you pay for things. Plus, University costs too much. Especially when you want me to go to one on the other side of the country. No. You already bought my brother a truck. You cannot buy my education, too. I'm flattered that you want to do all this for me and my family, but no Zac. No, it's too much." She said. Zac sighed. His body slumped. There goes that option. Now what? Would they have to break up?

"What am I going to do?" He said. He put his head in between his hands. Hailey rubbed his back. She had no answer for him. Only he could choose. At least she got the sign she wanted. No matter what he chose, she felt it in her heart that he would come back to her.

"Choose what is best for you and only you. Focus on the future. If we are meant to be, i'll still be here. Go and live your life." Hailey said. She felt her heart crack in half. She didn't want to push him away, but he needed to choose his best option, even if that means he was move to Michigan.

"Hails, I love you." He said. He turned towards her. She bit her lip. Tears were flowing down her face. He cupped her cheek, wiping some away.

"I love you Zac. Now, choose your dream." She said softly. Zac sighed, but nodded. Maybe she was right. If they were meant to be, they'd find each other again. He just wished he wasn't the reason for her tears and heartbreak.

~~~~~~~Two more chapters and the Epilogue!xoxo,Liv814ps. i have been lazy & unmotivated. i'm not sure why, but i just watched To All the Boys I've Loved Before & it motivated me to finish, so here you go.
~~~~~~~

Chapter 19 | Walk with Me

The crowd of people were loud with excitement. Everyone was decked out in their future school's colors and gear. They were in the high school's auditorium, ready to watch all the student-athletes sign their lives away for the next four years. At least Zac was signing to his dream school.

He looked up at the stands and saw Hailey. She was wearing a green t-shirt with Michigan State's logo on it. When he realized what he had to do, he bought her one. He wanted her to be supporting him from home. His heart didn't feel whole when he thought about her being so far away. But Hailey was right, he couldn't keep buying her things, especially her college education. As much as he wanted to, he knew he couldn't.

The moment he met her, he knew she was different than all the other girls he had ever met. She wanted to be independent and earn things on her own. She had goals and plans for the future. She wanted to reach them by herself. She didn't want to be anyone's burden. He loved that about her. He wished she could understand that he would buy the moon for her if that's what she wanted. He'd travel mountains and oceans just to reach her. That's why in his heart, he knew that he had to choose Michigan State.

Hailey would make a life on her own. She wouldn't need him. He knew that at the end of school, she'd still be there for him. They loved each other too much to just all let it all go to waste. They were going to do the long distance thing. It'd give Hailey the chance to do things herself, while still being with him. It'll all work out. It needed to work out.

"Alright, can all the athletes please report to their assigned table." Someone said over the speakers. There was rustling as everyone took their seats. He looked up and smiled at the love of his life. She grinned back. Just seeing her made him sure that this was all worth it. It would all be for her.

He fixed the hat on his head and looked out at the crowd. He saw his friends' parents sitting with happy grins. Nate was also in the stands supporting him. Nate hadn't agreed to any school. He wouldn't be playing football. Nate liked the sport, but not enough to continue playing it for four years. He still wasn't sure what he wanted to do with his life. For now, he would go to school undeclared.

Evan was somewhere in the room at his own table. He would continue to play football while learning. He was definitely the one to most be looking forward to furthering his education. Mariah also had her own table. She was signing to play college soccer at NYU. She screamed when she received the offer. She didn't think she'd continue playing, but knew it was fate to when she received the email from the coach.

While he searched the crowd of people, Zac saw his mom. She was sitting a few seats away from Hailey. That reminded him. They were yet to meet. He watched as his mom whipped out her phone and began to snap photos of him. He chuckled to himself. Those would surely be all over Facebook within the hour.

He looked back over at Hailey, feeling his heart race. She looked gorgeous in green. He just wanted to have her in his arms and kiss her until the end of time. He didn't know how he would last without her once he was at university.

"Alright, we will begin with the football portion." The announcer said. It was one of the many vice principals of the school. He didn't understand why so many were needed. Was there really that many jobs for them to do? They already have a big enough stuff as it is. Why do they need 6 vice principals?w

"Our first student is Zachary Logan. He was our star quarterback and team captain for three years. He is at the top of his class, with a 4.0 GPA and on the path to become our class of 2019 Valedictorian. Zac has chosen to attend Michigan State University, where he plans to continue playing football as well as major in Biology. Congratulations Zachary Logan."

The whole room erupted in claps and whistles. He grabbed the pen that was waiting for him. He placed it on the line to sign. He looked up at Hailey. She was smiling at him as she wiped tears away. This was breaking her heart as much as it was breaking his. He took a deep breath as people waited for his signature to appear on the sheet. He watched as she mouthed "I love you" to him. He then signed. That was the last little push of encouragement he needed.

The room got louder as he finished the N in his last name. He looked up and smiled at the camera. These pictures were going to be all over the news. Everyone wanted to know where the son of Mr. and Mrs. Logan would be attending college. At least there were people that cared for him because of his ability to throw the ball and not because of who his parents were.

Zac switched his gaze from the camera to Hailey. She had her own phone out. Her tears seemed to have stopped. He could see the torn emotions within her. She was proud of him, but he knew she wanted him to stay as much as he wanted to. But, they both needed this. She was right. He might regret giving this chance up.

"Next we have Evan Green. Evan was a starter on the football team as well for three years. He excels in the classroom as well as on the field. He will be attending the prestigious Princeton University. He will be continuing his athletic career as well as earning a degree in English. Congrats Evan on becoming a Tiger." The announcer said. Zac watched as his best friend signed the paper. He looked weird in orange. He chuckled to himself.

The announcer continued on with some of the football players and then went to some of the cheerleaders. Sasha, surprisingly, was amongst the crowd. She was signing to Oregon to become a Duck. Zac was glad to see she'd be moving far away from him. She was still crazy and in love with him. The threat about her sister ha definitely kept her away.

The announcer then began to say all the basketball players. Jordan was also there. He was signing to the University of Arizona. There he would be playing as a Wildcat. At least he wouldn't be near Hailey. She didn't need that kind of negativity in her life. The next group of athletes were the soccer players.

"Next we have the girls soccer team captain for two years, Mariah Carter. She has a 3.8 GPA and will be attending NYU for psychology. She will be continuing with soccer as well. Congratulations Ms. Carter." The announcer said. She gave the camera a bright smile as she signed. She was all decked out in the purple colors. She had blabbed about the the colors at lunch the day before.

Soon, all the athletes had signed. The only ones missing had been the spring sports since they were just beginning. They took even more pictures and talked to their college coaches. The Spartan coach was more than ecstatic to know Zac would be attending their school. He reminded him of all their big wins and how he would help achieve the Big 10 Championship. Zac chuckled to himself, only dreaming of that.

"Oh Zachary, I cannot believe you'll be living on your own in a different state." His mom said as she pulled him into a hug. She squeezed him tight, threatening to end his oxygen supply. He began to squirm out of her hold.

"Mom." He said in a very pained voice. "I can't breathe."

"Oh, sorry. I just have so many emotions on this day." His mom said letting go. He took in a big breath of air, trying to calm his lungs down. His heart had been racing and not like the way when he sees Hailey.

"I know mom. I feel the same way too." He told her. He turned and saw Hailey trying to weave her way through the crowd. His heart began to race again as she walked over. His grin was extended as she smile back at him. "Hi baby."

"Hey Zac." She said softly. Hailey felt a boatload of emotions as she saw Zac sign. She wanted him to stay with her, but going to his dream school was what he needed. He needed to have fun and live the life he's always dreamed of. She would still be there in the end. She would never be able to forget Zac Logan, even if she tried.

"Mom, I want you to meet my gorgeous girlfriend, Hailey Foster." He said. His mom's eyes traveled the length of Hailey. She was wearing a pair of ripped jeans with a Spartan shirt. She paired it all with some Vans and a black Nike jacket. Her hair was down in waves.

"Nice to finally meet the girl he's been gushing about. I was starting to think he made you up. Come here." She said. Hailey was then pulled into a death defying hug. Her eyes bulged out of her sockets as she took in her last breath. So this was how she'd die. She can see the news now: 'Teen Dies from Bone Crushing Hug by her Future Mother-in-Law'.

"Mom, you are going to kill her." Zac said separating his mother. Hailey gasped for air as Mrs. Logan let go. "Are you okay Hails?"

"Yeah." Hailey said, still trying to get enough oxygen in her lungs. She felt her heart begin to beat at a normal race again. "It is nice to meet you too, Mrs. Logan."

"Oh hunny, call me Abby. Mrs. Logan is my mother-in-law." Abby said.

"How do you feel about Zac moving away?" Hailey asked.

"Oh, sad of course. But, I knew that he'd want to move away eventually. His father and I are hardly home. Business just seems to run us instead of us running the business." She joked. Hailey saw the sadness in her eyes. "But what are you doing? I see you don't play a sport."

"Oh no. I am not very coordinated. I play catch with my older brother, but my arm was never great enough to be on an actual team. As for school, i'm not entirely sure yet." Hailey told her.

"Hun, if you need financial aid, i'd be willing to help. I had money donated to help Zac buy that truck for your older brother. By the way, how did he like it? I hope it wasn't too much. Zac just always talks about you and your family. I wanted to help in someway." Abby said. Hailey felt her heart grow with even more love for Zac. She turned towards him and saw he had a sheepish smile. She giggled.

"He loved it. Thank you so much for that. I will have to decline on your offer. As I explained to Zac, I want to get to college on my own, even if that means having to wait a year or two. My parents taught me to do things on my own and that's what I am planning on doing. But thank you, it means immensely that you would like to help." Hailey said. She was finally able to see where Zac got his compassion from.

"Of course. If you ever need anything, just call me. I know Zac would kill me if I didn't help his girlfriend out. So, shall we get going?" Abby asked. Hailey turned to ask Zac if he was ready and saw that he was with his friends. He must have excused himself during their conversation. Hailey watched as he laughed at something Evan must have said. Bella, Nate and Mariah were with them too. They all looked like the belonged with each other. Hailey smiled. Not only would Zac be away from her, but he'd also be away from his friends. They all would. At least the twins had each other.

"Go over there. Enjoy what time you have left with them." Abby said giving her a slight push. Hailey smiled at her before doing that.

"There she is! How was it meeting your future mother-in-law?" Bella teased. Hailey's cheeks flamed as she gave her a small push. Bella only laughed.

"So, what is the plan for tonight?" Nate asked.

"Sleepover at our house? We can finish having that movie marathon." Evan suggested. Everyone nodded in agreement.

"You just want to see what happens to Jenna. Spoiler alert, she turns thirteen again." Mariah teased. Evan rolled his eyes. "But, let's do it. We didn't get to watch Magic Mike."

"Oh no. Not happening." Nate groaned.

"Nate shut up." Bella said to him. Nate pouted. "We can each choose a movie. Now come on. I'm craving kettle corn."

-

Slamming her tray down, Hailey saw the twins in a deep conversation. She debated interrupting but chose to fill her stomach with fries. She had bought a cheeseburger as well and a yellow Gatorade. Did anyone know the actual names to those or did they just call them by their color too?

"Oh hey Hails." Bella said. Hailey gave her a closed smile as she swallowed her bite.

"Hey twins." She said. Evan rolled his eyes, taking out his English book. "Did we have homework?"

"No. I'm just getting ahead." Evan replied. Hailey sighed in relief. She couldn't start to slack with graduation so close.

"Hello my beautiful girlfriend and ugly twins." Zac said sliding into the seat beside Hailey. She giggled at his words while the twins glared. "I'm kidding. Hi Bells. Hey man."

"Hey." Evan greeted. He proceeded to stuff himself with his own lunch.

"Alright, we need to talk Spring Break plans. I'm think we throw her a huge party at her beach house." Bella said. Zac thought about it. She would be turning eighteen. They had to go all out.

"Who are we throwing a party for?" Hailey asked. She had no idea who they were talking about. It was the first she heard of someone's birthday. She should probably ask Zac when his was.

"Mariah." Bella replied. Evan then spit out brown liquid. He was drinking a bottle of Dr. Pepper. "That's disgusting."

"Sorry, but why are we throwing my girlfriend a party?" He asked. He had stolen some napkins from someone nearby and began to clean up his mess. He just kept moving around his slobber. Hailey grimaced.

"You forgot, didn't you." Nate said as he sat down. He was on the other side of Hailey. "Hey guys."

"Forgot what?" Evan asked exasperated. Bella narrowed her eyes at her twin brother.

"It's her eighteenth birthday you asshole." She said with anger. Evan's eyes bulged from their sockets.

"Fuck. I did forget." He whispered to himself.

"Now, since my brother here forgot about his girlfriend's birthday. I have created a plan for us." Bella said, flipping her head to her brother in annoyance. Evan glared.

"I get it. I'm a terrible boyfriend." He said with frustration.

"Beach party at her house, during the day and then we can have a sleepover at night. It'll be awesome. Mr. Carter already approved." Bella said ignoring Evan.

"That will work." Zac said. Everyone agreed.

"This spring break is going to be legendary." Nate smirked. The group had the same look. Hailey began to feel nervous. She had never really done much except go to her brother's baseball games. She would just work more hours and spend time with her siblings. She was looking forward to having something to do, but she didn't know what to expect from her crazy group of friends. Especially with Mariah's birthday around the corner.

-

Bright sun and splashing waves were perfect for the party they were throwing. They had decorated the entire Carter mansion with a beach and hawaiian theme. There were leis on everyone's necks and grass skirts decorating the tables. Energetic pop music was blasting from the speakers. Teens were in their swim attire, red solo cups in hand, enjoying their life.

It was the last break they would all have before summer and then they were off to college or university. Hailey giggled as she swung her hips side to side. Zac was beside her, encouraging her. She was enjoying the moment because she knew it would end very soon.

"Guys! Mariah is coming!" Bella shouted over the speakers. Everyone ran to hide. The music was shut off and the lights were turned off, not that it mattered. The sun was shining in through the all window walls.

"She is going to flip." Nate chuckled. They were hiding behind the couch near the front door. Hailey suspected that Mariah knew about the party. It was the talk of the school and cars were lining up her street.

"She's here." Bella whispered. She was the only one not hiding. They all peaked over the couch and saw Bella open the door for Mariah. Mariah had a look of confusion.

"Bells, why is my house dark? What are you even doing here?" Mariah asked. She had just come from a day at the spa. Bella had convinced her to go for the day. They needed her out of the house to be able to decorate. Bella then flipped the lights on, revealing everyone.

"Surprise!" The entire room shouted. They all jumped out of their hiding places. Mariah's eyes went wide before her mouth formed into a giant grin.

"Guys! Is this for me?" Mariah asked as she looked around. She waved at a few people before she focused her vision on her friends. "I am so lucky to have you all."

"Happy birthday babe." Evan said. He wrapped his arm around her waist and kissed her cheek.

"Thank you Evan. And thank you all. This is amazing." Mariah said. She then gasped. "I need to go change!"

They watched as Mariah and Bella disappeared up the stairs. The guys all drifted away, mingling with their other friends. Zac focused on the girl beside him. She was admiring how everyone got along with everyone, even if they weren't truly friends. He knew she still found it unbelievable that they weren't the typical popular group of friends that everyone feared. They were nice to everyone, well Nate still had his moments.

"You look gorgeous." Zac said. Hailey's cheeks tinted pink. He raked his eyes over her body. She was wearing a black swimsuit with an open back. She had black shades on her head for when they go outside. Her hair was in a high ponytail. She didn't have any makeup on, besides lipgloss.

"I can't believe you convinced me to wear this." Hailey said. She was beginning to feel self conscious again. She didn't like showing so much skin. She had shown up in a loose top and jean shorts, but somehow, Zac persuaded her to take them off. At first she felt alright. The entire party consisted of people in their swimwear. Even Zac was shirtless. She enjoyed that view.

"Babe, you look hot." Zac said as he wrapped his arms around her. She giggled into his chest. She began to feel all warm. It was one of the few times she had touched his bare chest. They hadn't gotten that far yet.

"Separate! We don't want any children yet." Bella's voice said from behind. Hailey and Zac pushed away and turned to see the rest of their friends. How did they leave and all unite again?

"I'm ready to party now." Mariah said flipping her blond locks over her shoulder.

"Then let's do it." Evan smirked. Mariah grinned.

"Let's get this mother fucking party started!" Mariah shouted. The entire group within the house screamed in agreement. The windows slightly began to shake which caused Mariah to giggle. "You guys are awesome. I can't believe you guys did all this for me."

"You are. We love you." Bella said squeezing Mariah. Hailey took a moment to look at their outfits. Bella was wearing a loose white tank top tucked into a pair of light wash jeans. Her hair was down in its normal waves. She was so casual. Mariah was wearing a blue crop top with a white skater skirt. She also put her hair into braids at the top of her head with the rest of it loose. She added a flower in her hair.

"I can't believe you guys did all this. How did you do all this without me finding out? How did you manage to convince my dad? I thought he was going to be home?" Mariah began to blabber on. Nate rolled his eyes at her dramatics. Hailey and Zac only giggled.

"Babe, chill." Evan said trying to relax her. Mariah blinked before nodding. She was always the drama queen.

"Sorry, Bella just made me take a few shots upstairs and I think I may be slightly tipsy." Mariah giggled. Evan swung his head to his twin. She was smiling sheepishly.

"Not that it matters, but we know how to keep secrets. Now come on! We need to dance." Bella said. She grabbed Mariah's hand and led her to the dance floor that was situated in the middle of the living room. Every thing was pushed away towards the walls or taken to storage. Mr. Carter did not want to come home to everything destroyed.

"Let's go play a game of beer pong." Nate suggested. Evan shrugged.

"I'll beat your ass. See ya!" Evan said as they both disappeared.

"Why are we always alone?" Hailey joked with a giggle. Zac only smirked.

"Because they know when to leave." Zac teased. Hailey rolled her eyes. She grabbed Zac's hand and led him out of the house. With all the bodies, the house was beginning to feel humid and claustrophobic. She stopped when they reached the small balcony. It had steps that led out to the beach. There were more party guests down there. Some were swimming while others were play beach volleyball. It was all a part of the party.

"This is my first time at the beach without just sitting on the sand and thinking." Hailey confessed. She then sighed. It was weird. She never thought of the ocean being a spot for drunk teens. It was always a spot for her to relax and think. It was her getaway.

"I'm glad I get to experience your first. You know Hails," Zac said. He placed himself behind her and wrapped his arms around her stomach, pulling her into his chest. He laid his head on her shoulder, feeling her shiver. He smirked. "I like being the one you share your firsts with. I convinced you to go to your first party. I was your first kiss. Your first real boyfriend. I get to be with you at your first beach party. I'm a lot of your firsts."

"I can feel your smirk." Hailey said with an eye roll. She didn't bother to confirm it by turning around. Zac confirmed it when he began to chuckle against her shoulder.

"Why are they throwing sand?" Zac asked. They were staring at the group of volleyball players. They resorted to sand throwing instead of hitting the volleyball. Zac was confused as to the type of people he shared a school with. Some didn't seem to have real brains. People like this is what he wants to get away from. They're just spoiled brats without a care in the world.

"They're drunk." Hailey giggled. She watched as one began to make sand balls, like snowballs, as if they were made out of snow.

"Come on. Let's go join our friends." Zac said. He grabbed Hailey's hand and led her back into the loud house.

-

"I'm tired." Hailey shouted in Zac's ear. They had been dancing while those nearby were grinding. Hailey never understood that. If they were going to have sex, can't they do it in private?

"Let's get a drink." Zac replied. He led them back out of the dancing teens and into the kitchen.

"There you two are. We've been looking everywhere for you." Bella said exhausted. Nate gave her a blank look. "Alright, we were just about to go looking for you."

"Now that's more realistic." Nate said. Bella glared at her boyfriend before turning back to Zac and Hailey.

"We are about to do cake." Bella told them. They nodded.

"Where is Mariah?" Hailey asked. It was just the four of them. The kitchen was still packed with people. Most were just standing and talking, while others were getting food and drinks. They had chips, fruits, dips, and treats placed around the room. Coolers were filled with waters and sodas, while the "adult" beverages were in the fridge or on the kitchen counter and island.

"Evan went to go get her. She somehow was roped into a game of beer pong. Evan doesn't really know how it happened. Mariah doesn't even like beer." Bella informed them.

"So, what were you two up to?" Nate asked with a smirk. Hailey's cheeks became hot. "Did you guys disappear upstairs?"

"Shut up Nathanial." Zac said in annoyance. He could feel Hailey become uncomfortable. Why didn't his best friend know when to shut up?

"Hey guys!" Mariah said. She was giggling uncontrollably.

"I think we need to get some water into you." Evan said coming up behind her. Bella went over to one of the coolers and picked one out. She unscrewed the lid and handed it to Mariah.

"I don't want water." Mariah pouted. She handed the bottle to her boyfriend. Evan glared in frustration before shoving it back.

"Drink babe. You need to sober up." Evan reminded Mariah. She sighed but placed the bottle on her lips. She managed to drink about half before she shoved it back into Evan's chest.

"I feel better now." She said with a bright grin. Evan and Bella watched her carefully before sighing. Hailey came to learn that Mariah was really good at holding her alcohol. She would drink a few drinks before downing them with water. She'd be back to being her bubbly self.

"We're doing cake!" Bella shouted. The music was turned down, but still playing. Everyone within the house started to gather in the kitchen. It was beginning to hold more people that it should. Evan went towards the refrigerator and took out a giant cake. It was pink all around with white lettering. They quickly placed the candles and let them. In unison, everyone started to sing happy birthday to her. She was grinning from ear to ear as they sang the last verse. She then shut her eyes before blowing out the candles. Cheers filled the room.

"Happy birthday babe. May all your wishes come true." Bella said hugging Mariah tight. Mariah then wiped her eyes. "What's wrong Mar?"

"Nothing. I'm just so grateful to have you guys in my life. I am definitely going to miss you all in the fall." Mariah said. She wiped her eyes as stray tears fell. "Enough of that. Let's get drunk!"

"Your girlfriend is a handful." Nate said as Mariah proceeded to grab a liquor bottle. She tipped it back, draining it of its liquids.

"I know bro, but I wouldn't have it anyway. It's what made me fall in love with her." Evan said. He was gazing at Mariah in a loving manner. Hailey began to wonder if that was how Zac looked at her.

"Damn, you are all so whipped." Nate said. Bella then proceeded to smack the back of his head. "Ow! What the fuck was that for?"

"You are also whipped. Now come on, let's go swimming." Bella said. She grabbed Nate's hand and pulled him towards the backdoor. Zac chuckled as Nate's eyes went wide. He was about to get it from Bella.

"I swear those two are such a weird match." Evan said in a low voice. He began to shake his head. "I still cannot get used to them together."

"Now, imagine if Nate were with Hailey instead. Now, that would be a weird match." Zac said looking at the girl he loved. Hailey's eyes widened at his words. He did not need to go there. That was a part of her life she'd regret. But, at least it got her and Zac together, even if it took longer than needed.

"Dude, don't." Evan said walking off. He was still shaking his head as Zac laughed. Hailey gave him a look of concern.

"What?" Zac asked. She was glaring at him now. What did he do wrong? He just joked about what could have been. He's glad she is in love with him.

"Can we not talk about that? I can't believe I almost dated Nate." She said in disgust. Zac began to laugh again.

"You dated that jerk Jack, too! But, at least it led you to fall in love with me." Zac teased. She hit his bare chest. Her skin began to tingle at the sudden touch. The butterflies in her stomach fluttered.

"Shut up." She said looking away. Her face was now warm from embarrassment. She loved Zac, but she still wasn't used to his bluntness about his love for her.

"Walk with me." Zac said. He took Hailey's hand and led her out to the beach. Tiki torches were now lit. The sun had set and most of the guests were drunk and having their time of their lives. That was what it was like to be a teen without responsibilities.

"Where are we going?" Hailey asked. Zac continued his little mission, not telling her anything. She frowned. She hated being out of the loop. "Zac! Where are we going?"

"It's a surprise Hails." Zac said. The sand between her toes was usually calming, but she was on edge. She wanted to know where he was taking her and why they were far from the party. You could still hear the faint screams and the music. A small bonfire had been started near the ocean while teens danced around. It was a safety hazard, but no one seemed to care.

"Are we there yet?" Hailey asked. She wasn't paying attention to where she was going, running into a hard wall. She placed her hand on her nose as she ached in pain. Maybe she should have been watching where her annoying boyfriend was taking her. She groaned.

"Shit, Hails, are you okay?" Zac asked. He had felt her body bump into his back. "We need to stop bumping into each other. It's beginning to feel unlucky."

"You are the funniest person I have ever met." She said with annoyance and full of sarcasm. She rubbed her nose as the pain began to subside. She took a moment to look at Zac. He was wearing blue and green board shorts and a matching blue button up. It was left open which left nothing to the imagination. His abs were on full display and she just wanted to count each and everyone. "What the heck did I bump into? A wall?"

"My back." Zac said. He placed his hand over his mouth, attempting to stifle his laughter. Hailey's glares only increased in intensity. Why was her boyfriend such a jerk sometimes?

"Who the heck has a steel wall for a back?" Hailey mumbled. Her face was beginning to go back to normal, that only stopped when Zac triggered her blush.

"I know i'm hot babe. You can touch my abs if you'd like. They're all yours." Zac said with a smirk. Hailey wanted to reply, but she was at a loss of words. How was he so comfortable in his own skin? She just wanted to put on sweats. She should have put on shorts before they left the house.

"So what are we doing?" Hailey asked. She was trying to change the subject and forget about running her hands down his body. He was so tempting.

"I just wanted a quiet place to talk with the most beautiful girl in the world." Zac said honestly. There goes Hailey's cheeks. Zac then sat down, wiggling his butt into the sand. He wanted to be comfortable. He looked out at the ocean. It was crashing against itself, yet it created the most peaceful sound. It was one of the things that would make him stay, but he can't.

"Zac, stop." Hailey said as she prayed for her cheeks to lose their color. She hated how easily he made her blush. She was never going to become accustomed to his compliments. She sat down beside Zac, enjoying the comfort the sand gave her. It was like a second home.

"I'm serious Hailey. I love you so much. I feel so lucky to have bumped into you because you are the most important person in my life. You have been so comforting and understanding these last few months that it only made me fall in love with you more and more. I know that it'll be difficult at first, but we'll make it work. You are the one for me." Zac said. He looked down at Hailey. She was grinning from ear to ear, looking out at the ocean. "I love you."

"I love you Zac. You honestly have no idea how much you mean to me. You changed my life for the better." Hailey said. She cuddled into his side, forcing him to wrap his arm around her shoulder. "I have walked alone, no one by my side. Now I walk with you. I finally have someone to share my life with."

"Even though, we have a few months left before I sadly need to leave, I promise I am going to make them worth remembering." Zac said. He loved having her in his arms. He knew he was going to miss that feeling. He'd have to buy a teddy bear and spray her scent on it.

"Any moment with you is worth remembering." Hailey said through giggles. Zac laughed.

"I thought I was the cheesy one." He joked. Hailey shrugged, not being able to shake her grin away. Zac always made her feel happy and whole inside. It was something that she had lost when her parents died. "But, I did have a real reason for us to be out here."

"What?" Hailey asked. Zac unwrapped himself from her and stood up. Hailey did the same. She was even more confused than before.

"I swear that if it weren't for that dickhead John, I would have asked you first. But now that he's out of the picture and you are my wonderful, beautiful girlfriend, Hailey Foster, will you go to prom with me?" Zac asked. Hailey stared at him. Was he serious? Was this really happening?

She looked into his eyes and saw so many emotions. The browns swirled together as he showed his happiness, excitement, hope, and love. He had begun to be so open about his feelings and that only added to what she felt for him. She knew he was the one. She was going to marry Zac Logan.

"Zac, of course i'll go to prom with you." She said. Zac let out a yell as he wrapped his arms around her waist. He then begun to spin them around as she flew through the air. She giggled as he looked up at her. She was grinning from ear to ear, giggling. These were his favorite moments with her: when she was enjoying life and forgetting about all the other problems.

"I love you so much baby." Zac said placing her back down on the sand. Her feet touched the softness right before she stood on her tippy toes. Hailey snaked her arms around his neck as he squeezed her waist to steady her. He was still a head taller than her.

"I love you Zac." She said. She stared up into his eyes, closing her own. His lips then touched hers. Each kiss felt like the first. They were full of electricity, fire, passion and love. They were able to showcase their emotions, those that words would never be able to do them justice. They were able to get lost into each other and only focus on themselves. They were the only two people in the entire world as their lips meshed together.

Their tongues fought for dominance as Hailey pulled Zac closer to her. She knew they were out of distance but even then, she'd try to get rid of it all. One of Zac's hands wormed its way down to her butt, giving her a squeeze. She moaned into his mouth. Her hands played with the strands of his brown locks causing him to groan.

Hailey's eyes then flipped open in alarm. She knew she had to stop the kiss or they would be doing more than talking on this beach. She wasn't ready for that. She untangled her arms from his neck and placed one hand on his chest. She gave him a slight shove. Zac opened his eyes in confusion. His eyes were darker and she knew what emotion he was feeling: lust.

"I'm sorry." Hailey whispered. She ducked her head down in embarrassment. It was one of the things she wasn't able to give him. She knew he was physical with his past relationships, but she wasn't ready for that intimacy. She still wanted to take it slow.

"It's not your fault Hails. It's mine. We will get there when the time is right. I'll wait years, even decades for you." Zac said. He placed a hand on her cheek, staring into her hazel eyes. They were full of doubt and worry. He hated it. He hated seeing her burden herself. "I love you Hailey. I love you so much."

"I love you too." She whispered. Zac leaned in and gave her a small kiss. He wanted to deepen it, but he knew it wasn't the time. This would suffice and he was more than happy to oblige. Anything for this girl. Anything at all.

Zac took her hand and began to lead her back to the party. They walked in peaceful silence as they got nearer to the house. They were supposed to be having a sleepover, but the house was still bouncing. As they got closer to the craziness, Hailey couldn't stop her brain from going into overdrive.

How was she so lucky to have found Zac? He was compassionate, sweet, genuine, respectful, and adorable. He knew what to say at the right time and he cared about everyone. He was understanding and reasonable. He didn't try to push her into things she wasn't ready. She smiled as they got near Mariah's home. Bumping into Zac was definitely pure luck. She didn't even want to imagine life without him.

Zac and Hailey went up the steps from the beach onto the balcony and into the house. It was still crowded with people, but slightly less than before. They pushed through the crowd until they found themselves in the kitchen again. Girls were dancing on the counter top as a group of guys salivated. What happened to all the alcohol that was there before?

"It's about damn time!" Mariah shouted. She was dancing on her kitchen counter with other random girls. She hopped off and smoothed down her skirt. She then walked past Zac and Hailey. They watched as Mariah grabbed a mic from the DJ they had hired for the night. "Hi! I just wanted to say thank you for coming and celebrating my eighteenth, but I do have one request. Get out!"

"She's so harsh." Hailey whispered. Zac nodded, chuckling at his friend's actions. She was also sweet. It was weird to see her so rude and blunt. Bella was definitely rubbing off on her. They watched as everyone began to grab their stuff and walk out the front door. Word began to travel fast as they were left with a huge mess.

"And then there were six." Zac stated. The rest of their friends began to gather around.

"This has been the most epic party we have ever thrown." Bella said in amazement. She began to pick up cups. Everyone soon began to follow suit. They had thrown the party, so they should help clean.

"You know I appreciate this all, but all I ever wanted was to be with you guys. I don't need a big birthday bash. Dinner and a movie would have sufficed." Mariah said. She had a garbage bag in hand as she pushed all the empty bottles from the table into it. They clashed into one big bang.

"Next year, we'll go see a movie." Evan said. Mariah grinned. She then placed a kiss on his cheek. It turned red. Zac had never seen his friend blush before.

"I love you guys." Bella said. She was wiping the counter tops free of feet marks.

"I love you all too. I'm going to miss having you all around. It's going to be hard not driving over to your guys' houses to hangout." Mariah sighed. The light atmosphere began to get thick. They had all been avoiding the topic of school, but that had become difficult when signing day was only a week ago. It was becoming real, too fast.

"We will always be friends forever." Bella said. She hugged Mariah and Evan. Soon Zac, Nate, and Hailey were hugging them too. It was one big group hug and they didn't want to let go. "Promise that we will always come back to each other."

"Promise." They said in unison. They separated and went back to cleaning. They joked around, pretending to shoot baskets with trash. Evan and Nate even had a race as to who could mop the fastest. Nate one which led to a series of groans from Evan.

During this all, Hailey couldn't help but think about the future. She only hoped that they would always remain friends. She knew she wouldn't be able to live without their friendship. They had made her life fun and exciting. She didn't want to go back to her old ways.

She sighed as she looked at her boyfriend. He was laughing as Nate chased Evan with the broom. He looked happy and carefree. He was just like that very first day she met him. That had been the luckiest day over her life. Bumping into him had caused her to meet him and the amazing people she calls friends.

~~~~~I know. I'm sorry. I move into my dorm tomorrow. Hopefully I can update after settling.xoxo,Liv814
~~~~~

Chapter 20 | Marry You

The school was buzzing. Girls were gossiping and trading beauty tips. The boys were dreading it. Prom was the next day and most had skipped school. They weren't even really learning since mostly all the seniors were gone. They were off getting perms, mani-pedis, and facials. Hailey was one of the few that didn't, but that was mostly because she had no clue where to get any of those things. Oh, and she didn't have the cash. She was going to try to save as much as she could for nursing school. She had gotten accepted into the same college as Ben to receive her associates degree. She still hadn't decide what her plan was, but she was going to take it one day at a time.

"Remind me why we are in school instead of at the spa?" Mariah said. She let her tray of food drop onto the table. Some of the lettuce from her salad flopped onto the tray. "I don't even feel like eating this."

"I still don't understand why you eat this leafy substance." Bella said with a grimace. She flicked some of it around. Hailey giggled.

"What are you two yapping about?" Evan asked. Zac and Nate followed his lead and sat down.

"About your girlfriend's horrible distaste in food." Bella said. She then bit the burger she had gotten.

"You have lettuce in the burger." Mariah pointed out. Bella rolled her eyes. She reached for her water bottle.

"So, where do I get the croissant?" Nate asked. Bella then spat her water all over Nate. She even managed to spray her twin. "What the actual fuck babe!"

"Seriously Isabella!" Evan shouted. They were soaking wet with water and spit. It was amusing and disgusting.

"Do not call me Isabella." Bella said through gritted teeth. Evan rolled his eyes.

"Now that that is done with." Mariah mumbled. She then sat up straight and put on a serious face. "Nate, I already ordered our corsages, knowing you three dumbos will not."

"What the heck Mar? Why am I brought into this?" Zac said. He had been beside Hailey, admiring her. She looked even more gorgeous than the day before. She was only wearing workout pants and a crop top.

"Because, I know you still didn't get one." Mariah said with an eye roll.

"Fine." Zac mumbled. Hailey laughed. She loved seeing Zac pout. It hardly ever happens, so she makes sure to bask it all in.

"Anyway, we have hair and makeup at noon. Pictures are at four and dinner is at six. Prom starts at eight and then we have the best time of our lives." Mariah said. She picked up her water bottle and unscrewed the lid. She placed it in the middle of the table, in the air and gestured for everyone else to do the same. She gave them a smile. "To us."

"To us." They said in unison.

"Remind me again why I agreed to this?" Hailey asked. She was restraining herself from itching her head. Her hair was currently being done by some hairstylist. She was nice and didn't talk much.

"Because Hails, tonight, you get laid." Bella smirked. Hailey's eyes widen.

"Bella!" She shouted.

"What?" Bella asked as if she didn't say anything wrong.

"Enough you two." Mariah said. She was laying back as a makeup artist did her face. "We are going to have fun. Now shut up."

"Sheesh. Control freak much." Bella mumbled. Mariah opened an eye, giving them a look. "Sorry."

"You look gorgeous." The hairstylist said. Hailey sat up with anticipation. Her chair then swung around to face the mirror.

"Woah." Hailey said. Her makeup was done flawlessly with a nude lip and fierce brows. Highlight was placed strategically over the high points of her face with contour emphasizing her jawline. Her hair was straightened with a few front pieces tied back.

"You are going to look smokin' once you have your dress on." Mariah said. Bella was nodding her head in agreement.

"You two are done too." The hairstylist said. Mariah had a satisfied smile on her face while Bella sat in awe.

"Bells, stop staring at your face. You look pretty too." Mariah said with a giggle. Bella rolled her eyes. "Now let's go."

"Thank you." Hailey told the hairstylist. Mariah paid her as they made their way out of the salon. "So, now what?"

"Now, we go back to your home to get ready." Mariah said. They piled into her black 2017 Audi.

"Remind me why we are getting ready at my house?" Hailey asked. When Mariah proposed that they get ready in her home, she questioned it. Mariah said her home was being deep cleaned and Bella's father was home.

"Because, we always get ready at Bella's and my house is being cleaned, thanks to that party you guys threw." Mariah said. Hailey rolled her eyes.

"Your house wasn't even that trashed." Bella said. She turned around and gave Hailey a smirk. Mariah looked in the rearview mirror and gave her a blank look.

"Anyway, we're here." Mariah said. She parked the car in the Foster driveway. They quickly got out of the car and walked up the front steps. The front door then swung open.

"Well if it isn't my little sister and her friends." Ben said. Hailey giggled. She gave him a small hug before pushing past him. The girls followed. It seemed like all her siblings were having a get together without her. They were sitting around the living room with drinks and chips on the coffee table.

"What's going on here?" Hailey asked. Josh smiled up at her.

"You look beautiful Hails. You look just like mom." Josh said softly. Hailey felt her heart drop.

"I agree. You will be by far the prettiest girl at the prom." Ben said. He had closed the door and was crushing her into his chest. Their words were making Hailey want to cry. They always told her how much she looked like her mom.

"Stop guys. You are going to make me ruin my makeup." Hailey said blinking rapidly. She was trying to stop the tears from flowing. Mariah would have a fit if she started to bawl.

"I don't want to be rude and empathetic, but we need to finish getting ready." Mariah said. She grabbed Hailey's arm, pulling her away from her brother. "The boys should be here in an hour."

"As you say." Ben said bowing down. Hailey giggled. Her tears were long gone and replaced by smiles.

"Your brother is so funny." Mariah said in a bored tone. Hailey laughed.

"So, are you ready for tonight?" Bella asked. She grabbed her dress from Hailey's closet. They had brought over their gowns when they picked up Hailey for the salon.

"No." Hailey said honestly. She tugged on a loose hair, still admiring her look. She really did look like her mom. She wished she was here to see her leave for prom with an amazing guy. She knew her mom would have loved Zac. Her dad probably would have been against his little girl having a boyfriend, but he would have warmed up to him instantly. He fit in his family perfectly.

"Put the dress on babe. You will be." Mariah said. She grabbed her gown and disappeared into the bathroom. Hailey reached for the bag that had her dress. She unzipped it and gasped. She remembered purchasing it, but it seemed even more beautiful now that it was hers.

The girls had picked her up a few weeks ago and took her to the closest prom shop. They spent hours looking for their dresses. Bella was the first to complain before she found the perfect one. Mariah had more difficulty, considering she was super picky. Hailey just didn't have an idea what she wanted or what color. She browsed rack after rack until spotting the purple magenta dress. She pulled it off and instantly regretted it. It was a two piece with cutouts. It was too provocative for her. Bella had come over and gasped.

"Hails, you need this. This is the one." Bella said. She grabbed it and headed over to the fitting rooms. Hailey groaned, knowing that unless she tried it on, Bella would not let her place it back.

"What did you find?" Mariah asked coming over. She also had a dress in hand.

"Hailey's dress." Bella answered. She then turned to Hailey. "Try it on."

"I love this color. I agree with Bella. Try it on." Mariah said. She then disappeared into her own dressing room. Hailey sighed but took it into the room. She slipped out of her jeans and top.

She put on the dress. It was tricky at first, considering it had thin straps that went around her stomach, connecting the floor length skirt to the halter crop top. She tied the strings around her neck and looked at the wall mirror.

She couldn't believe her eyes. She looked pretty. The skirt emphasized her hips since it was slightly high waisted. The halter top let her clavicles show while the small cut out in between her breasts was just the right amount.

"Hails, let us see!" Mariah shouted. Hailey unlocked the door and let them in. "Oh my god! This looks amazing on you. You need to get it."

"I agree. This is perfect!" Bella said. Hailey looked in the mirror again. They were right it was gorgeous. She needed to get it. "How much is it?"

Hailey reached for the tag on her back. She turned her head, reading the price. Her heart plumbed to her stomach when she saw it. She couldn't get this. It was much too expensive and she still had to pay for college.

"Now that's a bargain." Mariah said, taking the tag from her to read it. Hailey shook her head.

"Guys, I can't afford this." Hailey said. She scrunched up the skirt and slid on her jeans. She then pulled off the top and put her white tank top back on.

"Yes you can. Josh gave us some cash, plus Zac gave us his card. I swear that boy would buy you the world if you asked. Mariah said in awe. Hailey's cheeks grew red. Why was Zac always perfect to her?

"Now that we have that dealt with, let's go. I am starving." Bella said with eagerness. She placed the gown back in its bag and began to walk off to the register. Mariah grabbed her own dress and followed. Hailey stood still. She loved that dress but she didn't want Zac or Josh paying for it.

"Come on Hailey. Just live in the moment, worry about the price later." Mariah shouted. Hailey sighed. There was nothing she could do now.

Hailey smiled at the memory. She had to remind herself to never go shopping with her fashion obsessed friend. She would spend hours at the mall if Bella and Hailey let her. Hailey had confronted Zac about giving Mariah his card and offering to pay for the dress. He simply shrugged and said he didn't care how much it cost. He only wanted her to be happy which in return, made her happy.

She took the dress and walked out of her room. She would change in Ben's room. She opened the door, walking in. She scrunched up her nose in disgust. She looked around and saw a few beer cans and empty bags of chips. When was the last time those two cleaned in here?

She placed the dress on the bed and slipped out of her baggy t-shirt and shorts. She had showered before the salon and was already wearing a strapless bra for the dress. She was also wearing seamless underwear. The girls had suggested lingerie, but she quickly denied that option. She did not want to plan for that. If it happens, it happens because the time is right and not because she was anticipating it.

She slid on the dress and walked back to her room. Mariah was sitting at the vanity, adding lipgloss to her lips. Bella was in the bathroom. She was probably putting her dress on. Hailey hung the bag in her closet, reaching for her nude strappy heels. They were about five inches and still made her shorter than Zac.

"Oh my god! This looks perfect on you. You look insanely hot. I'd screw you." Mariah joked. Hailey rolled her eyes. Her and Bella's bluntness was something she would never get accustomed to.

"You need hoop earrings." Bella said walking out. She pulled on the ends of her dress and walked over to her bag. She then handed a silver pair of earrings to Hailey. She also handed her a few silver rings. "Now you look perfect."

"I feel pretty." Hailey said. She twirled in the floor length dress and giggled. She felt like a princess.

"You should! You look like a fucking princess babe." Bella said. Bella slid on her own shoes before cocking a hip. "So, what do you guys think?"

She was wearing a red spaghetti strap gown. It cinched at her waist and flowed down. It was made of a satin material. Her hair was in loose curls with it parted to one side. She wore a bold red lip with defined brows. She had gold jewelry on her wrists and matching pumps.

"I love this color on you." Mariah said. She then flipped her hair back. "Now me."

Mariah was wearing a pink dress with a crystal encrusted belt at her waist. The skirt was made out of a tulle like material. Her hair was like Hailey's. Top pieces were pulled back while the other half was down in curls. Her makeup was simple and elegant with some gloss. (pretend it's Evan)

"Girls. I think we did good." Bella said. She grabbed the bottoms of her dress and began to walk out of Hailey's room.

"Where are you going?" Mariah asked. She sprayed body mist on her.

"The boys are here. I can here Nate's voice." Bella said. Mariah nodded and grabbed her own things. Hailey did the same, feeling the butterflies in her stomach start to flutter. She hoped tonight was a night to remember.

When Zac arrived, Nate and Evan were punching each other in the Foster driveway. Zac rolled his eyes at his immature friends. He didn't even want to know what they were fighting about now. It always led to them punching each other in the face. It'll be over soon.

"Hey guys." Zac said interrupting them. Nate was about to sock Evan in the cheek but stopped. They both did. They had cheesy grins on their faces.

"Wow. You didn't try to stop us." Nate said. He ran a hand through his hair before straightening his suit jacket.

"I don't care enough. You two are children." Zac said honestly. He walked up to the front door and walked in.

"What the fuck Logan? We had been waiting for twenty minutes for you to show up to ring the doorbell." Nate said. They walked into the living room and saw the Fosters. They were playing Monopoly on the ground. Hailey and Trinity were the only ones not there.

"Language Nate." Josh's intimidating voice said. Nate straightened his body out. Zac smirked. That was why those two didn't come in. They're still scared of Josh. He would never tell them that he was a really a big teddy bear.

"You guys look well." Ben said. He sipped back a bottle of beer. Josh then pulled it out of his grasp. "Hey!"

"Nice try Benjamin." Josh said with narrowed eyes. Ben sighed and reached for a can of pop. "The girls are still getting ready."

"You guys want to play?" Seth asked. Nate shook his head while Evan looked like he was contemplating.

"We don't have time Evan." Nate said annoyed. Evan groaned.

"But I love this game." Evan argued.

"Who knew you were such a girl Green." Luke teased. He had a smirk on his face. Josh then picked up the dice and rolled them in his hand. "Yes. Pay up Joshua."

"Lucas." Josh threatened. Luke only stuck his hand out for the fake money. Josh sighed and handed it over.

"And we're the children." Nate scoffed. Zac only rolled his eyes.

"Presenting the pretty princess!" They all turned to see Trinity at the top of the stairs. She was dressed in her tutu, waving a wand. "I'm their fairy godmother."

"Well Trinity, present us with your creations." Ben said, encouraging her. She giggled.

"First we have Bella Green." Trinity said. Bella then began to walk down the stairs. Nate took in a breath as he watched her come down.

"You look beautiful sis." Evan said complimenting her. Bella smiled, walking over to Nate. He placed his hands on her hips and whispered something in her ear. She giggled before kissing his lips.

"Now we have Mariah Carter!" Trinity shouted. Mariah descended the stairs with a grin. She was always the one dreaming of being a princess. Even as a teen, Zac recalled she wished to find her prince. He believed that she did. She walked over to Evan. He stared at her starstruck. She giggled, waving her hand in front of his face. He blinked rapidly before placing his hands on her cheeks. She giggled as he leaned in. Zac looked away, not wanting to see them locking lips.

"Now, my favorite princess! My sister Hailey!" Trinity shouted. She then ran down the stairs. Zac stared up, waiting for Hailey. When she finally started walking down, he couldn't breathe. She was perfect. His heart was threatening to jump out of his chest. She was the most beautiful girl he had ever set his eyes on. And she was his and only his.

Hailey walked down the steps. Her heart was beating a thousand miles a minute. The way Zac was looking at her was making her want to go weak at the knees. She couldn't lose feeling, she was walking dow the stairs in five inch heels. She stepped onto the main floor.

"Wow Hails, you look like an actual girl." Luke said. Hailey narrowed her eyes at her brother. Why was he such a jerk sometimes?

"Luke, cut it out." Ben said. He then turned to look at Hailey. He gave her a wide grin. "You look great Hails."

"Thanks." She said. She gave him a hug.

"We need to take pictures." Mariah said. She handed her cell phone to Ben. Evan had his arm wrapped around her, pulling her close to his side.

"Yeah, before Nate takes off his suit." Bella said teasing. Nate rolled his eyes. Bella and Mariah proceeded to take pictures, making Ben their photographer. Evan was talking to Seth about who knows what while Nate stood by the door. Josh was staring at him with a brooding look. Those two were never going to get along.

"You look beautiful princess." Zac whispered the compliment in Hailey's ear. She took a sharp breath in at his sudden proximity. She hadn't even heard him approach her. He placed his hands on her hips, slowly tracing them upwards. As his fingers grazed her open skin, she gasped. Zac quickly spun her around, securing her at the hips. "This dress look amazing. You look sexy."

His voice maintained at a low octave. It was sending goosebumps down her arm. She looked up into his eyes. They were darkened. She bit her bottom lip. His stare was making her insides squirm. She's seen that look multiple times, but this one was more intense than before.

"Separate you two." Josh's voice demanded with authority.

"Come on. Pictures and then dinner!" Mariah reminded them. Hailey nodded, separating herself from Zac. Her nerves for tonight increased. Was Zac expecting it tonight? She shook that feeling away and smile for the camera.

-

Walking into the hotel, Hailey was amazed. They had decorated the ballroom elegantly with twinkle lights. The theme was Once Upon a Time. There were balloons everywhere. A castle near the DJ and a carriage near the entrance. The center pieces were fake trees, decorated with fake red apples. It had all the fairytales around the room.

"You're just missing the tiara." Zac joked. Hailey smacked his chest as they got deeper into the dance.

"Student council did good. Last year's theme was lame." Bella said. She was holding Nate's hand. She began to pull him towards the dance floor. He stopped her. "Come on Nate. Please."

"Izzy, we just got here. Can we just hangout for a sec?" Nate asked. Bella groaned.

"Come on. I'll dance with you in a bit. Let's go get food and some punch. One of the guys is spiking it." Nate said whispering the last part.

"Dude, who?" Evan asked. Nate chuckled. He then pulled Bella to the refreshments. Evan grabbed Mariah's hand and pulled her to the dance floor. He did always like to dance.

"And then there were two." Zac teased. Hailey giggled. It was starting to become a regular routine where their friends would leave them alone. She wouldn't protest against it. She didn't know how long she had until he'd be off. She didn't want to think about that.

"So, shall we dance or eat?" Hailey asked. She was looking around, trying to decide. She knew prom was a dance which meant that they should dance, but the food across the room looked equally as inviting.

"I want to eat." Zac said in a low voice. Hailey jumped as his breath fanned out on her shoulder. She could feel his heat radiating onto her.

"Let's go then." Hailey said, she began to walk but was stopped when Zac wrapped his hand around her wrist. "What's wrong?"

"Not that Hailey." His voice seemed to deepen even more. Hailey didn't know what to say. He had never been so open about that before.

"Hey Hails!" Hailey turned and saw Mariah. She was holding a clear cup with red liquid. Hailey had a feeling that wasn't just punch.

"Hey Mariah." Hailey said. She was glad Mariah had come and broken the tense atmosphere. Hailey didn't want to be alone with Zac. He was acting weird.

"Come dance!" Mariah said grabbing Hailey's hand. She nodded. They both started to walk off. "What was that back there?"

"I have no idea." Hailey said truthfully.

"He looks very possessive. Way more than usual." Mariah said. They had made it to the dance floor and started to move their bodies. A song by Drake was playing over the speakers.

"Hey! There you guys are." Bella shouted. The music was definitely louder in the pit. Nate was behind her. He was holding her hips as they swayed to the upbeat.

"Hey!" Mariah and Hailey shouted.

"Mariah, you left me!" Evan shouted. Mariah giggled and swayed. Evan rolled his eyes and stood behind her like Nate with Bella. Hailey then began to feel like a fifth wheel. The song suddenly ended as a pair of arms wrapped around Hailey's waist. She let out a screech before the familiar warmth settled around her.

"Baby, have I told you how gorgeous you look?" Zac whispered in Hailey's ear. Hailey bit her lip. His hands were now at her hips, holding her in place. She moved her body to the current song. She didn't want to turn around and see the dark irises in his eyes.

They continued to dance. Hailey was enjoying herself with her friends, being in the arms of the guy she loved. They were all having fun and not thinking about the future. Her back was still turned to Zac. A slow song began.

"Hailey, you have to turn around." Zac said in a teasing voice. She rolled her eyes but obliged. She placed her arms lightly around his neck as his were placed on her hips. They rocked slowly with the song. The lust in his eyes was long gone and replaced with love and happiness. "You're so beautiful."

"You're quite the catch too." She told him. Zac chuckled. She giggled.

"I know you think i'm hot." Zac said. He spun them around. Hailey laughed.

"Who said that?" Hailey played along. Zac smirked as he pulled her closer into his chest. She gasped at the sudden movement.

"Don't worry babe. I think you're hot too. Especially in this dress." Zac said. His eyes raked over her body, causing tingles to go up her arm. The butterflies that had been asleep began to flutter.

"Zac." She said softly. She bit her lip. She never knew what to do in situations like this. They had been occurring more and more lately.

"I love how innocent you are Hails." Zac said. One of his hands left her waist and was placed on her cheek. She leaned into it, closing her eyes. She was enjoying the warmth he provided. "I love that you have never done this or had a boyfriend before. I love that i'm your first."

"I love that you're my first too." She said softly. She opened her eyes and saw that the lust had returned.

"I fucking love you." Zac said, looking into her brown eyes. His hands were on the each side of her face. She was looking up at him with the same intensity he knew his had. Zac then crashed his lips on top of hers. He was kissing her with as much emotion he could muster. He loved this girl and he wanted to show her how much she meant to him. He deepened the kiss, biting her lip for entrance. She gasped, allowing him access.

Zac let one hand travel down to her hips, pulling him into her body. Her hands which had been on his face traveled down to his suit. She bunched up the sides and pulled him closer to him. She kissed him back with the same fire. She loved him, so much.

His hand that was on her waist traveled down and landed on her butt. She gasped which seemed to encourage Zac. She then felt him squeeze it, causing her to moan. She wanted, no needed more. She pulled away. Zac stared down at her with confusion.

"Let's get out of here." Hailey whispered. She was trying to regain her breath. That had been the best kiss of her life. She only wanted to continue it. She let go of his suit as Zac looked into her eyes. He was looking for any signs of doubt. He found none.

"I thought you'd never ask." Zac said pulling her away from the dance. He had other plans for them tonight and Hailey for once couldn't wait.

-

She had never been as nervous as she was now. She began to pace. She could feel her classmates eyes on her. She wanted to roll her eyes at them, but didn't. She needed to focus on calming down. It's not like she's the one giving the speech. She could only imagine how Zac felt.

Just the thought of him instantly calmed her heart rate. Ever since prom, the two had been inseparable. They knew that with graduation near, they'd have to say goodbye very soon. So, they made it their mission to fit in as many dates, hangouts, and sleepovers as they could. Hailey even managed to convince Josh to let Zac sleepover. That consisted of him allowing Trinity to sleepover at her friend's to allow Zac to stay the night with her.

The first few times, Josh kept coming into her bedroom. He seemed to not even sleep when Zac was there. After the fourth or fifth time, Ben suggested that Josh sleep downstairs. That seemed to stop her protective older brother. Although, Ben wasn't too happy about the situation either, he said he'd allow it as long as they had protection. Hailey was mortified and didn't let Zac come over for two weeks. Josh was overjoyed at that.

"Hailey! Stop pacing!" Bella demanded. Hailey stopped and gave her a sheepish grin. Since them and Mariah were a part of the honors classes, they were grouped closer together. Mariah was in the Honors Scholar group which was a few classrooms down and the first group of students to graduate.

Zac was the first of the entire class since he was Valedictorian. Hailey was immensely impressed. She never seemed to see him do any work, yet he was the top of the class. His testing skills must be excellent. Evan was also graduating amongst the first groups. He, too, was a Honors Scholar. Nate was the only one that wasn't graduating near the front. He took honors classes, but did not have the GPA needed to graduate amongst them. Plus, his last name was Price, so he was towards the end.

"I'm so nervous." She told Bella. Josh had dropped her off earlier. She was wearing a yellow body con dress underneath her white gown. She had straightened her hair and did minimalistic makeup. She didn't want to try to do anything extravagant in the hopes of messing up. She just did what she knew.

What she did know was that she didn't trust herself in the brown wedges. She had walked in heels before, but never on grass. They were graduating on their varsity football field. That was what made her most unsure. She didn't want to trip and have everyone laugh at her.

"Hails, everything is going to be fine. We're fucking high school graduates." Bella smirked. Hailey giggled, turning towards their supervising teacher. It was one of the freshman math teachers. She was sitting at the teacher's desk with her phone. She was also dressed in a black gown. All the teachers were wearing them.

"I just don't want to fall in front of everyone. That's my worst fear." Hailey told Bella. She sighed.

"If you fall, i'll fall too. You receive your diploma before me." Bella said. She flipped her brown locks over her shoulder. Hailey rolled her eyes in a playful manner. She had no doubt that Bella would embarrass herself more for her sake. They were best friends.

Just that thought made Hailey sad. Bella and Evan would be moving to New Jersey at the beginning of August. They were going to be renting and sharing an apartment. Evan wanted to be in a dorm, but Bella insisted that she couldn't do communal. Evan only agreed when Bella insisted that he'd get herpes in the dorms.

"Girls, it's time." The teacher said. She was now standing and her phone was put away. Hailey began to search her gown, wondering if it had pockets. There were none. She would have to place her phone in her boobs. She should have listened to the speaker at the graduation practice. She suggested leaving all personal belongings with parents or relatives. Now, she'd have to carry it.

"It's happening." Bella said grabbing Hailey's hand. They lined up in alphabetical order, leaving the classroom. Hailey finally saw Mariah. Her hair was in curls and she was grinning. Bella was right. Hailey should relax and enjoy this moment. In just a few hours, they wouldn't be in high school anymore. The rest of the groups began to combine. Even the guys stood beside them. Hailey got a glance of Zac before he disappeared out the doors. He was the leader since he was the top of the class.

As Zac led his entire class down from the classrooms to the football field, he felt like he was about to see his lunch. He had never been as nervous as he was now. Not even when he played in the championship had made him nervous, nor when he ask Hailey to be his girlfriend. He had no clue why he was feeling this way. He was only going to say a three minute speech to his classmates and their families and friends. It wouldn't be that bad.

"Oh god." He mumbled. He placed his hand on his mouth, hoping to prevent his upchuck.

"Hey man, are you okay?" He turned and saw his salutatorian. He was a shy guy that he had only talked to a handful of times. Zac regrets not getting to know him. He was too involved in the high school drama of hating the nerds and bullying them. If he could go back in time, he'd stop himself from his friends bullying him and everyone else.

"Slightly nervous." Zac said once his food didn't threaten to reappear. He continued leading his class, coming nearer and nearer to the football field. He was able to see the stands filled to the brim with people even lingering nearby. There were at least a thousand people in the stands. His class was over eight hundred students. It only made sense.

"Hey Zac." The salutatorian, Randy, called. Zac turned, but continued walking. He couldn't hold up everyone. "I know that I should be mad you are the valedictorian, but if I was beat by anyone, i'm glad it was you."

"Why?" Zac asked. He rounded the corner and walked through the entrance. The bright lights began to shine down on them. He walked down the sides of the track to where they're starting point was. They would walk down to their seats once the music began.

"Because you were the only one on the football team and that hung out with Sasha that didn't bully me. Yes, all your friends did, especially Nate, and you never did anything. But, you were always nice to me. I appreciate that." Randy said. Zac gave him a small smile. He did wish he could have prevented that from happening, but he knew he couldn't change the past. He could only change the future.

The music and speakers then began. Zac walked down the grass towards his seat. He felt nostalgic as he walked down the field he once played on. It was the last time he'd ever set foot on it. Next, he'd be on the Spartan field. He couldn't wait. He reached his seat and stood in front of it. The graduates had to remain standing until the last one met their seat.

He turned slightly and was able to see Hailey. He hadn't seen her since their morning practice. That was brutal. They were forced to be on this field at five in the morning. The practice took two hours and it mostly consisted of walking. They practiced how they'd arrive on the field and how they'd get to their seats. They also practiced the pace as to which they'd received their diplomas.

Hailey had been a nervous wreck earlier. He could only imagine how she felt now. He wished he could hold her hand and assure her that everything was going to be alright. He wasn't sure what terrified her more. If walking in front of thousands of people or having to say goodbye to high school. At least one would be gone at the end of the night.

He smiled as he saw her stand in front of her assigned seat. Bella was a chair over and was speaking to her. Hailey only nodded, biting her bottom lip. Zac was able to see her uneasiness. It almost made him forget how frightened he was for his speech.

"You may all be seated." Their principal said. Zac blinked a few times, registering her words. He then sat down. He stared straight ahead, ignoring everyone's words. They were unimportant now and they'd be after the ceremony ends. He just needed to hear for his name so he'd give his speech and again to receive his diploma.

"Now, for our next speaker. He is our starting quarterback, honors scholar and Valedictorian, Zachary Logan." The principal introduced him. Zac stood up, making sure his cap did not fall. He was careful to not trip over his light blue gown and stepped onto the stage. He shook his principal's hand before smiling at the camera. He walked over to the podium and slid out his speech. He unraveled it and took a deep breath. It was now or never.

"Hello everyone. I am Zachary Logan, but to my friends, i'm Zac. I want to take the time to thank everyone in the crowd of graduates as well as those in the stands for being here. Today is a very special moment in history. We are graduating high school! As we started to come near the end of the school year, I couldn't help but think of all the wonderful things that it has provided. For one, we all met friends that will last us a lifetime. I met my best friends when I was in elementary school. They have been with me throughout this entire journey and I only hope that everyone had that opportunity as well. I don't think I would have been able to survive without them.

"We also learned. That was the point of school, right." Zac said. He chuckled as the crowd laughed. "We learned things that we would need in the future. Not only how to find the area of a circle, but how to write essays and resumés, and how to speak a different language or make a meal. These are things that will help better our career, even if they did seem pointless at the time. I know i'll make a mean lasagna now."

The crowd laughed again. His nerves started dissipate. As he looked down at his speech, they began again. He would be talking about a future and one without Hailey by his side. He looked out at the crowd and instantly spotted her. She was in the fourth row with Bella beside her. She was already looking at him with an encouraging smile. God, he was going to miss her so damn much.

"As many as you know, I had been given such an amazing opportunity to continue playing football at the school I always dreamed of. I'll be able to major in biology while being where I belong at Michigan State University. I worked hard for what I earned and I can only thank our teachers and families for the support they have given us. They were the ones to push us to get what we want and now finally have.

"Today, is the last day we will all ever be together. It's sad and depressing, but it's also exciting and nerve wracking. We are now officially out in the world. Some may go off to college to further their education while others will go onto find jobs. No matter what you all decide to do, just know that you already achieved this tremendous milestone. You can achieve whatever else you want in life. You are your own person and can do whatever you like. Go out there and be the best person you can be. There are no limits.

"As we reach the end of my speech," Zac said. He looked back at Hailey. "I just want to thank high school for giving me the best gift in life. When I look back, I know i'll remember bumping into the love of my life and how I became the luckiest guy alive. So, thank you Freedom High School for the best four years of our lives. We did it guys. We finally graduated. Thank you."

The applause and cheers began. He smiled before ducking down. His heart rate was finally back to normal. He stepped down from the podium and off the stage. He walked back over to his seat and sat. He turned and saw Hailey. She was wiping away what looked like tears. She looked over and smiled.

"I love you." She mouthed. Zac grinned.

"I love you." He mouthed back. She bit her lip to stop herself from grinning. He chuckled.

"Now, we will begin to commencement of the diplomas." Their principal said. Zac looked forward. He was the first one. He got up and began to walk back to the stage. He should have just stayed up there. "To our Valedictorian, Zachary Logan."

Zac walked across the stage and received his diploma. He shook his principal's hand and smiled for the camera. There was loud screams and clapping. He laughed. He only hoped Hailey was one of those screams. She was definitely proud of him. He then walked off as they called the salutatorian Randy. He grasped the little book in his hand. It was crazy that he went to school for thirteen years just to receive this paper with his name on it. But, at least he meet the best people in his life. That, he would never change.

"Graduating with Honors, Sarah Elliot." Their principal called. Hailey watched as the girl in front of her was called. She walked up the stairs and then received her diploma. Her and Bella were on the field, in a line with other people behind them. Hailey managed to not trip on the unsteady grass but that didn't stop her from becoming even more nervous. What if she tripped walking up the stairs or when receiving her diploma!

"Relax Hailey. Just walk up to the principal as if she were Zac. Relax. Everything is going to be okay." Bella told her. Hailey took deep breaths. She was right. She learned how to walk when she was one. She had been doing it for seventeen years. It wasn't that hard. "Besides, Mariah is wearing freaking stilettos and managed not to sink in the grass."

"Graduating with Honors, Hailey Foster." Hailey widened her eyes. She was called. It was her turn. She grasped the railing as she walked up the ramp. She took deep breaths as she reached the top. She then only focused on receiving that paper. She put on a wide grin nearing her principal. "Congratulations Hailey."

"Thank you." Hailey said as the diploma was placed in her hand. She saw the flash go off so she turned towards the photographer. She smiled and another flash was seen. She giggled as she heard Zac scream that that was the love of his life. She also heard Mariah and Bella scream that that was their girl. She chuckled, exiting the stage. She felt powerful as she walked down the ramp and back onto the football field. She had made it without embarrassing herself. She continued to walk back to her seat. She passed near Zac.

"Congrats princess. You did it." He said. Hailey bit her lip, hopefully stopping the crimson in her cheeks. She continued walking to her seat, hearing Bella's name be called.

"Graduating with Honors, Isabella Green." Hailey screamed as Bella walked across the stage with a bright smile. She then did a little wave as she walked off. Hailey giggled. Her friends were always so extra.

After around five minutes, Evan was then called. They clapped and cheered for him. He also waved like his twin. Those two were always going to be inseparable. After about another fifteen minutes, Nate was called. Hailey giggled as they said his full name. She also clapped and yelled for him. Even if he still was a jerk half the time, he was still one of her best friends.

The handout of the diplomas continued for the rest of the class. Hailey would clap for the few people she knew. She even clapped for Jordan. When Sasha went up, she stayed still. She still didn't trust her, but at least with Zac's threat, she had left them alone. Now, she would never have to deal with her again.

"You many now turn the tassel to the other side." Their principal said. Hailey turned it, feeling proud. She had survived high school. Her parents would be so happy. She only wished that she could be sharing this day with them. They never got to see any of her siblings graduate. She knew that was what her parents wanted most. "You are all now alumni of Freedom High School. Congratulations class of 2019. You did it!"

The hats were then thrown in the air. Hailey threw hers nearby while Bella full on chucked it. They giggled, wiping away the tears. It was a rather bittersweet moment for them. They were now officially done with high school and there was no going back. Now, they had to focus on the future and build the life they want.

"We fucking did it Hailey!" Bella said throwing her into a hug. Hailey hugged her tight. "I'm going to miss you so freaking much."

"I'm going to miss you too Bella." Hailey told her. They hugged tight before separating.

"I want in on this girl hug." Mariah said. She had walked over from her seat. They all began to hug again. They laughed, still wiping away tears. Hailey was glad she chose the waterproof mascara today.

"Woah. Are we doing a group hug? Because, I want in." Evan said. He opened his arms wide and soon the girls were in his arms.

"Let go over my girl Green." Hailey heard Zac say. She saw Evan roll his eyes, ending the hug. Hailey then turned to see Zac. She felt her heart want to fall out of her chest. The look he was giving her was full of so much power and intensity. She could see the amount of love he had for her and it made her insides turn to jelly. "Hailey."

"Hi Zac." She said timidly. She walked over to her boyfriend. He grabbed her hips and pulled her into his chest. He wrapped his arms around her torso, hugging her tight. She then reciprocated the hug with just as much force. They knew what this graduation meant.

"We did it princess." He whispered in her ear. She shivered as his breath fanned her neck. He then pulled away, only far enough to look at her. Her heart skipped a beat again.

"I like your speech." She said giggling. Zac chuckled. He had worked on it for days, never finding the correct words. He wanted it to be perfect and showcase just how much high school will always be a part of his story.

"Hailey I am so glad I met you at that grocery store." Zac said. Hailey giggled. He had mentioned their bumping into each other.

"You changed my life for the better. Senior year was one heck of a ride." Hailey said. Zac grinned. He placed one of his hands on her cheek. She leaned into it, smiling at him. She had so much love for this boy.

"I want to marry you Hailey Foster." Zac said staring into her eyes. Her heart was now beating a hundred miles per second, hearing those words. Was he serious? Right now? They just graduated! "I know that we're still young and have our whole life ahead of us, but I promise you that I will marry you Hailey Foster."

"Zac, stop." She said looking away. His hand fell from her face. She felt a rush of emotions invade her heart. Thoughts of becoming Mrs. Logan flooded her brain. If her cheeks weren't red from his previous words, they were now.

"Hailey, i'm serious." Zac said. He placed his hand on her cheek, making her gaze up at him again.

"Zac." She said softly. He quickly cut her off.

"Hailey Foster, I promise that in four years, I will be asking you to marry me. I promise Hails. You are the one for me and I cannot wait to spend the rest of my life with you." Zac said before placing a tender kiss on her lips. Hailey fell into the kiss, thinking about how lucky she got bumping into Zac and falling in love with him.

Epilogue | Perfect

Clappter and yells were heard all around. Hailey felt the butterflies in her stomach begin to flutter as she saw the man she loved stand up. She watched as Zac accepted his diploma, smiling as he stepped off the stage. He was finally graduating from Michigan State University with a double major. He'd be receiving his Bachelors degree in Management as well as Biology. He'd have to run the family business soon, but he also had the degree in science in case being a CEO didn't pan out accordingly.

Hailey was proud of him and everything he had accomplished. It had been difficult for the two of them to get accustomed to not being in the same state. Hailey would pour herself into work and her family to forget he wasn't home. There were times where all she wanted was to be in his arms. They wouldn't even have to talk to fill up that space in her heart, but they were thousands of miles apart, so she knew talking would be all they could do. But, Hailey knew it would all be worth it in the end. It had to be.

Zac had it the worse. He would crave being near Hailey every day. He'd go to class and then football practice. Every second he'd be thinking of the girl he left behind. He thought he made the wrong choice of chasing his dream school because he was losing his dream girl. He began to search for ways to keep his mind off of her.

When football started to become more intense and classes started going deeper into their subjects, the thoughts of Hailey slowly started to disappear. He still loved Hailey and wished to be with her, but he was starting to let himself enjoy university life. He started making friends and hanging out with them. Overall, he was beginning to enjoy his new life.

He'd always make sure to call Hailey when he finally did make it back to his place after a long day. They had a three hour time difference, so no matter what time he called, he knew Hailey would answer. They would talk endlessly about anything and everything. Zac didn't even care if she was ranting about how Luke got on her nerves. He just loved listening to her voice. When they did talk, he'd imagine that she was laying on his chest, in his arms. He missed her, a lot. He'd count down the days until he'd see her again.

As the fourth year came, Zac and Hailey knew the drill. They'd call each other late at night and talk about their day. If Zac was playing in California, Josh would drive Hailey to the game, no matter how far. Hailey loved seeing Zac play the sport he loved. That's how she knew he made the right choice by moving to Michigan. It was only a small sacrifice they made in order to be even happier in the future.

Zac managed to help his team make it to the championship. It was the best possible way to end his football career. As much as he loved the sport, he didn't want to play professionally. He had a wonderful girlfriend he couldn't wait to come home to. Plus, as much as his father didn't approve of his choice in school, he was handing over the family company to him. Zac was nervous, but he knew he was destined for that. He'd try his best to be as great as his mother and father are when it comes to running it.

Over the years, his mother tried to be a mom. She would fly out once a month to visit him. Zac enjoyed that time with her. He would always cherish whatever time he had. Even if it did take her some time to start acting like a parent, Zac loved her and wouldn't change her for the world. Now for his father, he was still a strict and scary businessman, but he did call ever so often to ask how he was. Zac knew how awkward it was for his father, so he tried to make the most out of it. After all, they were his parents.

Another reason his parents were passing the company over to him, was because they were finally planning on getting a divorce. His mom had a great guy she wanted to marry. He had got to meet him a few times over FaceTime and once when he came with his mom to Michigan. Zac hated that his parents weren't a loving couple, but he knew his mom deserved that happiness. So, as soon as the name of the business is in Zac's name, his mom would be filing for divorce. Once that was set, Zac could start doing whatever he pleased. Zac was excited to finally start living his life with the girl he loved.

"Class of Two Thousand Twenty Three, congratulations!" The president of Michigan State said. Zac smiled bright. The day had finally come and he couldn't be happier. The president then allowed them to walk off the stage and find their families. Zac had remembered which section he had given his family. He pushed past a few kids and squeezed in between seats. He was determined to find the girl he loved. As he walked up another step, he finally saw her.

She looked even more stunning then ever. She was perfect in his eyes and he couldn't wait to ask her. He ran a hand through his hair and smiled bright. She still hadn't seen him. Her eyes were squinted as she stood on the tips of her toes. He loved that she was shorter than him.

"Hails!" Zac shouted. Hailey's eyes widened as her gaze followed the sound of his voice. Her heart began to beat erratically as her eyes connected with his. It had been almost five months since she had last seen him. That was definitely by far the longest they had ever gone. Usually they would fly out to see each other once a month, but Hailey had a reason for not coming.

"Zac!" She shouted. Zac's grin widened as he ran up to her. Hailey stood in her spot, giggling. Zac grabbed her waist and picked her up. She let out a high pitched squeal as he spun them around. He didn't even care that he may be ruining a classmate's picture. He was finally with the love of his life.

"I missed you so much baby." He said as he placed her down onto solid ground. She smiled wide. He was definitely the love of her life. She hoped he was excited to start their new life together. They had been planning it since the beginning of his senior year of university.

"I missed you too." Hailey said. She bit her bottom lip, trying to fight her cheshire grin from widening even more. She was sure she looked crazy.

"You know you're perfect right." Zac said. Hailey giggled. They hadn't even been back together for five minutes and he was already complimenting her. She only imagined what the rest of her life would look like. She cleared her throat.

"I have something I need to tell you." She said. She felt her stomach move. She took a deep breath as he watched her. Zac didn't know what to think. She looked nervous. Even four years later, he could read her like a book. He loved her with everything in him. That was why he was willing to sacrifice everything for her, but he loved her even more when she was the one who wanted to do the sacrificing. He knew that they would be able to get through anything.

"Hailey, what's wrong?" He asked. She looked down, not meeting his piercing gaze. He began to worry. Why the sudden change in mood? What is she hiding? What's going on? "Hails."

"So I know that you had plans for us of getting married and such, but can that wait?" Hailey asked. Zac nodded, not understanding where she was going. Was she breaking up with him?

"Hailey." He stated slowly. She took a deep breath. It was now or in five more months. It couldn't be in between.

"I'm pregnant." She said. Zac's eyes widened. He stood still. She began to feel nervous and scared. She knew he wasn't ready to be a dad. She wasn't even sure she was ready to be a mom and she had known for four months now.

"I'm - you. Me. Oh my god. Hailey!" He shouted. She squealed as he took her in his arms again. "I'm going to be a dad! You're going to be a mom! We're going to have baby! You're pregnant! This is amazing. Oh now, we need diapers. Will you need a bigger car?"

"Zac." She giggled. He quickly put her down, kissing the life out of her. Every kiss felt like the first. Bombs still went off every time they touched. She was more in love with him every day. She knew he'd made a great father.

"I cannot wait to start a family with you Hailey. I swear, you have been the luckiest bump in my life." Zac said. Hailey looked away, his stare becoming too intense.

"I love you Zac." Hailey said. She looked up at his eyes and felt a load of new emotions.

"I love you Hailey. I love you so much." Zac said. He placed a hand on her cheek before leaning in. Their lips touched, creating fireworks like never before.

-

She threw another pillow onto the couch. She wanted nothing more than to throw the lamp at the wall, but she knew she couldn't. There would be a gigantic hole that she would not be able to fix. Plus, she shouldn't be throwing furniture at the wall, no matter how angry she was. She let out a sigh of annoyance and frustration, letting her and her nine month pregnant belly drop onto the couch.

It had been four months since Zac graduated. They moved into a small apartment outside of the city in LA. He was busy working for the family company doing who knows what. She just knew he was high up there with other successful, rich people. She tried asking, but Zac told her to not worry about it. So, she didn't. At least she knew it was nothing illegal. The Logan's just ran one of the most powerful companies, owning almost everything.

"This is annoying." She mumbled to herself. She had been at home for the last month, doing nothing. The doctor had put her on bed rest for the last part of her pregnancy. She was bored and annoyed. She was even angrier that her siblings were off snowboarding up north. They offered to take her, but she had to decline. Doctors orders. Hulu and Netflix were not doing it for her anymore and there was no good shows on tv. She even did online shopping since she couldn't go to the actual store. She was desperate for some excitement in her life. She knew she'd regret not relaxing once the baby was born, but at least the baby would entertain her and keep her busy.

She got up again and walked out of their living room. She stepped into the kitchen and reached for a banana in the fruit basket that was placed on the counter, next to the bright blue toaster. She began to peel it when she heard the front door slam. She turned around and smiled upon seeing her fiancé. Now, she wouldn't be bored and alone.

"Zac!" She attempted to shout. She had just bitten the fruit, stuffing her mouth.

"Babe, the doctor said you are supposed to be in bed." Zac said coming to her side. Hailey rolled her eyes, biting her food.

"I'm fine." She said. She took the banana with her into the living room and sat back on the couch. She reached for the remote to power their tv. Maybe there was a marathon of some sort streaming.

"Hailey, you are supposed to be taking care of yourself and the baby." Zac said, reminding her. He loosened his tie and sat beside her. Even after five years, she was still the most gorgeous girl he has ever seen. Not a day goes by that he doesn't thank fate for bumping into her and changing his life. Now, they were officially engaged and expecting a child.

"Zac, I don't need to be in bed. I'm not allowed to do anything. Plus, i'm bored out of my mind. I was looking forward to going to the snow." She began to pout. Zac sighed. He sat beside her and pulled her into his chest. He could feel her body fighting his touch, until she relaxed in his hold.

"Baby, I know how hard this is, but in a few weeks, our baby will be here. You won't have any free time. Enjoy it while you can. We still need to choose a name by the way." Zac reminded her. She sighed. She had been putting that off because she didn't know the gender of the baby. If she started thinking of names, she'd favorite one name over the other and she wanted to equally love them all.

"No." She said. She turned back to the tv. A reality show about a family becoming famous because of their daughter's social media was playing.

"Hailey, come on." Zac said. He had a few names in mind and was dying to share them with her. He didn't know why she was protesting against it. He just thought it was because so many of their friends and family want the baby to be named after them. As much as he loved them, there was no way he was naming his kid after Luke, Nate, Ben, and Evan. Those four were the most persistent. Although, Trinity was making valid points last time they spoke.

Trinity grew up to be a very energetic teen with just as much sass as he first met her. She tries to visit Hailey as much as possible when she isn't at school. She joined the cheer team and was making friends left and right. She definitely was the more social sister.

Seth graduated high school a few years ago and was attending Dartmouth. Josh was hesitant at first since it was far away and expensive. Seth managed to get enough scholarships and financial help, that he didn't have to pay a cent. Josh was happy to hear that, but even more overjoyed to know Seth was going to his dream school.

Luke attended UCLA, until he decided to transfer to SDSU. He graduates in the spring and is planning on going into business. Zac offered him a job at his company for once he's done. Luke denied it, but Zac knew he'd want it then. The business world is quite difficult to succeed in, without connections. Luke and Tasha are still together, surprisingly. She is studying at UCLA still and was majoring in education. At least that was what Luke said last time Zac spoke to him.

For the next Foster sibling, Zac was surprised he wasn't staying with them. Ben was the overprotective brother who would not let Hailey live. When Ben first found out that Hailey was pregnant, he began to read and study every parenting book known to man. Zac appreciated his help, but needed to let him know that he would be there. That he was the father. Ben did start to ease up, but when the doctor put Hailey on bed rest, he was at their home every spare moment. Zac could tell in annoyed Hailey.

"Josh sent a picture of them." Hailey said. Her phone had rang in the middle of their little dispute. She unlocked it and revealed a picture of her siblings in their gear. She sighed. She missed them all, but she was glad Ben was gone for the week. He had been an annoying fly she couldn't seem to shoo away. He was at her beck and call, which she liked, at first. Then, he began to ask her silly questions and not let her be. She loved Ben, but he needed a girlfriend to focus his attention to. Maybe he'd be the one with kids next.

"You told Josh were are naming our kid after him, right. Besides, it could be a girl." Zac said. Hailey nodded. Josh was still the only father figure she had in her life, but even he didn't know what it was like to be carrying a child. He did have a girlfriend of a year who owns a restaurant in the city. They met when her place needed repairs. Josh now owns his own company and fixed it up. Guess love at first sight did exist.

"Fine Zac. Since you are not going to let this be, what do you want to name our child?" She asked. She turned the volume down and placed her free hand on her stomach. She could feel their daughter or son kicking. She smiled. It was still surreal to her to be carrying another human being within her.

"If it's a girl, I was thinking of Rachel." He replied. Hailey bit her bottom lip. She didn't really like that name.

"I thought of Zoey. Since your name starts with a Z." She said. She waited for Zac's response. She didn't want to hope for a specific gender, but she secretly wanted a son. She wanted a boy first so she could have a protective brother for their daughter. She wanted her to know what it was like to have someone there for you in a time of need. She doesn't want to think about a life without Ben and Josh.

"For a boy, I was thinking of Cody or Preston." Zac said. Hailey kind of liked those names.

"What about Xavier or Cole?" Hailey offered. Zac sat back in thought.

"What about we mix Cole and Preston? What about Colton?" Zac asked. She was about to reply when she felt a hard pain in her stomach. What is going on?

"Ow!" She cried out. Zac's eyes widened. Why was she in pain?

"What's wrong?" He asked. Hailey tried to reply, but another sharp shooting pain erupted from her stomach again. "Did you just pee?"

Hailey looked down and saw that her sweats were soaked. She didn't remember having to pee. She felt another pain and gripped Zac's shoulder. He grimaced but ignored it. He then reached for his phone, dialing. It was time.

"Hello?" He heard come from the phone.

"Bella, it's happening. Call everyone else." Zac said before hanging up. He then dialed a new number.

"Zac, what's wrong?" Josh's voice said. He turned to see Hailey gripping the pillow. She was in labor and he needed to get her to the hospital now. He stood up with the phone pressed in between his ear and shoulder.

"Hailey, we need to get you to the hospital." Zac said. He was speaking to Hailey, but Josh needed to know.

"Zac, what's going on?" Josh asked again. Hailey nodded, breathing fast.

"In through your nose and out through your mouth Hailey. You're going to have our kid." Zac said. Josh's breathing stopped on the line.

"We'll be there as fast as we can." Josh said before hanging up. Zac slid his phone into his pocket. He grabbed Hailey's hand and wrapped the other around her back.

"Are you ready to see our beautiful creation?" Zac asked. Hailey turned to look at him with deadly eyes. He had never seen her so angry.

"Get me to the fucking hospital Zachary!" She shouted. She went back to her breathing exercise, gripping his hand. Zac nodded. They made their way to the front door and grabbed her bag. They had made a hospital bag when the doctor put her on bed rest. It had the essentials needed for her hospital stay.

He shut the door behind them and made their way to his car. He had traded in his Challenger for a more suitable family car. It already had the baby seat and everything. He would miss his sport car, but the safety of his kid, would trump that. Now, he was a soccer dad in a Chevy Tahoe.

"Help me in." Hailey said through gritted teeth. Zac dropped the bag onto the concrete and helped her get in. Her placed the seatbelt around her and shut the door. He picked up the bag and threw it into the back seat. He then ran to the driver's side and started the car.

"I love you Hailey." Zac said as he reversed. Hailey was screeching in pain. He hated that he couldn't make her feel better. That was the one thing he hated the most: not being able to protect her or prevent her from being hurt.

"Drive Zac." She said when the pain seemed to have stopped. Zac nodded, accelerating the car. They were about to have a baby.

-

Zac let out a breath, slipping off his mask. The was the most gruesome and tiring thing he has ever seen. He wasn't sure how Hailey was able to be in labor for over ten hours. He thought it was just the water opens and here comes the baby. He had no idea about her having to be dilated.

"Alright Mr. Logan, you may go out and introduce your baby to your family." The doctor said. Zac nodded, feeling his body yearning for sleep. It was now around six in the morning. He had been up for over twenty-four hours.

Zac pushed the hall doors open towards the small waiting room. He looked around and saw that his family and friends took up the entire area. He chuckled. Of course they would all be here. He walked up to him and they all stood up with excitement.

"How is she?" Ben asked first.

"Great. She's really tired, but she did great." Zac said with a grin. And she had been. She was the most amazing person he had ever met and it only made him fall in love with her even more.

"Can we see her?" Josh asked. Zac nodded. "Come on Trinity."

"We're here!" He heard his best friend's voice. He turned and saw his best friends running into the waiting room. He chuckled. They probably snuck off to the cafeteria. "Is baby Nate born?"

"It's baby Evan!" Evan shouted. Nate rolled his eyes.

"It's neither of those. It's Isabella." Bella said next. Nate wrapped his arm around his wife. They had gotten married a year before and living together nearby. They had a gold retriever and were trying for kids. Nate was busy working for his father's company and Bella was psychologist.

"You guys are so immature." Zac said chuckling. Even though his friends lived close by, he hardly saw them. They were busy with their adult lives, but they did try to at least meet up once a month.

"Where's Mar?" Zac asked. Evan sighed, scratching the back of his head.

"Work. She wanted to be here really bad, but she had some big client coming in for an interview." Evan answered. Zac nodded. Mariah would have definitely been the first one here. She has had baby fever for years. Her and Evan still aren't married, but they do live together. So, for now, Mariah's baby is her magazine. She was one of the writer's for US Weekly. When she graduated with her journalism degree, she had been writing for multiple newspapers and magazines. Evan helped her write sometimes. His English degree definitely came in handy.

"Are you guys done with your reunion?" Ben asked with annoyance.

"Sheesh. Sorry I haven't seen my best friend in a few weeks." Nate said with an eye roll. Ben gave him a blank look. They still didn't get along.

"Alright. Come on. Let's go." Zac said. He turned on his heel and walked back through the double doors. The seven of them made their way down the hall. Luke was on his way, while Seth was still at school.

Hailey felt calm and at ease, knowing that her baby was finally here with them. She gazed down at her mini me. Zac and her made a beautiful baby. She grabbed the small little hand, smiling. Crazy to think how a small human was within her stomach. It's a miracle.

"Your favorite sibling is here!" She heard Ben's voice say. She turned and widened her eyes in shock. Her family and friends were all blocking the doorway, sliding in. Had they all been here the entire time?

"Wow. All of you are actually here so early." She said chuckling. Zac quickly made his way over and leaned down. He gave her a chaste kiss before standing straight.

"So, can we see the baby? Is it a boy or girl?" Bella asked with excitement. Hailey giggled. She pulled down the soft, blue blanket.

"This is baby Colton." She said. She cradled him into his chest. He had bright blue eyes and brown hair. He was beautiful. He looked like his dad, but with his mother's nose.

"He's so cute." Trinity said. She was eyeing the baby with adoration. Hailey smiled. They had made a beautiful baby.

"I love that name." Bella said.

"I'm salty you didn't name him after his godfather." Ben said in a pout. Hailey rolled her eyes.

"Who named you that?" Nate asked with a glare. Josh scoffed.

"I'm the godfather." Josh said. All the boys in the room turned to look at Zac and Hailey. Hailey bit her bottom lip. She knew this would happen. The boys are all so territorial.

"Actually, we decide to name Seth the godfather." Zac answered as he dialed the brother. He quickly put him on FaceTime as he said those words. Everyone was in shock. "He helped me win Hailey's heart."

"I'm honored." He said as he came onto the screen. Hailey smiled as she saw her youngest brother. He was so much older and wiser now. He was definitely perfect for the role. When they first discussed it, Zac had instantly said Ben. She wanted to agree, but she knew Ben would soon be even busier. He had graduated a few years back and was working at some company. He was making some money and still playing baseball. He definitely would not have time to take care of a child. Zac then suggested Seth.

Hailey remembered when Zac first met him. Seth was instantly in awe with him for inviting him to the library. She remembered that he was Zac's little spy. It's crazy to think that when she was crazy about Zac, she believed he didn't reciprocate those feelings. Yet, he did and he used Seth to help. That's why they chose him.

"So, who wants to hold him first?" Hailey asked. Hands and arms flew at her. She chuckled before passing her son to her eldest brother first.

-

Hailey's heart grew as she saw little Colton walking. He was nearing one which made him start crawling everywhere. Just recently, he discovered that he could stand on his two feet and walk. It was rather convenient since he was the ring barer for the wedding today.

She looked down at her dress. She felt beautiful in it, more than she has ever felt before. It was a rather simple white dress. It flowed down to her feet, hugging her body. The top was a simple strapless, sweetheart neckline. There were no embellishments or detailing. There was no train either. They were going to have a small, intimate ceremony with their closest family and friends.

Zac's mom had fought her on it since Zac proposed. She wanted to have a big, royal wedding. She wanted to invite everyone they knew and some they didn't. She wanted it to be the talk of the town since Zac Logan was finally getting married. Even though, they were only twenty-three, it was a big deal apparently. People thought Zac would never find a girl. Guess they didn't know about Hailey.

"Hailey, you look so beautiful." Mariah said. She was curling her brown locks while Bella did her makeup. Abby, Zac's mom, walked in, wiping away a few tears.

"You are the most stunning bride I have ever seen." Abby said. Hailey's cheeks rose in heat. She knew to expect compliments today, but still didn't know how to actually accept them.

"Zac is going to die and go to heaven." Bella said as she placed some pink lipgloss on Hailey's lips. "And, i'm done."

"Me too." Mariah said unplugging the wand. She then picked up Colton. "This little fellow is the cutest baby boy I have ever seen."

"He is." Hailey said seeing as her son giggled in her friend's arms.

"Are you ready?" Bella asked. Hailey looked at the clock and saw that the ceremony would be starting.

"Yeah. I am." Hailey said. She grabbed the bottom of her dress and began to walk. The girls and Abby followed behind with Colton. Hailey's nerves were beginning to spring life. She wasn't sure why she was anxious. Zac and her had been talking about marriage since their high school graduation and here they were five years later. She was ready to become his wife.

They began to walk out of the building. They were having their ceremony outside and on the sand. It was summer and breezy. It was going to be perfect. She could see her family and friends gathered around. They were busy chatting amongst themselves.

"Hails, you look beautiful." Josh said as he walked up. He would be walking her down the aisle. She wished her parents could be here today, but she knew they were watching from above. She could imagine her dad beside her while her mom held back tears.

"Thank you Josh." She said. The music began to play. Everyone took their places. Usually, the bridesmaids would walk down first, but they were just going to stand at the end. Only Colton would walk down. She watched as Abby held Colton's hand. He was giggling as he walked. He had the rings on a necklace, tied around his neck.

"Are you ready?" Josh asked when Colton reached the end. Hailey took a deep breath, nodding.

"I have never been more ready." She said. She wrapped her arm around Josh's and they began to walk. She took notice at those with them. She smiled, feelings her tears start to threaten. There were only about thirty people here, watching them with happiness. Zac was at the end, staring at her with love. Nate, Evan, and Ben were his groomsmen while Bella, Mariah, and Trinity were her bridesmaids.

As Zac watched Hailey walk towards him, he felt his heart stop. He was finally marrying the girl of his dreams and the mother of his son. He couldn't wait to make her officially his wife. He imagined this day since the moment he knew he loved her. She was perfect.

"We are gathered here today, to celebrate Hailey Foster and Zachary Logan in holy matrimony. You may all take your seats." The minister said. Hailey stared into Zac's eyes the entire time. She only paid attention to the words being said when it was time for the vows. "Zachary, you may go first."

"Hailey Foster, you are the love of my life and I think I knew it since the moment I met you. I didn't think that bumping into you at the grocery store would ever make such an impact in my life. Yet, here we are. These last six years, I have been the happiest man alive. We have gone through long distance for four years and only fell more in love. I cannot thank you enough for giving me a chance. I am so happy to finally call you my wife. I love you so much Hails." Zac said. Hailey wiped away a tear.

"Hailey." The minister said. Hailey sniffled before speaking.

"Zac, I think you made an even bigger impact on me. I was this shy, closed off girl since my parents had passed away. Bumping into you, while you shopped for party supplies, opened up my eyes. You introduced me to people who are now my best friends. You showed me what friendship and love was. You showed me how to live. Thank you Zac for being there for me since the start. I love you so much and I can't wait to start our life together. Besides, Colton over there is ready for a diaper change." Hailey said through a giggle. Zac grimaced before laughing.

"Do you, Zachary Logan, take Hailey Foster as your wedded wife to live together in marriage? Do you promise to love her, comfort her, honor and keep her for better or worse, for richer or poorer, in sickness and health and forsaking all others, be faithful only to her so long as you both shall live?" The minister asked.

"I do." Zac said. His mom passed him the wedding rings that we around his son's neck. He took one and placed it on Hailey's finger. She was staring at him through teary eyes.

"Do you, Hailey Foster, take Zachary Logan as your wedded husband to live together in marriage? Do you promise to love him, comfort him, honor and keep him for better or worse, for richer or poorer, in sickness and health and forsaking all others, be faithful only to him so long as you both shall live?" The minister repeated. Hailey nodded.

"I do." She said. Zac passed her the ring which she placed on his finger. She felt a tear slip down her face. Thank god Bella used waterproof mascara.

"With all the power vested in me, I now pronounce you husband and wife. You may now kiss the bride." The minister said. Zac didn't waste a second. He placed his lips on hers. They moved in sync as claps and whistles went off around them. Hailey giggled into the kiss. She was definitely the happiest person on earth right now and it was all thanks to him.

"I can't wait until we're alone." Zac whispered. Her eyes went wide. She looked down at her stomach. Zac was going to flip with the news.

"I can't either. I have a surprise for you." She said. Zac grabbed her hand and they walked back down the aisle. Their reception was inside. They would celebrate with their family and friends, before whisking off to a hotel nearby. They walked into the hall and saw the whole placed adorned. It was elegant and beautiful. Flowers were placed as center pieces and twinkling lights were strung around the room.

"This is gorgeous." Hailey said.

"You're gorgeous." Zac replied. She rolled her eyes in a playful matter. "Let's dance."

"Right now?" Hailey asked. Zac pulled her to the middle of the dance floor as their guests walked in. They all began to take their spot. Zac pulled his wife into his arms. She wrapped hers around his neck.

"I love you Mrs. Logan." Zac said. He looked down at her, making her heart skip a beat. They began to sway to a song. It was 'Perfect' by Ed Sheeran.

"I love you Mr. Logan." She replied. She gazed up at her husband. Yep, definitely the happiest woman on earth.

"Baby, I'm dancing in the dark, with you between my arms. Barefoot on the grass, listening to our favorite song. I have faith in what I see. Now I know I have met an angel in person. And she looks perfect. I don't deserve this. You look perfect tonight." Zac sang as they twirled. She giggled. A smile was on her face and she knew she'd never be able to get rid of it.

"You're the perfect one.." Hailey said with a giggle. Zac chuckled.

"I'm supposed to be the cliché one." Zac said. Hailey shrugged.

"Well, then I am so happy I bumped into you." Hailey said. She gazed into his brown eyes, seeing all the love he had for her.

"And, i'm happy I bumped into you." Zac said before dipping his head down. They kissed, feeling every emotion coursing through their veins. They were finally getting their happily ever after.

-

"Colton!" Hailey shouted. She was tapping her foot. Her son had been a trouble maker since he hit puberty. With his dad's looks, he seemed to be out of control. Girls walked in and out of this house, and Hailey had just walked into her own home to see one parading in a bikini.

"What mom?" Colton shouted. He was walking into the kitchen with a towel wrapped around his body.

"I leave to get groceries and come back to a pool party!" She shouted. Colton rolled his eyes. "Do not be disrespectful young man."

"Sorry mom. I asked dad if I could have a few friends over." Colton said with a shrug. Hailey's temper began to flair. Colton definitely knew how to work his dad. When Zac found out that Colton wanted to play soccer, he was devastated. He tried to convince him to at least try it for a season, but Colton was good at kicking a ball. Not so much at catching it.

"Just get them out of here." Hailey said in defeat. She could feel Colton's smirk. He was just like his father. Hailey turned away and began to unload the groceries and placing them in their respective places.

"Babe, your home." She heard her husband's voice. His arms wrapped around her body. She giggled as he placed his chin on her shoulder.

"I'm mad at you." She said, fighting a grin.

"What did I do now?" Zac asked. Hailey giggled.

"You let Colton have a pool party! What if Lily was here? Would you let her parade around like those girls he brings home?" Hailey asked. Zac tensed at the mention of his daughter. She was over at Evan's for the night. They had a daughter the same age and the two were best friends.

"No." Zac said in defeat. Hailey smirked in triumph. "But, i'm sorry. I thought when he asked for a few friends, he meant some of the guys from the soccer team."

"When you asked to have friends over, did you mean some guys from the football team?" Hailey asked. Zac shrugged. She rolled her eyes. Zac's parents were careless when he was younger, so he was definitely teaching his son differently.

"So, what's for dinner?" Zac asked. Hailey opened the freezer door and pulled out a pizza. "Again?"

"When we first met, I told you I didn't really know how to cook. We've been married for over seventeen years, do you think that's really changed? Besides, I have a shift at the hospital tonight." Hailey said. She placed the pizza on the baking sheet and place it in the oven. She did learn how to cook, but she liked reminding Zac that she didn't. He was always the better cook anyway. Plus, she had the late shift as an ER nurse.

After they found out Lily was on the way, Hailey began to study to be a nurse. She took some classes and did some interning. She had to stop when her belly began to really grow. After Lily turned four months, Hailey returned to school and got her degree in nursing. She did simple things at the doctors' office while her children grew. When they were old enough to be in elementary school, she took up a job at the hospital. She's been there since and she's loved every second of it. She knew her mom would be proud of her.

"Fine, we'll eat pizza. We'll have a guy's night." Zac said taking a beer out of the fridge. He unscrewed the lid and took a sip. "I promise no more naked girls, unless they're you."

"Oh my god. My ears! What the hell did I just walk into?" Colton asked. His hands were covering his ears as he walked in. Zac smirked while Hailey looked mortified. Hailey would never get used to Zac's bluntness.

"Not like you didn't have naked girls here." Zac said pointing his bottle at his son. Colton grimaced.

"But, they aren't mom!" Colton shouted in disgust. Hailey shook her head. This was a daily discussion in the household. Zac didn't have a filter and Colton always walked in at the worst times. Lily was always the one with the cleanest ears. She never walked in nor would Zac allow it. She was a daddy's girl for sure.

"Just shut up and set the table." Zac said. Colton nodded, still in disgust, grabbing some plates.

"How many do I need?" Colton asked.

"Four, Nate and Isaac are coming over." Zac said.

"So when you meant guys' night, you meant it." Hailey said as she took out a bowl of salad.

"We're watching the game tonight. Michigan State is playing USC." Zac said. Hailey rolled her eyes.

"Can we watch real football?" Colton asked. Zac gasped. "That's getting old dad."

"We are not watching soccer, especially when my alma mater is playing. Now, go put on Spartan shirt." Zac said. Colton frowned but left the room.

"He is never going to like football." Hailey said. Zac sighed.

"He can at least tolerate Michigan State for me. Besides, that's where he's going." Zac said. Zac walked out of the kitchen and into the living room. He switched the tv to the game.

"You know he wants to go to Stanford for soccer." Hailey said. Zac gave her a blank look before switching his gaze back to the tv. "Whatever he chooses, at least he's getting an education."

"Hails, I know. But, I wish he'd go there. He'd love the campus and the atmosphere." Zac said.

"Maybe, but his heart is set on Stanford. Plus, he'd be close to home." She reminded him.

"You're right. You always are." Zac said. He reached for Hailey's hand, plopping her into his lap. "I love you so much."

"I love you." Hailey said. Zac placed his lips on her. She smiled into the kiss. Each kiss was better than the last as mini explosions went off.

"Ew! Not again!" Someone shouted. Hailey and Zac separated and saw Nate with his son Isaac. "I swear uncle Zac and aunt Hailey, I am never coming back."

"Chill Isaac." Nate said slapping the back of his head. He was a replica of him with the model like features. Colton and him were the talk of the town. "You'll know what love is soon."

The two of them let their bodies drop on the couch. Hailey giggled as she slid out of Zac's grasp. He stood up with her, walking her to the front door. She pulled her coat on and grabbed her purse and keys.

"Have fun at work babe." Zac said, placing his hands on her hips. She wrapped her arms around his neck, leaning in. "I'm so happy I bumped into you."

"It was our lucky bump." She said, placing her lips on his.

"Oh come on! Mom! Dad! Stop making out." They heard Colton shout. They laughed as they separated. This was their life now and it was all thanks to the lucky bump.

The End.

www.ingramcontent.com/pod-product-compliance
Lightning Source LLC
Chambersburg PA
CBHW061101210726
48294CB00001B/246